Tapes of the River Delta

TAPES OF THE RIVER DELTA

Peter Cunningham

CENTURY

LONDON SYDNEY AUCKLAND JOHANNESBURG

First published 1995

1 3 5 7 9 10 8 6 4 2

Copyright © 1995 Peter Cunningham

Peter Cunningham has asserted his right under the Copyright, Designs and Patents
Act, 1988 to be identified as the author of this work.

First published in the United Kingdom by
Century Limited
Random House UK Limited
20 Vauxhall Bridge Road, London, SW1V 2SA

Random House Australia (Pty) Ltd
20 Alfred Street, Milsons Point, Sydney, NSW 2061
Australia

Random House New Zealand Ltd
18 Poland Road, Glenfield, Auckland 10,
New Zealand

Random House South Africa (Pty) Ltd
PO Box 337, Bergvlei 2012, South Africa

Random House UK Limited Reg. No. 954009

Papers used by Random House UK Limited are natural, recyclable
products made from wood grown in sustainable forests. The
manufacturing processes conform to the environmental regulations of
the country of origin.

ISBN 0 7126 56839

Typeset by Deltatype Ltd, Ellesmere Port
Printed in Great Britain by
Mackays of Chatham plc, Chatham, Kent

For
Peter Cunningham
17 October 1974 – 22 September 1990
*'Et erit tamquam lignum quod plantatum est secus decursus
aquarum quod fructum suum dabit in tempore suo.'*

(And he shall be like a tree planted by the rivers of water,
that bringeth forth his fruit in his season.)

Book of Psalms I

Fire and Ice

Some say the world will end in fire,
Some say in ice.
From what I've tasted of desire
I hold with those who favor fire.
But if it had to perish twice,
I think I know enough of hate
To say that for destruction ice
Is also great
And would suffice.

Robert Frost (1874–1963)

Preface

I have lived six weeks now in the river delta. No other man lives on this floating plain, no road runs through it. The great heartland is sealed by its vegetation from any boat and presents to aircraft a four- hundred-square-mile, unbroken mat of wilderness. Wildfowlers will come out in winter from Monument. Wildfowlers will break through when the frost has done its work and when every thing that had the breath of life in its nostrils has died.

You have to have spent time in this marsh to appreciate it. As I speak, the rain has stopped and the Deilt Mountains have appeared, a hazy fifty miles in the distance. Living on berries and clear water, I can easily imagine that I am still the boy of a lifetime ago who learned the secrets of this vast place over many summers.

I have become strangely detached from the fact that I am the subject of a manhunt. The spectacle of me presented by the media has excluded any possibility of my being fairly dealt with. It's not Mountjoy I fear, it's Dundrum. I know how the system in Dundrum works. No trial, no embarrassing evidence. 'The prisoner is being assessed in Dundrum.' I could not take it. I could not live without at least the distant prospect of my freedom.

These are the tapes of the river delta. Many lives are contained here. Many years of happiness, and also of sadness, run through these little spools. As I listen to them one thing above all others predominates: life is like this river delta. On the surface it seems solid, but press hard and it will always give way, revealing itself to be other than what you thought it to be.

In the end, all you can do is make peace with yourself. That is what I did. That is why I am here. I deny nothing of the truth but ask only that I be remembered for what I really am. The truth is, I knew what I was doing. The truth is, I picked up the gun and I put an end to it.

PART I

One

On the day of the funeral, he stood alone for once without the usual plethora of handlers. Down went the coffin. Over the grave's dark mouth was rolled the green plastic meant to look like grass.

After a hesitant start, the crowd broke ranks and surged to him up the narrow concrete path. I had to admire him, despite everything.

Pax Sheehy said, 'We can go whenever you're ready, Theo.'

Pax knew I might find the situation difficult. He's a sensitive man.

Then the crowd parted and he came straight for me. Even when we were children he had commanded the general attention as if to prove that stature has nothing to do with size. He held out his hand with its thumb cocked like the hammer on a gun.

'Theo, you came,' he said.

'I'm sorry for your loss, Bain.'

He hugged me. Cameras whirred and clicked. I could smell his piquant body, one of the smells of my youth. As if I had not known him for more than fifty years, as if he were a figure known to me only from newspapers and the television, I found myself examining him.

'We'll put everything behind us, Theo.'

'Of course.'

'Life is too short.'

'All right, Bain.'

His eyes, furtive and blue, clicked away, then back.

'I am going to ring you.'

He moved off, glad-handling, recognising old stalwarts with a smile and a touch, moving instinctively from the role of bereaved son to that of chieftain, the possibility that this one morning might be different to a thousand others lost for him in the imperatives of power.

I didn't think I'd hear from Bain again. I thought it was just the sort of talk you make at funerals.

But ten days later in Dublin Castle my assistant's voice came over the intercom saying, 'Theo, the Taoiseach's office for you.'

The dead often change how the living relate. Death re-creates constellations.

'Hello?'

'Theo. I said I'd be in touch.'

Outside, February was begrudging the daylight. I asked, 'How are you, Bain?'

'Fine, fine – well, nearly fine. You would not have heard about poor Brendan's mare.'

'Mare?'

'A pet he had. A lovely old thing. Hooligans ripped her up with carpet cutters. We had to put her down.'

'God.'

'Animals wouldn't stoop to it. Poor Aggie was in a bad way.'

'Who did it?'

'You know the way. The guards probably know but can't prove it. That's how it goes. How're you?'

'Same as ever.'

'Still swimming?'

'Now and again.' I had cut the pictures from the newspapers, the ones taken at the funeral. I had glued them into a photo album, not to show off at some idle moment, me-and-the-Taoiseach, but to lay down for some non-existent witness the long, straggling thread of life, with at one end box Brownie children at a swimming place and at the other middle-aged men in overcoats.

'I remember the swimming river in Eillne,' Bain said as if he had caught my thoughts. 'No one could ever keep up with you. Me least of all.'

I got a tentativeness over the phone as if he had misgivings about why he had really rung.

'Do you go down much?' Bain asked.

'In summer.'

'It's like going back in time.'

'Yes. I have photographs.'

6

'Do you? We must get together again, have a night just the two of us, like old times, go back over it all.' A pause followed as if the principle, although agreed, would be subject to delay in its enactment. 'I'm in the air more often than I'm on the ground. All over the place, at this meeting and that. I'll ring you.'

'Sure,' I said but the line was dead and he had gone, away to something more important. You expected that in Bain, we all had, me, my Uncle Hugo, the people who worked for us in Eillne, even my mother, whom everyone called Sparrow.

Eillne's flowers in their old names still come easily to my lips: bedstraw, bird's-foot trefoil, lady's-fingers. The tiny, begging faces of forget-me-not. Sweet William. Snapdragon. Pursh with its pink underleaves. Thrift of bees' ruby. Dandy in its prickles. Smells still smear the palate of my memory. Bath sponges that whiffed of sweet rot. Peppy mats of cork. Swirling pungency of old calico in a tall, narrow room beside the kitchen where china was wrapped and stacked. In Sparrow's wardrobes the elusive code I smelt from furs into which I plunged my feral nose, a code that no matter how hard I tried I could never break.

Eillne – the name referred as much to the house as to the place – had, I knew, been built by my long-dead grandfather, Sammy Tea. It was a great house with long windows and the other necessary proportions one might expect, but on one level only, thus creating a great house with the rest of its floors missing, in which conundrum lay its charm.

'Time to oxygenate the brain, Theo!'

Uncle Hugo began to pump his elbows. He wore three-piece suits of check, a collar and tie, and a cloth cap with a button-down peak. His black moustache lay glossy as a caterpillar.

'Hold your breath and say, "Well, Mam, is the dinner ready?" '

'Well . . . Ma . . .'

'You're getting there. Good man. Come along.'

Uncle Hugo walked with a limp, gangling, all knees and elbows, running his hand along the top of a hedge like someone inspecting a freshly groomed horse.

'By Jove, that's straight, Dalton.'

'Yes, Mr Love.'

Pipe tobacco clung powerfully to Dalton.

'Should keep up.' (Uncle Hugo on saying this always frowned skywards.)

Dalton's face was closed as a nut. 'No fear of it.'

'Any sighting of young Mr Donald this morning?' enquired Uncle Hugo, re-examining the hedge minutely.

Donald Blood, Uncle Hugo's junior by twenty years, lived at Drossa Park, a mile from Eillne. Donald was round and smooth with curving, ambivalent lips.

'Norra sign,' Dalton spoke. I could see how Dalton's little blue eyes snooped curiously from their bonnets of flesh at Uncle Hugo.

''Tis early yet for Mr Donald,' Dalton said.

'Hmmmmm. Come along Theo or we'll have all hell to pay.'

Dinner occurred in the dining room at one and was served with silver, in three courses, on linen. Hand in hand we made our way inwards by the yellow-gold of senecio, by stout mallow trees, by sheep's-bit (*Jasione montana*). Uncle Hugo gave Sparrow the sort of margin one allows a filly whose ears suggest she may kick. As if attention of any kind might provoke her, he would begin before the soup to sing aloud 'Ecce Panis', continuing through the main course with the 'Tantum Ergo' or 'Ave Verum', and accompany the tapioca pudding with 'All People that on Earth Do Dwell', which Uncle Hugo always referred to as 'The Old 100th' because, he said, it was based on the Psalm of that number. Uncle Hugo ate rabbit stew with the sparingness of a kitten, although I heard Nanny laugh in the kitchen that when invited out he put away the food of three men. 'O Salutaris'.

They say that when Cromwell had ravaged Monument he came west to Eillne and found all the land there loyal and owned by the Countess MacFerris, the spinster descendant of the old Norman family who had built Drossa Castle. Fearful that if the line died out the land would fall into the hands of papists, Cromwell ordered the Countess to take a suitable husband, and when the good lady professed herself unequal to this task, England's Lord Protector lined up twelve of his men, faces to the wall, and bade the Countess choose.

It must have been a memorable sight. A windy February day about to turn to rain, the dozen tunicked backs like the spines of so many different books, the spinster helped in terror down the choosing line by two of her ladies-in-waiting whilst Cromwell stood to one side with that impassiveness so well recorded by history. The Countess, with feminine discernment, reached her faltering hand to a shoulder that seemed to hold the most promise: not the widest nor the loftiest but shoulders with a gentle slope that in the poor woman's mind suggested sympathy and an element of breeding. The boy turned, grinning. He had but one eye. He was Reginald, or soon to be Sir Reginald, Blood.

Donald Blood was the umpteenth descendant of that memorable match between a noble lady and the son of Yorkshire cotters. His father, Reggie, had a brother over at Cruachan who was something of a hermit, and a sister who had gone native and had been walking out with a Catholic from Monument before he suddenly upped and went off to fight Hitler, but apart from Reggie and those two of his siblings, no other Bloods had remained in the county after Irish independence. Donald was to the bottom end of Reggie's offspring from three wives, the Anglo-Irish being free, thanks to Cromwell, to chop and change as fancy took them. Two older sons had followed tradition and joined a regiment. A daughter had married a duke. Charlie, younger than Donald, was at school in England and would drown at nineteen in Oxford, coxing an eight.

Eillne was such an accessible house for me. Rooms abounded without a staircase to complicate the issue. Bedrooms held views over the swimming river. Beyond the bathroom was a cold spare-bedroom, and across the hall, beyond the hall door, was found the drawing room, from which the river could best be seen. The dining room lay west, the breakfast room east. Smaller rooms with different purposes existed: Uncle Hugo's library, the games room with its billiard table, a boot room, and a dim place known as the cellar, full of junk and buckets with summer's eggs preserved in water-glass. A long, unlit corridor led to the echoing kitchen and the staff bedrooms where slept maids and Nanny Morrissey.

From Uncle Hugo's gramophone beat out dance-band music. November, I think. Sparrow must have been in Monument. From where I lurked in the hall outside the games room I could see Uncle Hugo at billiards with Donald Blood.

Uncle Hugo and I were comfortable with one another to the extent that often he went about his idle routines largely unaware

9

of my presence. I found him a source of endless curiosity. The more I observed Uncle Hugo the more he seemed to be other than whom I saw. From within his eyes, which were brown, sometimes emerged yellow, smaller eyes, not Uncle Hugo's. Sometimes when the attention of the room was firmly on other than Uncle Hugo, I noticed his gaze drift, sorrowfully, and in that unguarded moment a most un-Uncle-Hugo-like person was looking out. It was as if out walking you turned suddenly to your house and within a window you knew well you saw a stranger standing.

Framed by the games-room door, the billiards proceeded with knocks and dull thumps. When Uncle Hugo came limping into view, cue balanced at the tips of his fingers, his engrossment emphasised by fluted lips and the languid way he curved forward to inspect his options, he seemed of one long piece, like a river reed moving delicately with the stream. At the moment of decision the reed collapsed into a number of previously unconsidered angles, at one end the tip of the cue, at the other his sharp bottom. Smoothly the wood came back through the trellis of his bony fingers. With chalk-softened click, the ball flew on its way. By contrast, Donald's relationship with the table was an assault. A heaving-up and stretching. Roundy knee cocked on the table, like a dog at a bush, he stabbed.

One moment they are stalking in silent concentration or softly grinding the head of their cues in chalk thimbles; the next moment the doorframe holds nothing more of interest than the canopy lights left on.

Sounds leaked out under the spare-bedroom door. From the other end of the house came kitchen noises and talk that, at another time might have filled me with solid comfort, but which now, for reasons mute, filled me with fear.

'Darling.'

I could not breathe.

'Oh dearest, divine.'

Nor stop myself.

In swung the door to my touch. Sprawled across the bed so that her face hung upside down in my direction was a woman in a dress of Sparrow's. She'd pulled it up so her bare knees peaked in drumsticks either side of Donald Blood, who knelt there with his clothes off, his head down.

He started upright when he saw me and said, 'Oh Jesus!'

For the woman to see me she had to let her head hang further upside down. It was one of those trick faces like they used in the Mac Smile ads. She'd painted it and the mouth was a desperate grin above a glossy black line of hair.

As a child everything was assumed. There was no past to worry me, I was a citizen of the present, whole and intact. But in later life whenever I probed the past a little, whatever I had previously discerned went always abruptly out of focus. That is the reason I became an amateur historian, I think, to see what lay behind the comfortable assumptions on which my life was based.

As a child I assumed it normal that whilst my Uncle Hugo's name was Love and mine was Shortcourse, that my mother's should encompass both. I assumed that Sammy Tea, the father of my mother and of Uncle Hugo, had simply materialised out of the fog of the nineteenth century, which in the case of Sammy Tea was true. He sailed up the River Lyle to Monument in 1888 on board a steamship out of Liverpool intended for Cork. The ship's captain, a prey to drink, confused the promontories that marked the egress of the Lyle, it seems, with similar headlands a hundred miles south. Sammy, a commercial traveller in legal stationery, took lodgings that night on Monument's Small Quay, where he met the landlord's daughter, Miss Sweeten. By dawn Sammy had ensured his own succession, so when the ship's captain was revived and his vessel got underway, Sammy Love remained.

Monument – a town of hills where legend has it Saint Melb once lived, and to whom a great monument was once, allegedly, erected only to slip without trace into the river, leaving but a tenuous link between the name of the town and the saint – was in those days a sleepy port and a market town into which the landed families of the surrounding countryside rolled for their provisions and amusement. In summer, mud flats along the Lyle steamed like succulent brown loaves either side of energetic eights. Troop carriers from Portsmouth often hoved to, discharging or receiving men and artillery from Monument's barracks. An officer at your table was usual.

Sammy Love became a Catholic and married Mary Sweeten. Within eight months Mary Sweeten's father had died, Sammy had

11

fallen in for the premises on Small Quay, and Mary's first child, a son, Bernard, had been born. The Love residence, as it now became, abutted a derelict corn mill last used before the Famine by the last Sweeten to have shown enterprise. When Sammy Love came into this property on marriage, he initially considered setting up a printing works and continuing in his recently interrupted profession. He went so far as to invite tenders for machinery from England. But the year after Bernard's birth, with that happy synchronicity which in those days marked Sammy's life, the same steamship that had inadvertently taken Sammy Love into Monument, turned up again.

The ship's captain had been making the same mistake for thirty years, although sadly this occasion would be his last. Bringing his vessel up the Lyle on the wrong side of the marker buoys, believing himself to be heading down rather than upriver, he holed her badly below the water line, within sight of the town.

The cargo was Mazawattee tea. As the stricken state of affairs became obvious, the off-loading of the chests began on Monument's Small Quay – yet another navigational miscalculation; all vessels at the time discharged on Long Quay –at three o'clock in the morning amid great unrest from the dozen or so passengers and near mutiny from the long-suffering crew. It began to rain. Sammy Love was awoken and came downstairs in his dressing gown. In later years he would claim to have seen the clear path of his fortune laid out there and then, but whether or not this is true, he opened up, supervised the transfer of the fragrant tea into his empty premises, and went back to bed.

A hundred years later the archives of the Monument harbour commissioners speak of the substantial debt incurred at that time for port clearance. The passengers dispersed to lodgings along the waterfront, just as Sammy Love had done eighteen months before. The crew absconded. The captain passed out in his quarters and the ship sank.

My grandfather became known as Sammy Tea. Where once tea had been brought by road to Monument from greater ports, now Monument became the source. The fact that Sammy claimed the ships cargo as salvage, and that there was no one who could give evidence to dispute this claim, allowed my grandfather to begin in the tea business fully stocked and debt-free. In 1891 a daughter, Mary, called Baby, was born, and a son, Hugo, in 1896.

Sammy Tea was a dandy. He was known around Monument for the cut of his clothes, for the shine of his pomade and the lustre of his moustaches. He had a way with him, particularly with county ladies, for whom tea from anyone but Sammy Tea became out of the question. Young girls in from the country were employed on the Small Quay, packing Mazawattee from chests into paper bags, but often some of them returned abruptly and unexpectedly to their families only six or eight months after they had taken up their employment.

The first inkling that tragedy would also play its part in my grandfather's life came in 1900. His second son, Hugo, aged only four, contracted a muscle-wasting disease said to be carried in the droppings of the rats that swarmed along the river. Poor Hugo indeed became wasted, all down his left side, and could never walk again without the support of a steel right angle. Sammy Tea vowed to move his family out of Monument and to this end purchased ten acres on the river at Eillne from a man named Onsley Blood.

The Lyle is a complicated river. It rises in the Deilt Mountains fifty miles north-east of Monument and flows south for its first twenty miles with the utmost convention. Then a branching takes place. The Lyle proper continues as it began, widening by virtue of its tributaries and obliging the town of Monument on its way to the ocean, but the Little Lyle heads west for thirty miles from the point of its divorce and then, as the map shows, bleeds, as it were, in a thousand different outlettings to the coast, creating in the process an enormous river delta.

Eillne occupies the last decent land before the river delta. The site for my grandfather's house was part of Drossa Park, the home of the Blood family, and had been sold to Sammy Tea in the first of many dismemberings made necessary by the shrinking of the Blood fortunes. Onsley Blood, as is often the case with the Anglo-Irish, could see no harm in a man with an English accent. He certainly did not understand that my grandfather was then a Catholic. Above a section of the Little Lyle at Eillne a site was cleared and levelled and the foundations for Sammy Tea's great house laid out.

There then follows a period of murky history, which in truth most families are prone to at one time or another. My mother,

13

Martha, was born in 1905, the same year that her sister, Baby, emigrated to America, aged only fourteen. Mary Sweeten Love, my grandmother, died. Sammy Tea became resident in the Monument mental hospital, which housed criminals alongside the genuinely ill and the simply inconvenient. Explanations there are none. Two generations later these years were still glossed over. Suddenly it is 1910, my Uncle Bernard Love is running the family business and Martha, my mother, is five years old.

Bernard Love, big and handsome and twenty-two, a business-man to his core, had doubled the profits of Samuel Love & Sons in those five years and now set about finishing the house at Eillne. Bernard had a shifty way with him, a furtiveness across the eyes that I well remember and that my mother was unlikely to forget. She noticed this look in Bernard on the Small Quay when he looked up from his desk and saw her playing in the corridor, or when he put his head in on Nanny Morrissey bathing Martha before her bed. That look from Bernard was always followed the same night by a game. Bernard called it polony, after the long and meaty sausages of the time, the product of a recipe from Bologne. In Bernard's game, played in the darkness of Martha's room, he gave her liquorice and she held his polony. He gave her more liquorice to squeeze it. More still and she kissed his polony with her sticky mouth. For a whole bag of sweets Bernard could push his polony up between Martha's legs. One night Martha bit Bernard's polony hard until her teeth met and Bernard's roars of pain brought Nanny Morrissey and Hugo running. The next days were bad days for Martha, locked in her room, waiting for Bernard to die.

Martha knew Sammy Tea only as a man in a tweed suit shuffling around the grounds of the mental hospital. She climbed the high wall and sat looking down at him, whilst Sammy Tea, occasion-ally, returned her stare, but it was obvious he had no idea who she was. He never spoke and had not done so in years. But Martha liked to *imagine* they had conversations. She sat for many hours on the wall, watching Sammy Tea pick the threads from his pocket-less jacket, imagining they were discussing plans of mutual interest.

The way from the Small Quay to the mental hospital was up a hill known as Captain Dudley's Hill and through a dog-rough area

14

of Monument called Balaklava. There were more hovels in Balaklava than raisins in a sack, Hugo had once said. On a summer afternoon Martha headed for her spot on the hospital wall. She smelt the woodsmoke, the horse dung and the ale as she came into Balaklava. An infant sat in an open drain, water from its slit arching like a silver blade. Martha passed caged canaries. Through the open doors of a gut-house she saw entrails hanging. On level ground, on the square where they built scaffolds for Long Drop, the hangman, Martha paused. 'Long Drop doesn't let them die hard,' Hugo had whispered. 'He uses the best Italian hemp.'

The falsetto of stuck pigs rose from behind a terrace of houses. Shortcourses' sausages have pork leppin' out of 'em, Martha had heard it said. She almost didn't see the boy hiding in the lane. She knew him only as Pa. With dirty pegs for toes and his collar askew, he held in his hands a tiny, newborn kitten.

> *'Dearie, dearie me, where is Sammy Tea?*
> *Dearie, dearie me, where is Sammy Tea?'*

Martha's pinafores caught up behind her as she ran, a balloon. At Buttermilk, a peaceful terrace of elms, Martha looked back up Balaklava.

> *'Put a little girl in the family way*
> *Now Sammy Tea has gone away.'*

Martha ran the final hundred yards. Tommies in their gaiters lounged by trees, sucking their pipes. Big horses hauled drays in from the countryside; the coats of cobs glistened between the shafts of traps. Stooping zigzag up a dappled path, Martha came to the roots of a crab-apple tree that were one with the foundations of the massive wall. Each branch from the next was even as a steps. Martha broke upwards to daylight, to the wall's rounded top. Distantly the cathedral bell pealed the half-hour. Today sun would pour through the altar window that Hugo said was older than Monument, making coloured pools on the warm cathedral floor.

My mother's life was shaped on that wall. All her subsequent actions, everything she became, began there.

A garden lay below Martha, in shadow, empty. A long, dark building ran the length of the far side and in a corner a cut-stone

15

chapel sat like an ornament. Sharp on three out came Sammy Tea, walking with a little spring, slapping his hands together and laughing, just like in his snapshots. He stroked up his moustaches with thoughtful caresses of his folded index finger. Martha smelt his linen and his boot polish, his pomade and his tobacco. They had long walks together, just the two of them, then they went to Mass in the chapel where all eyes were on them, Sammy Tea, how well he looks, and Martha, my, how happy they are, that pair, did you hear that they are going far away from here together?

The cathedral bell struck three. One by one, out from the long building came the males of the place. Some curled up on the ground near the door and were moved on by turnkeys in tunics; some ran to spots of no obvious importance where they stood shifting from foot to foot as if anxiety were a condition of their existence.

On that day in June Martha, as was her normal practice, was acting out her fantasy when, for reasons unknown, she pitched inwards from the wall and landed in an unconscious bundle at Sammy Tea's feet.

Turnkeys ran to the spot. Sammy Tea had gathered up Martha in his arms and as if the incident had for the merest instant unlocked his ability to speak, cried, 'A sparrow falls!'

The turnkeys wrestled Martha away and brought her inert and unidentified body to the hospital. No doubt misunderstanding the thrust of Sammy Tea's remark, they gave her name as Sparrow. My Uncle Bernard and Nanny Morrissey eventually and after many anxious hours tracked Martha down and to their great relief found her well and oblivious to her ordeal. They brought her home from the hospital that night, but the name Sparrow stuck.

Two

I was born in Atlantic City, New Jersey, where my mother had gone for reasons unclear (pregnant but unaware of the fact, she said) in late 1939, returning in the latter part of 1940. From an early age I learned that where my paternal family was concerned, unspoken and unbreachable barriers existed. Although a child like myself, Bain Cross was my nephew. He was the son of my greatly older sister, Mag, and they lived with my father, Pa Shortcourse, in the Balaklava part of Monument. But Bain wasn't a Shortcourse. His father, I vaguely understood, had been from the North. When he visited Eillne, Bain arrived aboard Sheehy's omnibus or was fetched in the trap by Dalton, or occasionally he was deposited anonymously at the gates of Eillne by someone in a rickety black car who waited on the road until our door had been opened to the child. Bain could have been three years my senior. He was better at everything, at riding Mikey, my pony, at having bigger muscles and a taller penis. It was only in the swimming river abreast of Sparrow, with Bain wallowing twenty yards behind us like a cork, that I could bathe in my mother's smile of admission that one area did exist in which I could outclass him.

Summer saw Charlie Blood home in Drossa from his English public school. You always knew when Charlie came home: you climbed the hill behind Eillne and through the trees, half a mile away, you saw a Union Jack draped out one of Drossa's upstairs windows. It meant nothing to me. In hindsight, I believe the flag was intended as a provocation to Pius Sheehy, a de Valera man whose omnibus went past the front gates of Drossa and who was Reggie Blood's sworn enemy in some old dispute about water that no one could remember.

One July day Dalton reported a U-boat hauled up in Monument and the crew surrendered to the guards.

'A line of 'em marched up in handcuffs to the jail,' said Dalton slyly and shot a ball of spit beside us. 'The captain had orders on him from Hitler himself. The Germans will rule Ireland within the month and more power to them.'

Later, as Bain and I sat behind Eillne, Dalton made his way out the gates, pushing his bicycle slowly up the hill. You never knew with Dalton. He imparted information maliciously, as if it were his only means of getting even.

'Pa says Hitler is Ireland's best friend,' Bain said thoughtfully.

He sat so that our legs touched and Bain's salty smell became a part of me. Far below us, the swimming river shone like a new road.

'Pa says when Hitler wins the war every boy in Ireland will get a bag of sweets as big as he wants,' Bain said.

'What's Balaklava like?'

'Balaklava's the best. Our house is much bigger than this one. The garden is bigger too.' He rocked his leg.

'Sparrow told me your house in Balaklava is much smaller than here. It's got rats. She said you come out here because she wants you to have fresh air.'

Bain shook his head. 'I hate coming out here. Balaklava's a whizz. Pa gives you a tanner every time he sees you. Uncle Lyle once gave me a half-dollar when he was home.'

Now and then I had heard mention of Lyle, the brother of my sister Mag, my own brother, that is. Lyle worked for a bookie somewhere in England.

'Pa says Lyle drives a Rolls-Royce car.'

'Sparrow says Pa has never spoken a word of truth in his life.'

'Pa says your mother is a dirty old bitch.'

'Sparrow says Pa is a sewer rat.'

'Sparrow is a prostitute, Pa says,' Bain remarked, as far below us hidden coots started up a screeching from the rushes.

'What's Pa like?'

'The best. He killed fifty Brits out at Deilt once.'

'Serious?'

'He shot them first, then he cut their throats with the knife he keeps under his pillow.' Bain drew the edge of his hand across his throat. 'Fifty times,' he said and allowed his bare elbow to come to rest on my knee.

'Why?'

18

'What?'

'Why did he kill them?'

'It was war, you eegit, still is. They stole our country until fellows like Pa fought to get it back. His brothers were all murdered by the Brits, shot in the back of the head when they were asleep.'

'I don't believe you.'

Bain shrugged. 'You're more the fool. Don't take my word. Ask Dalton. Ask anyone about the Deilt Ambush.'

My problem was not so much in believing what Pa had done as in understanding my mother's attitude to such a hero.

'God, I'd love to kill a Brit,' Bain said. 'He'd squeal like a pig before you make sausages out of him, I'm tellin' you. I'm strong enough to kill one, aren't I?'

Bain's elbow bone was trying to find a way upwards between my trousers and my thigh. He did, I had to admit, in his salty way smell of something like strength.

'Why don't you, then?'

'There are no Brits in Ireland any more, more's the pity.'

'I know where there's Brits,' I said, rolling away from him on to my stomach and cupping my hands over my eyes to focus on Charlie Blood's distant Union Jack.

Parts of Drossa Park could be traced back to the early fourteenth century. Through matted creeper the neglected remains of a castle were attached to twisting Tudor beams, which in turn buttressed early Georgian, then late, until finally one came to a box of a flat-roofed kitchen tacked on a few years before like a tiny party hat on the side of a disorganised old dowager's head. Reggie's previous cars and tractors rusted peacefully in a field all of their own and we used them as cover, Bain and I, to get within fifty yards of the laurel bushes that separated the fields from the lawns and the house. A warm wind got up and carried a baby's cries to us; the same wind lifted the hem of the flag from the top corner windowsill and rippled it colourfully. Bain's mouth was a small, tight triangle of apprehension. He took a deep breath and scurried across open ground to the bushes, me behind him. Out from a side door of the house came a uniformed maid and put her hand to the big pram that contained Juliet, Reggie's daughter by his latest wife.

19

'Juliet, Juliet, wisha now girl.'

Charlie's room was at the same end of the building as the new kitchen. We were desperately near. The maid went back in, leaving the silent pram. Suddenly from inside the house came the sound of a gong, followed within moments by the sound of women's laughing voices, light and musical and unmistakably English, and then by Reggie Blood's voice, a nasal, nonchalant drawl with its Yorkshire inflections still clinging like barnacles after three hundred years.

Bain's strong body smell was intense. So rigid he was shivering, his tongue was caught out between his front teeth. The flag seemed much bigger than we had expected.

'I'll keep guard,' Bain whispered. 'You do it.'

I, who had come as a mere spectator, said, 'I can't.'

'The creeper won't hold my weight,' Bain panted. Standing up in the bushes he caught me by the collar and pushed me out on to the lawn. 'Hurry up!' he hissed.

The flag flapped lazily above my head. I made it easily up a trellis to the flat roof, then kept going. The boughs of creeper were solid beneath my sandals, its leaves like silky hands on my face. As I paused at my new height, the lawn stretched out and around the house like a deep, green carpet. I saw hoops for croquet and the mallets lying like matchsticks where they had been dropped. I saw the pram. I could see no sign of Bain. Then, catastrophically, the pram's occupant began to cry again.

I dragged up the last few feet and caught hold of a corner of the Union Jack. Despite the worsening situation, my fingers could distinguish its stitched hem. I yanked, but it remained fast. Trying to put from my mind the inevitable return below me of the maid, I let go and climbed another three feet. Resting my elbows on the granite sill, I worked the flag out from beneath the window. Then I saw Charlie Blood, standing there, smoking a cigarette and staring out at me. Such moments, crystallised for ever, tend to become so at the expense of those immediately following. Thus, how I got down so quickly, I cannot say. Perhaps I jumped. One moment I was face to face with Charlie, watching smoke drool up his face so that he had to half close one eye, the next I was bolting through shrubbery and making for the field of old cars and tractors with Charlie's outraged voice

20

somewhere behind me. But where was Bain? I actually *worried* about Bain!

'You'll pay for this, you little fart!'

He was fast, Charlie Blood. His centre of gravity was near the ground and he moved well. By the time I reached the scrapped cars, Charlie was only twenty yards off. I felt the ground momentarily sag and splinter beneath my foot. I ran on. Charlie's breath beat in the spaces between my own. Where was Bain? There was a crash and a curse behind. I ran and never turned until I reached the top of the hill behind Eillne, where, heaving, I looked back down over the valley between us and Drossa. Except for a few horses on yellow grass, it was empty of life.

Bain was playing draughts with Uncle Hugo when I came in. He barely raised his head to look at me and I thought, how calm he is in the circumstances, how wise he is to keep our secret. Then I felt where my leg had been sliced open on the buried, rusty metal.

Uncle Hugo's limp foretold his arrival. It was Uncle Hugo who laid cool cloths on my forehead and smiled down at me while my poisoned blood boiled. Uncle Hugo held my hand and winced when old Dr Armstrong dug me with a needle, and when Charlie Blood came bursting out of the ceiling, yelling, it was Uncle Hugo who held me close and whispered comfort. I had foul dreams in which I was always being abducted. Even when I woke up the dreams persisted, right through the day. The nights were worse and would have been unbearable without Uncle Hugo. One night I sat up in bed and screamed and screamed at Sparrow, my mother, to go away. She did, but Uncle Hugo stayed.

'Hugo, we are now six months behind with Wise.'

'He'll get his usual "on account" shortly.'

'We owe the poor man three times what we did before the war.'

'Poor man? There's nothing poor about Wise. He's clever as paint.'

'Please pass the bread to Bain, Theodore, without dropping the basket,' Sparrow said sharply, a rebuke merited by my attention to the conversation.

Sparrow's mood was something I watched as closely as a farmer watches weather. Sometimes when she sat, sewing in her lap and her gaze on the swimming river, I would steal a look and catch her smiling secretly. For me that was as wonderful as opening a book and finding flowers that had been picked and pressed in other summers. But such secret smiles, like sunshine, were all too rare.

Bain took a slice of bread and buttered it whilst holding the bread in his palm, a method frowned on in Eillne outside the kitchen. Sparrow's mouth went tight, but then, as if redirecting her irritation, she turned back to Uncle Hugo.

'Surely that's not the point,' she said dryly. 'We have our reputation to consider.'

'Are we to conjure money from air?' asked Uncle Hugo vaguely. 'We must await our dividend from Bernard. Wise must await his.'

Once a week Sparrow was brought into Monument by pony and trap to dictate her order to Mr Wise; once a week young Mr Wise came out to Eillne in a motor-driven van with a bulbous dirigible on its roof that made it look like a dromedary.

'How convenient for us,' Sparrow said sarcastically. 'I think you should realise that Wise has been overpatient with our account.'

'And so were the people of Monument patient, let me tell you, when Wise's family came here with only the cloth on their backs.'

'That kind of talk does not suit you, Hugo,' Sparrow snapped.

Uncle Hugo looked at Sparrow and blinked.

'Do you realise what has been happening in Europe?' Sparrow asked. 'Do you have *any* idea? Scandalous things. Wise has told me. His cousins, the children of his grandfather's brothers and sisters and their children, those who still live where his family came from, these people have *dis*appeared.'

'These people,' said Uncle Hugo slowly and shifting in his chair as if his piles were suddenly playing up, 'these people are *diff*erent, Sparrow. Foreign. Different rules, you know?'

'*Diff*erent? How different?'

Uncle Hugo's mouth mimicked well-bred distaste. 'Chap's not a Christian,' he said with a nervous laugh.

'Christian? I know no one more Christian!' Sparrow seethed.

'Nanny?' Uncle Hugo frowned.

I thought Nanny was Uncle Hugo's candidate for the distinction, but then I saw her standing in the doorway.

22

'Excuse me, Mr Hugo, but Dalton wants you in a hurry,' Nanny Morrissey panted.

Uncle Hugo limped out; Bain and I trailed behind him. It was after supper and Dalton should have long gone home. He was waiting out in the yard in his bicycle clips and drew Uncle Hugo around so that their backs were to us.

'Oh, damn it, are you sure?' Uncle Hugo said.

Dalton nodded.

'Nanny,' Uncle Hugo said, turning around, 'the boys are to remain here,' then he and Dalton made their way out by where the vegetables were grown, towards the paddock.

Nanny Morrissey was very old. Aside from her trembling chins and her regular confusion with names, she wheezed greatly as if her body was most uncomfortably parcelled into its linen uniform. Sparrow was always drawing back from the brink of explosion as far as Nanny Morrissey was concerned, which suggested to me a small but hard core of affection between them. I liked Nanny, of course, and she was kind to me, but in the end I found her a neutral person, someone who had grown too old for new attachments to take root.

Nanny Morrissey shooed Bain and me back into the house. The bell from the dining room rang, the old woman bustled up the dark hall, Uncle Hugo's instructions forgotten, and we made a break for it. Clinging to the wall of the vegetable garden, we edged along until we could hear voices. We dropped low and had a look. Mikey the pony lay on his side, bloated. His eyes were wild and foam oozed from his mouth.

'There wasn't a bother on him when I came in this morning,' Dalton was saying.

'But you didn't see him since?' asked Uncle Hugo.

'Not since early morning,' Dalton replied. He took out his pipe. 'If we tube him with treacle it might work.'

'Damn it, but how did it happen?' Uncle Hugo exclaimed and picked up a green stalk with a head of faded yellow flowers.

'I've been here thirty-four years and I've never let so much as a sprig of ragwort in,' Dalton said.

'I know that, Dalton,' Uncle Hugo said tersely, 'but someone has, someone pulled this stuff and threw it in here and now this wretched animal is going to die. Who?'

Dalton's face took on the mask of ambivalence that some people say is how the Irish managed to survive seven hundred years of oppression. His eyes wandered in the direction of Drossa. 'That's the question,' Dalton said blandly, 'and that's the question I can't answer.'

Reggie Blood came over to supervise the tubing, horses being something he knew more about than anyone. He said later it would be a close-run thing for Mikey. He sat with a whiskey and soda as a new moon hung over the swimming river and told me and Bain, while Uncle Hugo smiled quietly, that once he'd had a horse that could jump it cleanly from bank to bank. They talked about how careless the Irish are, as if the Irish were another race, which of course to Reggie they were. Before he left he gave Bain and me sixpence each. I heard him in the hall tell Uncle Hugo that Charlie had gone back to school in England earlier that day.

In early 1948, Father O'Dea, a young curate just appointed to Eillne parish, came to lunch. Small, dark and trim, wearing a cape with an embroidered hem and a rustling soutane, he conveyed an air of diligent good humour.

'So this is himself.'

'Theodore, come in and say "how do you do" to Father.'

'Hello, hello, Theodore. I'm Father O'Dea, another "d" and I'm dead,' the priest said cheerfully.

I looked emptily at him.

'He's all right, he's grand, a grand fellow. You're great at two of the Rs, your mam tells me, Theodore,' Father O'Dea said and sipped his sherry. 'Your mam's been the best teacher you could have had, there's no doubt,' he said and smacked his lips.

Through the breakfast-room window I could see dead bog iris enshrined in frost. Later I would bump stones along the ice of the swimming river.

'He's lost his tongue as usual,' Sparrow said.

'Sure, he'll find it soon enough like all these boys do,' Father O'Dea said happily. 'Good man, Theodore, there you are.'

There was an air of foregone conclusion to Father O'Dea that I did not like.

'Have you no little pals out here, Theodore?' he asked.

'He has his cousin, Bain,' Sparrow replied.

24

'Ah, yes, yes,' said the priest thoughtfully. He nodded with sudden vigour. 'Mr Redden turns them out ready for the modern world, Mrs Love Shortcourse. Mr Redden and his like are the backbone of the new Ireland. Ah, how are you at all, Mr Love? I'm in your chair, I'd say.'

'Don't stir, Father,' Uncle Hugo said, loping in and helping himself to an unexpected glass of sherry.

'You're all well here?' Father O'Dea asked.

'One mustn't complain,' Uncle Hugo said. ' "Age will not be defied". Bacon, of course.'

'Theodore wouldn't agree,' the young priest beamed.

'Nanny Morrissey has asked that you call into the kitchen before you leave, Father,' Sparrow said quietly, as if the question of age mainly concerned Nanny Morrissey, or perhaps because she misunderstood the reference to Bacon.

'Ah, yes, yes,' Father O'Dea gravely acknowledged. 'Miss Morrissey. Yes. A fine woman. What age is she at all?'

'Seventy . . . two?' Sparrow replied, with a glance to Uncle Hugo.

'Four,' Uncle Hugo said.

'She told me after Mass last week, no, I tell a lie, after Mass a fortnight ago, that's right, she told me she found it difficult to get around,' Father O'Dea said.

'Yes, I know,' said Sparrow with the hint of irritation that always accompanied mention of Nanny Morrissey.

'How long has she been with the family?' Father O'Dea enquired.

'Oh years,' Sparrow said.

'Our poor mother died,' Hugo said, 'and Nanny Morrissey appeared. Or so it seemed.'

'Ah, dear, what year?' asked Father O'Dea.

'What year what?' Uncle Hugo scowled.

'Did your poor mother die?'

'Ah, it was, ah . . .' said Uncle Hugo, suddenly confused and looking at Sparrow, 'it was, ah . . .'

'The year I was born,' Sparrow said.

'Of course,' Uncle Hugo said.

'Ah, God be merciful to her,' said Father O'Dea with a sad smile.

'Her brother is good to her,' said Uncle Hugo, recovering.

25

'Her brother is . . . is he?' Father O'Dea frowned.

'Nanny Morrissey's brother,' Uncle Hugo said. 'Patrick Fox. Her half-brother in actual fact. He's very good to Nanny.'

'Ah,' said Father O'Dea.

'You're good to her too, Hugo,' said Sparrow, displaying rare support for her bother.

'One does one's duty,' Uncle Hugo said.

'I'd say now there's more to it than duty,' Father O'Dea said knowingly. 'Ah, there's a smile at last from Theodore.'

I was smiling because Nanny had appeared at the door behind the priest's back with beside her a girl a year or two my elder who was smiling at me.

'Lunch, ma'am,' Nanny said with a little dip in the priest's direction.

'Ah, Miss Morrissey,' said Father O'Dea. 'And who have we here, at all at all?'

'Eleanor,' beamed Nanny Morrissey. 'A niece of mine, Eleanor Fox, Father.' She gave the child a reminding nudge to acknowledge the priest, but Eleanor Fox could only blush.

I waited as they went ahead of me into the dining room.

'I was just telling Mrs Love Shortcourse that Mr Redden will be only too pleased to take young Theodore into class,' Father O'Dea said to Uncle Hugo.

Mr Redden combined virtue and vice in equal parts, in most people not at all unusual, but in his case unfortunate, because when the good in him was to the fore he displayed an almost excessive love for the English language that was touching and contagious, but when the bad in him came out it did so as a violent and sadistic temperament. Eillne's national school stood in a windswept field on the road to Monument. In a room impregnated with the rank body odours of a hundred years sat twenty-five children between the ages of six and fourteen, segregated first by age and then by sex. Mr Redden was a small man, old in our eyes but in reality not more than in his mid-thirties. He lived with his mother in Monument. Bald, he had grown his ginger hair long above one ear so that it could be trained across his head to meet the other. I remember him in later years in Monument, malodorously drunk, his pathetic queue lying over his shoulder.

He had been retired early because of the drink and all the good he had done in showing children the beauties of language had been forgotten.

'Shortcourse. Will we be all right for sausages so?'

Sniggers of laughter.

'Can you read?'

I nodded.

'Oh, be the hokey. Read this for us, then.'

I was handed an open book, its spine embossed like those in Uncle Hugo's library.

' "I have just returned from a visit to my landlord – the solitary neighbour that I shall be troubled with. This is certainly a beautiful country. In all England, I do not believe –" '

'Enough, enough. Sit down there beside big Pax and if you talk to him within the confines of this room I'll skin you alive.'

Before we went home that, my first day, a girl older than me and bad at her sums had her legs beaten by Mr Redden with an ash-plant.

Big Pax, who I discovered was Pax Sheehy of the omnibus family, was quiet and calm but sometimes too slow for the liking of Master Redden. Pax needed to digest new information at his own pace. This process worked badly when we were required to commit formulas or poetry to memory. Mr Redden punished Pax by beating his hands with a stinging leather strap, or, when it became obvious that Pax's calloused hands could outstay the master's energy, by catching the boy by the hair in front of his ears and hoisting him upward until his eyes wept. (The method of standing pupils beside their desks with their hands stretched horizontally had the desired effect with most boys, and with the girls, who often fainted, but for Pax the position was as comfortable as sitting.) For the most part I enjoyed my days in Mr Redden's school, but equally there were many of my peers who entered adulthood with a profound aversion to books and knowledge.

Pax began to drift up to Eillne. The swimming river, which to me began when it came into view near the house and ended where it curved and became hidden, was, I learned from Pax, the last stretch of the Little Lyle in this area to flow between solid banks before it joined the vast delta. The Sheehys' land, a mile downstream of us, was poor and regularly flooded. Over the years the lives of precious Sheehy bullocks had been claimed by vigorous currents and Pax had grown up learning how to navigate beside his father through the treacherous, unending wilderness. Pax taught me how, by lying on a timber, we could penetrate places a punt never could. Pax showed me how, with a few flicks of the hands in the water, we could get out of adult earshot. I showed Bain.

In the first week of the summer holidays we paddled out, following a maze of covered waterways and rested at last where a huge bog oak, one of many in the delta, had become anchored to an island of weed. Bain's face had changed: it was fatter than I remembered and the eyes moved more quickly. Pax and I sat and watched as Bain extracted a cigarette from a twist of brown paper. He cracked a match and sulphur hung deliciously on the air. Inhaling deeply, Bain passed the cigarette. I watched as my lips brought the ash magically aglow. The new sensation of smoke in my mouth was exhilarating and seemed suddenly to hold the key to wider opportunities.

'Where did you get it?' Pax asked in wonder, smoke shooting from him.

'Bought it,' Bain said. 'In Monument.' He took the fag back from Pax's clumsy hands and lay in the reeds, his eyes closed. 'Where do you think I fucking got it?'

'But where did you get the money?' Pax asked.

'I have money saved,' Bain replied.

I could taste the strong grains of tobacco on my lips. Pax was staring openly at Bain and suddenly I found myself ashamed of my artless school companion.

'Bain works in Pa's shop in Monument,' I said to Pax, 'I've been there,' a statement which, though true, was only technically so; I had sat outside once in the trap when Dalton had gone in to collect the order. 'Isn't that right, Bain?'

'That's right,' Bain said lazily and stretched in the sun. 'Theo and I have been lots of places together. D'you know Monument – what's your name?'

'Pax.'

'*Do* you?'

Pax's face went into the expression I knew so well from Mr Redden's classroom. He said, 'I go in on me Daddy's bus.'

'Me Daddy's bus,' Bain jeered. 'Is that the clattery old yoke on the Long Quay that looks broke down? Jesus. Me gran'father says it's like something the tinkers left behind.'

Pax's consternation made Bain laugh.

'When Theo comes into Monument he and me smoke all the time,' Bain said, cementing our sudden alliance. 'We chats up young ones too in Balaklava, don't we Theo?'

I nodded. 'Yes.'

'D'y'ever kiss a girl, what's-your-name?' asked Bain.

Pax looked caught in a great dilemma.

'They takes their knickers off for me and Theo,' Bain drawled. 'D'you know what's on them down there, what's-your-name?'

Pax's forehead was seized into two great knots of bewilderment.

'Cunts,' Bain explained. 'Like red lips. You wouldn't know that, would you? Tell us, what d'you do when you're not snaggin' turnips?'

A lifetime later I would see the same desperation in Pax when, as one of the keepers of the nation's secrets, he would have to choose between friendship and duty.

'We have a wireless!' Pax blurted and jumped into the water and paddled off in the direction we had come from as Bain laughed until he had to cough and I sat there trying to show I had set the whole thing up for his amusement.

'Have a fag, Theo,' Bain said when he found his composure.

He put a match to my cigarette, then lit one of his own. 'I didn't give what's-his-name one for himself, he can't smoke,' Bain said. 'You know how to smoke, Theo. Lie back here, beside me.'

I had seen snaps in the paper of soldiers after D-Day, lying back in battledress like this, smoking, their guns beside them.

'D'you like being here, Theo?'

'Yes.'

'Being here with me, I mean?'

'Yes.'

'It's good, isn't it?'

'Yes.'

Bain's voice had grown deeper and seemed to come from his stomach.

'Did you feel good when I told your man about the young ones?'

'Yes.'

'When I told him about cunts? Did you see his face?'
I laughed.
'How did you feel good, Theo?'
'How do you mean?'
'How did you feel good? Where did you feel it?'
'It was . . . just super.'
Bain was so near me I could hear his heart. 'It's our secret, Theo,' he whispered. 'Everything we do. All right?'
I wondered suddenly if Pax would be my friend again.
'Theo?'
I looked down and saw Bain's hand working the length of his bared erection. There was no shock that I can remember. Although I had previously been shown Bain's member, I could not recall him attending to it with such energy. Even so, the sight of his upright flesh, springing from a bed of hair and ending in a raw, red head, seemed unremarkable. Like his briny smell. Bain jiggled the tip of his penis between his index finger and his thumb.
'You do it,' he said.
I did it. I wondered if Pax would sit beside me in school.
'Faster.'
I did it faster. After a bit a tiny cap of froth welled out, in appearance like cuckoo spit.

Pax was not seen in Eillne for weeks afterwards. He must have established from the chitchat of our servants, from the likes of Dalton who passed Sheehy's every day, that Bain was still in residence. From Monument came Mr Turner who went around with a little stool, winding and adjusting Eillne's many clocks. Small and organised with a thick but trim moustache that was black whereas his hair was white, Mr Turner wore wire-rimmed glasses and always the same suit of tweed. He walked stooped and never spoke unless addressed, as if his management of time had resigned him to endless introspection. Eillne's gardens hung sweetly consenting in warm afternoons. Days were long and bright and ended in fiery sunsets, vectors of burning light.
Between the two bends of the warm river, Bain struggled in his oddly upright fashion, resembling someone with a bell pull in each doomed fist. He never protested his strange powerlessness, as if

30

prepared to confront even drowning to be part of the same element as me.

I floated in bulrushes. The water churned. Borne up by great force I gasped air.

'Now swim!'

One arm paralysed my upper body, my shin was encircled by his fist.

'Mermaid.'

'Ouch . . .'

Bain's chest muscles, round and distinct as dinner plates, shone. Releasing my ankle, his hand, rising through my legs, was both hard and soft. He immobilised me. Out on the bank, beneath orchids, he strained with a strange, dream-like gentleness, begging me to show him the same grace as I had the water.

Later, a heron came in and perched, flapping, beside where we lay.

Later, through glossy, upright reeds, I could see Uncle Hugo's face, tiny, at one of Eillne's high windows.

My Uncle Bernard, the businessman in the Love family, announced a camping expedition to Leire. Uncle Bernard was as different from Sparrow and Uncle Hugo as those two were from each other. He was a big, handsome man with flowing blond hair and a lazy, laughing manner that made you forget the sly hardness of his eyes and the fact that he expected his orders to be obeyed. He had the most white teeth. By relentless diversification he had changed the tea business he had inherited more than forty years before into a little empire, unloading his many products from boats directly in front of the premises of Samuel Love & Sons. Whilst ignoring Uncle Hugo in the main, Uncle Bernard treated Sparrow with correctness. His wife, my Aunt Delia, was pretty, but I heard Sparrow describe her as 'foolish'. They had big sons, including one called Johnnie, the image of his father.

Sparrow and Uncle Hugo seemed quite happy to have Uncle Bernard organise the expedition to Leire, a coastal place thirty miles away.

'Bathing twice a day,' Uncle Bernard explained to me. 'Salt water, not like that stuff you swim in here. Tennis and cricket on the beach. Rummy at night. Sixpence to the first boy who catches me a mackerel.'

For a week employees of Samuel Love transported tables, chairs, beds and wardrobes, curtains to divide ladies from men, washstands, a coal stove, innumerable boxes with storm lamps, cutlery, crockery, and rugs to cover the grass, to a canvas tent set up behind the sand dunes in Leire. Mr Wise made two trips with provisions. When Sheehy's omnibus arrived for us in Eillne, Uncle Bernard's family and their retainers were already aboard. We squeezed in with our trunks and carryalls, Sparrow, Uncle Hugo, Nanny Morrissey, Bain and me, and the bus rattled out Eillne's gates to a great cheer. With us too came Nanny's niece, Eleanor, who had begun to come more often to Eillne to help Nanny. We called her La. Up in the driver's cab beside his father I saw Pax pretending not to notice me. The engine fumes as we snaked north turned many of us, Nanny Morrissey especially, the colour of flour.

'Me gran'father says Sheehy shouldn't be allowed a licence,' Bain said loudly and fanned himself with his hands.

'Now, now, none of that,' Uncle Bernard rapped.

'I'm *sick*, Uncle Bernard,' Bain complained.

'You'll be there in an hour,' Uncle Bernard said dryly. 'When I was your age it took two days to get to the seaside – that's if we were brought at all.'

'I wish I wasn't,' Bain muttered.

The bus lurched around a corner.

'Jesus,' Bain gasped.

'No *lang*uage from you!' Uncle Bernard snapped. 'I'm warning you now. Another word and it's back on this bus to Monument you'll be sent.'

'If I'm not dead first,' Bain retorted.

'The wrong element entirely,' I heard Uncle Bernard mutter to his wife. 'I wish somebody would speak to Sparrow.'

Apart from a nun's convent perched on a distant cliff, Leire was nothing more than sand dunes and a shore. Our tent awaited us, its canvas flaps tied back, as if the final performance of a circus had happened in this deserted place and the enterprise had then been abandoned. When we had unloaded ourselves and our belongings, Mr Sheehy revved for home with Pax looking out at us from the cab.

'I'm sure Pax would love a few days at the seaside, Mr Sheehy,' said Sparrow, stepping forward.

Pax's father appeared to be flattered by the suggestion and Pax, with a big grin, jumped down.

Those days in Leire were marked by the worst weather of that summer, or of any summer. Gales came at night, thrillingly, and blew out the storm lamps. We sang songs as Uncle Bernard and his sons went out with mallets to secure the tent stays. Every night Uncle Bernard's wife said this night was her last, whilst Uncle Hugo taught us card games and La brought tea with whiskey to Nanny Morrissey, who spent a lot of time in bed.

Bain refused to join the hearty swims that Uncle Bernard led or to gather firewood or pick periwinkles. Bain remained aloof from games such as charades, which he considered to be the antics of the feeble-minded, and declined to surrender his disbelief for the duration of Uncle Hugo's bedtime stories, to which Pax and I looked forward unashamedly but which Bain considered further proof of Uncle Hugo's senility. Pax's omnipresence denied Bain the access to me he enjoyed in Eillne. The three of us shared a cubicle in the tent and went everywhere together. Even the sea, which might have presented Bain with surreptitious opportunities with me in the way of the swimming river, was not an option as its waves were more than he was prepared to face, even on my account. He became moody and sullen. The private occasions he might have seized for jiggling his big cock, a pastime to which he was devoted, were denied him in Leire. One evening, behind the ditch where everyone's toilet was performed, he had me to himself long enough to direct my hand to its appointed task, but even this was a failure as scarcely had Bain begun to whisper 'Faster!' than Uncle Bernard's (suspicious) voice rang across the field.

'Theo? Bain? Are you lads out there?'

Bain cursed and buttoned up with difficulty.

'Where's that boy Bain?' Uncle Bernard asked, and I heard in his voice a long-held disapproval of who Bain was and where he came from.

'Cunt,' Bain said and back to the tent we came.

Uncle Hugo had transported his gramophone from Eillne, one that you wound by hand and was called His Master's Voice. On an evening when the walls of our abode were sucked in and out by fierce wind like giants' cheeks, a strange, jumpy sound came from Uncle Hugo's gramophone.

Pax grabbed my arm. 'Charlie Parker!' he whispered.

Bain gave him a look intended to humiliate.

I asked, 'Who?'

'Charlie Parker. Jazz, Theo,' Pax said.

I listened and for the first time heard a saxophone.

'Jazz!' Bain laughed, looking around for some support.

'You know Charlie Parker, eh?' Uncle Hugo wore a smoking jacket and had the comfortable demeanour of a man who has paced his whiskeys correctly before bed. 'Who else d'ye know?'

'Woody Herman, Miles Davis,' said Pax eagerly. 'There's this new fellow, Dizzy Gillespie.'

'Dizzy!' cried Bain as if suddenly among mad people.

'I know him, trumpet player,' Uncle Hugo said. 'Glenn Miller?'

'You have him?'

'Of course,' replied Uncle Hugo languorously and strolled off to his part of the tent.

'You'll love jazz, Theo,' Pax told me as Bain slouched away to find better company. 'It's music broken up in little pieces like someone opened up old music and found new notes in it. It makes your feet tap.'

'It's nigger music,' Uncle Hugo said benignly, returning with a record in a paper sleeve. 'It's in their bones.'

Giving his machine a furious twist, Uncle Hugo dropped the record on to it. There was a scratchy pause, then trumpets filled the tent in brass pulses that made my neck prickle with excitement. Deep strings followed at the same pace, like currents of water. Then came saxophones, sidling up in their nasal tones to the bobbing strings.

'*Pennsylvania 6–5000!*'

We formed a circle around the gramophone. We could no longer hear the storm. Uncle Bernard's sons began to clap in rhythm and I saw Sparrow sway from her hips, clapping, her face alight.

'*Pennsylvania 6–5–0–0–0!*'

Pax was unable to contain himself. Big, shy Pax Sheehy leapt into the ring and, using just his heels and toes, made his way around our circle as if mounted on casters. His hands, which were

34

splayed and fixed to his knees, kept time with his feet. When he reached the point from which he had started, which coincided with a pause in the music, Pax stopped, dead as a statue, and then, as the beat picked up once more, he reversed the circle he had just made, his movements so much one with the dance-band beat that you thought not of Pax Sheehy there before you, but of some trick of modern magic that made a dancer appear from nowhere as soon as a record was dropped on a gramophone. There was no one in the tent, not even Bain, who in the brief space of a few seconds did not feel a surge of wonder. Pax had achieved an instant union with the music that transcended any obstacle one might ever imagine had stood in his way. La joined him, mimicking Pax's hands, heels and toes. Uncle Bernard's sons joined La, as did their own maids, two little red-haired women with wild eyes. Uncle Bernard stepped in with Sparrow by the wrist, and then Uncle Hugo, with a nod in my direction, and Uncle Bernard's foolish wife, until suddenly there was no circle, just everyone waggling in time to the music, even Bain, shrieking and laughing under the fluttering storm lamps. We took our lead from Pax, sensing as we did so in that happy moment that we were all suddenly part of a much larger world, that we had struck a chord that connected us in an instant with people and places we had previously only heard of and that our lives as a result had been permanently altered.

'Pennsylvania 6–5000!'

Half a mile from our encampment, in a lonely cottage near the strand, an enterprising soul had bravely stuck up a sign for Woodbines and operated a makeshift shop selling penny sweets. A few days after Pax's dance, which had not been repeated nor even referred to again, as if we had all allowed ourselves in an unguarded moment to get out of hand, we walked along the shore, Pax, Bain and I, until the shop loomed out of the dunes like a turf rick. Pax and I thumbed out our ha'pence for sweets but Bain threw a florin down on the counter and with a cocky grin asked for cigarettes.

'Where did you get that?' I asked.

'Oul' Hugo's pockets,' Bain explained. 'He doesn't miss it.'

I lacked the means to separate right from wrong where Bain was concerned. When he described stealing, as he just had, it arose in

35

me a shiver of excitement, the same as when he went on about the anatomy of girls or as when we were alone and a desperate look came over his face to tell me what he wanted. He caused whatever judgement I had to be suspended and that little quiver of excitement to become my dominant concern. We smoked all his cigarettes that day, huddled behind seaweedy rocks and flicking our butts into the incoming tide.

Uncle Bernard's obvious dislike of Bain became an issue in Leire on which people took positions. Uncle Bernard's sons sided with their father, and where a kick or a punch was possible Bain got me from them. Their family servants took much the same line, as Nanny Morrissey would have, one suspected, had she been well enough. But Sparrow, for reasons that for many years lay hidden, would not so easily forsake her grandchild, and for Uncle Hugo to take a public position in conflict to his sister was not a possibility. I tagged along the way I always had, open to Bain's suggestions, and Pax tagged along with me.

I have not smoked for decades, but the tobacco smoked that summer in Leire is perhaps the fondest memory of its type I will ever have. I still yearn for it. I can still relive the sense of anticipation of opening the foil from a new row of Woodbines.

'We'll go to the shop tomorrow and buy more,' Bain said.

Neither Pax nor I had reason to object.

'But it's your turn this time, Theo,' Bain said quietly.

'I've no money.'

' "I've no money," ' Bain said, girlishly. 'You have to get it from oul' Hugo the way I did, Theo.'

If the fact of robbing a man who had been nothing but decent to me presented me with a dilemma, then it was a dilemma I was blind to. No great drums of foreboding sounded, no cannons of moral warning fired. Nothing more than the opportunity to please Bain occurred to me and with that came the familiar tug of excitement.

Nanny Morrissey had been sent home with La to Eillne that day, shivering, and after supper the adults sat around a kerosene fire discussing whether we should abandon any remaining hopes of good weather and follow her. Because it was a tent, you could hear what was going on from every point within it. Ropes traversing the roof provided the means for hanging curtains to

36

box off various quarters. As Bain and Pax lay on a rug, innocently dealing out hands of cards, I sloped off to where plates and glasses had been washed, polished and stacked on a massive deal table. Uncle Bernard's red-haired maids had retired. When I came to wet canvas with wind blowing at my ankles, I began to edge along between it and the wall of curtains that marked the bedroom area. Hidden from sight, I could hear the sea and curlews. Dimly, as in a dream, I proceeded. Which was Uncle Hugo's room? People's chat sounded eerily close and was no help in fixing my position. Judging best I could from the roof of the tent and from the poles and various ropes that kept us upright, I dropped to the grass and crawled in under a curtain.

The bedroom was almost totally dark. Unlike ours, this box had had a lid added – yet another curtain – and there was a faint smell of perfume. I struck into the iron frame of a bed with my knee; pain reduced me, mutely. I began to discern outlines, hidden boxes and chests on the ground. Rummaging over the bed and under the pillows, I came to clothes hanging –again the strange if slightly familiar perfume smell – and raced through them, looking for Uncle Hugo's proven pockets, or for jackets wherein a pocketbook might reside, or, at this stage, anything of value to salvage my mission. Then I hit gold. Wedged between two suitcases beside the bed I felt a leather bag with a strap. The many items Uncle Hugo had of which I knew nothing! I wrenched back a clasp. Smooth, round shapes blocked my fingers. In the gloom I tipped the bag on to the bed, then sat back on my heels in wonder at the sight not only of shining coins, but of a wad of orange ten-shilling notes. With only a triumphant vista of tobacco before my eyes, I began to stuff my pockets with the coins, then the notes on top of them. In what would later be seen as compounding my premeditation, I put one note back into the bag, but then, with a sickening swish, the brass curtain runners were pulled across and dark became light.

'What are you *do*ing here?' cried Uncle Bernard's foolish wife.

I tried to run out the way I had come, an action assured to crown my guilt had it not already been manifest.

'You're *steal*ing!' cried Uncle Bernard's wife, anything but foolish.

I could think of nothing to say.

37

'Well, look at what we've caught our little cousin Theo at,' said Johnnie Love, coming in and catching me by the ear. He hauled me into the body of the tent, his mother clucking behind us.

'What in blazes' name is this all about?' shouted Uncle Bernard.

'He was stealing from Mammy's bag,' Johnnie said.

'He's hurting my ear,' I whined, the archetypal thief.

'Mammy?' asked Uncle Bernard slowly, taking in Sparrow and Uncle Hugo as well in his search for confirmation.

'Oh, Sparrow,' my aunt trembled, overwhelmed by the political pitfalls of the situation and reverting to type.

I could see Bain and Pax some way off.

Uncle Bernard stood up. '*Were* you stealing, Theodore?' he asked, somewhat unnecessarily, as coins spilled from my fists.

'Answer your uncle, Theodore!' said Sparrow coldly.

No words came to my mind.

'I must say I *am* surprised,' said Uncle Bernard, looking surprised and disappointed. 'What could you want for here?' he asked, looking around the damp tent, cornucopia, as it were, of the world.

'He smokes, Daddy,' Johnnie said.

'He smokes? Do you *smoke*, Theodore?'

'No,' I replied.

'Empty your pockets.'

Gingerly I began to shell out the coins, one by one, knowing what was coming. Johnnie saw my hesitation and, catching me around the chest, pulled first one pocket and then the other inside out. Silver, copper and notes made an impressive heap on the rug, topped off by my matchbox, which when opened yielded yellowing Woodbine butts.

'A liar too,' said Uncle Bernard grimly. He turned to my mother. 'You find something like this, there's only one thing to do. You must nip it in the bud.' Standing up hugely, he began to unbuckle his belt.

'Give him a good thrashing, Daddy,' Johnnie said.

'Shut up you, Johnnie,' Uncle Bernard growled.

'Hang about,' Uncle Hugo said from the side of his mouth. 'Chap's only a child.'

That the original target of my thieving should be the only one to speak in my defence overwhelmed me with guilt.

'That's the whole point,' said Uncle Bernard patiently, as if his childless brother could always be relied upon to make the wrong remark. 'He won't do it again after this.'

I looked in terror to my mother, but by the hard set of her face I knew that she had deserted me.

'It's not Theo's fault!'

In one of those moments whose drama the people there would later recall with great precision, Pax Sheehy stepped forward. Perhaps it was his proven ability to come up with the unexpected that made Pax's intervention crucial and not just the words of a child.

'It's not Theo's fault,' he repeated. 'He thought it was Mr Hugo's room.'

'He thought it was Mr *Hugo's* room,' repeated Uncle Bernard incredulously, again including all the adults in his look of stage surprise. 'Did he, by the Lord Harry!'

'Anyway, it was all Bain's idea,' Pax gulped.

Slowly all Uncle Bernard's long-held suspicions about Bain played out their themes across his face. 'Bain's idea,' he said softly. 'I always knew it.' He made a lunge across the tent. 'You're in for it now, you little schemer!' he cried, catching Bain. 'We all know you don't have to scratch far to find dirt in your tribe!'

'Bernard!' Sparrow had come to her feet. 'Bernard, don't lay a hand on him, I warn you!'

Uncle Bernard's blood was up, but on hearing Sparrow a strange uncertainty seized him.

'He's nothing to you,' Sparrow said. 'You've no right.'

'He's a thief!' Uncle Bernard protested. 'He stole from Aunt Delia!'

'He didn't,' Sparrow said calmly. 'It was my own son who stole and is the thief.'

'Put up to it by this maggot!' cried Uncle Bernard, his face crimson.

'Bernard. I'm warning you,' Sparrow said with finality.

We all stood there, petrified. I understood that something far more grave than shillings and pence or cigarettes had made its way into our midst. Uncle Bernard was trembling.

'Very well,' he heaved, 'but he goes home tomorrow morning, first thing, out of here.' He pushed Bain from him. 'He's bad,' he panted, 'they're all bad, the Shortcourses, I shouldn't have to remind you Sparrow, of all people. I remember the day –'

'Bernard!' cried Uncle Bernard's wife, stepping forward with one hand held out, like someone in a theatrical production.

'I remember the day I *begged* you not to marry Pa Shortcourse,' quivered Uncle Bernard, beyond restraint. 'I im*plored* you, Sparrow. I said, come and have your child and live with us, but don't marry Pa Shortcourse just to have the child of another man. I loved you. We all did. They're rotten to the core, I told you, the Shortcourses. They're parasites, the worst of the worst, so help me God. But you went and married him because you were too proud to take what I had to offer.'

That night in Leire the past came out of hiding for a moment, and once out, could never go back. Uncle Hugo gave me money anyway when Bain had gone, and Pax and I smoked the shrinking days away, blowing smoke rings into the damp air and flicking our butts into the tide.

Sparrow Love was bored. She boiled to leave Eillne. Each time her brother Hugo, a shy, inoffensive man, attempted to engage her in conversation she felt crushed. Nanny Morrissey's bromides were worse. Horticulture, charity and horses, the mainstay of female gentility, all made Sparrow nauseous. The young men of Monument bored her. The ridiculous Pa Shortcourse was the worst. Outside the new ice-skating rink that had been opened the year before, he usually lay in wait, too gauche ever to consider entering, and when Sparrow emerged, he always doffed his hat and bowed like one of those devices on a grocer's counter you put a penny into.

Captain Harry Amis had served an Indian term of duty with distinction. His regiment, the King's Own Warwickshire Fusiliers, had been posted to Monument the previous December. An accomplished ice-skater, Harry Amis was drawn to Sparrow Love with a well-bred inexorability that set Monument chattering. Harry Amis, with his slow, easy way, his inky pat of hair, his pencil-line moustache and his cigarettes, had met many young ladies endowed with one interesting name, but never with two. Sparrow Love had never quite mastered the rink and when Harry one day materialised alongside her, she overcame her surprise and accepted the services of this darkly handsome postilion.

Protocols existed. Pretty young girls of sixteen were deemed to need rings of steel in 1921, even when the young man involved was an officer and arrived in Eillne by gleaming Studebaker complete with a driver whose moustaches alone must have taken hours to wax. Hugo, in the nervous way he affected when he was with people he perceived to be of a higher class than himself, went on at length about Irish ingratitude, and the security in being part of an empire, and Sammy Tea's own background, which made Sparrow and Hugo British by virtue if not by birth. Never once during Hugo's theorising on the military situation – intensely offered advice about the best approach to skirmishing on Irish topography – did Harry's polite attention falter from Hugo's long, lopsided face. Later, walking out to the car where sat Harry's driver, Franks (who leapt out at their appearance, magnificent in breeches and gleaming boots and those marvellous spiked moustaches), Harry stopped Hugo dead in mid-flow with a gesture of his gloved hand and said, 'I say, listen! You have a stonechat!'

They listened, all four of them. Harry turned Sparrow gently to the call, which called to mind two pebbles knocked together. Sparrow could feel Harry's fingertips through his glove and she realised that all along his real attention had been for her.

'Chock! Chock!' Harry called.

There was the pause of a pulse, then the bird answered.

'Chock! Chock!'

'Exactly the same as we have in Warwickshire,' Harry Amis said.

My mother was a woman whose attachment to her concept of freedom cannot be exaggerated. Perhaps her childhood experiences of people leaving – first her mother, then her sister, Baby, then Sammy Tea – were the cause of the restlessness in Sparrow, or perhaps it was the sense of adventure she felt whenever she saw a ship. Or perhaps it was simply Sammy Tea's blood that had brought him up the Lyle in the first place that made Sparrow want to sail down it again and away from Monument for ever. In times of such political uncertainty as existed in 1921 she

41

was suddenly prepared to do anything that might secure her attachment to Harry.

Letters began to arrive every other day, and in the days between, if the postman shook his head on the hill, smiling as he carried on up for Drossa, Sparrow knew that in the afternoon she would hear the sound of the car coming from Monument, filling Eillne with its deep throb. On bicycles they probed the hidden tracks of the river valley. After swimming they lay out on Harry's coat and watched sedge flies mating on the evening water.

From the telephone apparatus Bernard Love's voice piped into the hall in Eillne.

'There is great tension here, Sparrow,' Bernard said. 'Rebels took a portion of the town and were bombarded. No one knows what will happen next. Under no circumstances are you to come into Monument, do you understand?'

'What about our groceries?' Sparrow asked.

'Whatever you require can be dispatched to Eillne by Wise,' Bernard said. 'Is that clear, Sparrow?'

Sparrow said the easiest thing: 'Yes, Bernard,' but her voice betrayed her amusement at Bernard's apprehension.

'I should not have to make this communication,' Bernard said as his voice dwindled, then surged back. 'It is our lives that are at risk, not yours.'

Sparrow walked the length of the hall to her room, kicked off her shoes and undressed, stepping from her clothes and dropping them on the floor behind her in little islands. In the sky above the swimming river a hawk hung, engraved. When Sparrow told Harry her secret, fondness had spilled from his eyes. All at once he was busy with plans for Sparrow: shipping out, the date, the need to procure travel documents. His sisters, his mother, his estate in Warwickshire with its tenants and workmen and all the servants of his household, all were introduced with exquisite urgency, including a stout, old Nanny Morrissey type, although it was made clear that should Nanny Morrissey be needed to ease the pain of Sparrow's relocation, she too would be welcome. It was Harry's *excitement* that was so wonderful! He told Sparrow that up to then he had never dared to think he might be a father.

Day broke with the heat of afternoon. Nanny Morrissey placed a tray at Sparrow's bedside and pulled one curtain so as to illuminate but not blind. Bees worked on wisteria; a rake worked on pebbles.

'I'd love a swim,' Sparrow said and stretched.

Nanny Morrissey stooped to pick items of Sparrow's clothing from the floor.

'Has the postman been, Nanny?'

'He has not,' replied Nanny Morrissey, straightening up, red-faced. 'Nor won't be never, maybe.'

'What is it now, Nanny?' asked Sparrow and poured tea.

'Because, child, the gunmen have won,' Nanny Morrissey said.

'We'll be all right out here in Eillne, Nanny,' said Sparrow lazily, her cup propped between her hands. 'All we need sent out to us by Mr Wise.'

'I don't know,' Nanny Morrissey said. 'Dalton is in this morning with such stories. Scores dead. Monument destroyed and the only hope we had of keeping things halfway right, the army, out as fast as ever they can for England.'

'For England?'

'Mother o' God, Dalton says even the altar window in the cathedral's gone,' Nanny Morrissey said and blessed herself.

Sparrow sat up. 'What did Dalton say about the army leaving?' she asked sharply.

'Oh, child!' Nanny Morrissey cried. 'Put him behind you! All ever a poor girl got from a Tommy was a broken heart.'

'For God's sake!'

Erasing from her mind any travel contingencies that might involve Nanny Morrissey, Sparrow leapt from bed.

'Child –'

Sparrow dressed hurriedly and strode down the hall and outside to the source of the raking. Dalton, waxen and ever bent, whether over rake or spade or a bicycle's handlebars, raised his cap. 'Miss.'

'Dalton, what news is there from Monument?'

'A wicked scrap entirely,' Dalton replied. His eyes, like tiny blue eggs in nests of pink skin, took Sparrow in. 'The winda's gone in the cathaydril. Bloods' groom told me he seen dead men in the street an' soldiers lyin' plugged in a Lancia car.'

'But they're still fighting. I mean, the army are still fighting the rebels.'

'Norratall.' Dalton unpocketed his pipe with its metal cap over

43

the bowl, and put a match to it. As he sucked you could see he had no back teeth. 'They're runnin' like rabbits, commandeerin' ships. No one knows whether or not there'll be compensation.' Dalton dwelt on the word as if by association he might somehow benefit. He said with smoke and a hint of vindictiveness from the side of his mouth, 'Evacuation.'

In through the gates the postman was pushing his bicycle. From his untroubled face Sparrow knew that what she had heard was uneducated gossip; the very existence of the postman proved it. Triumphantly, she held out her hand for Harry's letter.

'The one only, miss,' the postman said. 'For Nanny.'

Fearful that the postman, if asked, might confirm what Dalton had already said, Sparrow ran back into the house and met Nanny coming from her room with her tray. Sparrow banged the door as terror gripped her. Plugged. The detail about the car, a Lancia, from the mouth of Dalton had had about it a quality of authenticity. Sparrow's plans had been based entirely on Harry remaining alive. Sparrow kicked off her shoes and buttoned up calfskin boots. She took the first hat she came to, fastened her hair up beneath it, grabbed from their trees a pair of light gloves and ran out into and down the hall.

'Child –'

'I'm going to Monument,' Sparrow said stiffly, making for the hall door. 'I won't be back. Say goodbye for me to Mr Hugo.'

'Child –'

Even Sparrow's unveering determination checked.

'Child . . . we'll look after ye here.'

Although Sparrow feigned surprise flawlessly – a pausing, a faintly puzzled smile – the knowledge implicit in Nanny Morrissey's offer, the common 'ye' that made Sparrow more than one, shocked her, and although Sparrow vowed as she took her bicycle from the shed that she would flaunt her condition to the world if need be as proof of her love for Harry, such resolve wavered each time it came up against the realisation that she had just been seen as someone in need of charity.

The hot day lay windless on the countryside. Dead. Heat produced a droning, sometimes a lowing. Sheehy, the farmer's son, saluted Sparrow from the back of his mare, clean and white as a cloud. Sparrow passed Eillne's national school and heard children within it. She pedalled madly, and if the truth be told, began to recall old wives' tales about how overexertion often precipitated the termination of pregnancy.

On the outskirts of Monument broughams proceeded, as did the occasional automobile. Houses on Captain Penny's Road that had formed an elegant terrace to face the Protestant cathedral were now roofless and oozing smoke. But the lead tips of the mental hospital's roof rose solid and reassuring as ever and midway down Oxburgh Street a group of men were calmly smoking pipes. Sparrow recognised one, an old stager from the Small Quay. He came forward, doffing his bowler hat.

'Two grand cheeks you've brought us in this mornin', miss.'

'What is happening?'

'Divil a bit.'

Sparrow laughed as if her attitude could minimise the impact of history. 'We heard you were all in flames,' she said.

'Two nights ago we were. There's a few dead all right, them's more the fools.'

From the direction of the river came sudden music.

'What's that for?' asked Sparrow.

'Seeing th'army away,' the man said. 'There's many sad to see them go and I can't say I'm happy myself.'

It would be unfair to my mother's intelligence to deny that by now she had doubts about the wisdom of her strategy. She recognised the great flux that she was suddenly just a small part of, and every time she thought of Warwickshire she felt, in place of recent happiness, loss. But neither would it be fair to Harry to doubt him at this stage, she thought as she pedalled. Harry was, after all, fighting a war.

At the head of Long Quay ropes of flags were slung from lampposts on the wharves across to a troop ship. Several hundred men and women, dressed as for regatta day, were waving and cheering to soldiers, deck over deck of them, a pyramid of heads. Sparrow dropped her bicycle and squeezed through. Young girls from Balaklava, for generations the stand-bys of Monument Tommies, stood hatless, calling up brazenly to the ship. Sparrow could see a group in the shade of the aft deck, officers, reserved in

45

their demeanour. She thought she could see Harry. The ship put up a huge, drowning head of steam.

Two naval ratings held the entrance to the gangway. Sparrow could see the worn planks with their horizontal laths, she knew exactly how it was going to feel to walk up from quay to ship, how the gangway would sway, how she would steady herself on the rope handholds.

'Sorry, miss, all visitors 'ave gone ashore.'

'Captain . . . Amis,' Sparrow panted.

'Sorry, miss.'

'Captain Amis is ex*pect*ing me. Miss Love,' Sparrow said. She went to step on the gangway but the sailor blocked her with his arm.

'You can't go up there, miss. Sorry.'

'It is *you* who will be sorry when Captain Amis learns you have kept me down here like someone at a tradesman's entrance,' Sparrow blazed.

The ratings exchanged looks. One shrugged, the other made his way up into the ship.

'Just one moment, miss, if you please.'

Sparrow *knew* Harry was on that ship. She searched the top of the gangway. 'Thank God you made it!' Harry would say, making her stomach leap at the very thought, as it just had. It was inconceivable that someone about whom she knew so much, with whom she had made such detailed plans, *the father of her child*, would allow her to wait in this fashion. The sailor bantered unintelligibly with girls in the crowd. Sparrow heard hobnails on wood. Back down the plank came the other sailor and behind him a soldier whom Sparrow at first did not recognise. He saluted.

'Miss.'

Sparrow smiled. In regimental trousers and tunic, Franks, the driver, without his breeches and gleaming boots seemed to have lost something of his dash.

'Franks,' Sparrow beamed.

'Miss.'

Sparrow said, 'I was almost late.'

The band's cymbals and the carrier's hooter between them made the gangway quiver.

'Beg pardon, miss?'

'My things will have to follow, Franks,' said Sparrow with an air of unstoppable momentum.

'Is you lookin' for the captain, miss?' asked Franks quietly.

Sparrow laughed. 'Of course I am,' and saw Franks through air bending.

'Miss, Cap'n Amis shipped out four days ago, miss.'

'Shipped out? Was he . . . wounded?'

'Left before the fightin' started, miss,' Franks said.

'Left?'

'As I understand it, miss, he had requested a transfer to Aden an' it come up.'

The ratings went aboard and pulled the gangway up behind them. The ship's hooter pipped like a trumpet; the flags tightened, then snapped as the vessel moved first a foot and then a hundred yards from the quay.

Sparrow remained face to the river. She watched the grey ship shrink into the bend and disappear. Then, finding within her that resource for survival she had first discovered when sitting on the wall of the mental hospital, she turned to pick up her bicycle.

An old man was sweeping the empty quayside of confetti.

'God bless those lads,' he said and tipped his head towards the river. 'I hope they make it home in one piece.'

'I hope they drown in their own vomit,' Sparrow said and began the journey back to Eillne.

Three

Bain never forgave Uncle Bernard for Leire. Years later, when Uncle Bernard was long dead and Bain was Minister for Justice, a son of Johnnie's who had tried to join the Garda Síochána but had failed on some technicality tried to enlist Bain's support for his case. Bain pretended at the time to help, but in reality Johnnie's son's chances of becoming President of the US would have been better than of becoming a guard once Bain knew of his existence.

We never camped out in Leire again – or anywhere – but in the same way that people use a war or a death to fix events in place, I came to think of my childhood as before Leire and after. Thus, we never saw much of Uncle Bernard after Leire; and before Leire Bain used to come a lot to Eillne; and it was the year after Leire that Nanny Morrissey died. Bedridden for a year with a failing heart, nursed in Eillne by La, she died one April morning before the sun rose with Sparrow and Uncle Hugo, as well as La, at her bedside. She was buried beside my grandparents in Monument, and is included on their tombstone as 'Their Friend'. Her name was Alice, I learned. Her funeral was on a wonderful spring day when it was hard to think of death. All the Loves turned out, as well as awkward but kind country people called both Morrissey and Fox. A shy man who was the brother of the man who had married my mother's sister, Baby, came over and gave me sixpence.

I asked Sparrow why, although the headstone gave Samuel Love's dates, in the case of his wife, my grandmother, only her age was given, and Sparrow explained that it was because there was no room. Dalton died too, but not until 1953. He just tilted into the hedge he was cutting. Sparrow found him, shears in hand. Everyone said how lucky Dalton was to have gone like that.

Those winters now all seem shrivelled into a single day in Mr Redden's classroom, whilst the summers are seamless and ever bright. Pax and me cut straight furrows between the two bends of the swimming river, and later sat at one of Eillne's big windows, listening to jazz on Uncle Hugo's gramophone. I often had the strangest dream and told Pax about it. About entering and leaving the same building many times, about that building's walls and gardens, its pieces of furniture and its peculiar smell of starch. I spoke of the woman who lived there, about her strange perfume. I hinted at but could not dwell on the size of her ample, fur-clad breasts as Pax might be disconcerted. But I was glad there was someone I could discuss it with: less a dream, more a gigantic effort to remember, it was accompanied by a sense of the most acute frustration, as if someone was trying to tell me something and I was trying to listen, but a membrane of time had grown between voice and ear and made the communication impossible. The dream always ended the same way: I lay between the woman's breasts as we both floated out of her house on a plank similar to the ones we used in the river delta.

Where rhubarb leaves sprouted big as sails I sat in May and watched La through a window at laundry. She shone with intelligence. She'd cropped her brown hair close to her head and rolled up her sleeves. I relished La's grace as she pummelled shirts.

My relationship with Sparrow was dependent largely on my daily management of her affection. If we sat together reading of an evening, I would in reality be half reading and half watching Sparrow, trying to anticipate by her expression, or from the way she sat, whether I might bell the kitchen for a pot of tea, or whether a window should be opened, or closed, or whether she might like a walk before retiring. To misinterpret contained as many pitfalls as to ignore, for to drag her from the depths of a book with a silly question about tea or a window could produce a wave of irritation whose ripples could still be felt hours later; and even when she was not reading, when a smile took over her face and her eyes were on the swimming river, I knew it was not the river Sparrow was seeing, but a place known to no one else but herself and Sammy Tea.

Correspondence left on tables, or on Sparrow's bedroom desk, contained clues as to how days should be approached. I came to know the letters of Father O'Dea, with whom Sparrow was involved in projects of a charitable nature. My Uncle Bernard, I read, sent Sparrow cheques, accompanied by ever terser notes. A statement from Wise and Sons amounted to over seven hundred pounds and bore a handwritten note across the bottom, *To be paid entirely at your convenience. D. Wise.* There were photographs of Sammy Tea, in addition to those in frames that stood in the drawing room. I found old newspaper cuttings from the war which told of the death by bomb in Antrim of a Billy Cross, wed only the month before to a Margaret Shortcourse from Monument in the Free State. It was some time before I realised that Billy Cross was Bain's father.

In Sparrow's remarks I began to catch a changing policy towards the Shortcourses. She began to order her meat there. It was sent out on Sheehy's bus, neatly wrapped in brown paper and tied with twine. Bain began to crop up in Sparrow's conversation; as a student of my mother's form, I knew that such events did not occur randomly.

'Bain has a new shop,' Sparrow said.

Uncle Hugo looked up politely from his newspaper.

'Very modern and impressive, I was pleasantly surprised to see,' Sparrow said.

Of course, what she meant was that Pa Shortcourse, her husband, had a new shop, but to mention his name in Eillne, even when some long-term strategy was being unfolded, was not acceptable.

Sparrow said, 'This joint is excellent, don't you think, Hugo?'

'Yes.' Uncle Hugo looked up again, this time with a grin. 'What used we say? "Pork leppin' out of 'em", eh?'

'They're making money, Hugo,' said Sparrow sharply, 'which is more than can be said for some.'

'Selling sweetbreads for the frying pans of Balaklava,' Uncle Hugo mused.

'How bad that is,' Sparrow said.

'Someone has to do it,' Uncle Hugo agreed.

'Someone to whom work is not a foreign language,' Sparrow snapped.

'I am most frightfully sorry,' said Uncle Hugo. 'I hadn't realised that we have rallied to the Shortcourse banner.'

'Sarcasm is the wit of fools, Hugo,' Sparrow replied and turned away.

My mother's will was inexorable and radiated from the severity of her beauty. We rattled out of our landscape in a gig in Easter week, Young Dalton at the reins. (He was not related by blood to his predecessor, but his name was regarded as unavoidably auspicious and he got the job.) Following the severe winter of 1952, small fields along the road were bare where poor farmers had been forced to graze the very first shoots. On Captain Penny's Road we were the only horse-drawn vehicle among motor cars. The noise of factories drubbed from the newly cleared area of Palestine, once a slum worse than Balaklava. Hopping off, Young Dalton led us up Balaklava past houses low and cramped. The way levelled. A tin lean-to shop on the gable end of a larger building had half a dozen women with bags lined up outside it. I got down so that horse and trap were between me and the shop as Young Dalton went in with our list. A burly young man came out, wiping his hands on his butcher's apron. Sandy hair rimmed his upper lip like curd.

'Gran.'

'Bain love.' Sparrow bent to let him kiss her cheek. 'Do you not see Theodore?'

'Hello, Theo,' Bain said across the shafts.

'Bain.'

I saw his red-flecked arms and wrists. I realised I was the taller by head and shoulders.

'You still at school, Theo?'

'Yes.'

Bain looked at me knowingly, then at Sparrow, who smiled ever indulgently at him.

'It's well for them that has the time,' said Bain with a little wink in Sparrow's direction.

'Did you give it up?' I blurted.

'I'm studying by nights. I'm doing business courses by correspondence. You still swimming, Theo?'

'He does nothing else,' Sparrow replied.

'On your own, I suppose?' said Bain cockily.

'He has the coots, don't you, Theodore?' Sparrow remarked.

'I'm a great swimmer, Gran, Theo'll tell you.' Bain smirked.

'Oh, I remember you all right, Bain,' Sparrow said. 'You were always good at everything.'

A familiarity to their conversation put me outside it. Bain, for reasons I had long known of but could not understand, had a special place in Sparrow's affections. He could infatuate her with a remark that coming from me would be dismissed as silly and she would always accept what he said, even in matters such as swimming, which required she deny the proof of her eyes.

'You should come into Monument some time, Theo,' Bain said. 'I'd show you around.'

'Theodore would like that, thank you, Bain,' Sparrow said.

'I'm serious,' Bain said, meeting my eye. 'Don't believe everything you hear about us.'

He kissed his grandmother and went back into the shop with its sawdust floor. I saw him take down with one hand a big hunk of meat from its hook and throw it on the wooden counter.

'The shop was busy,' Sparrow said as we went home.

By a tiny lake the haunches of cattle were like gibbets with the evening light behind them.

'Three women inside and six waiting their turn,' said Sparrow quietly. 'Money is being made.'

Eillne appeared in the distance.

'Money is being made in *our* shop, Theodore.'

'I don't want to be a butcher,' I said.

Throughout the summer Sparrow's campaign of chance remarks, of references to property rights, money and lost opportunities, increased.

'I have good news for you, Theodore,' Sparrow said in August. In frilled and rounded collar she sat upright. 'Good news for us.'

Mr Wise's van had just disappeared out the gate. Good news, I knew, came spontaneously and without such formality.

'Your father's health is poor,' Sparrow said quietly. She slipped a lace handkerchief from her sleeve as if to anticipate a further immediate deterioration in my tabooed father's health. 'I know we see very little of them, and that I have tried to rear you differently, but he is your father, which means that he must pass to you what is now his.'

'I don't want to be a butcher,' I said.

'Oh, so you're off on that spree again. It's not *butch*ering. It's business. Our business. You are your father's son. You must look to what is yours. Your nephew Bain's the *butch*er, you'll be the . . . businessman.' Sparrow laughed, as if despite herself. 'They've bought a motor car.'

It was a statement that somehow carried within it terrible possibilities for our defeat.

'Bain's studying to be a businessman,' I said. 'By correspondence course.'

'Of course he isn't,' Sparrow said. 'You take whatever Bain says and you believe the opposite. It's no reflection on him, it's simply the way he was brought up.'

'I don't –'

'We live here with kitchens and gardens,' Sparrow pressed on. 'Am I a cook? Is your Uncle Hugo a gardener? But I once learned to cook and Uncle Hugo knows more about the shrubs and trees in Eillne than any paid hand. You must first learn what your business is about.'

'I don't want a business,' I said. 'I hate it.'

'*Theodore!* Shall I tell you the alternative? Very well. We are selling Eillne. Tomorrow morning.'

I looked at her. She had stood up and her face was thrust at me and smooth with rage.

'Tomorrow morning I am going to Monument and seeing Mr Wise to arrange it. Your Uncle Hugo and I will move to stay with your Uncle Bernard. Your Uncle Bernard has no room for idle boys. You have no purpose to your life, no wish to work, to please me, to do anything constructive but listen to nonsense with that apish Sheehy boy. What a contrast to your nephew Bain, who has been working in your shop for years. Taking it from under your nose. I hope you're pleased with yourself.'

'Has Mr Wise suggested all this?'

Sparrow's expression perfectly encapsulated bewilderment. 'Why on earth should Mr Wise be a party to our business?'

'You discuss everything with him.'

'Oh, so you eavesdrop, Theodore, I see.'

'No.'

'Then how do you know what I discuss with Mr Wise?'

53

We sat in unresolved silence. Sparrow abruptly began to cry. 'I haven't had an easy life, Theodore,' she sniffed. 'Do you think it's easy for me to see you go away? All my life, people have gone away and left me. Do you know what it is like to have only memories left? Of course you don't, you're too selfish to understand. Now, when we are faced with a necessity, you are going to turn against me.'

I had never been able to solve the problem of the mysterious, intrinsic failing I knew was at the root of why I disappointed Sparrow, which was why in the end I always agreed to everything she suggested.

You seldom notice love in your life, just its absence. Whereas I constantly circled Sparrow, like a mouse seeking the weak point into a stockade, I scarcely heeded Uncle Hugo, taking his presence for granted. Mostly everything he said was on a wavelength I had learned to screen out. He was discreet in his weaknesses and led a lonely, isolated life, waiting for the days my mother was away to indulge his solitary pleasure from her wardrobe. A man of no measurable malice, parsimony was his only fault, that and a stubborn unworldliness. One February day in Drossa he had hurled Juliet Blood's entire gramophone collection one by one into the air for her brother Donald's shotgun practice.

'Less than a foot between us now, by Jove. Must be something in the air.'

He had come down without my seeing, fly rod in hand, to the sweet and scented hollow near the water, the last night of that last Indian summer.

'Sorry to interrupt.'

'You're not.'

'You're the image of your Aunt Baby, you know.'

The past lay achingly out of my reach.

'What was she like?'

'Tall. You have her eyes. Gentle eyes, Baby had.'

'You still remember her?'

'By Jove, yes, you never forget, you know. Jumping in down there from the bank of the swimming river.'

54

'Why did she go away, Uncle Hugo?'

Uncle Hugo's secret yellow eyes emerged to peer at me. 'Just one of those things, you know. The New World and all that. Took off with Fox, Nanny Morrissey's nephew, when she was just a child. Probably his idea, yes, that's it, I daresay, God rest her.'

'I remember everyone dressed in black, and a drive in a coal-driven car,' I said. 'Was that Aunt Baby?'

Uncle Hugo's brow went into tight wrinkles.

'Funny you remembering that, January '41, Sparrow had just brought you home.'

'From New Jersey where I was born, Where Sparrow had been staying with Aunt Baby.'

'Yes.' Uncle Hugo frowned.

I felt a desperate need that I knew Uncle Hugo could not satisfy. 'So why? What happened?'

'The Red Cross brought Baby's body home from London,' Uncle Hugo said slowly. 'She was killed in the Blitz, poor thing. December 29th, 1940. She'd just come from America, you know, on her way home here. Booked into an hotel and fell asleep. That night everyone evacuated, but Baby mustn't have heard. The hotel took a direct hit from a German incendiary bomb.'

Why did I feel so dismayed when I heard of my poor Aunt Baby's fate?

'She's buried in the Fox plot,' said Uncle Hugo. 'In her will she wanted to be buried in New Jersey with her husband, but we couldn't get her back with the war and all, so down with the Foxes in Monument she went, poor Baby.'

'But she had a son, hadn't she, Dan Fox?'

'Yes, just an infant.'

'She didn't bring him with her to London in 1940?'

'Lucky for him, poor chap, no.'

So Aunt Baby, a widower with a tiny son, left him behind her in New Jersey in December 1940 and sailed to London, which was probably the most dangerous place in the world, the month after Sparrow came home with me.

'Why, Uncle Hugo?' I asked. 'Why did Aunt Baby want so desperately to come home?'

Uncle Hugo's inner eyes made another brief appearance. 'Who knows why any of us do anything?' he said. He smiled at me. 'We were chums, your Aunt Baby and I, the best. You see, we were very alike.'

What he was trying to tell me, in his shy way, was that I was like him, and indeed in some matters of gesture and appearance, I am. Unawares, I catch myself in a glass door, or in a shop window, and there's my tall, slightly stooping Uncle Hugo of forty years ago looking back with that strangely seeking look, as if returned to ask me what has happened to his soul.

Facing each other, all the years we had stored between us seemed suddenly laid out in the twilight.

'Big day tomorrow,' said Uncle Hugo.

'Yes.'

'Big step into the world.'

I could sense rather than see tears in his eyes. Stepping in, he embraced me. 'She's so cold,' he whispered haltingly. 'So terribly bloody cold. But it's not her fault, always remember that, it's not her fault.'

We stood together until Uncle Hugo's face had dried and he could show it to me again without danger of embarrassment to either of us. He limped back up into the shadows. Fish rose. Coots came clattering into the reeds for the night. Uncle Hugo's generosity of spirit is what I treasure so much now. His meanness was all in the small change of life, the coins he fingered away into the pouch of time.

I couldn't leave the swimming river that night. It groomed my body knowingly. Lying out on its banks, I looked up at the stars and saw how each fitted perfectly in its appointed place. La found me, long after the others were in bed. She lay beside me without a word.

If by remaining for ever we could have stopped the sun rising, we would still be there.

Four

Before I, shall I say, discharged myself from Dundrum, the visits I received were largely confined to those from my legal counsel. She was a young lady named April, a junior at the bar, and her outstanding qualification as far as I am concerned was that she believed me. April described to me in detail the occasion on which she applied for my discharge from Dundrum and for my case to go to trial.

A familiar landscape of polished mahogany greets the visitor to the Central Criminal Court. The judge, a man of no pronounced qualities or defects, sat above the clerk of the court. Arrayed before him were Dr Croke from Dundrum, Garda Síochána Assistant Commissioner Pax Sheehy, my defence team of one, and an eminent but out-of-place pair of senior counsel.

The court clerk called out my case. The judge looked out over his spectacles. 'Miss . . . ah . . . ?'

'My lord, my client appeals to the court's sense of justice and asks the court to discharge him from the totally inappropriate ministerial order under which he is currently incarcerated in Dundrum,' April said. 'He wishes to stand trial in a court of law.'

'Dr Croke?' enquired the judge.

Dr Croke I know well. A cheerful fifty, a family man, he was also a hill walker. A boyishness about Dr Croke made you think his best days lay ahead.

'Thank you, Your Honour. The Review Board hasn't as yet had a full opportunity to examine the case.' Dr Croke sat down.

'Assistant Commissioner?'

Sheehy was a big, strong fellow, April told me, as if I needed to be so told, but as the months wore on she felt he began to carry about him a sense of having known better times. The way he got to his feet. The way, as he stooped forward, that his suit draped. The look of his new spectacles with their startling, off-blue frames, chosen you had to believe, by his wife. He said, 'May it please Your Lordship, the prosecution supports the defendant's application for a discharge from Dundrum,' and sat down. Dear, dear Pax.

'I am afraid I am in the position of being unable to do what neither Miss April's client nor the prosecution want me to,' the judge frowned. 'In fact, so far as I can see, I have no power whatsoever in this matter. Due to his alleged unfitness to stand trial, the defendant has never been tried or convicted and is therefore held entirely at the pleasure of the Government, in this case the Minister for Justice. The Minister for Justice is advised by the Review Board, which is itself accountable to the Minister for Health. I can do nothing.'

'The Review Board to which Your Lordship refers is appointed by the government it advises,' April reported. 'It exists to review cases where the defendant has been found guilty but insane – in other words, has stood trial. My client has not even been allowed to stand trial, my lord. He is lost without remedy.'

'And judged unfit to stand trial,' the judge remarked.

'But by whom?' April asked. 'My client is the helpless victim of a system whereby he can be detained indefinitely on the instructions of a Government Minister whose interest in my client's freedom is at best inimical.'

'That is not for me to comment on, Miss April,' warned the judge.

'My lord, the Government has had nearly two years in which to evaluate my client's condition,' April said, 'during which time my client's rights have been totally ignored and his freedom forfeited. He has not been examined once. He has never been evaluated. He has been ignored and left to rot in Dundrum because it suits the Government of this country. It is a national disgrace and an affront to human dignity.'

'Please, Miss . . .' the judge murmured as if everyone's morning was being spoiled.

'I will apply for a writ of habeas corpus,' April pronounced.

'Apply all you wish,' the judge said, turning to Pax with an exculpatory expression.

In the rumble of standing the calling of the next case was lost and had to be repeated.

The two senior counsel usually went around the back of Morgan Place to emerge on Ormond Quay, April told me. Their wigs and gowns lent a certain dash to an area notable mainly for decay. What they discussed must remain the subject of speculation, but the portlier mostly talked whilst the loftier mostly listened. They parted and the smaller, thumbs hooked propitiously into his waistcoat, strolled towards the Four Courts, whilst the taller walked to the Ormond Hotel, fifty yards short of Capel Street Bridge.

April confessed that on that last occasion, angry with the impenetrable nature of justice, she raced ahead and installed herself under an empty telephone hood next to where she knew her colleague would come as he had on every previous occasion. In he came, the taller half of the severed pair, to the adjacent booth. He dialled a number, then said, 'Henry here.'

He said, 'The application failed,' and gave a chuckle.

He said, 'No, nothing to worry about.'

He said, 'Thanks, Taoiseach.'

When I think of Monument I see Pa's great head in the sky over it, like a depiction of the wind in old atlases. He was very old to my eyes. His hair was lank and oily, his moustaches stained, his clothes gleaming from wear. From his chin you would think he had been outside in a fall of snow. The slightest exertion was a trial, causing him to proceed about with cheeks puffing. In the first days of our encounter, sobriety was his condition. He ignored me.

'All these pictures you see nowadays of the new English queen,' Pa told Bain. 'It's just a peepshow compared to when a pope is put on his throne. A peepshow. The cardinals in their scarlet, the bishops from every country of the world. We're the old religion, never forget that. The old religion. The Protestant Church is built on the balls of Henry the Eighth.'

Bain grinned furtively across the dinner table to see had I heard. Pa leaned back, thumbs in his waistcoat.

'The world has gone mad,' Pa explained. 'Mad, mad. No one has any time for you any more. Rushing, rushing. I was asked to stand for Monument twenty times. I always said the same thing: "Lads, leave me alone, will ye? What d'ye want with an oul' soldier like me up in Dáil Eireann?'' I'd be damned with callers to the door looking to get them indoor toilets, to get them this and that, rushing here and there for them, driven mad like they are. Up on my hind legs seven days a week talking tripe in public like Oscar Shortcourse. No way.'

The reference to Oscar Shortcourse was, I learned, a running sore. Pa's brother had become a local councillor, but representing those whose political attachments were the opposite to Pa's.

Residences in Prince Consort Terrace contained two small rooms each on two floors, with in addition a box-size kitchen downstairs. In Pa's backyard was a water pump and a privy. If Pa and I met in the narrow hall, I stepped into the wall to allow his wordless passage, or reversed down or up the stairs as appropriate. I wondered those first days if in fact he noticed me at all, or if to acknowledge my presence would involve some admission that he was not yet prepared for.

'Ireland cost John Bull his empire, and bad cess to the bastard. He'll never forget that. Never. Somewhere in London there's a bullet with Pa Shortcourse's name written on it. Don't ever forget that. I always sleep with a knife under me pillow. Always will. If you don't believe me, ask your mother.'

Bain looked to Mag, who turned up the corner of her mouth.

'Oh indeed he does.'

'Knew what the tripes of a Brit tasted like, that knife did,' Pa nodded to Bain. 'They'll have your name on a bullet too, mark my words. Never forget who you are, because the Brits won't.'

I saw Pa and Mag of an age: her hair was long and grey and her eyes were small and mostly obscured by the swells of flesh around them. In the back room the first morning, Bain ate puddings of black blood fried in margarine by Mag, still in her night attire.

'Hurry up or you'll be late opening,' she called from the kitchen.

I could see how her wrap fell from points of her body, making deep hollows.

'Give me a pudding,' Bain said.

'You've had three,' Mag told him. 'Think of others.'

'I've had two,' Bain said and winked at me.

Mag came with the pan, bringing with her warm bed smells and a little spiky waft of gin. A receptiveness about the flesh of her throat and arms was at odds with the coarseness of her face.

60

'Have you ever worked before?' she asked me, looking at my spotless clothes that La had packed.

I shook my head.

'Never?'

'I work at my lessons,' I said.

'God help you, you little crater.' Mag sighed and gave me the last pudding.

Bain and I went down Prince Consort Terrace together, under a cold September sky heavy with soot.

'Jeez, Pa's some man,' Bain said admiringly. 'He killed more Brits than pigs, he told me once. He's in the history books, you know.'

The Deilt Ambush had been briefly mentioned in one of Mr Redden's classes, but what happened in books always seemed very far removed from what happened in life.

'What exactly did Pa do?'

'Pa and three of his brothers – Sidney, Anthony and Lamb – were in a special unit that laid traps for the Brits in places like Deilt,' Bain explained. 'One day they were going from Deilt to Baiscne, British troops on a mission to kill, but they were ratted on.'

'By who?'

'Pa would never say,' replied Bain. 'But someone ratted on them and the Brits ambushed them in a cowardly spot. They put up the blazes of a fight. Sidney and Anthony and Lamb were killed.'

'How did Pa escape?'

'He shot his way out,' Bain said grimly. 'With a revolver in each hand, he went right through the middle of the bastards. Wham! Bang! They fell like bottles. Wham! The Brits scarpered off to get reinforcements. Between both sides there were two dozen dead – lying on the ground. Pa walked all the way back to Monument.'

'I never knew he did all that,' I said in genuine amazement.

'Now you do,' Bain said and kicked open the door of the abattoir.

The walls glistened. A central bulb shone through a mist of dampness. There were no windows. A low, wiry man sat near a pen of lambs, the first of their number across his leather apron. Bain took keys from a hook beside the hatch to a filthy makeshift office and said, 'He's workin' here,' before letting himself into the shop, its door banging behind him.

I looked around me. At a wooden worktop whose sides sloped upwards in a grainy 'V' stood a fat youth with a smooth, sly face. All eyes were on me: those behind the glasses of the who inhabited the office, the eyes of the sheep, frozen in their holding pen, those of the men either side of me. The fat one whipped his knife up and down a steel and sang out, 'Poor girl is lost, is she?'

'Shut up, Nero,' said the man with the lamb on his lap and punched a stiletto under its jawbone. 'Are you the fuckin' mayor of Monument or what?' he asked me.

'I'm Theo Shortcourse,' I said.

'Your Honour,' he said and made a show of mock submission. 'I'm Humph, Mr Shortcourse, beggin' your pardon.' A helpless bleat came from his lap. 'Could you get me the next beast, if it wouldn't be too much trouble, like a good man.'

'Like a good girl,' Nero purred.

'In your own good time, of course,' Humph added and levered the lamb's head back to make a solid arc of blood into a trough.

The flock bunched as I entered the pen, their sharp feet slipping. Their fate was all in the set of their heads. I made to grab, but they broke beneath my hands like foam.

'Tighten 'em fuckin' up!' Humph shouted.

Nero's knife flowed in languid strokes. 'As tight as your sweet hole,' he called.

The sheep dashed madly to the other end of the pen, spattering me with dark green dung. I then fell.

'My clothes!' I cried, scrambling up.

'The girl's dirtied her dress!' Nero cooed madly.

I made another lunge, but back up the pen charged the lambs. I squelched in pursuit; the lambs passed me at speed, adapting quicker than me to the situation.

'*I'll take you home again, Kathleen,*' crooned Nero.

I caught oily fleece and a lamb swung under me, bolting.

'*Across the ocean wild and wide.*'

'Catch him under the chin, Your Worship!' Humph called.

I could see that the lamb on Humph's lap had grown drowsy. He gently coaxed it, like someone working the last tiny note from bagpipes. Then he tossed the woolly bundle across to Nero's bench.

62

'To where your heart has ever been . . .'

Nero's knives clattered as he exchanged them. He turned the carcass with a swift incision. Out splashed hot viscera.

'Oh Mother o' sweet Jesus, bring me the lamb an' get another,' Humph said. I dragged through my bucking lamb.

I saw that under Nero's hands, instead of wool was steaming meat.

'Since first you were my bonny bride.'

Nero nudged his lips into a smiling kiss. My charge had gone suddenly quiet in my grip, as if it trusted me. Humph's eyes and mine met. Mine, I know, showed naked fear, but Humph's held nothing, not even the suggestion that he found slaughter amusing.

'The lamb, Your Honour,' he spoke.

The lamb twitched.

'Oooohhh!' trilled Nero and caught himself two-handed at his crotch. 'The girl needs a ha-hand!'

'For fuck's sake,' sighed Humph and grabbed the lamb. 'An*other*, Your Honour. An*other*.'

I returned to the pen. My lamb made a long, despairing bleat; the trough drank.

I craved sleep those first days. On the mattress laid on the floor of Bain's room I could imagine myself everywhere except Monument and the abattoir, in places free from blood.

'Theo?'

Bain had climbed over me into his bed.

'Yes?'

'What d'you think of Nero?'

'Nothing.'

'Don't go with him to the lav.'

'Why?'

'He's a cunt. He'll drop the hand on you.'

'Thanks.'

'I've seen Nero at it with himself,' Bain said. 'He dips his fist into a bucket of blood, then he comes into the bucket saying, "Oh Jesus that's grand!" '

Pa's voice droned through the adjoining wall in low timbre. The house was like the tent in Leire; you got used to hearing where everyone was and by the tone of their voice you learned the quality of their disposition. Sleep folded over me like the arms of a warm woman, like La's arms, the night before I left home.

'Theo?'

'Yes?'

'D'you know Juliet Blood?'

'Yes.'

'What d'you think of her?'

'I don't know.'

'I'm ridin' her.'

We lay in silence. I had last seen Juliet Blood, very blonde and bright blue-eyed, now at a boarding school in Monument, the summer before in Eillne when she had been in her brother Donald's car. The school was known locally as the Prison.

'All Protestants ride,' Bain said. 'It's not a sin for them.'

I thought of the Bloods and their kind, joined all over Ireland by a network of promiscuity. I remembered Juliet's smile from the back of Donald's car, and suddenly realised that what I had seen as mockery was in reality importunity.

'Imagine oul' Blood if he knew his young one was eating it off the butcher in Balaklava!' Bain giggled. 'She's a fantastic fucking ride. She can't wait for it, man. She begs you for it.'

'She's in school here,' I said.

'The Prison. Some school,' said Bain. 'Out the window and over the wall. A riding school.'

'Where?' I asked. 'Do you do it?'

'Behind Love's yard,' Bain said. 'I cross her over the railway line.'

'What if you're caught?' I asked, thinking of schoolteachers and patrolling railwaymen.

'I pull out,' Bain replied quietly.

Pa had begun to snore.

'Bain, do you love Juliet?' I asked.

'I love riding her,' Bain said. 'Yes, she's sound. She wants it bad, I can tell you.'

There was a qualification somewhere in Bain's voice, as if a hidden problem existed in this otherwise successful relationship.

'Theo?'

'Yes?'

'D'you want to ride Juliet?' Bain asked huskily.

I couldn't answer no for fear of being misunderstood. I said, 'I don't know.'

'She'd like it,' Bain said.

'What d'you mean?'

'For it to go on and on, like.'

'When?'

'After me.'

'*Oh, Jesus Christ!*' shouted Mag through the wall, as if awoken from a dream.

Bain whispered, 'Juliet'll be our little number, Theo.'

I sluiced coagulating blood into a drain. With gravity's help it would gurgle under Balaklava and down into the River Lyle. Humph stirred a knee-high vat of blood; Nero scoured from bedded blood the wood of his worktable. Blood lived stickily in every crevice. It shone from the concrete floor I had just washed. Blood old and new was spattered across the window of the office, from where the anxious face of Teddy Batty, the clerk, peered. He lived next door in Prince Consort Terrace. Teddy's father collected scraps that his big-bosomed mother fed to the pigs she then sold to Pa for execution.

In came Pa. He had broken two days before. Now in place of his grudging dryness was ire alternating with happy garrulousness. He had sung the previous night in a sweet, surprising voice. His hands, forgetful of my company, had strayed to my sister Mag sitting on his lap, to her thighs and breasts, in absent-minded affection. But Bain forecast to me a closing window of fondness as Pa's imperative became more drink, which meant more money, which accounted for his early presence at the business.

Pa's shirt collar was peppered red, in keeping with the surroundings. His bowler was tilted back from his hot face and he carried a walking stick.

'I suppose,' he puffed at Nero's scouring, 'there's money in that.'

'Bain said to kape ever'tin' clane,' Nero whined.

'Bain said,' Pa whistled. 'Bain said.'

'I'm only doin' what I'm told,' Nero said with a hint of protest.

Pa made a sudden jump at Nero, the stick high over his head.

'Who's the boss of this place?' he cried.

'Sorry, Pa, sorry,' Nero cringed.

Humph fished a dripping lump from the heart of the red vat. Pa rounded on him.

'I want to see you in ten minutes, up the road,' he snapped. 'Bring the car.'

'Understood, boss,' Humph replied smugly.

'And *Lord* Shortcourse himself,' said Pa slowly. 'How is his lordship this mornin'?'

'Well thanks, Pa,' I answered.

Nero giggled.

'Are you not out at the meet of hounds that's in Drossa Park?' asked Pa moronically.

'No, Pa.'

His eyes were small and vindictive.

'You should see the carry-on,' Pa told his audience. ' "How *naice* to see you", an', "How is poor so-and-so coping with life in Lon-ding?" '

Nero was collapsed over his bench.

' "Have you read about the *dread*ful weather in Essex?" '

'Good man, Pa,' chortled Humph.

'Back to "Lon-ding" with 'em!' Pa cried as if my part was paramount. 'Over the fuckin' cliffs and into the *say* with 'em!'

Nero let out a high-pitched shriek.

Pa whirled. 'What's the fuckin' matter with you?'

'Nuthin', Pa.'

We all stood, frozen by the situation's unpredictability.

'Get on with yeer work,' Pa heaved. 'Ten minutes, mind!' He nodded at Humph and made for the door to the shop.

I stayed until four that afternoon. Nero, assuming charge when Humph had gone, made me scrub all the floors and walls, sometimes twice, as he sat back, one hand pressed between his legs, smoking cigarettes. Rain slanted on to the river at evening tide, but the river, as I walked along it, meant nothing to me. I was used to water as part of my personal domain, to water creatures who knew and trusted me. Wet and cold, I turned back up narrow steps for Balaklava.

*'Bold Robert Emmet, the Darling of Erin,
Bold Robert Emmet, will die with a smile,
Farewell, companions both loyal and daring,
I'll lay down my life for the Emerald Isle.'*

The song came from the door of Pa's house as I made my way

along Prince Consort Terrace. Creeping in, I saw Pa, Mag and Humph with hands linked at the fireplace. A woman unknown to me lay across the table we ate off, one hand outflung. The table itself was strewn with bottles and flagons and glasses half-filled with water. Drink and smoke conjured false warmth into the house.

> *'I was arrested and cast into prison,*
> *Tried as a traitor, a rebel, a spy . . .'*

Pa's voice sang the words with a sweet distinction, as if song transcended his condition. A silent shadow, I edged up the stairs.

> *'. . . But no one can call me a knave or a coward!*
> *A hero I've lived and a hero I'll die.'*

Bain sat on his bed. On one side of him a nest of vinegary paper flowered, on the other lay dark bottles. A snapshot in a silver frame showed the head and shoulders of a handsome man: Billy Cross, Bain's deceased father. Bain offered me the paper and I picked up hot cartilage, sticky as blood.

'It's fuck all the food we'll get here tonight,' Bain said and drank stout from a bottle.

I ate the crubeens and flat, salted potato chips.

'Goodbye old Ireland . . .'

'Robbed every shilling from the till,' Bain said quietly.

Rain came to our window in urgent drops.

'I'm getting out of here, Theo,' Bain said. 'Going to America. I have me passage paid.'

'When?'

'Soon. America's where the money is, Theo.'

'When are you going?'

'I don't know.'

'You said you have your passage paid.'

'I meant I had enough to pay my passage,' Bain said harshly. 'More than your Aunt Baby had when she fucked off from here,' he added with a laugh.

'What do you mean?'

'Come on, Theo.'

'I don't know what you mean.'

Bain's eyes were calculating. 'Some gobshite called Fox poled her,' he said quietly. 'She had a baby. Don't tell me you don't know that.'

'I didn't know that,' I said.

'That's what happened.'

'I don't believe you.'

'I heard Pa telling me mother one night he was drunk,' Bain said. 'Sammy Tea gave them a packet of money and told them never to come back.'

'What happened to the baby?'

'How do I know?' Bain shrugged. 'I suppose she reared him.'

'The only child Aunt Baby had is my age,' I said. 'His name is Dan.'

'Jesus knows,' Bain said candidly.

We sat unspeaking, listening to the rain, our interest in Aunt Baby run its course. Bain finished one bottle and drew the cork from another with his teeth.

'Do you want to come out with me tonight, Theo?' he asked.

'Where?'

'Out.' Bain suddenly reached and caught me between the legs. 'Our little number, Theo!' he said, laughing, when I jumped up.

'No,' I said.

'Are you afraid?'

'I just don't want to.'

'She won't know the difference, if that's what's worryin' you,' Bain said.

'No.'

'You'll like it, Theo. Nobody will say a word.'

'Lay off, Bain.'

'So you really are a fuckin' nancy like you were in Eillne?'

'Who's fucking talking?' I said.

'Get outa here, you gobbler!' Bain cried and threw an empty bottle after me.

'O Blessed Virgin Mary,
Mine is a mournful tale,
A poor blind prisoner here I am,
In Dublin's dreary jail . . .'

68

Pa squinted into the hall's shadow. 'Ah, me own son,' he beamed, speaking in his soft song voice. 'Come in, come in.'

Mag was slumped by the remaining ashes in the grate, her flickering attention employed in bringing a glass to her mouth. Side by side, Pa and Humph swayed like a pair of old-faced infants fresh on their feet.

'This is my son', Pa pronounced.

'AyeIknow'im,' Humph said, needing his whole jaw to speak.

'Your boss,' Pa said.

'Yersun,' declared Humph.

'Come here to me,' Pa spoke and I stepped up to them, Pa and me about eyelevel, Humph hanging on to Pa's elbow. 'I love you, you know,' he said and kissed me wetly.

I could make out the open pores in his face, hundreds of shouting mouths, and his moustache, stained yellow from a thousand nights like this.

'My son,' he said with such feeling that I wondered with a rush how anyone could object to him in drink if it produced such depths of affection. He was gripping my elbow. 'I'm your father,' he said.

'I know, Pa.'

'You know?'

'Yes.'

'How d'you know?' he asked, tilting his head back and squinting keenly at me, as if prior knowledge about anything represented a threat to him.

'I just know you're my father.'

Pa looked at me for a long time. 'More than I know,' he said eventually.

'What do you mean, Pa?'

'More than I know,' he repeated elaborately. He checked around him (needlessly) for eavesdroppers. 'I *like* you,' he said. 'But . . .' He made a little play of being very daring. '. . . But I don't think you're my son.'

'Then whose son am I?'

'Does it matter?'

'To me it does, Pa.'

He spent many seconds in unsteady deliberation, like someone trying but failing to thread a needle.

'You're my son,' Pa said at last.

'I know,' I said, completing the circle.

'What else d'ye know?'

'That you're a real hero, Pa,' I said. 'That you shot your way out of trouble in Deilt.'

'Oh ho!' Pa said. 'You know all about that, do you? Who told you?'

'Bain,' I said and noted the satisfaction on Pa's face. Feeling, perhaps, that I might not get another opportunity to do so, I asked, 'Who betrayed you that day, Pa? Who ratted?'

Pa's mouth went slack. What I thought he said was, 'Veal.'

'Who betrayed you, Pa?' I repeated, assuming his mind had strayed back to his business. 'The day your brothers were shot? Who?'

'Brothers,' Pa muttered. 'D'ye know you have a brother? D'ye know that?'

'Yes, Pa.'

He shook his head slowly from side to side and his eyes did something strange and chemical. 'Your brother, maybe. But not my son,' he said, a martyr to the subject.

Humph took one step forward and two back, threatening our common structure. I caught Pa as Humph melted to the floor.

'What were we saying?' Pa asked.

'I don't know.'

'Ye're a liar.'

'My brother.'

'Not my son,' repeated Pa, looking at me with curiosity bordering on suspicion. 'No way.' He intensified his grip and his moustache prodded my ear. 'Captain Bull's son,' he confided, then seesawed, his bottom lip rolled out smugly. 'It's in that family,' he nodded cutely. 'Oh, be the boys!' Anchored to me he looked slowly right and left. Mag's mouth had become incontinent, the effort too much. Pa swung in on me again. 'Sammy Tea, too,' he whispered. 'Oops. Now I've let it out.' Fingers to his mouth in a stage gesture, he grinned, the watery way of incorrigible boozers. I could see a whole array of Pas taking their turn, old charmers and seducers, bitter old soldiers, confidence men and vengeful drunks.

    ' *"Dearie, dearie me, where is Sammy Tea?*
    Put a little girl in the family way
    Now Sammy Tea has gone away."

'D'y'ever hear that one before?'

'No.'

'But ye heard o' Sammy Tea?'

'Yes.'

'Your *gran*'father,' Pa said and squeezed my arm as if the connection still eluded me.

'Sparrow's da.'

'Oh ho!' Pa chirped. ' "Sparrow's da". Mr Big Boots!' A continual sizing-up and resizing-up of me seemed to be going on as Pa's eyes focused on me again. 'Died in the madhouse. Why? Because he put a young one up the pole. But who? *Who?*'

'I don't know, Pa.'

'You don't know, Pa. But I know, Pa. I know. I know where Sammy went to stir his tea.' Swaying like a pendulum, Pa's hand had no other purpose for him than its attachment to my arm. Across his face, like storm clouds, raced a succession of reflections and ruminations, as if the subject of Sammy Tea's ravaging more than fifty years before was still something that even a very drunken man considered carefully before he pursued. Suddenly Pa's expression changed again to that of bothered begrudgement.

'Of course, Sammy was a Captain Bull too.' Pa came in very close. 'Sammy Tea sailed in here and – bang! Oh she wanted him all right, Miss Sweeten. Hah! He sweetened miss, the English Bull. To her hilt. You know what? They'd sit down there for ever, Monument women, tight as hoggets, no one here'd do. But Captain Bull!' Pa's free hand cupped itself to his crotch and he yanked upwards. 'Captain Bull gives 'em one look at it, Jeez, they can think o' nothin' else. Why is that, eh? Why is that? What has Captain Bull got that I haven't? D'you know what?'

'No, Pa.'

'No, Pa. No, Pa.'

Pa suddenly became reflective, as if neither of us had the answer to the question or if we had, it was best left unanswered. He appeared to loose his train of thought and cast around him, perhaps to source drink. Then he surged back again, his grip on me redoubled.

71

'So what does he do then, eh, Captain Bull? He fucks off. Puts his rod back in his trousers. What are *we* left with? Eh? You fuckin' know *who* I mean – eh?'

'I don't, Pa.'

' "I don't, Pa." Me arse, you don't Pa.'

'I *don't* Pa.'

'Hah hah! He wants a fight! I'll give you a fight. Me arse you don't know who Captain Bull left behind. Why don't you have a look the next time you go out to Eillne? Eh? Then you'll see what *I* was left with. *Soiled goods!*'

I pushed Pa away from me. He teetered for a moment, then, with a few quick little backwards steps, he tipped over Mag and into the grate.

Bursting out the front door, I gulped in cold air and felt the rain on my face as I hurried down the length of the terrace.

'I knew you'd want to come in the end,' said Bain, falling in beside me.

Bain led me the long way down from Balaklava, throaty water gullys on either side. The houses had retreated inward from the rainy night. Pa's sly voice replaced my pulse. I shared with Bain the sudden wish to escape to America, to get away from Balaklava and Pa and from all the dismal uncertainties on which my very existence seemed to be founded.

Bain laughed quietly. 'Poor oul' Pa,' he said. 'He'll be grand for another hour, then he'll start breaking the place up when he realises the drink is gone. He'll kick my mother out and out she'll go because she knows she's dead if she doesn't get him more whiskey.'

We passed the Esplanade with the old barracks heaped behind it like a mountain. The lights of the Prison appeared. It really had been a prison, a square fortress under the eye of adjoining soldiers, but the soldiers were long gone and ten years earlier the landed families around Monument, in the face of war and of their shrinking means to educate their daughters in England, had acquired the derelict place for a Protestant girls' school. Despite attempts to alter its appearance, it still looked like a prison, and the Prison it was universally called, except by those families with money and offspring at stake, who spoke of it as Oxburgh School for Girls.

'What'll happen if we're caught?' I whispered.

'On a night like this?' Bain asked and made a face.

The Prison wall buttressed Military Parade in impregnable cornerstones that had done for criminals and should therefore prevent the break-out of young girls, or so I thought. Within the narrow arches of the railway station glowed yellow light, the way dim light is held in old people's eyes. Rain hung like fine wire above stacked planks in Love's lumberyard. We climbed a wall and slithered down an embankment to the hut of railway linesmen.

'Jesus, it's wet,' Bain said and produced a bottle, this time a flat one with a screw cap. 'Here.'

'I'm all right.'

'Drink it. I have another.'

I drank and burned. The tin shed had three sides, its front open to its business. A bench took up the back wall. The smell was of old piss.

'Wait here,' Bain said and slid away down towards the track.

Rain against light made a swirling emptiness. The only noise, somewhere off behind, was a ship on the river taking on cargo. Whilst I drank I pondered my severing from Eillne with unusual detachment. I thought of Bain and myself on a westbound ship, perhaps as deck hands, narrowing our faces into the spray and drinking whiskey in our cabins. Where I had been cold, now I glowed. The rain made crazy patterns. I drained the bottle as laughter came from the embankment.

Bain came into view first. I crouched in a corner. Bain leant down and pulled someone up behind him. It was Juliet. She stood out in the rain, angel-like, as Bain handed her a bottle. Juliet tilted back her head, making of her neck the most beautiful slope of flesh I had ever seen.

'Come in,' Bain told her.

She did so with a stumble. She giggled.

'Have another drink,' Bain said.

'I've had far too much,' Juliet said and made a little cornet with her lips.

Bain said, 'I will so.'

'Oh for the love of heavens, ride me.'

I sizzled in the rushing fat of desire. Not just the private parts of me but all the flesh that my bones came wrapped in stood upright. Juliet had stepped from her skirt. Her shining legs were perfect enough to eat. She was impatiently at Bain's waistband and all at once his trousers were dropped on his ankles. Juliet's hands stayed at Bain's midstation and he let out an agonised groan and fell to his knees, where she smothered him. Engulfed in a mist of longing, I saw Juliet draw Bain up with a tantalising mixture of softness and strength.

'Come *on*!' she cried.

On the bench.

Bain gasped, 'Just . . . wait.'

'I. Can't.'

I heard them from under boiling water. Saw Bain's frantic extremities. Thought of La and the sideways, inviting way she looked at me. I swam unstoppably with my most exquisite lancing, thickly delicious.

'Theo!' Bain was over me. '*Theo!*'

'What?'

'She's yours!' He jabbed his thumb. 'Now!'

Juliet, I could see, was bucking; bucking and crying, her hands digging.

'I can't.'

'How d'you mean you fucking can't?' Bain snarled. 'Why're you here then, you freak?' He dragged me over to where light fell like a yellow veil across Juliet's lower body. 'Help yourself to that!' he hissed, then looked to my trousers. 'You dirty cunt!' he cried.

I ran out. Back up the embankment and over the wall, I ran across open space, over cracked cement and thistles. The ship I had heard earlier was still working. Pa's voice was the one I kept hearing in my head; Pa's face was the one that kept appearing out of the rain, repeating over and over, 'Not my son'. If life so reduced its heroes, what place in it was there for somebody already as diminished as me?

Young Pa Shortcourse was in love. More, he was obsessed and infatuated. He spent his days in the shed wherein the famous family sausages were made, broiling with love. He could think of nothing else. The ticklish brush of gristle between the hind legs of a hanging pig carcass was enough to make Pa dizzy. The Sunday before, when they had all been late for Mass and he caught a startling glance of his mother's naked lower body as she had struggled into her clothes, of dark, springy hair against marble-white skin, Pa had gone to church and knelt in extreme discomfort up to the Consecration.

Pa sat in his backyard, both feet soaking in a bucket. With a gut on him like a porker, at twenty-eight Pa wheezed and puffed and sweated the way men twice his age tended to do. Wheezing now, blowing up alternate sides of his carroty moustaches with little gouts of effort, Pa brought his right foot up from the bucket to his left knee and with a razor specially kept, he pared gingerly the calloused tip of his inner foot.

Sparrow Love. Big Pa, little Sparrow. Her green eyes as she turned half away at the ice rink, although she had seen Pa lift his hat, yes she had. So ripe, so ready for children. Oh, Pa, you're much too big, Pa. Welcome, well-come. With delicate thumb, Pa burnished his trimmed flesh. Bernard Love would catch mice at crossroads. The younger brother – what was his name? Hugh. No, Hugo, that was it, hobbledy Hugo Love – carried a leg. Drink dirty water and you'll be like little hobbledy Hugo Love. Pa shaved white, calloused sole skin. Tea for the gentry. Good idea if only you could have it first. Pa shook water from his foot and by means of a looking glass examined his sole. No clouds marred the sky over Monument. From an upper field of half an acre, a place called Brambling where sheep and pigs were garrisoned between purchase and slaughter, you could see upstream on a morning like this to where the Lyle forked. Sammy Love came up that river over thirty years ago. Cute little whore. Most pious Catholic in Monument, the Old Man used to say. Turned Catholic to marry a local girl. What was her name? Sweeten. Hm. He had, the joke went. Sweeten with Love. They say the Englishman makes women weep for it. Fell in for her father's place on the Small Quay, then boxed her. Pa frowned. When? Something about that headstone, no date, just *Mary Sweeten Love, Died at 41 Years*. Pa dressed his left foot.

In the nearby kitchen, the mother clinked between her range and sink. Pa's mother, a widow, was a round, dark little woman who walked like someone used to a life at sea. They never spoke, her and Pa, their communication was of some lower order than speech. Pa slept in a bed with his younger brother, Ernest, a pale boy of twenty. Pa's older brother, Sidney, slept with Bartholomew, or Borneo, so called because his hands hung to his knees. Lamb, the youngest, still slept with the mother. Oscar, the youngest but one, slept in Palastine over the fishmonger's wherein he was apprenticed, butchering not being good enough for Oscar. Anthony, at twenty-seven the next down to Pa, had married and moved. Pa, Sidney and Anthony, Oscar, Ernest and Lamb. And Borneo. The night Borneo had been dragged out, feet first and purple for want of air, people said he should have been smothered.

Sidney emerged, a rolled newspaper beneath his arm. The trouser ends of his brown serge suit were turned down over the heels of his brown boots. His shirt-front was starched and he wore a seasoned bowler.

'Who'll win the Lincoln?' Pa asked, carefully barking his deformed foot.

'Weston,' Sidney nodded. 'His filly's well in.'

Pa rolled out his bottom lip. 'I'll sail under Donoghue's banner.'

'He has top weight,' Sidney said, shaking open the racing page.

'Donoghue's worth a stone any day,' Pa reminded his brother.

Sidney pushed the bowler back on his head. 'I'll stay with Weston,' he said and shoved the newspaper into his pocket.

A bright spout from Pa's foot made him plunge it back into the bucket.

'Bloody yoke!' yelled Pa, throwing the razor across the yard. He saw Sidney turn away to hide a laugh. 'I've no pigs to kill this morning, Mr Beau,' Pa snarled. 'We'll stand still today, I suppose, so that you can parade around the town dressed up like a Presbyterian.'

'We couldn't go to the fair in Gleann yesterday, Pa,' Sidney said. 'There was no train. The line is blown.'

'We couldn't do this, Pa, we couldn't do that, Pa. But Pa has to run the shed with no pigs,' said Pa vehemently, applying ointment from a bottle. 'There's Veale's hackney car, did you never think of that? No, Pa.'

'Veale wouldn't drive,' Sidney replied.

Pa's eyebrows went up sceptically. 'Veale wouldn't drive?'

'Veale says the Shinners have a Thompson machine-gun in Gleann, turn it on every car they see,' Sidney said.

Mollified, Pa poked his toe delicately into a stocking and rolled it up his leg. 'Ruinin' the country, ruinin' us,' he muttered. 'Can't even go to fairs in our own country any more.'

'I heard talk of Jews stirring trouble. Sucking money out of the land like blood,' said Sidney eagerly.

'Where there's Jews there's trouble,' assented Pa. 'Did you ever see old Wise except with a good belly on him?'

'Wise?'

'Wise now,' said Pa with a grimace. 'The Old Man remembered him with a little yoke like a saucer on his head and "Wiezmann" over the door. Turned Catholic because no respectable woman would marry a Jew.'

'I never knew that,' Sidney said, frowning at the undependability of even the familiar. 'Now that you mention it, they're going around in a brand-new motor car.'

'There you are,' Pa said and coaxed a stocking up the other foot. 'What did the British ever do but keep us from each other's throats?' He sat back and raised his head as if scenting the air. 'What else did Veale say?'

'Said he was up in Gleann last Wednesday. Said he was stopped by three boyos, could have been anyone, officials of the new Irish Republic they told him, collecting money for dog licences,' Sidney said.

'Dog licences,' Pa said. 'How much?'

'Half a dollar.'

'Half a dollar.' Pa whistled a monotone of air. 'And they could have been anyone?'

'One of them had a Browning automatic. Veale told them he had no dog and drove the blazes out of it.' Sidney laughed.

Pa put on the only pair of boots he owned and slowly laced them up as Sidney walked down the yard and out into the lane behind it. How was money made? Pa wondered. How did you *start*? Why was it given to some, like Sammy Tea, to get a money idea, and not to others? Over the wall came a bugle call from Monument's barracks. Pa's chest suddenly tightened as he was seized by the vivid and unexpected prospect of opportunity. He had no grasp of history, but instinctively Pa realised that behind every fortune is an act of daring.

They left Monument in heat unheard-of for early May just as a destroyer appeared around the bend of the river. All the month before troop carriers had been discharging men and artillery in Monument. Now, with the appearance of the warlike vessel, the presence of new troops, the ceaseless rumours of engagements in the nearby countryside, and the unexpected weather, Pa and his brothers had a sense of law and order suspended and an exciting but fatal perception that bonanzas were awaiting. Only Oscar stayed behind: Oscar had left the Shortcourse business for cods' heads and dogfish and could forfeit opportunity now, as far as Pa was concerned.

Pa sat in the front seat of Veale's car. Sidney drove. Lamb in the back seat broke the chamber of a Mauser parabellum, then snapped it home again, *crack!*, detonating the consonance of the Morris-Cowley.

'Put that yoke away!' Pa bawled.

'Sir,' rapped out Lamb, military style, and winked to Anthony.

'People bein' shot every day through tomfoolery,' Pa muttered.

Lodged between Anthony and Ernest, Lamb's knees poked the roof. Sandy curls rolled under the rim of his bowler and over his starched collar. He lacked a moustache. People said his face was an elf's: it twitched this way one moment, then that, it was never still. Lamb would never have been called Anthony's brother; Anthony wore a tight moustache, a serious demeanour.

They steered by green bursting hedgerows. Twin asses peered from a gate. The terrain climbed, turned. Suddenly the road ahead was held by a cart, a white horse and two farmers.

'Look like ye're Sinn Feiners!' Pa snapped and settled into a scowl.

Gas of dead whiskey competed with the astringent Pa had used that morning to staunch the nicks done with his Mac Smile. The curious farmers peered in at the big, bowler-hatted men crammed into the little car that was straining to reach the crown of the rise. Sidney kept his foot steady. Then they began to gather speed downward in a long roll through stands of beech with boles like stone, leaving the pair of farmers open-mouthed.

'Sinn Feiners!' cried Lamb and clapped his hands. 'Be the hokey!'

'Pull in,' Pa ordered.

They glided into a gateway. Pa, sweating like a porpoise, uncorked an amber flagon and wobbled it to his mouth.

'Give us a belt of that,' Sidney said.

The whiskey went one round, only Ernest abstaining. Pa looked at him: he had never even gone to school. Smooth face of a girl, smooth, white girl's limbs that lacked hair. Each night for years as Pa got into bed beside him, Ernest had meekly turned on his side into the wall and allowed Pa his way.

'Ahhhh-hhhh!' Pa took the last swallow.

'Go over it again,' Sidney said.

Anthony said, 'I have the book.'

'I have the gun,' grinned Lamb.

Pa rounded on him. 'If I hear gun again I'm damned but I'll skin you!'

'Leave the gun out of it,' Anthony concurred.

'But when did y'ever see Shinners without a gun?' protested Lamb.

'Keep it in the belt of your trousers,' Pa said and closed his eyes in a demonstration of great patience. 'If they get contrary, open your coat.' He nodded to Anthony. 'Go on.'

Anthony said, 'I have the book.'

'I ask the name, you write it down,' Pa said. 'I take the money. Say, "God save Ireland". If it's a woman, lift your hat. Ernest, you stay and mind the car.'

'What if they've no dog?' Lamb asked.

'Everyone has a dog,' Sidney said and depressed the pedal.

The countryside became abruptly raw, a raised bog. Mountains suddenly filled the forward sky with azure, pagan power. Where the road forked left for Baiscne, roofs to the right came into view and chimneys with regulation columns of smoke. Deilt.

'What if we're asked our name?' asked Anthony.

'Then Lamb open your coat,' Sidney said and Lamb giggled.

'Keep your hat on your eyes and your mouth shut,' Pa instructed.

Deilt was a huddled square. The police barracks, once central to the village, was a blackened shell. Beneath a sign for Players Please, an old man rested. A woman polishing a window stepped down from her chair at the sound of the car and hurried in.

'Turn ready for home,' Pa puffed, illustrating with the movement of his finger.

The car slowly followed the parameter of the square, Sidney

79

killed the engine and one by one they got out. Pa felt the way he did sometimes at cards, or when the morning paper was awaited and the day before he had wagered more on a horse than prudence allowed. Ernest remained, foot on the running board, his face nervous and pale. Oozing fear and whiskey, Pa knocked at the door of the first cottage.

'No one in,' Pa said.

'Knock again,' said Sidney.

Pa's feeble knock bespoke the draining of his courage, but Sidney hammered on the door, his teeth clenched. There were unbolting sounds. Lamb tore open his coat.

'God save ye.'

A man in belted trousers and stockinged feet stood in the doorway. Unshaven and grey before his time, he emitted a calm dignity. Behind him the eyes of his children shone like lamps.

'Dogs,' Pa said, then coughed and said much louder, 'Licences for dogs!'

With big hands the cottager gathered the heads of his children to his knees.

'We're from the new Government of the Irish Republic,' Sidney revealed.

'God save Ireland,' added Lamb with menace, one hand on his hip, the other on the butt of the Mauser.

The cottager made no sign of accepting what he had been told but with a cool gaze analysed each of them. Suddenly the transparent nature of their enterprise overwhelmed Pa. All of Deilt was behind him, unseen but all-seeing. He could imagine the shock from a bullet in the back. He longed for whiskey. He was about to turn back for Veale's car when Anthony produced the book. A solid ledger with a bright red leather spine, it was the detail needed to convert the faltering tableau into an official delegation.

'Name?' Pa gulped.

The man gave his name and Anthony entered it with over-wrought precision, looking up with a frown at the number on the door to emphasise the conscientious nature of officialdom in the new republic.

'Half a crown,' Pa said, confidence trickling back into him.

The man retired into the dimness of his cottage, leaving his children, now bolder, to stare at the men, particularly at Lamb whose face alternated between dark scowl and lopsided grin. On Anthony's arm the ledger remained open as if to close it would sink their credentials.

'Half a crown.'

The coin gleamed. Pa took it. It was warm from the man's hand. Anthony snapped the book.

'God save ye,' Pa said and raised his hat.

'God save Ireland,' the cottager replied.

As they moved to the next door, Lamb turned back to Ernest and gave him a cheeky cocked thumb.

Like most small-time swindlers, Pa was drawn easily into grandiose projections. Deilt had yielded six quid, no questions asked. Not a word since and over a month had passed. Deilt was just one tiny village full of dogs and half-dollars. Dozens of others existed within a radius of fifty miles from Monument: Clithar, Focherd and Sliab Erris. Sibrille that is by the sea, and Irrus. Fuait. Baiscne. Baiscne was half as big again as Deilt and would yield ten quid minimum.

This time Veale drove. An old campaigner from the Land League days, this time the jarvey had insisted he drive his own car. They changed down a gear as the foothills of the Deilt Mountains were reached. Pa, feeling a new sureness, looked over at Veale's apprehensive face. Old men loose their nerve, loose the hold on their bladder. They had stopped twice already and Pa had heard Veale's water coming in spurts like a pipe with a blockage. When Lamb told Veale to knock it on the gate, Veale said, 'God be with the days it's under the gate it'd have to be to stop me pissin' in me eyes.' Now Pa looked back at Lamb, wedged between Anthony and Sidney. Pa had once heard Veale talk in drink about Turkish women. Ate it off ye, Veale had said. Filthy that in the mouth of an old man. They crept out from under a canopy of June beech and the land changed as if boned.

Like Deilt, Baiscne's barracks had been abandoned, its constabulary withdrawn. Veale would have to get a deuce, but they could afford a deuce since Ernest had stayed behind. A deuce would make Veale part of it and solve the problem Veale's presence created in the first place. But why, Pa wondered, had

Veale insisted? Smelt money with that old nose, the jarvey, those greedy eyes behind the glasses spotted opportunities. But how had he heard? Lamb and he drank sometimes. Lamb mouthed too much. Lamb and Veale.

They forked left for Baiscne. The bog was wide and empty, a place of distant horizons and crumbling beehives of turf from the wet summer before. The road dipped, climbed. Pa saw a lone tree standing in the distance like a man.

'How much further?' he asked.

'Couple o' mile,' answered Veale, eyes ahead.

Pa whistled impatient air. He thought of the money they were about to make and would make in the days ahead. A car for himself would be possible. Pa thought of Sparrow Love in his car, of her gold hair, her secret hair. Pa thought of Sparrow carrying the child of his loins and became aroused. He thought of gold and money, of cars. Of Wise the Jewman's car. Pa was thinking of how he had heard that white women love the peeled flesh of a Jew when Veale lurched off the road at the tree and down a track.

Pa cried, 'Where're ye going?'

'She's overheatin',' Veale said and Pa saw sweat like pebbles on his lip.

'Jasus,' said Lamb as they hit a stone.

High walls pinned them tunnel-like in a long, bumping turn.

'Watch out!' Pa cried.

Men were blocking the way. Men in breeches and gaiters and slouch hats. The car skidded up. Pa's first instinct was to rebuke Veale, but the jarvey's door was open and he was gone, stumbling past the men whose guns were now aimed.

'You . . . !' Pa began to shake. 'We've nothing to say to anyone . . .' he hissed.

'We're tricked!' cried Lamb and tore out the Mauser.

A rifle cracked and Lamb's eyes went round as coins. He slipped down to Anthony's shoulder as if he wanted to whisper something, the white back of his neck showing between his curls and his collar.

Anthony began to scream.

'All right! All right!' Pa yelled.

They were hauled out, two soldiers dragging Anthony, howling and drenched in Lamb's blood. A man stepped forward.

Pa blustered, 'Who are you?'

82

'I am Captain, "F" Company, First Battalion, Monument Brigade,' replied the man quietly and pushed up his hat an inch from his eyes. 'And you're a thief. Ye're common thieves, all of ye.'

Pa recognised the inhabitant of the very first cottage in Deilt.

'We gave the money in!' Sidney cried.

'Where to?' asked the captain coolly. 'To some shebeen in Balaklava?'

'Ah Jesus ye can have it back, for the love o' God, come on, we're all on the same side,' Sidney said, his bottom lip gone loose. 'We're all Irishmen, for the love of God.'

'We are,' the captain nodded grimly, 'and some of us die for love of our country whilst more of us, scum like ye, suck her dry.'

'You have the wrong people!' Sidney cried.

Anthony knelt, hands over his face, repeating, 'Oh my God, my God forgive me.'

A youth in hat and patched-up gaiters, no more than eighteen, with rifle slung, carried over from the Morris the incriminating ledger. Amidst the browns and greens of the place its red spine stood out like a fatal wound.

Pa began to nod vigorously. 'We were wrong. Very wrong. It's not my fault, but I see it now. We'll make it up to you tenfold, a hundredfold, by golly yes.' He managed a little laugh of self-chastisement, then, as if it had been obvious to everyone but him, he continued, 'An army marches on its belly, by God it does. You need food and we've plenty of that, plenty, plenty. Tell us what you want and don't be the least bit shy about it. We'll bring you the best, the very best. Nothing but.'

The eight men in the semicircle looked curiously at Pa, some of them drawing on cigarettes. Pa clapped his hands in a gesture intended to reinforce his magnanimity.

'Oh be the boys!' Pa cried. 'Skirts and lights! Back rashers by the stone! And puddings to beat the world!'

The captain stepped back crisply and spoke an order. The soldiers stubbed and pocketed their butts and shuffled into a line.

'Oh Jesus,' Pa called out, 'oh Jesus, what are ye goin' to do? It's not me that's to blame!'

The captain said, 'Patrick Shortcourse, Anthony Shortcourse and Sidney Shortcourse. Ye are found guilty of theft against the

83

citizens of the Irish Republic. Ye have been apprehended this morning on yer way to repeat yer crime. By the power vested in me by Dáil Eireann ye are to be shot. Ye have one minute to make yer peace with Almighty God and may He have mercy on yer souls.'

Pa's hands found Sidney's arm. He took a step forward, then back. His legs gave way and like someone in a peculiar party game, on his knees he made for the captain across the rocky ground, belly and jowls shuddering. 'It wasn't my idea, I beg you, it was theirs. I implore you to give me this chance.' He sat back, wet-faced, on his heels. 'I have big funds no one knows about, ready cash. I beg you, take it, for yourself and your lads, for the love of God . . .'

The captain placed his boot on Pa's chest and kicked. 'Heap o' shite,' he said grimly. 'Prepare to fire!'

Sidney was the only Shortcourse on his feet. As rifle bolts clattered like padlocks, Sidney made a break. Hands outstretched, he rammed a youth on the end of the firing line and ran the only way he could, past the Morris, back up the grassy lane. A first ragged volley missed him. The walls hid Sidney. Suddenly he reappeared, a lonely figure up near the road. Perhaps sensing a final opportunity for mitigating his own fate, Pa jumped to his feet and began to shout, 'No, Sidney! Come back! These men are our friends!'

As if to prove the baselessness of Pa's every utterance, another volley sounded, a more even note, and Sidney, up on the lip of the high road, threw his hands at the sky and fell forward.

'Let's hurry it now!' said the captain, frowning as if he had heard something in the middle distance.

'He was a fool – ' Pa began.

'Shut up!' the officer snapped, motioning Pa aside with his revolver. He peered anxiously over the wall towards Baiscne, then towards Deilt. Anthony swayed where he knelt, his lips moving, Lamb's blood on him like a shawl. The captain, now hastening, faced his men.

'Take aim. Fire!'

There was, it seemed, the merest connection between the gunfire and Anthony. He went slowly over on his side, as if adjusting to a more comfortable position.

The captain's lips moved but to Pa his words were as noiseless as snow. He saw the shabbiness of the gunmen's get-out, the top of their vehicle beyond the turn of the boreen, the clear divisions of air in the walls around them where stones did not exactly meet. Pa saw everything in deafness. The soldiers wrenched back then snapped forward and down their rifle bolts, but despite everything Pa still could not believe their intentions were beyond altering. As if by the very sins it represented the incriminating ledger might somehow divert the gunmen down another path, Pa scrambled to the discarded book, then, holding it before him as both shield and offering, he knelt. The soldiers took aim. The sky split open with a whoosh that left Pa incredulous that death could be so easy.

Regaining his bearings, Pa realised he was pinned face down by a weight and, furthermore, that they were under siege. Having taken a discreet poll of his limbs and principal functions, Pa levered upwards and the young soldier who had taken the force of the blast rolled off.

'Are y'all right?' Pa whispered, but the youth, whose last thought had been to execute Pa, stared glassy-eyed at the sky.

On all fours, Pa bolted. At the burning chassis of the gunmen's car where Veale's lifeless head protruded, Pa checked like an immense rabbit as without warning his ears cleared and he heard engines. Scrambling over the wall of the boreen, Pa fell again to his hands and knees and made a dash for a deep ditch running north, jumping down and scraping his way along the bottom of it until he came to a drainage gully, a narrow cutting that ran deeper into the field. Clambering inwards until he could go no further and nothing but his arse was visible to the ditch, Pa began to pray.

The wind changed. Accents common to the Monument barracks came across the field in airborne intonations. A series of muffled explosions, a revolver fired at close range, punched the otherwise still morning. Then engines revved and there was silence.

Pa prayed to God for whatever was required to transform his life from the venal. Even though he was not to blame, even though the whole thing had been Veale's fault, not Pa's, still Pa forswore all ambition, clenched his teeth as past transgressions assailed him and cursed himself for his overdue recognition of God's mercy. Muttering prayers to give him chastity, Pa lay shivering the hours to twilight in his drain until all possibility of the return of the gunmen or the resurrection of the dead had been exhausted.

A horse and trap from Baiscne stopped on the high road and one man of two descended cautiously on foot. In less than a minute the cob was wheeled about with excited shouts and the trap flew back the way it had come at a mad gallop.

Pa took over the bog in a straight line for Monument. Night came and he lay by a bog oak, shivering in the twin grip of fright and frost, watching uncomprehendingly as distant fireworks lit the silent sky. Pa thought he had died that night. So did the besieged town of Monument, which made Pa's stark appearance there at noon the next day a sensation.

Five

The site of the Deilt Ambush is today a bleak acre of tarmacadam off the road to Baiscne where buses come from all over Ireland on 14 June each year. Men, women and children lay wreaths. There are speeches. Irish schoolchildren *learn* Deilt. In its immediate aftermath, the ruthlessness shown by the British to the wounded at Deilt came to justify many subsequent atrocities on our side – 'Remember Deilt!' – and served to turn men who had up to then been indifferent to British rule into implacable opponents of Empire. In later years Deilt would become a power base for a certain type of Republicanism, and would be used most efficiently as such by Bain on his long road to power.

Pa died in November 1966. Fog had rolled up the river that morning from daybreak. In the customs sheds on the Long Quay everyone was complaining of cold and if your office had a coal fire, as mine had, then you were counted lucky.

He had not been ill that I knew of. I had seen him once in the previous year, from a distance, leaving the Commercial Hotel between two men and being put into a car. I saw Bain often in the street. He had acquired the mien that comes with the early assumption of responsibility; he had married Aggie Sharp, a country girl from Deilt, and they had a baby, and wife and child had moved into Prince Consort Terrace with Bain, Pa and Mag. Bain, I knew, was supporting them all.

'Theo.' One of the officers put his head around the door. 'Your cousin is outside.'

I knew before I got up from my desk that someone was dead, I saw it in the lingering fascination in the young officer's eyes, the way in which people cannot help but take a cheap peep at the inevitable.

'Hello Bain.'

He was dressed in a dark suit.

'Theo, I've bad news.'

'Who?'

'Pa.'

'When?'

'He came downstairs at eleven. My mother said he just complained once about a pain in his head. The next thing she looked around and he was dead in the chair.' Bain suddenly began to cry. 'He never felt a thing. It was like . . . it was like he got the bullet with his name on it in the end.'

Bain clutched me there in the customs shed. He buried his face into me so that I could smell him there and then the same as ever. Nothing had changed. Pa had been my father only in the most theoretical way; for all practical purposes Bain had been his son, not me.

'We have to go to Eillne,' Bain said, wiping his face with the back of his hand. His ginger moustache seemed always to have been a part of him. 'I'll drive you out.'

I almost said, why?

'We have to tell Sparrow. You do.' Bain sniffed. 'I have the van outside.'

We went up Cuconaught Street and out Captain Penny's Road, our lights blazing although it was three in the afternoon. The van was filthy and stank of offal.

'He was seventy-three,' Bain said, peering.

Pa had always seemed more than any age he could be given, just as Sparrow seemed less.

'How is Mag?'

Bain threw up his head in a show of helplessness.

Pa had been no more a father to me for twenty-six years than he had been a husband to Sparrow. The only connection, apart from ancient marriage vows, was Sparrow's legal right to Pa's assets, my apprenticeship having failed so miserably nearly ten years before. There had been a ruffle of activity between Eillne and Monument following my retirement from the Shortcourse business: Sparrow had demanded of Pa that his political influence, if any existed, should be used to secure me a job in Monument's Customs and Excise, and Pa had succeeded, although I later heard Sparrow scorn this help, saying the only reason he had done it was to bolster his pride.

The landscape was cut from barrenness as a rut is cut from muck. Anonymous little hills and fields with abandoned dwellings hunched in them came at us now and then through the fog. These were the relics of homes, the people gone, like Young Dalton, to England, or, like Pax's brothers, to New York, or, like Nero from the shed in Balaklava to a sanatorium for tuberculosis from which he would never emerge.

'Poor oul' Pa,' said Bain grimly. 'If only he'd laid off the jar. He couldn't. He'd try for a week or more and then he'd go like parched leather. It was the fighting from long ago. Poor Pa. How could you begrudge him a drink after what he'd been through?'

The fog had spilled over the county, but whereas in Monument it licked sinisterly around street corners, in Eillne it sat in the pockets between little hills and wedged in a neat layer on the surface of the swimming river.

'It's feckin' lonely out here,' Bain shivered. 'No people.'

Nothing about the place had changed since our childhood. The gates and shrubberies, the gravel sweep beneath our wheels, the house on one level with its eyes towards the water.

'How's old Hugo?' Bain asked.

'The same.'

'Poor old eegit.'

'La is a saint.'

'I'd rather go like Pa, a single bullet.' Bain sighed and pulled up. 'I'd hate to hang on like that, depending on people to nurse me.'

We went in through the front door that was never locked. La was coming down the hall with a tray from the direction of Uncle Hugo's bedroom. Her smile when she saw me was one of the things I came home for. That and at night, in the long, dark corridor to the kitchen, when she kissed me. La saw Bain behind me, in his suit. She put down the tray and came forward anxiously, catching my sleeve.

'What is it, Theo?'

'Where is Sparrow?' I asked.

'In the front room. What is it?'

'My father's dead.'

La let me slip her grasp with a gesture of relief, as if to say thank God it is not news that can wound us.

Sparrow would have heard our car and seen our arrival from where she sat reading, but nonetheless, because to show

89

anticipation put one in debt, however lightly, to one's emotions, she went through the ritual of looking up, of recognising us with pleased surprise, and of gesturing us to where she sat with a look of playful puzzlement.

'Boys?'

'Pa's dead,' was the best I could come up with.

Sparrow's posture remained frozen. The light from the window, although dull, illuminated her face and allowed youthful beauty and late middle age to coexist eerily. Slowly she held out her two hands.

'Poor Bain,' she murmured.

He went to her, down on his knees, and she gave him the warmth he needed.

'He was a great man,' Bain sobbed. 'He fought for his country. It wasn't his fault that he couldn't do any better after. He put everything into that.'

'I know,' Sparrow said and stroked him. 'I know, I know.'

'He loved you beneath it all,' Bain said and gulped breath. 'I heard him talk about you before he'd get too bad. I heard him say, "My wife's a lady". I heard him say, "I married the beauty of Monument". He wanted to remember the old days you had together, when people respected him as a hero. He used to say that you and he were once the king and queen of Monument.'

'Poor Bain,' Sparrow stroked. 'Poor, poor Bain.'

La came in quietly and caught my hand and rubbed it gently to her cheek as if to say there were more ways than one to feel sorrow. It was exciting that she did that, there in the room in front of Sparrow. La had never done such a thing before.

Pa's death was as good to Monument as a holiday. By the time Bain and I arrived back, the well-practised rituals were already under way: Pa lay upstairs in his striped pyjamas, his hands clasped, already yellowly, around a rosary, whilst downstairs men and women began the business of reminiscence. Pa's moustaches and hair had been washed and combed out by big Mrs Batty, and his eyebrows groomed. Bain knelt to rest his head on Pa's arm and began sobbing. I knelt too. It was like someone had manufactured a good likeness of Pa and laid it out there. I could see the hair sprouting from ears and nose, the stains on the moustaches, the pores of the skin, the sunken eyes. For the first time from my new angle of observation, a petulant curve of the lips was also visible, lips that had remained hidden all Pa's life. They seemed to change his character completely and give him an obstinate dignity. Grief had stripped Bain and had brought out in him an integrity that had always seemed to be the virtue he lacked most. It was as if only a limited time was allocated for the untethered spirit of Pa Shortcourse to be rehoused in Bain Cross's sturdy, receptive frame.

That night of Pa's death, a succession of men and women added their touch to the tapestry of one life in progressive anecdotes that seemed to relieve their tellers of some final obligation. Lyle Shortcourse came home from England. My brother, whom I was meeting for the first time, was a bookmaker in Ealing, he said. He had a shifty way with him and talked a lot about the cost of living and how he would consider returning to live in Monument, if the right opportunity arose.

Pa was brought to the cathedral the next day at five. Like everyone who died in Prince Consort Terrace, he was carried down from his bedroom and coffined in the hall as the narrowness of the houses did not permit a coffin to be borne with grace down the stairs. Pa's fishmonger brother, Oscar, with whom Pa had exchanged scarcely a dozen words in forty years, stood spruced up and dandified at the foot of the stairs, receiving the remains as if in final settlement of a long-running quarrel.

'Sparrow's come in,' Bain told me from the side of his mouth.
'How?'
'Driven by your friend,' Bain said and did something sly with his eyes. 'By La.'
I blushed.
'Your Uncle Bernard wants her to stay the night with him before the funeral tomorrow,' Bain said.
'La?'
Bain laughed at me. 'Jesus, that's what Bernard'd like,' he said. 'The younger the better as far as Bernard is concerned. No, you eegit, Sparrow.'

*

91

What is it that makes death so fertile, that causes new hope to spring so readily in its place? Sparrow stayed that night with Uncle Bernard. Since La could not leave Uncle Hugo alone in Eillne, and I, in turn, did not want her driving back to Eillne on her own, I went with La. I imagined as we drove in the gates and saw lights spilling out in the direction of the river that we were returning to Eillne, La and I, as husband and wife. Headiness brought me to the verge of song, restrained only by decorum for the nature of the day. I stopped in the hall.

'The clock has stopped,' I said.

'We're all thrown out with the funeral, Theo,' La said, dragging a chair over and climbing up to retrieve the winder from above the clock's dead face.

'That's Mr Turner's job,' I said, drinking in the (novel) sight of the rounded backs of La's calves, the elegant way her legs gathered at the ankles and the arched expression her activity was now lending to her insteps.

Winding, La looked down at me over her shoulder.

'Mr Turner's not been here for over a year,' she scoffed. 'Too expensive, the missus says,' La said, in a voice to mimic Sparrow's.

Uncle Hugo was tipped over off his pillows, his head hanging upside down over the side of the bed in a way that was oddly familiar. His eyes, his only remaining method of communication, became animated at the sight of La.

'You should have been there, Mr Hugo,' La said, taking off her coat and drawing back his covers. Uncle Hugo, installed on rubber sheets beneath his linen, stank. 'Such a throng. They were all the way back from the door of the cathedral to the end of Military Parade.' La cradled the old man up with one hand and did his pillows. 'The Irish flag on the coffin, men from all over. No one had eyes for anyone but the missus. There we are. Theo'll take those dogs out for a minute, won't you, Theo? They've been in all evening, the creatures.'

Outside, the river played to the night. I wanted no second to elapse without sight of La. My infatuation was at such a peak that I was jealous even of the place an old, dying man held in her affection. The dogs were excited by the shadows and begged me to take them further. I was unsure if La's feelings for me were not just part of her general nature which gave equally to all things in distress, be they young men or dogs or uncles. I was terrified of diminishing myself in her eyes, of falling, on the night my father lay dead in church, into sins of baseness in her judgement. Yet the night was crucial because it was unique in that Sparrow was absent.

We ate together in the kitchen, an act that in itself was a statement acknowledging the temporary suspension of rules. Side by side, full of longing, I felt the terror of failure that came with images of Bain and misty, yellow rain and Juliet Blood.

'Is Uncle Hugo asleep?'

La nodded. 'All he wants is sleep. I think he wants to sleep for ever now.'

'He's dying, I know that.'

'What else do you know, Theo?' La asked with a sudden slyness.

My ears began their familiar boiling. 'I'm often afraid that I know nothing.'

'Are you afraid now?'

I nodded.

'Of what?' she smiled. 'Of me?'

'Of this house,' I croaked. 'I've never slept up there alone.'

'You won't be alone. Mr Hugo will be there.'

'You know what I mean.'

'So, where else might you sleep, Theo?' La asked wide-eyed.

My head went down so that I did not have to meet her eyes. 'With you,' I whispered.

'With *me*?'

I nodded.

'Well, well, well, Theo,' La said. 'All right, you can. But on one condition.'

'What?' I asked hoarsely.

'That you're able to catch me!' La cried and jumped up.

A new, mad look had entered her face. I grabbed at her across the table but she ducked me. I scrambled at her, kicking the chair aside. La made for the dark back hall. She wanted me to *hunt* her! All I could do was roar.

'*La!*'

I made it to the main part of the house. I could smell her and that brought me to the verge of blindness. I ran up the hall and into the front room where Sparrow usually sat; a boot flew over my head. La was panting as she unbuttoned the other. I dived as she sprang away, but I caught her leg.

'*Catch* me, Theo!'

I had her foot. I pressed my nose into her instep. La wriggled away and to the other side of the upright piano.

'Theo!' she screamed as I lunged unsuccessfully, falling upon and shattering the piano stool.

'La . . .'

I snatched at her apron strings as she ran out the door; the apron flew off over her head and the outline of her bottom wobbling madly was revealed.

'Mr Hugo! Help me!' La shouted. She burst into Uncle Hugo's room. 'Theo wants to rape me!'

The declaration by La of my intent in front of my invalided uncle drove me wild. I made a run at her around the end of the bed.

'*Theo* . . .' La hissed, pushing out Uncle Hugo's bedside table between us.

I could see the hunger in her eyes. Uncle Hugo was dribbling hugely.

'Mr Hugo, help me!'

La took the only route available, across Uncle Hugo. I saw the heel of her other boot catch Uncle Hugo's midriff. He sat abruptly upright. I leapt over him in pursuit, knocking him back on his pillows as I did so.

'Theo . . .'

I expected her door to be locked, but I entered her room unhindered and into semi-darkness. The room smelt differently to any other. La's body dwelt in the atmosphere, but pungently and strangely so also did the body of Nanny Morrissey, her memory in the safekeeping of her lingering essense.

'I love you,' I said.

'Come here, Theo.'

'La, I love you.'

'Stop talking,' La said.

Light came in from the kitchen through a high window. La removed pins and shook her hair out so that I saw her face sideways as if for the first time. She turned away from me, revealing again the high rise of her rump. I enacted the fantasy of many years and pressed myself to her bottom.

'Theo!' La scolded.

Her fingers seemed to dawdle down her blouse. She wore a cotton slip and was built much firmer than I had imagined, with wide hips. Her breasts spilled out big and ripe as she sat on the bed and let me remove her other boot and her stockings.

'There, Theo,' she soothed and let me suck each mouth-filling teat by turn.

La unbuttoned and gently undressed me as I sucked. I caught her around the thighs and hefted her up on the bed. Reaching for my scrotum she took me with a mixture of urgency and gentleness that left me abruptly swamped.

'That's nothing,' La whispered. 'Wait.'

La knew so much more than I did about life and death. She lay on my back, coaxing out my desire with soft language and the sweetest imaginable rocking against my arse with her moist cunt. When I told her I wanted to marry her, it was only by my tongue in the darkness that I learned of her tears.

The year of Pa's death and the one or two after showed little change in the run of life in Monument from the generations before. Joe Batty was killed by a car in Ship Street. Television sets became common. A Bartholomew Shortcourse of whom I had never heard died in the mental hospital. He was buried without fuss in the same grave as Pa and to my surprise Sparrow shed tears at the graveside for this man I had never met and to whom she referred as Borneo.

I stayed between Mondays and Saturdays in lodgings on Ladies' Walk with two spinster ladies whose father had worked for Sammy Tea in the old days. Perhaps because I had spent my life reacting to minute changes in my mother's disposition, I could pick out a smuggler on sight. I got quite a name for it and was always required to be present for difficult cases. I studied for a customs and excise examination. La nursed Uncle Hugo's husk in Eillne and one Saturday night as I pressed La to me in the shadows of the kitchen, Sparrow appeared soundlessly from the mouth of the passage a second before La saw her and broke away from me, dusting off the shoulders of my jacket.

95

I began to notice a change in Sparrow's attitude to La. La was suddenly and frequently to blame for all the minor trials of life, and by reason of her lack of education and low beginnings was held by Sparrow to be a burden tolerated on grounds of charity alone. Sparrow's belittling remarks invariably came in such a way as to make us both the patient victims of a bumbling peasant girl. Despite the obvious baselessness of Sparrow's inferences, despite the fact that I loved La and that she ran our household and attended to all the needs of a helpless invalid, Sparrow's campaign created a warm ambience where I was concerned and allowed me to bask fondly as my mother's ally.

Pa's house and business, the sheds and fields here and there accumulated from the time of his own father when they had been worth no more than a beast or two, but now suddenly, when you added them all up amounted to something, this ragbag of assorted titles, leases and unencumbered deeds went to Sparrow. Bain borrowed money from the bank and bought from Sparrow the house he lived in and half the business he had built up from when he was little more than a child, and the field above Monument called Brambling, the place where sheep awaited execution, probably unmindful of the splendid views upriver to the Deilt mountains. An attempt was made to block these sales by Lyle Shortcourse, my brother, whose interests were represented by a Dublin solicitor. The action was badly mounted and failed to reach a court.

Married, with a child, Bain was the proprietor of a business, and at twenty-six the elected choice of Balaklava to the Monument Council. There were days at lunch time when I saw Sparrow driving up to Balaklava and I knew that just as Bain privately went out to Eillne to discuss business matters as between two equals, so too Sparrow came to Monument without bothering to bid me the time of day. Sometimes after work I strolled up in the direction of the shed, hoping to find Sparrow there, and although such chance forays always led to disappointment, there were times on the backs steps, or on the winding Priests' Way, when I encountered Bain.

'What're you doing up here, Theo?'

'Just taking a walk.'

'Are you getting bored of all that paperwork? Are you coming back to work in the butchering business?'

'I'll leave that to you, Bain.'

'How's La?' he asked, sticking his tongue into the side of his mouth.

'I don't know,' I shrugged, ablaze. 'Fine, I suppose.'

'She's a grand little number, in her own way, Theo,' Bain nodded.

'What do you mean?'

'Lob the odd one into her if you want to, that's your business,' Bain said and looked away as if it was not something he would contemplate. 'But don't get carried away – you know what I mean?' He chortled and slapped my arm to show how his advice was founded on good-natured concern.

'It's my business, as you say,' I said.

'Theo,' said Bain and winced. 'Sparrow is a very clever woman. You should listen to her, OK?'

They had discussed me, it was clear. I suddenly saw a way to turn Sparrow on the subject of my love for La. If Bain were to be the supporter of my cause, then Sparrow, too, would accept my position.

'Look, I know Sparrow doesn't approve,' I said, 'but it's nothing to you, is it?'

Bain looked at his watch.

'The next time you see Sparrow,' I said, 'just say something to her like "I think La would suit Theo very nicely", or "La is a very nice girl". Will you? Please?'

'Of course I will, Theo,' Bain said slowly. 'No problem, old son.'

Growing up, I had always thought that Bain was driven mainly by the urge to be cruel, and maybe he was, but as a man that would be to underestimate his motives. Even in a simple street encounter he always had a strategy, he never saw people as themselves but as voters to be won over by him. To see them otherwise was a wasted opportunity.

'I heard', I couldn't help saying, 'that you could be the mayor of Monument next year. The *Gazette* said so.'

'If they want me, they know where to find me,' Bain said coyly. He gave me his half-smiling, curious look. 'What d'you make of that, Theo? I mean, nobody knows me half as well as Theo Shortcourse. Not even my wife.'

He might have been trying to see if the past, with its dangers, was forgotten, or he may have been probing my reaction, and the reaction of clerks like me, to his political progress, or perhaps he flattered every likely voter by enlisting their opinion of himself.

'I'm Pa's son and you're his grandson, Bain,' I said, 'except that nature put us the wrong way round.'

'That's right,' he said slowly. 'Everything I do is for Pa. For him and for all the people who've gone before us and died for their beliefs.'

'Don't forget what I asked you to do,' I called after him.

In April each year it was Bain who took the honours out at Deilt. He held aloft a pistol and cleft the empty heavens in the name of the dead. It was a matter in which he would always be both blind and true: true to the memories he had received intact, blind to their fallibility.

There were few opportunities when Sparrow was absent from Eillne, leaving me alone with La, but even these potential occasions for sin were thwarted due to La's terror of Sparrow. Once, remembering Bain's tactics in somewhat similar circumstances, when I resorted to cornering La near the coal shed and guiding her hand to my erection, her reaction was one of such disgust that I never tried that approach again. The infinite complexities of her emotions baffled me. Buoyed only by the memory of our single night together, I returned to Eillne each Saturday with renewed hope, but the most I ever achieved was a stolen kiss. She began to turn away from my touch. Her brown eyes saw me knowingly and I knew it was only for Uncle Hugo that she remained in Eillne.

'La . . .'

'No, Theo. No.'

'I want you more than my own life.'

La looked quickly to the kitchen door. 'It's no use.'

'We'll run away.'

'I couldn't leave poor Mr Hugo any more than you could leave Sparrow.'

'I could!'

'Where would we go? What future would we have? Your future is here, in Eillne and Monument.'

98

I held her and she turned her head away as I kissed her neck.

'I dream the whole week of coming into your room on a Saturday night,' I whispered. 'Look at me, La!'

'Theo!' La hissed.

'Please.'

She struck me across the head with a ladle.

'What if I gave you your way with me, Theo?' La jeered. 'Where would you be tomorrow morning after Mass? Up in the front room with herself, licking her boots. Why don't you stand up for me when she says "La, try and not bang the door every time you leave the room", or "La, the switch on the wall beside the kitchen door is for the light. Try and use it more often, like a good girl. We're not made of money"? When she goes on like that and then looks over at you, why don't you ever speak up, Theo?'

I usually came out to Eillne on Sheehy's bus after lunch on Saturday when the office closed. Pax's father had once had hopes that Pax would stay in the business, but Pax had gone away to become a guard. A new bus had been brought from England, in reality a fly-blown jamboree on wheels. At four o'clock on Saturdays the stout farmers' wives in their paisley boarded Sheehy's bus with their shopping, sucking ice-creams whilst their menfolk lurched against each other glassy-eyed from drink. We made out for Eillne.

Sparrow was standing at the hall door. I thought from the way she looked at me, from her sorrowful smile, that something was amiss.

'What is it?'

'Nothing, Theodore.' We kissed. 'I wanted to catch you before you went off on one of your little expeditions. We have a guest for supper, that's why I've been counting the minutes that bus has been overdue. You smell of it. I don't know how that man is allowed on the public road with such a thing.'

'Who is the guest?'

'A surprise,' Sparrow said and played the little girl by biting her bottom lip. 'Now the best thing you could possibly do, Theodore, would be to have a swim. You look hot, my darling. Hurry along.'

Sparrow seemed resigned in her attitude to me ; I wondered whether Bain had done his bit on my behalf. I put my head in on Uncle Hugo who was asleep, then got a towel and went down the hall and out through the kitchen. La did not pause when she saw me; she moved between pots and simmering dishes in a blur. I looked up the passage, then moved closer in and put my hand lightly in the cleft of her rump. La's face when she turned was set like that of a cornered vixen.

'Get away!'

'La?'

'*Get away!*'

I reached out to her.

'If you touch me again I'll spill this boiling water over you, so help me!' she spat.

'It's going to be all right!' I whispered.

La turned to her range. Preparation far beyond the normal was in train. La would be better later on, after supper, I decided. While Sparrow sat chatting with our guest, whoever that was, I would come down and find La restored and calm.

'Who is the guest?' I asked.

'Oh, that's not the business of the kitchen,' La said and slammed down a steaming colander.

I went out through the kitchen garden and down the steps betweens terraces that overhung the river. Since Uncle Hugo's stroke, no entertainment had taken place in Eillne, nor did Sparrow accept any invitations that I knew of. Other than her trips to Monument, and tea with Mr Wise who still came personally with her order, the society of people was something Sparrow made do without. The conical indentations that were as much a part of the river as surprises are part of life revolved drowsily in the aftermath of the baking day. I carried up my clothes and was dry before I reached the house. I heard the doorbell from my room and tied, as I had recently learned, a Windsor knot, then with a light step made my way down the hall. As I entered the drawing room two women looked up at me. Sparrow and Juliet Blood.

'Theodore, look who our surprise guest is! He's lost for words.'

Juliet laughed. I felt ill.

'Theodore will find us all a little Madeira, won't you Theodore? And then we'll go in for supper – that is, if supper is not burnt to a cinder,' Sparrow said, her eyes floating up as Juliet laughed again.

From the side table where decanters were put out on such occasions, I fiddled around with glasses and observed Juliet. She hadn't changed much. Her airy blouse showed off the long, smooth line of her neck where her very fair hair was collected in a red toggle before falling in a brush between her shoulder blades. She had kicked her shoes off and tucked her bare legs up beneath her on the couch so that from where I stood I could see her dirty soles peeping out from under her dress in my direction, like an invitation to share a scandalous secret. I poured the drinks.

'How is Donald?' Sparrow asked.

'Sitting on a high stool somewhere in London, I should imagine,' Juliet said.

'He should marry,' Sparrow said.

'*Don*ald? Who on earth would have him?'

'I miss him coming and going. So does Hugo, I know,' Sparrow said.

'I'm sure,' Juliet replied with a little smile.

'And your father?'

'Says he's going to hunt this season. He's mad. He'll kill himself.'

'Theodore would love to learn to ride.' Sparrow beamed. 'Theodore, you should have a horse, darling.'

'I'll teach you in Drossa, Theo, if you teach me to swim in Eillne,' Juliet said.

I said, 'All right.'

'Didn't you used to have a pony?' Juliet frowned.

I nodded and then tried in vain to think of something else to say because I knew what was coming.

'Bain rode it more than Theodore,' Sparrow said.

'I'm sure he did,' Juliet responded, looking directly at me.

All Bain's explanations of ten years before concerning Protestants and sin crystallised for me in the most painful head of desire. We went into supper and Sparrow took a small brass bell in the shape of a woman in a long dress and rang it. I didn't meet La's eyes, nor she mine, as she hurried in with the soup tureen. La looked hot against Juliet's blue-eyed cool; La looked bothered as she served us, whereas Juliet, for whom La was invisible, smiled and laughed. Even La's obvious intelligence seemed for a moment to be a primitive projection of something that people like Juliet had learned not to show, or, even more, to do without.

'What exactly do you do, Theo?'

'I'm an officer in the Customs and Excise.'

'Oh, is that interesting?'

'He runs the country, don't you, Theodore?'

'It depends on what you find interesting.'

'I'm afraid I understand very little about running the country. You prob'ly think I'm very boring, Theo.'

'Of course he doesn't. Mmmm. She's actually somehow managed to make half-decent soup.'

'From your recipe, Sparrow, I'm sure.'

I knew the easy way that Juliet could come into a house like ours and kick her shoes off went with a way of life that La could never understand. Yet for all her cool, knowing ways, I could sense beneath Juliet's skin a raging impatience. It showed between exchanges of conversation, when Sparrow was attempting to coax words from me by asking me questions that required an answer, and I, mumbling my reply, saw a sense of bottomless regret pass across Juliet's face, as if she were condemned for ever to remain in some way unfulfilled. Then Sparrow would say, 'Don't you agree, Juliet?' and Juliet would whirl back to the matters at hand, saying, 'Of course,' the smile on her mouth unable for just an instant to overtake the irritation in her eyes.

Juliet was collected after supper by Reggie's chauffeur. She kissed Sparrow, then came to me on the side that put me between her and Sparrow, and quick and efficient as a lizard, darted the hot tip of her tongue into my ear.

'Bye, Theo,' she sang, as the driver loaded and rugged her for the trip to Drossa.

'What a charming girl,' Sparrow said. 'How lucky you are, Theodore, to have such a beautiful friend.'

The next evening before I went back to Monument, La left six shirts ironed on my bed, one for every day that would pass before I came home again.

In 1969 Monument began a short burst of prosperity that in later years would be looked back on and thought of as a golden age. Factories were set up. Credit became widely available. Bathed at last in the backwash of the postwar revival, Monument heaped praise on its leaders and Bain Cross became not only the youngest mayor in the town's history but also the first to serve two terms in succession. He had built himself a new home up in Brambling, so that everyone could look up and see the home of the man they had (or had not) voted for.

La was no match for Sparrow and it became clear to me that La's presence in Eillne was guaranteed only as long as Uncle Hugo clung to life. Although Juliet was most attractive, with a quality of availability that, in bed alone in Monument, made me think of her almost as often as I thought of La, the sheer, overwhelming force of Juliet's sexuality created in me uncertainty and a fear of failure. One Sunday morning in early December, knowing Sparrow to be out, I went to La's room with its deep smells, and she let me lie with her on top of the bed and kiss her tears away, so that the next day I went back to a windswept Monument swelled with a resolve that when next I came home I would confront Sparrow with the full evidence of my love.

Reggie Blood lived according to the attitude and style of a Renaissance prince in exile. He never went outside Drossa. He saw his sister sometimes. She married a Monument businessman, a prosperous Catholic, so brother and sister harboured a mutual disapproval, as if their contrasting circumstances testified to an ancient interlude of treachery. In old age Reggie had become hunched so that he carried his face, which was always set in a half-smile of quaint amusement, level with his right shoulder. It was said that unlike his brothers in the years immediately after independence, Reggie had stayed put because he had been unaware of the commotion. Whatever the reason, his relevance to the affairs of the country in which he lived, and theirs to him, had been on courses of widening divergence for his entire lifetime and before, so that Reggie's attitude to Ireland and the Irish, although impeccably courteous, was founded entirely on the shaky ground of patronage.

On the Saturdays on which Juliet was not invited by Sparrow to Eillne, Sparrow and I were invited to Drossa. The sheer relentlessness of our mutual socialising was bent on making up for lost time and making the outcome between Juliet and me increasingly inevitable.

'Remind me what you do,' said Reggie Blood.

'Theodore works for the Customs and Excise in Monument,' Sparrow explained. 'He is an Assistant Preventive Officer.'

103

'Splendid,' Reggie said. 'Donald works for an accountant in Ipswich, you know. Same sort of thing. D'you hunt?'

'Juliet will teach him,' Sparrow said.

'Does he live in Eillne?'

'He stays in Monument during the week, but he will live in Eillne, won't you, Theodore?'

'Lovely house,' Reggie said. 'I remember as a child it being built, you know. I remember your father, Sparrow, Sammy Love, a small man; but full of energy. He came out here every Sunday for nearly two years before he decided exactly where to build. Then it was all business, walking up and down the bank of the river every day with plans, pointing here and there, giving instructions. Took twenty men six months to level the site, you know. You weren't born then, Sparrow. Even Hugo was with his nurse, but he and Bernard were brought out to see.'

'Do you remember my grandmother?'

Reggie and Sparrow both turned as if surprised that I could speak.

'Yes, I do,' Reggie answered slowly, although something guarded had entered his face. 'I'm so old I remember the Ark.'

It was the mystery of my grandmother's tombstone that impelled me. I asked, 'Did Sammy Tea bring my grandmother out here too?'

'Your grandmother died young, poor woman,' replied Reggie, confused.

'I know,' I said, 'but when exactly did she die?'

'When?' Reggie said. 'Good Lord, there's a question.'

'The year,' I said. 'It's not on her tombstone, Sparrow,' I said, turning to my mother. 'It just gives her name, above Sammy's, no date, it just says, "Died at 41 Years".'

'What a very morbid conversation,' Juliet said.

'Quite,' Sparrow frowned, although I could see the attention in her face.

'Alternatively, what year was she born?' I asked. 'Same thing, since we know her age.'

'Bloody accountants are all the same.' Reggie smirked.

'I mean, obviously she died after Sparrow was born,' I said to Reggie's increasingly scowling face. 'But when? Sparrow was born in February 1905, when Eillne was still being built. You remember

104

Sammy Tea out here. But did he not bring my grandmother out as well? Surely she would have been interested in what was going on? In her great house? Bernard and Hugo and even Hugo's nurse came out, after all.'

'Poor woman died,' Reggie said sternly. 'You let the dead rest.'

'So she never came out to Eillne?' I persisted.

'My dear young man, I can't remember what happened the day before yesterday, never mind half a century ago,' Reggie said. 'Juliet, darling, I'd like you to check my mare. Take your young man here with you.'

On a Friday afternoon in January, as Monument scurried to get its work done before nightfall, as ships could be seen from the transit-shed window standing at berth above the warehouses and new silos, I was called to the Surveyor's office in the Customs House and told the results of my examination.

The Surveyor sat one side of an empty, sweeping, redwood table. Behind him on shelves, were dozens of bottles containing model ships, his life's hobby.

'You've brought distinction to the district, Theo,' he said. 'First in the exam in all Ireland.' He got up and went to his shelves and selected a ship. 'It means Dublin, of course,' he said, returning to his chair. 'There's no future here for a lad that's come first in all Ireland. You'll be going up there as a UO, I'm told.'

A UO was an unattached officer with a roving role.

'How old would you say I am, Theo?'

'I don't know, sir.'

'Come on, lad. We're both men.'

'Fifty?' I ventured.

The Surveyor laughed. 'I'll be sixty-five next midsummer's day,' he said. 'The rules say I have to retire. I knew this town in the days just after your grandfather, Sammy Tea. I worked as an office boy in this very building when the Brits were in charge. I remember the smell of the Mazawattee when it came off steamships. Steamships, Theo. And d'you know what? It seems like last week it happened.'

We paused for a moment in due deference to the impenetrability of time.

The Surveyor said quietly, 'Those days have changed. There's a

105

new element in charge. You're better off out of here. Away from Monument. Away from . . . Anyway.'

He had almost said, I knew, 'Away from Bain.'

'You're going to go far, Theo,' the Surveyor said. 'You've got it in you to go all the way. Much further than I ever did, for example.' He held up his hand. 'No, I know what I'm saying. It takes a rare man to get to the top of our business. There are huge responsibilities involved. All the coins of the counting house flow through your fingers and many men are unequal to the task. You have to be many things when you reach that height, but above all, you have to be your own man.' The Surveyor stood up. 'For you to be your own man, Theo,' he said quietly, 'you have to leave this town. Now, I'd like you to have this as a personal memento. It's a Spanish galleon, but I'm sure you know that anyway. It's one of my better ones. Good luck, lad. You deserve it.'

Where my thoughts should have all been on my new career, they were on La. I rose on Saturday morning with a great sense of purpose. I would marry La secretly, after which there was nothing Sparrow could do; La would leave Eillne and come to live with me in Dublin. Having reached my decision, I was quite light-headed at the way the future had suddenly been presented.

The bus was cold and unusually empty. The weather had kept the farmers' wives and their husbands at home, or perhaps Christmas had swallowed the weeks of January in its excess. The landscape evoked Sparrow for me, the memories of all the times we had made this trip together, in gig and car and on bicycles, the toing and froing between home and town that had weaved the pattern of our lives like thread between bobbins. Only by keeping La's face foremost in my mind could I ward off the dread that leapt at me every time I thought of what I had resolved to do.

Sparrow met me in the hall. My antennae, forever alert to the smallest alteration in my mother's mood, took in something changed about the house.

'Poor Theodore,' Sparrow said. 'You must be tired.'

'Is there something the matter?'

Sparrow sighed. 'Come in, Theodore, please.'

My analysis of my mother's mood went beyond simply her as I followed in. I lost connection with the substance of her words and instead was listening for noises that I suddenly missed. From the hall. The kitchen. The noise made by Uncle Hugo's door when La, carrying in a tray, let it close behind her.

'How is Uncle Hugo?' I asked, and then, uncaring if my voice betrayed me, 'Where is La?'

Sparrow closed her eyes briefly. 'Theodore, I am extremely upset at the moment, so please try not to shout.'

I gaped at her. There were tears on her face.

'Your poor Uncle Hugo has had to go to the county home in Monument,' Sparrow said between breaths. 'There is no one here to nurse him any more.'

'La,' I gasped.

'La is gone, Theodore,' said Sparrow, her eyes black. 'She left without so much as an hour's notice, as Bain said she would. She is never coming back.'

I married Juliet.

That's what the record says twenty-nine years later. That's what's written in the book in the sacristy in Monument's cathedral, witnessed by Pax Sheehy and a friend of Juliet's called Dorothy from London, all rounded off in a flourish by Father Jack O'Dea's broad-nibbed pen.

My efforts to find La, to live out the warm twosome that I had imagined, were ineffective. I wandered streets, having convinced myself that La had come to Dublin too, and that we were both casting blindly, searching for one another. At times the stocky back of a young woman on a busy footpath would cause me to run up and glance sideways, but always in disappointment. I knew instinctively, in my heart, as they say, that despite Sparrow's story, La had been banished from Eillne and that Uncle Hugo's happiness, which I had considered the trump card for La's perpetuity, had been tossed aside when it stood in the way of Sparrow's will. I knew also that for his own ends Bain had not only failed to support my case to Sparrow, but had in fact done the opposite. I felt shame that I had asked him for his help. I felt that his involvement with me and La had somehow made dirty something that had been essentially pure.

One Saturday, between my train's arrival in Monument from Dublin and Sheehy's bus to Eillne, I went to the county home in the irrational expectation that Uncle Hugo could communicate to me what had really happened to La or where she had gone. Wind whistled through the frames of the long windows and the pervading smell was of polish on linoleum. A crisply uniformed young nurse led me along a corridor at a smart pace. The whiff of her starch, and its rustle, brought La back to me strongly, and there was a moment at a door when I longed to press my free hand to the pert rise of her rump, as I had with La, and bathe in her smiling admonishment.

They'd shaved off Uncle Hugo's moustache and I walked up and down the ward full of men twice before I recognised him from his pyjamas. I don't think he knew who I was: none of my questions about La led to any more than a dribble. On my way out, when I asked if Uncle Hugo had had a young female visitor, the staff frowned and shook their heads. No, Mr Hugo Love had had no visitors, they said matter-of-factly. Apart from yourself, not one.

La faded. I stopped in digs with a raft of others of my kind – that is to say, civil servants – on Baggot Street, where twenty people sat down nightly and ate boiled potatoes and pan-fried chops, whilst I alone ate cod. I always seemed to be too busy to do anything more decisive about La than indulge my recollections. There was the urgent, unceasing stir of Dublin Port; there was an emerging sense of the power of the organisation of which I was a part. The longer I left La – should I, for instance, advertise? – the harder it would be to explain my inaction if ever I did find her; and La thus faded from my mind, as is customary with guilt.

Sparrow's ambition for me was Juliet. Reggie Blood, too, was keen on the match, for despite the knack of the Anglo-Irish for making impecuniosity a virtue, he had faced the need to tap into a fresh source of funds. Changes occurred in Eillne in my absence. The house acquired new electric wiring. An outhouse was converted for a tenant, an agricultural inspector, a man in his late twenties by the name of Denny. A Morris Minor was purchased, and a refrigerator. I shared a carriage down from Dublin with my Uncle Bernard in Easter week.

'Your mother's in the money, Theo,' he remarked.

Despite Uncle Bernard's shifty eyes, his face was still wide and handsome and his silver hair crowned him lustrously. If he still judged me by the old episode in Leire, it didn't show.

'How so?'

Uncle Bernard looked at me sceptically; countryside rushed through the window-glass reflection of his face.

'She got over ten thousand pounds from Bain for her half-share in the Shortcourse business,' he said, as if I really knew but wasn't saying. 'Hell of a price. Too much, if you ask me. That Bain fellow will come to a sticky end if he borrows out of his depth.'

In my job I was learning the value of inscrutability. 'How do you know he borrowed?'

'Had to, had to. Ten thousand *pounds*.' Uncle Bernard groomed back his wad of hair with big hands. 'You'd never do that now, Theo. You're too much a Love, just like your mother.'

As with Sparrow, it seemed to be important to Uncle Bernard that I was a Shortcourse in name only.

'The business bent comes from your grandfather Sammy Tea,' Uncle Bernard assured me. 'You've heard of Sammy Tea?'

'Yes, I have,' I said. 'Do you remember him?'

'Oh yes,' Uncle Bernard said.

'What was my mother like as a child?' I asked, watching the handsome face.

'Much the same as she is now,' Uncle Bernard said, but the smile stayed fixed a moment too long on his lips. 'Don't tell her I said that,' and he laughed.

'Did your mother, my grandmother, die soon after she had Sparrow?'

Uncle Bernard blinked. 'Yes. Yes, she must have.'

'When exactly?'

'I'm very bad at dates.'

The azure outline of the Deilt Mountains appeared.

'What is the mystery, Uncle Bernard?' I asked this man I barely knew. 'It's more than sixty years ago. Why does the mention of that time, particularly of my grandmother's death, make everyone become withdrawn? She died young, I know. At forty-one years. Of what?'

'She died', said Uncle Bernard quietly, 'of a broken heart.'

I began to return to Dublin from Eillne with images of Juliet in my mind. The shape of her mouth – which always held a taunting suggestion as the uppermost of its possibilities – did savage things to my lonely imagination. Forget her light gold hair, or her blue

109

eyes; forget her skin and her body that I had seen begging Bain in all its lovely nakedness. Juliet's mouth, Juliet's lips, whose taste at night alone I knew, Juliet's tongue, which, with mine, leapt between our joined mouths like supple fish thrown together in a juicy pool, these images night after night threw my flesh into disarray. In my darkened Baggot Street bedroom, the merest touch of my hand – Juliet's touch – was enough. I lay in my limp aftermath, reliving my sense of failure in the railway shed and trying to remember the pleasure that La had told me I had one night given her.

Nowhere but Eillne would do Sparrow for the wedding breakfast, a decision on which Reggie Blood appeared to hold no strong views. He told me one evening that to do the job with Juliet's (estranged) mother, they had legged it over to Gretna Green. Sparrow revealed that she had commissioned a new altar window in stained glass to be ready for our September wedding day in the cathedral.

'As a little girl in Monument I remember the sunlight in coloured pools on the cathedral floor,' Sparrow explained to Juliet.

'Who's paying for it?' I asked.

'Oh, I am, for most of it,' Sparrow said. 'Father O'Dea says the parish funds will make a contribution. And Bain will see that the town council helps a little too. He's been marvellous,' she said and I saw Juliet lower her eyes. 'But it's mainly me.'

'Wonderful,' I said. It was Sparrow's money, after all. 'The old window went during the war of independence,' I told Juliet, who appeared slightly bemused by the whole project.

'The British destroyed it like they destroyed so much else,' said Sparrow reflectively.

Juliet's face told me that excursions into Irish history, particularly those parts of it that dealt with the green shoots of Irish independence, were not considered suitable table conversation in Drossa.

'Father says there's more fighting in the pub on a Saturday night than there was in Monument,' she remarked.

'Does he indeed,' said Sparrow archly.

110

'He was being entertained to dinner in the barracks by the general or something and the lackey came in and said that the chef had been shot through the kitchen window by a sniper, and what should they do. Close the window, the general said, and bring on the port,' Juliet finished brightly.

'I have insisted on a simple inscription,' Sparrow said to me, ignoring Juliet and displaying the first evidence I had seen of abrasion between them. ' "Erected by Mrs Sparrow Love Shortcourse" and the date of your wedding.'

Before we knew it we were into and almost through another summer. Often, on the train between Dublin and Monument, I had to look up from the drafting on my knee and concentrate for a moment to ascertain our direction, to establish whether the weekend was beginning or had just come to a close. Sheehy's bus was a *rite de passage*, a Styx in which I was immersed before surfacing in Eillne. I spotted from the bus window that July, a mile from the gates of my home, Bain in his car passing us on his way back into Monument.

'You're very punctual,' Juliet said coming out to greet me. Her appearance was somewhat untidy, her hair out on her shoulders and the look of someone who has been asleep, but then I saw the dust-sheets of painters that were laid all along the hall and realised the reason for Juliet's dislocation.

'I passed Bain,' I said. 'I would have liked to have said hello.'

'He just looked in for a minute, he was looking for Sparrow,' Juliet said brusquely. 'But she's off somewhere. Get rid of your bag and we'll have tea outside. The smell of paint is nauseating.'

I was less awkward with Juliet than in earlier days. My formula, whenever I felt intimidated by the implications of her lusciousness, was to think forward to September when her affections would be forced to accommodate themselves to what I had to offer. Teaching her to swim, for example, would be one of the first goals of my marriage. Fantasies of Juliet's body in water, of its versatility, had long played in my mind. A small, round car went around the back of the house; Denny, the tenant, was home from his rounds.

'What does he do, exactly?' I asked.

'No idea,' Juliet replied. 'Looks up cows' bums, I suppose.'

111

Juliet could become easily distracted in my company and often appeared to be listening to other than what I was saying. Now I saw her gaze off in the direction of the swimming river, and noticed the rise of her breasts, and thought forward lazily to the day when, at will, I would be able to collect them to my lips. Juliet's eyes were dreaming, their long lashes partly closed and trembling. Although our marriage would have a large element of convenience, I would work assiduously on fashioning a great love from the opportunity.

I heard a car, then a door banging.

'I've got you a cup out here!' Juliet called. 'Theo's home.'

My mother came from the shadows of the house.

'Stay,' she said, pressing me back down, and gave me her cheek. 'Oh, that Sheehy man! I don't know how I'm still alive. He came around the corner in his bus and I had to drive up the ditch to avoid him. I've a mind to tell the guards.'

'And his big son will come and arrest him,' said Juliet, amused.

'Did you bring your laundry, Theo?'

I said, 'Yes.'

'Monument was stifling,' Sparrow said and drained the teapot. 'I've been dreaming all afternoon of a swim.'

'I'll fetch hot water,' Juliet said.

Sparrow and I both watched her walk into the house. I could see the outline of Juliet's legs beneath her dress.

'I've been ensuring there will be no snags when the window is delivered,' Sparrow said. She looked like a child, sitting with the cup in both hands. 'Bain has been marvellous. I had an appointment with him this afternoon and the town's engineer is going to supervise the installation.'

I passed Bain earlier, I nearly said, but didn't.

'All those people waiting outside his office, there must have been twenty before me,' Sparrow said. 'But he took me first. He'd just dashed in from a meeting out in Deilt.' Sparrow leaned across and touched me. 'It will be a great day, Theodore.'

Juliet was standing in the shadow of the French windows, holding her breath as if unwilling to disturb the moment between mother and son. I longed for September. I longed for the priest's words that would change everything.

*

112

It was said there had never been a more beautiful bride in the cathedral. When I looked back down the nave from my place beside Pax and saw the river of fluid colour that the town of Monument had also come to see, with my wife to be gliding towards me like a dove across tinted glades, I felt singularly blessed. Her train of silk attended by a son of my cousin Johnnie and the granddaughter of an English duke made a leaf-like whisper as Juliet approached. Father O'Dea smiled at us frequently and spoke quiet instructions and words of encouragement that only we could hear. He said his Mass and gave a sermon. I took in little that morning, but what he said was all about Sparrow anyway, and the window, and how we were rolling back the years to when Monument echoed with mortars and guns. I glanced behind me. Sparrow and Bain were picked out in beams of light, but Reggie Blood's face had slipped down on one side as if his grin had melted in the heat and was about to drip on to the floor.

With one vivid exception, I remember no more about my wedding day than the next fellow. Outside, Juliet giggled about the crowds and the town council in their robes of fake ermine, with Bain the leader among them. She lifted up her veil to him and they pressed cheeks in a way that reminded me of people in a station saying goodbye. Ships at moorings hooted us as our car came out on Long Quay. Alone in a corner stood a stocky young woman, but she turned away before I could see her face.

It had been wet earlier that September. The water table of the delta had risen and overwashed into normally good land. Although the day of our wedding was gloriously still, with sun uninterrupted and the scents and sounds of the dying phase of summer profuse, the swimming river had forgotten any sluggish pretensions and was vigorously high, as if to show our guests its true potential.

Assorted Bloods from Reggie's various marriages came from all over England. Bernard Love came with his wife and their big sons and grandsons. Bain and his family were there. From Balaklava came my sister Mag. Uncle Hugo was brought out by ambulance. It was Sparrow's decision to err in the interests of benevolence and thus my once loved uncle – for who could love the shell he had become? – spent his last time in Eillne propped in a wheelchair beside the window of the drawing room, listening, or so it seemed, to whatever was being said to him by Mr Wise. A lot of what Sparrow called 'business Monument' was there, as was Father O'Dea. Determined jollity persisted with the Brits protesting they had drunk too much and the Irish pretending to be sober. Champagne was opened as we cut the cake. Donald Blood, upon whose fatness everyone whisperingly remarked, was held to be the most adept at untwisting the wire from the bottles and releasing the corks without ensuing loss. I saw Bain snare one and steer Sparrow into a corner, where he coaxed golden bubbles into her glass until her cheeks were ripe. My sister Mag went out to the terrace, stretched out on Sparrow's hammock and slept without a break until the evening turned a little chill and the guests began to drift off to their cars.

'D'you know what I'd love now, Theo?'

Bain and Sparrow were sitting in the last sun at the edge of the terrace. I heard Sparrow laugh like a little girl. Inside I could see Juliet arguing with Donald, who in the first stages of truculence an hour before had refused to bring his father home and was now persuading my wife – my wife! – to give him a final drink.

'I know exactly what you'd love,' I said to Pax.

'Will they think we're mad?'

'Who cares? Say nothing. I'll see you down there. I'll get towels.'

The river would wash the dust and fatigue away; we would benefit from its wisdom. I grabbed the towels and slipped riverward in the creeping shadows.

'Hey! Theo!'

They were all lined up above me, in their wedding clothes, Bain, the sun behind him, like a buddha.

'Why don't you join us?' I called.

'I don't want to show you up, Theo!' Bain laughed.

Pax was already stripped to his shorts. We dived in together and came up a rapidly lengthening twenty yards from our clothes on the bank.

'It has its mind made up today!' Pax shouted and we struck back upstream at the angle we knew from years of trial and error, a compromise worked out with the currents and flows that allowed everyone their way. I hauled up on reeds and pulled Pax behind me. On this side we still caught the sun, but the Eillne bank that we had left was in deep shadow.

'At its best, It knows the day that's in it, Theo.'

'I'm sure it does.'

'Are you happy today, Theo?' asked Pax, with concern exceeding polite interest.

'Deliriously.'

'If you're happy, then I'm happy.'

I could see that something was weighing on his mind.

'But you're worried on my account.'

'Why should I worry, Theo? My best friend is happily married. Why should I worry?'

'We are all different now to the children we were, Pax. All of us.'

'Maybe,' he said and looked at the racing water.

The invitation was there, if I wished to accept it, to explore the reservations that Pax had kept housed and ready for my benefit, like the custodian of our collective conscience. It was what made Pax so dependable; you could always dip into him like a bank or other depository of the soul.

'You have to look forward, not back,' I said quietly.

'OK,' Pax nodded. He put his hand on my shoulder and looked at me from that very serious place he inhabited. 'D'you ever think of being cremated, Theo?'

'I'm not looking that far forward.'

'Seriously.'

'No. And not today, certainly.'

Pax wasn't going to let the nature of the day deflect him from philosophy. 'I think it has a lot to offer. Imagine your ashes thrown in here on a day like this. Imagine being part of the river. It would make dying easier for me.'

'Pax, are you a bit drunk?'

'Holy Jesus tonight!' Pax said, staring across the swimming river.

A group had arrived on the opposite bank: Bain and Aggie and their two boys, Juliet and Donald, Donald with a bottle in his hand, and in a vivid red kimono, which as we watched she shed, my mother, Sparrow.

Sparrow waved.

115

She had on a pink swimming costume that sprouted a little gauze dress from around the hips and whose clinging upper fabric showed her flat breasts. Her legs were ivory white. She was putting on a bathing cap.

'It's too strong, Sparrow!' I shouted. 'No!'

Her audience seemed suspended in awe of the daring they lacked. Pax and I stood looking in horror.

'No!'

Donald Blood stuck the bottle in the air and shouted something; Sparrow sprang out, hands joined, gracefully as a gull.

'*Sparrow!*'

She hung for a moment, light enough, it seemed, to stay in mid-air. Without a splash she entered the river, disappearing into it as through a fault in the water.

Pax and I went in together. With complete prescience I knew what I would see when I surfaced. I saw the receding group on the bank and the now slyly hurrying surface of the water, empty except for Pax, whom I could see near me. There was screaming from the land. Pax and I duck-dived together, needing no advice. Underwater the current was less perceptible and only by swimming head on to it and glimpsing bits of flotsam whipping by in the murky depths was it possible to guess the strength we were subject to.

Our task was hopeless from the outset. She could already be half a mile downstream. And yet in the underwater world where I felt so at home, where it seemed the important aspects of my life had been shaped, instead of feeling dread at the thought of Sparrow dead there was a calmness. Finning with feet and arms to control my place, it was as if I had prepared from my first days for this moment. I found no need to dash upwards for air but knew of an infinite well of minutes in my lungs and a complete mastery of my environment. I could use the river to my cool purpose and analyse at the same time how even in a simple matter like a swim on the evening of my wedding, my mother had been unwilling to allow my primacy.

Up I came. Pax was kicking strongly to keep his place five yards upstream. We had rounded the bend, out of sight of the bank, to where a tree, fallen ever since I could remember, channelled the river even more narrowly and with compressed vigour. We went under again. I could see nothing. My hand caught a slippery, sunken bough. I hung like a pennant in a storm, straining to see, husbanding my air. As if shot from fog, an enormous black shape tumbled by me, winging my shoulder in the process. When I turned it had disappeared. Pulling myself further into the limbs of the tree, I wedged between two of them to allow my arms rest. Just about to surface again, I discerned, hooked beneath a branch, a piece of pink gauze. It was a damning testimony. I reached for it so as to bring back something, tugged, then realised sickeningly that it was not a piece but the edge of the whole dress with wearer intact, somehow dragged under the vegetation and lodged there.

I dug. Throwing up dense mats of weeds, I plunged. Her eyes were open. Her mouth. Chest bursting, I ripped her away and in my arms shot us up, then on my back let the river rush us to its next, widest stretch, gasping for Pax as I did so. In two strokes Pax was beside me. He guided me and my strangely heavy charge in through water lilies to the lee of a spur where his father's cattle came down to water.

Strong in the water, on the bank I could not breathe. Pax rolled Sparrow over. With big hands clasped he came down full strength on her back: there was a sound like walking in wet shoes and water burst from her mouth. He pounded her half a dozen times until the stuff from her mouth turned yellow. He tossed her over and repeated the treatment until I thought her chest would shatter. Falling to her face, Pax joined their open mouths. His big body filled, then emptied; Sparrow's stomach swelled. Pax pumped her. After half a minute he lay back and Sparrow slumped, dead and drooling. He straddled her, shaking his head, and again, with his hands in a cradle he smacked her with full force across the breastbone so that her heels jumped from the grass.

Then she twitched again. Without Pax. He looked at me with a tired grin and nodded. She was retching as I raced back to tell the others. The comforting sight of bile! I burst through briars gleefully. We had come easily a mile in seconds. The chances of achieving what we had were remote enough to make anyone laugh with happiness. I laughed. From a hundred yards I saw them all, I heard the children and Juliet crying. I saw Bain with his shoes off – his shoes off! – standing on the edge of the bank, his wife Aggie holding him back by the arm. I laughed aloud.

117

'It's all right!' I shouted and waved. 'She's safe! Sparrow is saved!'

Maybe they could not hear me. I shook my ears out as if that somehow accounted for their terrified stares.

'She was caught in a tree,' I gasped. 'She nearly drowned, but she's fine. Pax has her breathing. Sparrow is alive.'

Such shock in my poor Juliet's face. I reached for her, smiling. 'Sparrow is safe.'

She screamed. 'Donald!'

I must have looked stupid.

'Where's Donald, you fool?' Juliet cried. 'My brother jumped in after that silly bitch! Now he's drowned!'

Six

Eillne was never more beautiful than in that autumn. The light, especially the evening light on the swimming river, had a quality of sad delicacy, of sweet farewell, as if its duty was to attend with utmost sensitivity at the point where such tragedy had unfolded.

The week I had taken for my honeymoon was spent probing the marshlands of the delta for Donald's body with gangs of volunteers. Maps were pinned to the wall in Eillne and the many possibilities for an object borne by flood were pointed out. The task was hopeless. Men tried to cut their way inwards with boats, but after days their tiny progress in relation to the sheer size of the delta was enough to break a heart full of even the stoutest resolve and they gave up. Pax and I made forays of our own, using timbers, the method we knew best, and between us penetrated the furthest of anyone, but to no avail. I did not tell Juliet, but I knew that I had been the last person to see Donald as he hurtled like a meteor into infinity, brushing me in the process, his last touch of farewell.

I returned to Dublin but Juliet remained at home in Drossa, looking after Reggie, whom Donald's tragedy had considerably reduced. The circumstances of Donald's death had brought out in Juliet a rare expression of principle in whose defence she was unwavering: she would have nothing further to do with my mother. Sparrow, restored to health, would hear no blame for her part in the drowning of a man who for over twenty years had been drunk more often than he'd been sober. Subterranean wells of feminine dislike seeped surfacewards. My bride in name dwelt beyond my reach in Drossa and I returned to Dublin.

Dublin, I confess, was a relief. I met Pax some evenings and we went out to Sandycove on his new motor bicycle, which he taught me to ride. That was a thrill I had not expected: wind in my face and hair, power between my legs and Pax seated behind for ballast. In Dublin Castle there was the cool, impersonal balm of

119

draft legislation. Statistics and the elasticity of demand. Immersed in the search for the middle path between competing interests, I worked hard to reduce the future opportunities of those opposed to my aims, enhancing as I did so the esteem in which I knew I was beginning to be held.

'Theo, there's someone on the phone for you.'

Evelyne-Mary O'Grady was my nominal junior. She sat at the desk opposite.

'Says she's your wife,' Evelyne-Mary said.

'Hello?'

'I'm in Dublin, Theo,' Juliet said.

We met that afternoon in an upstairs café on the Green. Juliet was already there when I arrived, looking out at the traffic, a small suitcase by her chair. She wore a hat, a little thing in the shape of a dove with feathers at the back, which even though it was somewhat formal for the place, was nonetheless touching and gave Juliet's beauty a classical context.

'Hello, Theo,' Juliet said, as if being in Dublin was not something she did well.

I said, 'You look marvellous.'

'I didn't know what to wear. I've only ever been here for the Spring Show,' she said, touching the hat.

'You would look beautiful wearing nothing,' I said, meaning no hat, and saw Juliet look at me sideways and cross her legs and then take out and light up a long cigarette.

A pot of tea came, and shiny, sticky buns with currants in them, and butter whorls in a bed of ice.

'Have you been shopping?' I asked, although if she had there was no evidence of it.

'Perhaps tomorrow,' Juliet said. 'That's if you'll give me some money.'

In a rush of excitement I comprehended the strength of my position.

'We'll go back to the digs,' I said and heard my own heart like a tugboat.

Carrying Juliet's light suitcase, linked to her, walking down the busy Dublin street to the bus stop and conscious of the admiring eyes of passers-by, my anticipation had grown into a wonderfully hard curve like beach coral.

'Are we going to get in all right to your digs?' Juliet asked quietly. Implicit in her question was the voice of experience, of someone who did not expect to sail into a man's bedroom without subterfuge, and this pushed me to a new peak of excitement.

'You know your way around, Theo,' Juliet said and linked me closer as I took out my latchkey.

The woman who ran the boarding house knew all about my marriage and took to Juliet like a broody hen. She bustled us upstairs with croonings and cluckings of happiness. One light only hung from the ceiling. I put it off when I saw Juliet beginning to take off her clothes, and was going to pull the heavy window curtains across the yellow lace when she stopped me.

'I like to see.'

So did I, I found. I took off my jacket and shoes and in my shirtsleeves sat on the narrow bed watching my lovely wife undress. Her loveliness choked me. The slim yet utterly feminine body I remembered from the railway hut had filled, like flowers fill with pollen, so that every round part of her sang desirability. She stooped for the stocking of her left leg, balancing with one hand on the end knob of the bed, and her breasts as she did so touched the smooth rise of her belly, which in turn spilled down to her cunt. So many graceful turns and long sweeps of muscle and bone made up my Juliet. She changed hands and feet for the second stocking. The firm little valley in the small of her back was presented to me, and the gathering of her buttocks, one arched momentarily up with the angle of her leg, allowed me sight of her dark ravine, which, if I had ever done so, I had previously considered with no more than academic interest, but which now, in its many lurking possibilities, seemed infinitely sweet.

'Now you.'

She stood over me. Unbuttoning my flies, I wriggled from my trousers with Juliet at the same time attending to my shirt, until I sat on the bed in my underpants like a man in the last stages of a strip-search.

'You are enormous,' Juliet said.

She reached and unwrapped my final secret. In my maelstrom of excitement and terror I tried to think my way out of the tiny room, away from Juliet, so that my duties – what a fool I was! – could be honourably discharged. But it is hard to deny the immediacy of a

121

beautiful woman with her hands on your florid cock, commandeering your weight on top of her, burrowing herself so that her breasts are tight to your scrotum.

'Ride me!'

The shed! The same yellow light came through the bedroom window, except this time it was not complicated by rain. Juliet took me in her hand and with the first touch of my straining head to her succulence I shot my months of waiting with a prolonged roar that Juliet had to gag with her fist.

We lay side by side, Juliet looking to the window.

'I need more practice,' I mumbled.

Juliet's beautiful face contained a tightness.

'Theo?'

'Yes?'

'How much do you earn, exactly?'

It was such a relief to change the subject. I told her: eighty-five pounds a month.

'Every month?'

'Yes.'

'Golly, you're rich, Theo,' Juliet said and leaned over to catch me in her small fist. 'I'm married to a rich man.'

That was a Friday. The next day no bank was open and I had to borrow five pounds from my landlady for Juliet's shopping. On Saturday night our lovemaking was along the lines of the night before, a chemical disaster if success is counted other than in terms of the speed of an ejaculation. Juliet hummed desire. The sight of her body brought me on so quickly that I tried to look away from her in the tiny bedroom. Her merest touch made my flesh frantic. There was so much I wanted to do but couldn't: to suck her lovely breasts, to lick her skin where it was most lickable – on the insides of her thighs – to caress the curve of her neck and the moldings of her shoulders, to kiss the silky little flutes of her cunt. But she didn't seem to mind. When I buried my head in the pillows she patted me gently. She was against my indulging myself in her body when I was flaccid, putting down my hand with a firm 'Wait.' The very fact of me aroused was what excited Juliet, even though the commencement of action spelt its immediate and predictable conclusion. I borrowed a further five pounds on Sunday morning and put Juliet on the midday train for Monument.

It would be unfair to Juliet, whatever her motives, to deny the pleasure she brought me. Happiness, like beauty, can flower for a little season of its own, regardless of what went before or is to come; that is how I now look back and see those months. Juliet came to Dublin on Friday. I gave her what money she asked for. We made love. Juliet went home as the Sunday Angelus rolled down the Liffey. The landlady put Juliet and me in a better room; we ate our meals with her and she and Juliet discussed shopping, although Juliet always claimed afterwards that she had not understood a single word the woman had said.

At three on a Saturday afternoon in December, Sheehy's bus crawled between hedgerows where a million webs had been preserved in white, past gateways where pools of ice with iron collars of muck made anyone looking at them long for a fireside. I had not been home for nearly three months, my longest absence by far from Eillne. The scale of the place appeared to have changed. I walked in across the frozen, unyielding gravel. The terrace outside the house looked narrow, and from the front door as I looked down, the swimming river curled like an old scar.

My mother was reading in her usual place. An electric heater made the room overhot.

'Theodore, love.' She stood up and let me hold her. 'My, you look so well. I had forgotten how much a man you are.'

She had a tea tray ready and an electric kettle in the grate.

'Eillne seems strange,' I said.

'After Dublin, it must.'

'What have you been up to?' I asked.

Sparrow looked at me curiously. 'Up to.' She smiled and handed me my cup. 'On Monday I drove into Monument and gave our Christmas order to Mr Wise. He asked for you, as always. This is very much top-secret, but Mr Wise has endowed a ward of a children's hospital in the Holy Land.'

'Israel.'

'Yes, Theodore. Jerusalem. I made these mince pies especially for you.'

'They're excellent.'

Sparrow took me in from over the gilt rim of her teacup. 'On Tuesday, what happened on Tuesday? Oh, Mr Denny put in new shelves in the clothes hot-press.'

'Denny, the tenant?'

'Yes, Theodore. Mr Denny.'

'I thought he had a job.'

'He has some days off. He looks rough but he's got his own charm underneath. On Wednesday Mrs Sheehy made stuffing for the goose. I tasted it and you will love it.'

'Pax's mother?'

'Of course, Theodore. You haven't been to India, have you?'

'I didn't know Mrs Sheehy worked here.'

'You wouldn't want me to run a house like this on my own, would you?'

'No, no. I'm sure Mrs Sheehy is excellent.'

'They're nice people, Theodore. Mr Sheehy is a genius with motor cars.'

The mince pie had great depths of fruit and chunky sweetmeats. 'How is Uncle Hugo?'

'It's useless. I dropped in yesterday with his Christmas present. He never woke up the entire time I was there. They say he eats like a horse. The ice in the car park was so bad two men had to push me out.' Sparrow poured more tea for both of us. 'I saw Bain. I was in the cathedral – it's so much more pleasant to go into now that the window's there – and when I came out he was standing over at his grandfather's grave.'

'How is Bain?'

'I told him you were coming home for Christmas. He said he hoped to see you. I asked him to come out. He never comes near Eillne any more.'

'They say he'll be a TD at the next election.'

'Of course he will. Only Mr Sheehy thinks not. He says Bain is too much identified with a certain element, as he calls it, which is why Bain will be elected and Mr Sheehy will never be more than an obliging mechanic. I have invited your Uncle Bernard and his wife here for Christmas dinner.'

'I want to talk about Christmas.'

'Bernard has been kind to me since you left. He has always been kind, but particularly since you left.'

'I am married to Juliet.'

'Don't address me as if I were senile, Theodore. I know your circumstances.'

'Juliet will stay with her father for Christmas.'

'Juliet will please Juliet,' Sparrow snapped and stood up.

There had been a time when such a tone would have struck me as would a whip, but suddenly I was seized by great recklessness and a sense of elation as if the long years ahead with Juliet were a treasure awaiting, were gold compared to Sparrow's brass.

'And I will spend Christmas with my wife,' I said.

My first Christmas away from Eillne was spent in Drossa. In the New Year I returned ecstatically to Dublin, having slept with Juliet eight nights in a row.

'Am I getting better?'

'Sort of, Theo. You need to slow down.'

'Do you enjoy it?'

'Sort of.'

'I'm no good, am I?'

'You're good occasionally, Theo.' Juliet reached for me in the bed. Her timing was right, like a fish that knows when the river level is up. 'Golly, you're big again. Try it this way.'

On her elbows, her face buried in the pillows, she presented me her back, long and shiny as an otter's. Reaching back, she led me into her with her hand, except that instead of her thick oil, this time I felt only strange numbness. Nothing.

'That's good, Theo,' Juliet said, capturing me in that dark, blank place. 'That's really lovely.'

On other nights I felt her leave our bed and once woke as she crept back, frozen, dawn in the sky behind her. I brought her over to my warm side and held her tightly. Reggie was fitful, she explained with a yawn. He hated Christmas. She had heated port for him in a saucepan to get him through the long lonely night, and spent the night with him, sitting by the big fire in his bedroom.

'Then why are you so cold?' I whispered, but Juliet, her face angelic on the pillows beside me, was asleep.

In the summer of that year matters other than the riots north of the border occupied my mind. In Dublin Castle an important project team would soon be formed to smooth Ireland's entry into Europe; and I tried to wonder how I could solve the problem of Juliet's outright refusal to come and live with me in Dublin. She said they could not afford a nurse for Reggie and that the least she might do was let him die in his own home. Juliet knew that my transferring to Monument was not an option I would or could consider. When I tried to confront her about our unsatisfactory relationship, Juliet told me that if I had not gone swimming the day we were married, Donald would still be alive, Reggie would still be mobile and she and I would be living together in Dublin. I was lying on my bed one evening after supper when my landlady informed me that a visitor was in the downstairs hall.

I came quietly on to the landing to have a look. It's a sneaky trait I've inherited from Sparrow; we like our spontaneity to be forearmed. I could see Bain below me. He wore a green felt hat. There was an air to him of being out of place. As I came down the stairs he seemed to look behind me as much as at me.

'A surprise,' I said.

'Theo,' he nodded, with the furtive grin that had been very much part of Pa's armour.

'I didn't know you were up.'

'Holidays,' Bain shrugged. 'Everyone's on holidays.'

'Everything all right at home?'

'Not a bother on any of them.'

He was standing his ground, like a tangler at a fair waiting for the other man to bid.

'Have you eaten?' I asked.

Bain frowned. 'No, now that you mention it.'

'I'll ask if she'll fry you up something,' I said.

'Can I put this somewhere?' asked Bain.

A small suitcase had remained parked unnoticed beneath a depiction of the Sacred Heart.

'I'll put it in my room,' I said.

If I have not already mentioned my landlady sufficiently, let me now allow her her place. You must be long dead, Mrs Agnes Mullane. What a big, strong woman you were. Did you ever rest? (Can I tell you now, between us, that I found the sweat hoops that hung beneath your armpits arousing? What's the point of dis-sembling with the dead? Your sweaty excretions kindled some-thing, God knows what, deep in me.) Your husband must have died soon after you married because you seemed always to have the air of an entrenched widow and the only children ever

126

mentioned were the likes of myself, paying guests who over the years had enjoyed your commercial brand of motherly affection.

Bain was served up a platter of livers, kidneys, puddings and two eggs. He had a way, when he wanted something from someone, to give that person all the attention, so as I sat to one side of Mrs Mullane's kitchen table, Bain plied her with questions about her family and background, nodding sagely in time to his mastication at her eager replies, interjecting regularly to pick up on the name of someone who might have been a common acquaintance – a highly unlikely event since Mrs Mullane came from the Blasket Islands – and generally stoking my widowed landlady until she was fetchingly aglow.

'I've never eaten better and I'm in the butcher's trade,' Bain said, sitting back.

'You have to pick and choose to get the best nowadays,' Mrs Mullane said.

'People have no pride in their work,' Bain said.

'Not a bit,' my landlady agreed.

'The whole country's gone on holidays,' Bain said, 'as if their whole life wasn't a holiday.'

Mrs Mullane made broody noises and filled Bain's cup.

'We do a bit in wholesale, as Theo knows,' Bain said. 'I had to make two trips today, up and down to the market for meat.'

'Two trips,' Mrs Mullane lamented. 'From Monument.'

'No one to drive, out sunning themselves,' Bain said.

'You must be destroyed,' winced Mrs Mullane.

'Has to be done,' said Bain, the hero.

'You should stay,' the widow importuned. 'I'll put a bed down in Theo's room.'

'Can't,' Bain said, resigned. 'There's a thousand pounds' worth of stuff out there in the van. Can't leave it in the street.'

'But sure, can't you lock it in my garage!' the widow cried.

I knew enough of Bain to know that events had a habit of turning out to his foreshaping. Later that evening, his van under lock and key in the garage, he lay on my bed, smoking a pipe.

'Big things happening, Theo,' he said quietly.

'Yes.' I thought he meant our joining Europe.

He observed me through the smoke, his mouth sucking wetly on the pipe stem in tiny explosions.

127

'Our people up there are in trouble, Theo. Understand me?'

Quiet confidence in what he was saying is my memory. I wondered why he was really in Dublin, lying on my bed. Our people.

'We can't stand by. Whole streets have been torched. They must be allowed to arm themselves. They must have the means to fight back.'

In customs, we had all, of course, been briefed about the entry of arms and explosives, a possibility that had, when first mentioned, seemed more diverting than cigarettes or books of an unsuitable nature.

'The law is very strict on who handles guns and the like,' I said by way of caution, just in case he had anything in mind.

'The law!' Bain chuckled. 'Who made that law, Theo? Who wrote it?'

'Most current laws and statutes were in place in 1921,' I replied, now understanding his thrust. 'Britain made them, but –'

'Britain.' Bain nodded. 'Some act, isn't it? *We* must now obey *their* law which stops *us* helping *our* people who are being murdered in their beds by *them*. Some act.'

I gave Bain my bed and slept on Mrs Mullane's litter.

'Theo?'

'Yes?'

'I wasn't here, OK?'

It could have been a summer's night in Eillne, twenty years before.'

'OK.'

'And Theo?'

'Yes?'

'Thanks.'

I left him behind me the next morning, breakfasting with Mrs Mullane. I hoped his consignment of meat had not stewed overnight.

Juliet came up to stay irregularly, but the tension involving her marriage obligations to me and her decision not to come permanently to Dublin made our time together difficult. Pax and I met one late August evening out at Sandycove.

'Do you see much of Bain, Theo?'

'Some weekends I'm home he comes out. To see Sparrow. They've always something on the go, that pair.'

We sat drying on sun-warmed rock. Pax, when he asked questions, had learned to collect his black eyebrows together so that they hung like dark clouds of doubt over the issue.

'No sign of him in Dublin at all?' Pax asked. 'In the last few weeks?'

I almost told him. It was the forced casualness in Pax's voice that stopped me short. He hadn't quite mastered the knack of bleeding a question of official interest.

'No.'

'He didn't call to see you?'

'No. Why?'

'I just wondered.'

I marvelled at myself. I had no greater friend than Pax, to whom I had just lied. I felt more excitement than shame. Was my instinctive protecting of Bain just a thing of blood? Or of flesh's old obligations?'

'He's weak, Theo,' Pax said, and, side by side with the friend of my childhood, I saw in his face a sterner and more authoritative man, the Pax whose life was not dappled, as mine was, with moral ambiguities, but for whom right and wrong had been laid down with unerring simplicity in a cottage in Eillne. 'Weak and dangerous. He is corrupt, Theo.'

'Come on!' I laughed.

'There's a lot of lads like him going to be in trouble, Theo,' Pax continued quietly. 'Trucking around with guns and the like. Running them over the border. You must have heard.'

I suddenly knew how close I had come.

'A little,' I admitted. 'But there are so many rumours flying around. Guns from where?'

Pax looked at me curiously, then he shrugged. 'From the Continent,' he replied. 'Being smuggled in through ports like Monument.' He leaned over me. The summer's sun had tanned his forearms. 'We'll catch them all in the end, Theo. No matter who they are. There are no friends in this. No one is above the law.'

Funny the choices you make, how deceit allures. I would have trusted Pax with my life, but not with a simple truth. Not that it was a hard decision either. I took Bain's part as easily as a trout takes a dancing fly.

*

Although Juliet was patient with me, there were times she was not. Often she lay with clenched teeth, or rolled on her front with her hands beneath her, squirming and moaning like a beautiful, wounded fawn. And yet I looked forward to our weekends together in Dublin more than I had ever looked forward to going home to Eillne. Juliet made me happy. I made myself believe that my precociousness was something that would adapt. That the cash between us was incidental. And yet. And yet a tiny pulse of self-respect told me I was a fool and that the only woman who truly loved me was growing old alone in Eillne.

Weekends were missed by Juliet. Colds. Reggie. Men coming to value Drossa with a disdain for history that would have made Cromwell wince. Juliet always explained her inability to travel up too late for it to be worthwhile for me to make the southward journey. When she did arrive, with her little red nose, with news of her father, with the bill sheet of a Monument auctioneer describing the forthcoming sale at Drossa of lands, house and contents, I had lain awake so long in the intervening days thinking of her face, her body, of the fleeting but languorous moments when she would be mine alone for the taking, that I was prepared to accept her explanations without ceremony. These were the weekends when Juliet would be most testy. She would exploit the guilt she knew I felt at my own inadequacy as if to counterbalance her own guilt at having left me the previous weekend, or two, alone in Dublin.

Then one Friday evening in October there came a knock. My beautiful Juliet was due. She had not come from Eillne the previous weekend, so as I went to let her in, my mind was in its usual swirl of apprehension in which I fought to temper my own surging with the sober management of Juliet's needs.

'I've been counting the minutes,' I smiled, throwing the door open.

'Hello, Theo,' said Pax.

'Pax.'

'Can I come in?'

I stepped back to allow Pax enter; I think I then put my head out and looked down the passage, believing Juliet and he might have travelled together.

Pax had acquired an official mien for use in relaying bad news; he stood grim-faced, hands behind his back.

130

'I've nothing good to tell you, Theo,' said Pax quietly.

'Sparrow,' I said.

Pax shook his head. 'Juliet, Theo,' he whispered.

'Juliet?'

Pax nodded. He looked away. He looked around my one-roomed home, at my bed, at the kettle that I used to make Juliet's coffee.

I began to shake with fear. 'Dead . . . ?'

Pax's face had a fierce edge to it. 'Not dead, Theo. Gone.'

I sank. 'Gone?'

'To England, by all accounts.'

'Oh Jesus, I must follow her,' I cried.

'Theo, she went with that lodger in Eillne, that fellow Denny,' Pax said with a deep breath. 'They've been at it for a year, it seems.'

The weight of my worthlessness sat across my shoulders and kept pressing me into the cracks and fissures of the floor.

'What about Reggie?' I heard myself ask, as if Reggie Blood was the last piece of logic at my disposal.

'Gone into the county home, Theo,' Pax said, 'alongside your Uncle Hugo.'

I was most comfortable prostrate. A long time ago someone had taken something essential out of me and killed it for their amuse-ment. I remembered the tenant, Denny, and his wry, unshaven face.

'Theo, get up. Come on.'

Pax hefted me on to the bed.

'I'm taking you home.'

'No.'

'Your mother told me to.'

'No!'

Pax wiped his sleeve across his face. He re-examined the room, as if looking for an ally, or an idea.

'Theo, listen. You're better off. Jesus, imagine if there were children involved. I've spoken to Father O'Dea. You never actually lived together. There's a good chance you'll get a Church annulment. It's all for the best. No one is blaming you, Theo. No one.'

How badly I wanted to go to Sparrow at that moment, but how impossible it was to do so. If I could have just slipped like a phantom back to Eillne, and then, over weeks, like an object in

131

shadow finally resolved, been reformulated, so that my return would be as unnoticeable as the difference between seasons, then I would have done so. But I dreaded the certain surfeit of Sparrow's generosity. I despised her perfectness of spirit that would show me up for what I was.

'Theo.'

'No.'

'Theo, it's me'll be in trouble if I come home without you. Come on now, like a man.'

'*No!*'

Poor Pax.

'She was her own worst enemy, Theo.'

Pax's voice quivered with prudish secrets.

'How do you mean?'

'She just was.'

'What do you know?'

Pax looked away, regretting he had indulged himself.

I said, 'There were others too?' You know, I actually got a perverse thrill from asking that question. 'Who?'

'It's not for me to say, Theo.'

I had prayed that the truth would be everything but its name. It had flirted with me right up to the last moment, like an ugly old hag with the figure of a girl keeping on her veil till last. Breath was punched out of me. Knees to my chin, I lay foetus-like on the bed. I wept.

'She was a tramp, Theo,' Pax said. 'She was a nympho.'

'She's my wife,' I cried. 'I love her.'

I did, too. We had been like two people at the very beginning of a journey. Such a lot would have been learned: of life, of one another. Juliet had had almost no faults that I could not have overlooked in the cause of her beauty, and in such blind admiration would have lain the road to both our happiness.

'Who?' I cried. 'Who else?'

Pax sighed. 'If I tell you, will you let me take you home?'

I nodded.

'Bain,' Pax said quietly.

His mouth was the bitterest I had ever seen.

PART II

Seven

It is true that from my cell window in Dundrum there was a wonderful view. Beyond a screen of young, red oak, the mountains were mine; the shades of green up there were uncountable. I know, I tried. I thought sometimes I had green in all its categories buttoned down, then a cloud swam over the sun and my slate was wiped clean. I used to play the same game as a child in Eillne where the light performed tricks with the lower slopes of the Deilt Mountains, magnifying every last detail on mornings when later there would be rain, or pushing them out on hazy afternoons a hundred miles beyond Monument.

I tried not to dwell on my confinement. I had often stayed in hotels whose rooms were far less comfortable and did not have a heated swimming pool along the corridor. I was warm. I had a sink and a proper toilet. Outside, the twin tracks of jets were tooled incessantly across the white-blue Dublin sky. Watching them drift apart and become lost to the morning as even the most vivid dream is lost to memory, I gazed down at the older patients wandering about, men who had come into Dundrum fifty years ago as wild-eyed killers of some loved one but who were now just grey-haired old lags. Their movements lacked humour of any kind and bespoke a sad powerlessness; the upcoming millennium that everyone was agog at would hold for them, I suspected, little significance. At least I could not see the main building from my cell and that was a blessing: put up in Bram Stoker's day, it was as grim as anything conceived by the Victorian imagination.

Dr Croke, whom I have already described, was, I thought, converted to my case.

'We are all scapegoats for the past, Mr Shortcourse,' Dr Croke sighed. 'You are no different. We all think with our blood, as someone said, I can't remember who.'

Yet when it came to the question of my being released to stand a

135

proper trial, Dr Croke became evasive and thus our relationship consistently withered before it could ever take root. Broaching the subject of my identity with him made him go wary across the eyes and led to my keeping such concerns to myself.

I also kept private my dreams and my memories. Memory: beside Uncle Hugo's chair, a vase on a shelf. In summer it held marigolds, in autumn heather, in winter honesty, in spring primroses from the banks of the swimming river. The vase was the colour green as in moss. It had a slightly bulbous base and rose to a rim, eight inches high, through a series of circular riddles. Dreams: sticky. Frothing in the darkness, slime hatching out steamily, clawing to the shore when the level rose too much. Tadpoles with the ability to slip up- or downstream, back or forward, no journey too great, no moment ever truly forgotten, the stream as a whole the important thing, not any one tadpole in it.

The consultant had his rooms in Beaumont, a hospital on the north side of the Liffey to Dundrum. This consultant sat on a board that reviewed the cases of people like me; he decided in the first instance if we should be referred to the board at all and then, if so, the board made its recommendations to the minister. Ten weeks ago, perhaps as a result of my pretty counsel April's strenuous representations, I was removed across Dublin to be examined.

Three screws were assigned to my transportation. We left through Dundrum's electric gates in a big Honda Accord, myself between two screws in the back, the driver's eyes ticking to me in his mirror. Civilised relationships persisted in Dr Croke's regime. It was very much Mr This and That, and, if you would now care to step this way. Of course if you did not so care to step, they had restraining jackets and electric-shock machines and an ocean of injectable drugs at the ready. But by and large in my wing, from which two of these three turnkeys hailed, tasteful behaviour was the order of the day, and in my case such items as handcuffs were deemed unnecessary.

We swept down through Milltown and Donnybrook and across Ballsbridge towards the East Link toll bridge. It was uplifting to see children again, with their parents, in prams, playing. I would never father children, a minor regret in a tapestry of such

136

sprawling tragedy, yet I wondered if this application of mine failed, how many more times I would see the children of Ringsend, which we were then passing through, or those who lived in the shadow of the Pigeon House, or within sight of the Liffey?

Like schoolboys going to a match, the screws all smoked. Ships were moored either side of the toll bridge as we crossed it. Midsummer sun picked out every last detail of the decks and masts and deck hands at work. For years I had worked along those wharves and taken pride in what I had been about. Through Summerhill people swarmed in and out of the tenements. Beaumont was reached by a long avenue; we went to a side entrance and I was ushered in like someone famous going in the stage door of a theatre. There is not a lot to say about the consultation, except that I left it when my hour was up with a heart so low that not even the best day an Irish summer can offer could alter the infinite despair of my perspective. We set out to cross the city for, as the screws described it without irony, home.

The consultant's scepticism was exposed by his professional politeness. He did not really listen to what I had to say but rather observed the overall context I presented, of which my words were just one part. He examined me from a varity of angles, each one minutely different, as if searching for some elusive characteristic. His warm smile gave initial comfort until you realised it was a mask. My (reluctant) description of my dreams – that wonderfully comfortable bosom I knew so well; the furniture; the smell of starch – caused him to make his only notes, from which I had to conclude that the testimony of my waking logic fell on barren ground. I am sure he had kids in private schools and all the overheads that come with middle age; he had not made it to where he was by bucking ministerial suggestions.

We swung down by Fairview and took the canal road for the toll bridge. My carers puffed busily on their cigarettes and seemed more relaxed with the business completed. One of them even asked me how I had got on. The liberating sight of the river drove me further down; it bled the last drop of my self-esteem. Even the most obnoxious criminal could at least chalk off the days and call a point in the future freedom, but not me. I would be locked away for ever; I and what I had to tell.

The car stopped on the East Link bridge. The driver opened his window. I saw what I thought were gulls flying overhead from left to right, but then realised they were topsails and that we had stopped because the midsection of the bridge was up to allow the entrance into Dublin of a magnificent four-master. She was a sight! Her crew in whites stood all to attention along her main deck and her livery of canvas, brass and teak shimmered in the sunshine and bestowed on the Liffey an air of unexpected opulence. From the halted cars ahead drivers had got out for a better view. Fathers with children on their shoulders went to the railings. The screw on my left opened his window full down and leaned out.

'By God, look at her, Mick,' he said.

The screw on my right opened his door and stood, one foot on the road, whilst the driver screw peered out from under his mirror.

You don't ponder on these occasions. I took the standing man with my head in the chest and was twenty yards up the bridge before I comprehended how easy it had been. The ship slipped across my running vision, making it seem as if the bridge was moving. There may have been some shouting behind me. I climbed the railing. A tiny girl in a dress was perched on a man's shoulders.

'Love'y boat,' she said to me.

I jumped. As soon as I hit the water, I was free.

The Head Office of Customs and Excise is located in Dublin Castle, a hotch-potch yet comfortable fortification, a city within a city where the amassing of cash for spending by wastrel governments is undertaken in an ambiance of tranquillity. By the late 1970s great cranes had sprouted on our skyline and the roar of traffic outside the walls seemed louder, if you concentrated on it, than it had when I first came there. Not much else had changed in fifty, or even a hundred and fifty years, when inspectors – or the equivalent to my recently elevated position – wrote procedural directives for men in the field and contributed generally to cool, calming legislation.

I acquired a flat in Sandymount, overlooking Dublin Bay, which is to say the view was of water or of mud depending on the tide. Sparrow came up and helped me furnish it. Sometimes she stayed. In those days she would often be there when I returned from Dublin Castle. She would sit by the window at a full tide and watch

138

as I waded out then swam to the middle of the bay. For me it was a tantalising experience, the ocean on one side, my mother a black speck in a tiny frame on the other. Both directions exerted their feotal pull. Sometimes it was quite an effort to return to land, but I was always glad when I had done so.

I could look back on the bad years by then with equanimity. Just as Reggie Blood had died off, lasting no more than a few months in the county home, just as the current inhabitant of Drossa, a German businessman, lived there without the slightest reference to the Blood generations, so the memory of Juliet and I married was something I had to work at in order to resurrect and the only physical experience with her I could remember was the fleeting wetness of her tongue in my ear.

Having not met Bain for two years, I was surprised when I did that I felt no rancour. As it became obvious that I was not going to open old sores, Bain became eager to talk about himself. He had given up cigarettes. He had lost weight, he laughed and patted his large waist section. A TD, he was firmly launched on his political career, he told me, as if he wanted my approval. Perhaps what he really wanted was no old impedimenta in his flight path, no debris from the past or junk that might knock holes in his political fuselage. He gave me his private number in Dublin and, whether he meant it or not, urged me to get in touch.

In those days I regularly walked between Dublin Castle and Sandymount. Because I hated chlorine and because in winter the sea was not an option, the streets of Dublin became my place of exercise. I took in great exploratory sweeps of the city, much as I had explored the river delta as a child. Covering slums and leafy suburbs, parks and industrial estates, I clocked up thousands of miles and tens of thousands of faces. What I was searching for – because, if I am honest, it was a search – I do not know. Movement was everything. Faces were my reward. I forgot none and still retain them in a loose fashion: the momentarily interested eyes of a lovely young woman in Fairview; the smiling face of an ample matron in Clonskea. Maybe they, too, were searching. Maybe in the way of stars once in a million years I would make my crucial collision.

One winter evening in a dense jungle of a thousand matching doors, paused for my bearings, there came to me from nowhere voices in song with the words of the Old 100th.

139

The little church was like the one decent piece of furniture in a setting altered beyond recall. In richly corniced sandstone and granite it sat behind railings between a Catholic church and a public house, like an overwrought metaphor for the Protestant religion in Ireland. I entered quietly. The altar was contained within a number of enfolding arches at the end of a short nave, so that the lighted chancel with its choir resided as if in another dimension to me, distanced by a wedge of darkness. They loved their hymns, I could tell. In the gloom, with the old words coming back, imagining myself again at Eillne's luncheon table, remembering every detail of silver cutlery and linen and the taste of Nanny Morrissey's soup, I wept.

That evening I joined the choir of St Fel's. The music was like a river in which I could swim warmly to the past.

Little had changed on the journey from Dublin to Eillne. Once on the train I met my Uncle Bernard with his son Johnnie, now grown into his father's smiling replacement. They were returning from business; Uncle Bernard had lost a lot of weight and his skin reminded me of Pa's the day I had seen him laid out, a comparison by which Uncle Bernard would not have been flattered, but appropriate, because I would never again see him alive. Johnnie had inherited his father's sly look across the eyes as well as his big hands and mop of (already) silver hair. There was also the same suggestiveness that had been the clue to if not the proof of Uncle Bernard's loose reputation. For the whole journey Johnnie told stories that hung one way or another on women's anatomy, whilst Uncle Bernard stared, unhearing, at his approaching fate.

I saw my sister Mag once when some errand or other took me into the centre of Monument before I caught Sheehy's bus. She did not recognize me. An inner collapse had taken place in Mag's face as if, like acid, drink was corroding her bones, crumbling them with slow resolve, so that only Mag's eyes seemed to pin the dough of her flesh in place. Were it not for her perpetually reduced condition, there were questions I would have liked to put to Mag concerning the doubts about my origins that Pa had implanted in me whenever he had been drunk enough to suggest I was not his son. Sparrow would never supply me with that elusive information and the only other person I knew of who could was my brother,

140

Lyle, but no one had seen Lyle for years, and so it appeared I would have to live with my troubling questions unanswered.

It was still Sheehy's bus. Now there were two, huge, hissing things bought in England and operated by Pax's cousin, his father having died five or six years before. As you went out Captain Penny's Road stands of new houses had begun to creep, blocks of white and brown pebble dash, with the occasional new shop. Where once there had been only a holy well now there was also a zebra crossing.

Eillne's unperturbability, the sense that the house with its face to the river, and the river itself, would always be there as long as I needed them, was always reason enough to come home. Sparrow, of course, was also the reason, yet a fusion between woman and place existed for me, a codependence in the deepest sense in which I could not imagine the survival of one in the absence of the other. Stepping from Sheehy's bus on the hill, I looked forward to the first undercrunch of gravel in the way of an early but minor movement in a favourite symphony. I paused, still hidden from the house at the gate, and drank in the gluey-sweet scent of escallonia. At any moment there would be the roll of wheel rims and Uncle Hugo would appear in the trap, half slouched, switch in his hand like a fly rod, transported, like I was, back through time from his bed in the county home where he was now the most enduring tenant. Waking in Eillne in early summer to magpies or wood pigeons, or in winter to the harsh cough of a vixen in the darkness, I was able to imagine myself in the same bedroom as a child, listening to Bain's breathing in the bed beside me, or La's voice calling from the kitchen.

'Theodore, please try and be on time. Father O'Dea has to be back in to hear confessions on a Saturday evening.'

Although Sparrow was no more devout than I was when it came to religion, I noticed the increasing presence in Eillne of Father O'Dea. He was now, accurately, Monsignor O'Dea, working closely with the old bishop, bringing him back and forth to Rome and dealing with his correspondence, according to Sparrow.

'Tell me, *how* is Pax Sheehy?' Father O'Dea's lips suctioned vegetable soup from his spoon and his cheeks flattened and filled in little, bellows-like intakes. Nevertheless his brown eyes were observant across the table. Brown eyes and shiny, straight black

141

hair. 'I couldn't tell you when I last set eyes on him,' Father O'Dea said.

'He's a detective inspector,' I replied. 'They bought a house in Malahide.'

'Oh, so you've been out to it, Theodore,' Sparrow said.

'Once or twice, yes.'

'Comfortable?'

'Oh, very.'

'Pax was a great man for the jazz,' said Father O'Dea.

'Still is,' I said.

'Is that so?'

'He sometimes plays the saxophone.'

'I take my hat off to him,' said Father O'Dea.

'Quite abrupt the way he married and never even informed his old neighbours,' said Sparrow thinly to Father O'Dea. The long-standing antagonism between Pax and Bain meant that Sparrow could never hear Pax's name mentioned without adding her touch of spice.

'Oh, they were always very independent, the Sheehys,' Father O'Dea said. 'Very strong. He'll go far, Pax will.'

'Certainly to superintendent,' I said as Sparrow looked away.

'I would imagine,' Father O'Dea nodded. 'A great commitment to the law. A man beyond turning.'

'In that case I'd better go and have my car taxed,' Sparrow said and leant back with a brilliant smile that was just for Father O'Dea. 'If he comes home and finds me, you'll be in the courthouse putting up my bail.'

'An independent surety,' said Father O'Dea, returning the smile as if such personal exchanges were commonplace between them and my presence was incidental.

'Bain has little time for Pax Sheehy,' Sparrow confided, 'although he would never say so.'

'They're both ambitious, Sparrow,' Father O'Dea said. 'They see each other as competitors probably. Ambition can be a terrible burden.'

Sparrow smiled at the priest as if grateful that neither of them was prone to such affliction.

'You should get in touch with Bain, Theodore,' she said. 'Both of you up there in Dublin together. It seems such a shame.'

'I had lunch with him a few months ago,' I said. 'In the Dáil.'

'In the Dáil,' Sparrow said and nodded to Father O'Dea.

'He seems quite at home there,' I said.

'Well, well.' Father O'Dea beamed. 'The seat of power.'

Sparrow rang the little bell for Miss Turner, the woman who now did for her, sister of our long-deceased clock winder, to come in and take away the soup plates. 'He was out here during the week,' she said. 'He's all talk of an election.'

'Oh, he'll skate back in,' Father O'Dea said. 'The Balaklava vote alone will see to that.'

'He thinks he may be in line for a junior ministry,' Sparrow said.

'A family tradition.' Father O'Dea beamed. 'His father would be proud.'

A little silence fell on us as Miss Turner arrived with a tureen of stew. By Father O'Dea's tone it was obvious that by 'his father' the priest meant Pa, ignoring the fact that Bain's name was Cross and that Pa, who had been Bain's grandfather, had never held anything remotely resembling public office. Sparrow ladled out oily rounds of lamb cutlet and carrots with waxy pearl barley.

'How is Bain's business doing?' I asked. 'I mean, now that he's in Dublin so much.'

'Oh, I don't ask,' said Sparrow dismissively, busying herself with serving, as if I had managed to find the one subject on which she and the Monsignor were not thick as thieves.

'Business today is very difficult,' said Father O'Dea as his ha'p'orth, acknowledging that difficult ground had been reached. 'Goodness, Sparrow, that's more than plenty.'

'Father, if it's not too late, would you please say grace?' Sparrow asked and smiled her little-girl smile.

Father O'Dea put down his knife and fork. He joined his hands across his chest, tilted his head to heaven and closed his eyes.

'Bless us, Oh Lord, and these Thy gifts, which of Thy bounty we are about to receive Through Christ Our Lord. Amen.'

I suppose that period of my life was aimless in the social sense. I worked, I sang with St Fel's choir, I walked in winter, in summer I swam. I slept. There were the occasional contacts with Pax but social life is mainly a thing of couples and I was demonstrably lacking in that regard. Looking back, I wonder now how I coped.

How did I manage my sexuality between Juliet's absconding and . . . ? Sex became a hidden part of my personality. I stopped looking at the bare legs of young women and at the bosoms of fecund matrons, not because I did not want their legs interwound with mine or their breasts sweetly denying me air, but because I was unable to muster the energy for the ritual that is a necessary prelude to such trysts. My hunting instincts became subdued, even though I went through the motions. Nature bled me of troublesome semen at night as I frolicked in the safety of my unconscious. I became something of a hermit, I suppose, living within the bare world of my own construction, able, as a result, to give the full power of my mind to matters legislative and excisial, using a lone pint, here and there, and the uplifting chorus of anthems as my few points of reference with the world outside Eillne and Dublin Castle.

Bain Cross became Minister for Justice on 2 November 1979. He was popular in the way of rogues. People only disapproved of the stocky little butcher from Monument, who, it was said, had a way with the ladies, because they also envied him. His wife, Aggie, a big, strapping Deilt woman, rarely appeared in public and accepted whatever life brought with an ancient resignation.

I neither voted in the election nor followed the tense count afterwards; in truth it was not until I arrived in Monument on my way home to Eillne that it even registered with me that Bain had not only been re-elected by a landslide, but greatly elevated. A thousand people stood around excitedly although the midday was cold. Ships hooted. Even the Lyle seemed frothy and skittish. Sheehy's bus was landlocked by the crowd and as I pushed my way through I saw a banner with, daubed in uneven letters, the words: BAIN CROSS TD MINISTER FOR JUSTICE. Bain and his political cohorts had been on the same train and I had not even known!

A band struck up and Monument's councillors in their faded regalia lined up looking pleased with their vicarious power. Bain came out of the station, moving on the balls of his feet, the only man there without an overcoat. He clasped his hands over his head, climbed up on to the makeshift platform and, because the public-address system would not work, shouted, 'It's good to be home!'

I didn't wait for his speech. I went over to the river and watched its absorbing patterns, the eddies and whorls that testified to so much hidden strength. I felt happy for Bain, but in a calm, distant way. I hate crowds anyway. I would drop him a note of congratulation when I got back to Dublin and perhaps, if he had the time, he would reply.

Late spring and early summer arrived as one. After weeks of merciless rain rolling in cartoon-like squalls across my bleak Sandymount vista, suddenly one morning, before the onset of high-octane gasoline, the air was stippled with hints of lavender, and that evening, when I got home from work, families with buckets and spades and children with reddened shoulders were still clinging to the last sunny tracts of sand. I cannot say in honesty that I had followed the fuss surrounding Bain in any detail. I was aware that his appointment stood and that he clung fiercely to the ground he had reached despite the onslaught of derision from, it seemed, everyone. But once a decision is made in politics, however bad it may be, it is a bad politician who then changes it. Bain was dug in for the long haul. The media, contrary to general perception, had neither the talent nor the tenacity for extended vendettas, and the same papers that referred to my nephew as a gunman would, in six months' time, refer to his antiterrorist legislation as a milestone in the search for peace.

I say that most of the argument about Bain passed me by. There was reason for this, I think. To be too knowledgeable about Bain would have allowed me to discuss him ad nauseam with Sparrow on my weekends home to Eillne. When she had done with eulogising Sammy Tea, she would, if encouraged, speak of no one else but Bain. That irked me. It brought up again the whole spectrum of my relative place in her affections and reminded me of all the times I had been excluded from secrets shared by Bain and she and of the deep wounds I still carried. I know nothing of politics, I told my mother with a sigh. They bore me. Poor darling, she would say, we can't have that, and our talk together would turn to matters exclusive to us, such as our past, then, with my gentle probing, Sammy Tea and the Small Quay and the good old days would slip out in the twilight and Sparrow would allow me to drink from her momentarily unguarded cup of love.

One evening, walking between Dublin Castle and my flat, a man came up to me in the street.

'Are you Mr Theodore Shortcourse?' he asked.

I confirmed I was.

'Theodore,' he said, 'I am your brother Lyle.'

Eight

He was small and nearly sixty with a thin, white moustache and overcandid eyes that, in anyone else but a brother, I would have described as those of an inveterate liar. I recognised him from Pa's funeral fourteen years before in one of those great leaps of adjustment that does away with intervening time. He had the manner one might expect in the doorman of a club in Pigalle.

'I've seen you now and again walking along here, and I thought it might be you, but I didn't like to presume,' Lyle said and actually doffed his little hat.

He told me he had knocked about England all his life and that there had been many a rum old time. You knew by his face that mental arithmetic was his by second nature and that his agile brain, which might have been well employed in solving the great problems of the world, in Lyle's case had done nothing more all his life than perfect ploys for separating fools of the minor league from their money. But now it was time to settle down. He was always on the lookout for opportunities. He had some capital put away in waiting for the right idea, he said, having sold his bookie's business in Ealing. He told me this with a wily smile as if to say whoever came off worse in the deal, it certainly wasn't Lyle.

'I once met a lady who told me, when she heard my name, that she'd been married to you,' Lyle said.

'What was her name?' I asked.

'I'm sorry, I can't remember,' Lyle said. 'Quite pretty, smallish. She was driving a bus around Clapham Common.'

'Juliet?'

'I'm hopeless at names,' said my brother Lyle.

I could imagine Juliet driving a bus, swinging the big steering wheel. It was quite an erotic image.

'Did you ever marry?' I asked.

Lyle put his hand to his mouth to signify a whisper. 'Twice,' he

147

replied. 'And each one skinned me alive. I've a son somewhere. Changed his name, the knave, to Short. Then had the nerve to come and try and touch me for money. Can you believe it? Short?'

He reminded me of the old stagers on the Long Quay in Monument to whom a chat on a morning stroll was as important a part of the day as the racing page of the newspaper.

'And Oscar Shortcourse is still alive,' Lyle said.

'Still selling fish. Still taking the air on the Long Quay.'

'I like Oscar,' Lyle said. 'None of that old Deilt nonsense about him.'

'You must have grown up with a bellyful of that,' I said.

'And a lot more besides,' Lyle said. 'Pa was a depraved man, God rest him.'

I realised anew that Lyle, long forgotten by everyone, was the answer to the many doubts about myself that Pa, and Sparrow by her refusal to discuss such things, had long ago engendered. For the best part of twenty years Lyle would have been in Monument when matters crucial to my history occurred; Lyle had lived with Sparrow in the cramped house on Prince Consort Terrace where secrets personal to behaviour could not have existed.

'Bain Cross is coming up in the world,' Lyle was saying.

'Minister for Justice.'

'He was always a one to take his chance.'

'Politics suits him.'

'Doubt if he'd even remember me now,' Lyle said. 'How is his business getting on? I mean to say, he's a big shot now, up here in Dublin, flying here and there. Who's running the business? Who's making the sausages, know what I mean?'

'I understand he has a manager,' I said. 'Teddy Batty. Used to be the clerk.'

'Not the same thing,' Lyle said wisely. 'Bain should never have got that shop, you know.'

There was the old business of the court action when Pa died. Like rank odours, the bitter memory of such things long survived their demise. Yet I could suddenly see a way in which my brother's interest in the sausage business he had once coveted and my own hunger for the past could be driven in harness.

'I ran a successful enterprise of my own,' Lyle was saying. 'I came up the hard way, but I never did nothing underhand,' he added with the air of a man who expects to be disbelieved.

'One business is the same as the next,' I said.

'Spot-on,' Lyle said.

'Making a book, making sausages.'

'Now you said it.'

'But not politics,' I ventured.

'Not politics and sausages, no way,' Lyle agreed. 'Pity someone doesn't tell Bain Cross that.'

'Maybe someone will,' I said.

I took Lyle's card, which described him as a business consultant.

'I remember you, you know,' Lyle said. 'We used to drive young Bain out to Eillne. Pa had me nick the petrol coupons and I used to come along for the drive. Lovely old place. Is it still there?'

'Same as ever.'

'You were very small and skinny as I remember,' Lyle said. 'You'd be standing face to a window as Bain walked up to the door. You and he were the very best of friends. Are you still?'

'In a way.'

'We must get together properly,' Lyle said. 'To discuss the old days, Theodore, old son. Something tells me you'd like that.'

We'd only talked for ten minutes, but it was all he had needed to get my measure.

'Yes, I would. There are these gaps in my life.'

'I know.'

'You know?'

'Your old brother Lyle knows everything, Theodore, old son. All he wants is half a chance to spill the beans.'

'Sausages and beans,' I said. 'Reminds me of Balaklava.'

'Do you know what the past is?' Lyle laughed. 'I'll tell you. She's like an old prostitute forever waiting to turn one last trick. Turn your back on her for a moment, and bang!, she has you by the short and curlies.'

I felt it was time to be moving on. I looked at my watch.

'Do give me a ring,' Lyle said. 'But remember, that business of Bain's is rightly mine.'

'I'll remember, old son,' I said.

It was catching.

*

Twice a year I was sent to visit customs surveyors in the provinces. One was in Monument and worked behind the sweeping rosewood desk where once the coordinates of my life had been laid out. A single ship in a bottle sat on the shelf. The Surveyor was young and tidy and the many photographs on his desk of his children reminded you of the rounded nature of his achievements.

'This table should talk,' I said, when our business was concluded.

The Surveyor was first class at his job, but less nimble when leaps of imagination were required. He looked at me with empty politeness.

I said, 'It could tell a few stories, is what I mean.'

'Of course, you began in Monument, Inspector, I'd forgotten,' said the Surveyor, rallying to my theme. 'Do you ever get the urge to come back and live here on retirement? Not that that's near or anything, of course. What I meant was, you must have good memories.'

They were nearly all memories of women, for some reason, with some of Bain, but I said, 'I mustn't delay you.'

'You'll take the train back?' the Surveyor asked. 'I'll run you to the station. You have over an hour. Can I offer you tea, or a drink?'

'I think I'd like to walk, thanks all the same,' I said.

'Always at your service, Inspector,' said the upwardly focusing young man.

I strolled along Long Quay to the Commercial Hotel, where he and I had lunched earlier, and turned into Bagnall's Lane. I never alerted Sparrow to my official trips to Monument, preferring to do the business in one day by train. Despite being a man of forty, I felt my mother might try, as she always had where I was concerned, even in matters of customs and excise, to assert herself at my expense.

Unconsciously I was taking the route to the station by way of Balaklava. As I went through Moneysack, no longer a curving lane marking the boundary of Palastine, but a cleared site for Monument's main public car park and new courthouse, the past began to reassert its usual pull. I climbed Priests' Way with deliberate slowness, as if giving the steps and walls and handrails every chance to recognise me, or as if expecting some time-defying

150

metamorphosis of myself to occur. Near Prince Consort Terrace some houses that had always used their front rooms as sweet shops had now become shops proper with big square windows and plastic signs. Mag still lived in Pa's house, but she was more like a distant relative than a sister to me. To drop in unannounced and find her in God knew what condition would put an unfair burden on both of us and serve no purpose other than one of obscure duty.

Two black, ministerial Mercedes were parked outside the Shortcourse meat business. In one sat a driver, in the other a driver and two further men. I never thought very much about Bain's life, or how high office had affected him, but it amused me nonetheless to imagine what Pa would have felt to see his humble shed so attended. As I paused to look across – at the shop with its cold butcher's fittings and sawdust floor, at the shed that ran at right angles to the shop, its corrugated steel roof patched with asbestos in a dozen places – Bain walked out to his car and his driver jumped to hold the door. I turned to continue on my way, in case he thought I was snooping, but he had seen me.

'Theo?'

'I'm on my way to the station,' I said, and crossed the road to him. 'I thought I'd remind myself of my famous apprenticeship.'

'Aren't you lucky you gave that up,' Bain said. 'Were you in with my mother?'

'I thought about it, but I'd only be rushing,' I said.

'Heading back to Dublin?' Bain asked.

'Yes.'

'Then get in,' he said.

We swept northwards. I would have preferred the train and a cup of tea and a couple of hours to write up my file and read. Bain's car had deep leather seats. A radio-telephone was mounted near the handbrake and a little table with a light could be folded down should the minister decide to work in transit.

'How is it?' I asked.

'It's good and bad, Theo,' Bain said. 'This is the good. I know how to do this job, how to handle people. I wasn't picked for minister because I'm Einstein when it comes to the management of justice, but because of what I represent. I'm the last stop before Republicanism becomes disreputable – you understand? – or that's how I'm perceived. I suppose in some ways I have a leg

151

both sides of the border. How many Irish cabinet ministers can walk down Ballymurphy and call people by name?'

'Doesn't that mean you get pressure from both sides?' I asked. 'Doesn't it make your job difficult?'

'It may,' he conceded, 'but isn't that the challenge, Theo? These gunboys today, they're not like the lads that Pa knew. Not like Deilt. They're not even like the lads I knew in the sixties. They're dirt.' Bain chafed his hands. 'You wash dirt out, Theo.'

I could have asked about the dirt of history, but it was his car and we were in open countryside. The Deilt Mountains appeared to our left with the sun behind them making a long, black cliff against an azure sky.

'What's the problem, then?' I asked. 'What's so bad?'

'That fucking business back there is the problem,' Bain answered immediately. 'I feel such a relief every time I leave it and come back to Dublin. Does it make sense to you that it's easier to run the Department of Justice than it is to run Shortcourse Sausages?'

'Have you not got help?'

'I have Teddy Batty,' Bain replied, 'but he's just a clerk, he's not a businessman, and the unions walk all over him.'

Lyle and Bain were, after all, on the same wavelenth.

'I don't have the *time*,' Bain was saying. 'You've no idea the pressures in this job. The North, the courts, the Brits, everyone pulling out of me. And I'm meant to know what's going on in a fucking sausage business in Monument?'

'Sell it.'

'I've tried, believe me,' Bain said grimly. 'I'd nearly give it away now, if someone said they'd protect the jobs.'

'Perhaps if you expanded you could afford to employ someone who could lift the whole business,' I said tactfully. 'Trade out of the problem.'

'Do you want to know the truth?' Bain asked. 'I'm borrowed up to my bollocks and beyond. The business is in the Stone Ages, it's crying out for investment, but the money is simply not there to put in.'

We hurried along the night roads, lights from our protectors a constant distance behind.

'I might know somebody who might invest in it,' I said, regretting it immediately.

'Who?' asked Bain.

'Ah, I probably should mind my own business,' I said.

'Who? Who?' Bain asked. 'You've said it now.'

'I'd rather not tell you the name until I make some enquiries,' I replied.

'But there may be somebody?'

'Yes.'

Bain blew out his cheeks the way Pa used to. 'You'd be doing me a favour, Theo,' he said.

'Don't raise your hopes,' I said.

'Let me be the judge, Theo,' Bain said. 'I need cash like I need blood, OK?'

'OK.'

'Like I need blood,' he repeated.

As if the hope I had offered Bain also caused his memory to mellow, he talked softly about the old days and what he knew of them all the way to Dublin.

Pa came back from Deilt and found himself the hero of Monument. Grasping quickly that the birth of legend is not at all encumbered by fact, Pa's grief, suspended during his brothers' executions due to terror, and subsequently due to shock at his reception in Balaklava, was once more postponed by the prospect of opportunity. A business that had struggled to support eight, suddenly found its obligations halved. A congregation of which Pa, the Sunday before, had been just one, now knelt with eyes for Pa alone. Standing on the great spoil of yellow earth that the excavations for three coffins had raised, Pa looked out over many hundred heads and saw men eye him with furtive respect. His brothers' coffins sank, the earth rattled. What did men want, after all, except something to believe in? Pa grew until he imagined he could touch the spire of the cathedral. He was suddenly a new person with no past. To make the transformation complete, at his feet, smiling up coyly at him, was Sparrow Love.

Sparrow and Pa married in the early summer of 1921. Pa, although the virgin, was not long in realising that in Sparrow he had got more than he had bargained for; Sparrow never altered the view of Pa she had once formed outside the ice rink and clung to the piece

153

of vanity that it was she who had chosen him as her solution. My mother named my brother after the river, Lyle. Weakly and small, sallow-skinned and dark, he was clearly not a Shortcourse, whereas Mag, born ten months later, took after Pa in build and attitude.

If Pa had not been a drinker he might have been useful in politics to men cleverer than himself. But Pa was a drinker and his whole life was defined by this fact. He was abandoned soon after Deilt by the hard men whose job it was to shape the nation, and spent the rest of his life in the progressive ravaging of his own business and in a variety of attempts at swindling people more reduced than himself.

Sparrow came to detest Pa. Although she acted out the part of mother in Prince Consort Terrace, she had long abandoned that of wife, and from the time Lyle was a child had withdrawn to sleep on a cot in his room. But the older Lyle grew, the more like Harry Amis he became in looks and mannerisms, the more he resembled the cheat who was his father, and as far as Sparrow was concerned, anyone who resembled Harry Amis was himself a cheat. Thus Lyle, uncannily, began to slick his dark hair in exactly the same way Harry had and cultivated a pencil-line moustache. He even began to smoke cigarettes – Harry Amis to a T!

One of the things that kept Sparrow in Balaklava for eighteen years against her instincts was a sense of duty. Duty implied performing within certain limits but also contained the prospect of eventual discharge. In later years Sparrow liked to say this quality had had to do with an affinity to civics inherited from Sammy Tea; but Sparrow also had to admit that the predicament in which she had landed herself was in many respects of her own making and one for which there was a price. As mistress of the house, even one in Prince Consort Terrace, obligations arose outside the physical intimacy with Pa she had long abrogated.

'War, war, war.' Pa shook the paper out and turned sideways in his chair to catch daylight. At one o'clock, he was already in the day's first flush of drink. His eyebrows were arched, his moustache and mouth downturned so that his face was a series of quarter-moons. 'The world has gone mad. They say here that even the sup of tea will be taken from our mouths.'

'As long as it's only tea, Pa,' said Billy Cross with a grin.

Billy Cross came from Belfast. South with coal, north with pigs, ready cash, Pa's sort of young fellow. A lot of smiling when the newspapers told of dead policemen in South Armagh. A lot of sliding his brown eyes sideways and letting you draw your own conclusions. Small and square with a tan moustache, but handsome overall, if in a rough way, Billy sometimes gave Sparrow a cocky wink and Sparrow had to turn her head away to hide her blush.

'Daddy, you said you knew a fellow who told you he could get you all the tea you wanted out in Sibrille,' said Mag.

She sat in a frock that clung to her like muslin.

'They won't mind no war out in Sibrille,' Pa grunted. 'I seen them once eatin' slime off rocks and yokes in shells. Monkeys, bejasus. They even ate the postman, I'd swear that's what happened, poor oul' whore, all they ever found was his bicycle.' Pa squinted at his paper. 'Wing'll win the big race today. Where's that young fellow? I want to have a bet. Lyle!'

'He's gone to a flapper meeting with Jumpy Joe, Daddy,' Mag said.

'Bloody crook he's gone to work for,' Pa growled.

'What price does the paper give Wing at, Pa?' asked Billy Cross.

'Ten to one.' Pa rolled out his lower lip for wisdom. 'No one knows The Curragh like Morny Wing.'

'He has a big weight to carry, Pa,' Billy said.

Pa's lips fluted sceptically and he made a little impatient dance with his head. 'An' what'll beat him, tell me?'

'I've a sneaking regard for the bottom,' Billy smiled and gave Mag a little nudge. 'But Pa, forget the gee-gees for a moment and tell us again about the chamber of commerce dinner.'

Pa stood up, warming the backs of his legs. He shot a deep scowl at Sparrow as she came in and sat quietly down. 'The usual evening,' Pa began, 'not a decent drink to be had, half of them there in stuffed shirts, me in me suit o' Donegal homespun.' He tipped his face in a frown that caused his throat to re-form in a series of fleshy threads. 'Oscar Shortcourse, I need hardly add, was with the stuffed-shirt brigade.'

Mag took out her Craven 'A's. She lit one for herself, one for

155

Billy. Pa went to his pocket, unscrewed the top from a flask and drank.

'Up gets oul' Sir Clarence Fell,' Pa said, smacking his lips. 'Full of port, of course, he proposes the toast. "His Majesty the King!" says he. Back go the chairs.'

' "Back go the chairs," ' repeated Billy and winked at Sparrow.

'I sit where I am, which happens to be opposite Sir Clarence,' says Pa. ' "Sir! Your King!" he shouts. "Not my king, pal," says I. "Sir!" he roars at me. "My best friends have died for your king and your miserable kind." Says I, " 'Tisn't my business who chooses to die for a German in a homburg hat." '

Mag's mouth drooled smoke.

' "On your feet, sir, damn you!" Sir Clarence yells. "Right," says I and up I gets. Every eye is on me to see will I raise me glass. Instead I opens me mouth.'

Billy's chubby face shone. Mag pinched out the fat tip of her tongue at Pa between her teeth.

In a voice within which Sparrow sometimes heard strange sweetness, the voice of a deeper person, Pa sang:

> *'Breathes there a man with soul so dead*
> *Who never to himself has said*
> *"This is my own, my native land"?'*

Whiskey destroyed you in the end, Sparrow thought. He used to crow about his regularity, now it was either roaring for the bucket to be brought upstairs when he had the jigs, or Eno's. Three nuns sat him in bed the last time, saying the rosary like they did around the dying.

Pa reseated himself in warm glow and again fished out the flask. Smoke covered Mag's drowsy, acquiescent face like a veil.

' "I'm not dyin' for no German in a homburg hat",' Billy laughed.

'Where's that young fellow, I want to have a bet,' Pa scowled, wiping his mouth. 'Lyle!'

'He's gone off with Jumpy Joe, Daddy,' said Mag patiently.

'Bloody crook,' Pa growled. He scowled at Sparrow. 'Eats the fill of ten men, your son, then he's not even here when he's wanted.'

Sparrow looked beyond them to where she could see the blue midday sky.

'No respect for his elders,' Pa said, seething gently. 'Goes around the place like a lord. We're not good enough for Mr Lyle, no way!'

Sparrow's bowed head with its wisps of blonde hair presented to Pa the elegant line of her neck.

'Can't even be allowed to *sleep* on his own, Mr Lyle,' Pa said with rising pitch. 'Oh-ho no. Not our Mr Lyle!'

'At least he's bringing money into the house,' Sparrow snapped.

'Oh bejasus!' cried Pa brightly.

'Everyone's a crook but you,' Sparrow said.

'Oh, be the Lord hokey!' Pa cried. 'She's gone on the attack!'

'Jumpy Joe is a crook now,' Sparrow said. 'When Lyle was working for Mr Wise, Mr Wise was a crook.'

Pa let out a harsh laugh. 'Wise,' he said grimly to Billy. 'Wise me arse. Wizemann they were when they drifted up here first. Thrun out be their own beyond in Germany. Sucked the country over there dry, now they're stuck in here like grass ticks.'

'Ah now, Pa . . .' Billy began.

'There were many times food would not have been on this table were it not for Mr Wise,' Sparrow said to Billy.

'I'm sure, Sparrow, I'm sure,' Billy said, his eyes attentive.

'*Mister* Wise,' said Pa darkly. 'I want no charity from a Jew. They're the root of all evil, they crucified Christ.'

'Simpleton,' Sparrow said. 'Mr Wise is educated, and that drives you mad with jealousy. He is a churchgoer and a Christian whilst you are one without being the other. He is also kind.'

'Some Christians! They crucified Christ and now they're crucifyin' the new order.' Pa nodded to Billy, the definitive word. 'Money is all the Jewman has on his mind – when he's not thinkin' of women.'

'That's drunken talk,' Sparrow said.

'Wise turned, like the tide below on the Small Quay,' Pa sneered. 'Like Sammy Tea.'

'You see someone doing well and you're eaten with envy,' Sparrow spat. 'You were left the best business in Monument and you drank it dry and gambled what was left.'

'Oh listen to Sammy fuckin' Tea talkin'!' Pa shouted.

'Now Pa –' Billy began.

'A little, murderin' robber that sired . . .'

'Now Pa –'

'. . . that sired half the Eucharistic Congress, bejasus!' Pa yelled, standing up, shaking.

Sparrow set her face at Pa until he was forced to look away.

'Come on,' he blustered to Mag and Billy. 'We have more business than can be done in this company.'

Sparrow heard the street door bang. From where she sat she imagined she smelt freedom blowing to her from a point in the future she had not yet reached. On the kitchen range bubbled a sheep's head gone to sweet jelly. Sparrow went out and pummelled a pot of cottons and lugged it to the yard to drain off. Borneo saw her and ran for the privy, beside which he slept. He was actually the one Shortcourse Sparrow liked, because he lacked the brain to harbour rancour; because although he feared Sparrow, he was also prone to show her affection.

Sparrow began to peg out her wash on a hemp line. Ernest had been kind to Borneo, he had talked to him and said Borneo had a mind in there all the time. Ten years ago they'd cut Ernest down from where he'd done it in the shed. Between two pigs. Poor, pale Ernest, the weal on his white neck. Why had he done it? Had he died hard? Sparrow had helped wash him. Strong noises came from the privy. Sparrow sighed. She sometimes thought of Balaklava as one gigantic intestine, a huge polony sausage machine, meat oozing through meat, curling round and down through its winding drains and out into the ever-bending River Lyle.

Three in the front of Billy Cross's Riley, they went down Buttermilk so fast Pa's stomach was left in Balaklava. Mag was squeezed between Billy and Pa. Pa saw the white teeth in Billy's smiling, manly mouth. He felt his anger give way to the beginnings of an arousal.

Pa profoundly disliked Sparrow. She had not slept with him for years. In long, whispered confessions with Father Whittle, the parish priest, Pa told of his dilemma and Father Whittle told Pa he was not to blame for a state of affairs in which the woman's responsibility was paramount. God's plan was plain and those who went outside it, man or woman, risked damnation.

Pa's feelings for Lyle were more complicated. Aware that Lyle was the son of a British officer, Pa, sometimes in drink, became vicariously proud of my brother's breeding. Such confusion aside, Lyle's furtive nature alerted Pa to my brother's future potential in some of Pa's more ambitious dupes. Lastly, Lyle reminded Pa of his own deceased brother, Ernest.

The Riley passed parading Free State cavalry where Pa could once remember elms.

'Up Dev!' shouted Pa with the triumph of drink and both Mag and Billy grinned.

In James's Place they careered around the gable end of Wise's grocery. Root of all evil. Come between husband and wife. Past Turner, the watchmaker, on Half Loaf, then the hardware shop, the forge, the dairy. Then a block that had been burned in the war. No money to rebuild. How *was* money made? Pa saw Joe Batty tramping uphill with buckets, collecting scraps door to door. For his sow. Udders like one, too, the big Batty one. Pa saw them in half-sleep. Mouth like a sow on her, take you in for ever, lucky little fucker Batty.

Desire for a fecund woman began to burn Pa's head like fever. It made his scalp dance. Her boy, never forget, but sometimes, when he was drunk, Pa thought Lyle was poor Ernest sitting there. Pa felt Mag's thigh warmly on his upper leg. Out came his flask. Through Cattleyard, iron poles stood upright, used in the old days by the women who did the British Army's washing. Her boy and Captain Bull's. Pa had known on the first night eighteen years ago and even liked the thought of it from time to time. Pa could imagine the three of them in the bed, give her the bull, Captain, after you. Something respectable about an officer. Pa slurped whiskey and offered across his flask, but Billy's eyes were on the road and Mag's were on Billy. Desire.

'Where now?' Billy asked.

'Straight on,' Pa rasped. 'Straight on.'

Lyle had the same skin as Ernest, the same fine fingers. A wave of terror washed over Pa and left images in its wake, like rocks uncovered by tide. Ernest's pale body. Even now sweet comfort seeped perversely inward. Skin Alley took the Riley, just.

159

'Turn into Pollack Street,' Pa motioned.

Ernest had liked it all those years, never said he hadn't. Not Pa's fault, not Pa's fault. Pa drank. The shock. Ernest's feet only an inch from the floor. Pa thought Ernest had been standing in the killing line that morning. The shock, Jesus, the shock. Ernest's eyes had stared at Pa like Lamb's last eyes. A blessing the poor mother was gone. Oscar helped Pa cut Ernest down. Pa remembered Oscar's voice screaming murder. Jesus, if anyone had heard what Oscar'd said. He shouldn't have said that to Pa, Oscar shouldn't, he shouldn't have accused Pa of such filthy behaviour. Fucking lies, anyway. What did he know about Pa and Ernest? Pa had to threaten Oscar with a knife in the end. Pa's breath came in a shudder as Ernest and Lyle returned to his mind, two-headed on the one, smooth body. That was *her* fault, giving Pa bad thoughts he couldn't even confess to, letting Pa lie in dead of night straining for release. Was that right? The priest had whispered understanding. Ernest had been sick, Pa now knew, Ernest had only himself to blame.

They came to the low roofs of Palastine, another Balaklava, but sprawling in a dip between hills. Billy pulled in at a yard entrance and Pa got out. Air made his head swim. He leant on the car's roof to steady up and looking back in saw Billy's hand come out like a ferret from between Mag's legs. Pa turned his back to the car and came on hard. The images changed: Billy was suddenly and vividly in Pa's bed, big and oily blunt, and her face, Sparrow's, was struck with the shock of pleasure. Pa *knew*. He had seen the looks pass between them.

'You all right, Pa?' Billy put his arm around Pa.

'All right.' Pa caught Billy's neck and caressed it gently. Desire. Pa could feel the strength in Billy's neck. In *her*, with Pa looking on. Heaven. 'I'm fuckin' drunk, that's all.'

'You're a terrible mon, Pa.'

The doors of the narrow houses opened on to the cobblestones of Moneysack Lane. Pa watched Mag's motherly rump dancing in her light dress. He wanted to hurl himself on its warm mound and roar delight. The deeper into Palastine they went, the more flesh meant to Pa. A door was opened to his knock by a powerful, black-bearded man in a stovepipe hat.

'Mr Shortcourse. *Fáilte*.'

160

There was the light of a single lamp. A woman and an old man sat on a straw mattress beside a spittoon.

Pa said. 'God save ye.'

Tiny glasses and a bottle were already set out. With trembling hand, the bearded man poured six brims of clear liquid, then stood the rim of the little glass on his mouth.

Pa did the same. 'Christ,' he gasped. He felt drink rush all over him. The bearded man poured again, his eyes on Mag's throat. Mag stood legs apart, as if inviting the strange man's gaze. His long beard. Hers down there on her. Wet. Pa would soon burst. From the floor came a spasm of coughing.

'You'll kill that old man with this fuckin' stuff,' Pa gasped.

'Then the poor ol' whore'll die happy,' muttered the bearded man, slopping up the glasses again.

'So where's the wee bitch?' Billy asked.

The bearded man put down his glass and said formally, 'She herself was never beaten, sir. Out of three litters, none of her pups that fought was ever beaten. She's a reg'lar little gold mine, isn't she, Mr Shortcourse?'

Pa nodded and wondered how to cope with what refused to die beneath his coat. He hurt.

'Pups outa her'd fight with their throats cut. I seen 'em,' the bearded man said.

'They'd want to up my country,' Billy said.

'She'll not leave here for less than a ten-pound note,' said their host.

Billy made a face. 'Can we see her now?'

They went out into the rear yard. Holding up an oil lamp, the bearded man dragged back a wooden panel. There came deep growls. A bitch with a smooth blonde coat lay there, her pink dugs bursting in rose-like tips of promise. Pa caught himself beneath his coat and swooned. Out from under the terrier bitch teemed four-legged shapes, naked as mice.

'Ah, Jasus,' Mag said and caught on to Billy.

Grinning at Mag, leaning in, the bearded man caught up a pup, in size a sow's ear. It tore at his finger. 'Teeth's sharp as nadles.' The man laughed.

'It's dogs he'll have to fight,' Billy said.

The man picked out another pup, then squatted. He presented

161

the dogs head-on, nipping the skin on their backs. They lunged at each other.

'You're asking too much for the bitch,' Billy said.

'I'm not askin' half enough an' you know it,' said the man bitterly.

'I don't know any such thing,' Billy wheedled.

'Ten's the price,' the man said. 'Take it or leave it.'

'I'll give you seven for her,' Billy said.

'You're taking the bread from me mouth.'

'Seven's top.'

'No way, sir.'

'Give me a knife,' Pa commanded gruffly.

The bearded man dipped into his coat; he passed Pa a knife with its blade honed to a new moon. Pa lifted a pup and wedged it under his arm. Pulling out a front paw and fitting the blade under the lower joint, he sliced it off. Blood sprayed finely. Throwing down the thrashing dog, Pa reached for the other. He cut off the same butt of limb.

'Now fight them.'

'Mother of God,' Billy said.

They stood transfixed as the pups, paddling frantically in circles, tried to tear at one another. Mag fell senseless on her face.

'She must be comin' down with somethin',' muttered Pa as Billy slopped yard water on Mag's face.

'Pa,' said Billy, looking up with a sheepish grin, 'I've got something to tell you. I think Mag is in the family way.'

On the night before Mag and Billy's wedding, Sparrow had a powerful dream. She was on a train crossing water. Beside her on the seat sat a tall man in a black cloak that covered his head and face as well as his body and Sparrow's. Beneath the cloak he kept pressing Sparrow's hand to her womanhood. Outside the train, on the water, suddenly appeared Pa, Mag and Lyle. They were looking in at Sparrow and laughing, they were pointing at the man beside her and nudging each other, and Pa particularly was ogling him. Sparrow felt something cold and hard being pressed into her hand and knew immediately it was a gun. She pointed the gun and shot Pa and Mag. Then she shot Lyle. She awoke to a feeling of relief.

Undressed to her slip, Sparrow sat at the mirror in Lyle's room and brushed her hair out on her bare shoulders. Applying the barest coat of lipstick, the only adornment to her face, she dressed quickly in the costume and blouse, red and white, in which she herself had been married. From their box she took out shoes, given years before by Bernard but never worn. Bernard often gave her gifts, awkwardly, as if from an ancient obligation. The past sometimes came to Sparrow at odd moments, such as when she passed a sweet shop and caught the wafting smell of liquorice, or now when she put on Bernard's shoes. From tissues glowed a yellow, bud-like hat with a veil. Sparrow put it on and mystery looked out from the mirror. An old fox stole had been Hugo's wedding gift, no furrier's work, but that of some hound man with skills in taxidermy. Gathering its teeth and nails around her shoulders, Sparrow made her way downstairs, her unaccustomed heels clomping on the steps.

The third Saturday in that September of 1939 was a pet day. Pa had been out since early morning, tanking up for the occasion. Now he stood puffed up at the fire in the back room, Mag glowing from a tight, new blue costume beside him. When Sparrow came in Pa shot his frown in her direction, but then a ripple of appreciation crossed his face.

'Be the Lord Jesus,' Pa muttered.

The trio made their way down Captain Dudley's Hill. Burrowing her chin in the soft pelt, veiled, the beat of her expensive heels sounding on the long, downward steps, Sparrow felt detached from her husband and her about-to-be-married daughter. Suddenly her eighteen years in Balaklava meant nothing to Sparrow and she was once more someone just passing through the poorest area of Monument, observing the little doors and when someone met her eye smiling with well-bred courtesy. The feeling of detachment and, shamefully, the sexual exhilaration of her dream persisted for Sparrow throughout the Mass. She was unhearing of the words from Pa's confidant, Father Whittle. She sat when she should have knelt and stood when everyone else was sitting. The Communion passed by without Sparrow's participation, a detail that later would be widely seized upon. Sparrow left the cathedral in the belief that she had entered it but a few minutes before. All the others had gone on. Sparrow began to make her way in the direction of the Commercial Hotel.

The Angelus began as Sparrow crossed Mead Street. She stopped, as did everyone in the street, two drovers in charge of black cows, shawled women in donkey carts, everyone stopped in the sunshine, crossing themselves, their lips moving. The cows swayed on, unattended, splashing dung on to the cobblestones of Bagnall's Lane as the echo of the last strike died away.

'I never expected such beauty.'

Sparrow looked sideways. A tall, strange man with great muttonchops and curly black hair was standing beside her, his hat neatly beneath his arm.

'The way the town is part of the hill and the valley,' he continued, not actually speaking to Sparrow, but since there was no one else in the immediate vicinity, clearly speaking for her attention. His accent was that of an educated foreigner. 'The way the sea beckons one from the masts of ships. The way the river curls into its bend yonder. *Ja*, beauty indeed.'

He was so tall Sparrow had to step back to get a good look at his face. She was stunned. He was the stranger from her dream.

'Nothing would stop me from coming to a place where I could find such a pleasant marriage of people and place,' he said, then, as the bells ceased, replaced his hat upon his head and strolled away in the opposite direction.

Sparrow's sense of disorientation, like a dizziness that foretells a fever, went into high gear. From the Commercial Hotel, men with drink swelled on to the footpath. In the hall, beneath pictures of the Lakes of Killarney and the Battle of Bethlehem, Lyle, dressed like a spiv, orchestrated children's eyes with coins tossed neatly from the back of a comb. Music came from the inner bar. Pa sat on a high stool, Mag on his lap, a row of amber glasses marshalled before him and his face lit with the peace of a sailor faced with open sea. Mag's blue costume skirt broke across her thighs. Seeing Sparrow, she commandeered the cigarette from Pa's mouth, took it in her own and whispered something that made Pa laugh. Sparrow turned away and as she did so, a jackdaw with tripod and black cowl captured her likeness in a puff of smoke. Disdain, coquetry and apprehension can all be seen in that famous snapshot.

'Ah, Mrs Shortcourse.'

Father Whittle in frock coat was making for her. His face hung

164

lard-like under his silk hat, which in turn stood on his head like an obelisk. Sparrow pressed out a smile, as a machine does that stamps out pennies.

'How are *you*, Mrs Shortcourse?' frowned Father Whittle, as if Sparrow's wellbeing might hold some clue to her recent behaviour in his church.

'I am very well,' responded Sparrow brightly.

'No . . . distractions?' asked the priest closely.

'If there are, they're harmless,' Sparrow replied.

'The man downstairs always comes dressed up as harmless,' Father Whittle revealed, a little, knowing smile for the devil. Silver appeared in his hand and Father Whittle tilted back his face and pinched snuff into his nostrils. 'Ahhh. God made man and He made woman, Mrs Shortcourse. In His own image. We're a grand little country, you know. Our own government now. But it is not for you or me to anticipate God. He made nature. Ahhhhh . . . We have no choice but to do his bidding, Mrs Shortcourse. *Shoooo!'*

'Sparrow.'

Bernard and Hugo Love stood to one side with glasses of sherry, tokens of their conviviality. Their suits were well cut, their moustaches fitted trimly below their unruptured noses. Authority clung to them.

'One less for you to worry about, eh, Sparrow?' Hugo enthused.

'She's a young woman now,' Sparrow said in Mag's direction.

'She certainly is,' remarked Bernard with a long, sideways glance at Mag.

'I met an extraordinary foreigner on my way from the cathedral,' Sparrow said. 'Not a sailor. A tall, Teutonic man.'

'The town is full of them,' Bernard remarked. 'They come from England and from Europe to take in the Monument scenery and then to send picture cards home by post. I can't imagine why, especially when the rest of the world is fighting a war.'

'Nanny Morrissey can speak of nothing else,' said Hugo grimly. 'I know all her theories involving foreigners who creep into the district and have their way with young girls. She's led a very sheltered life, Nanny.'

'Why isn't she here?' Sparrow asked.

'She's getting too old for this sort of thing,' Bernard said vaguely. 'We sent her home with Dalton.'

'There is the most beastly chill around,' Hugo said, frowning fiercely and showing front teeth separated by a gap. 'Nanny should watch out. Reggie Blood tells me half the kennel staff in Drossa are laid low.'

'Do you you *know* anyone here, Sparrow?' Bernard enquired.

There were dog men and horse men, all familiar to Sparrow from Pa. There were small round women from Billy's family who glowed up at Sparrow like oven-ready dumplings.

'Sparrow?'

Billy Cross was shining with drink and excitement.

'I can see that Pa has no plans for stirring,' Billy said. 'That being the case, will you do me the honour of joining me for the breakfast?'

Sparrow felt the familiar blush that Billy caused in her; she thought of her dream, of the man in the street. She took Billy Cross's arm and he led her out of the hall and into the dining room.

The tables were set out for two dozen. By the cake, cigarette in mouth, sat Mag. Billy put himself between his new wife and her mother. Father Whittle and Oscar Shortcourse sat together. Then Lyle. Some minor civil dignitaries from the Monument town council were in their chairs beside men from the livestock trade, and next to them, the surviving two brothers and sister of Pa's own father, and a small, dark woman no one could put a name on. Billy's family sat in a line. Kitchen women brought teapots and platters with sandwiches and a huge pot of crubeens that had been insisted on by Pa, although he remained in the bar as Billy had predicted. A chomping and a slurping began.

'I heard someone talking about you earlier,' Billy muttered.

'Who?'

'One of the guests. A man.'

'What did he say?'

Billy's eyes were on his plate. 'He said, you could be the bride.'

Sparrow carried on eating as if nothing had been said.

'It's the truth,' Billy persisted, in the way that the truth comes to the surface when mixed with drink just as oil does with water. 'You . . . you deserve better than what you have, Sparrow.'

This was, of course, precisely what my mother believed, but again she ignored Billy, although this time she blushed.

'Why do you stay?' asked Billy, his confidence rising. 'Why don't you leave?'

Sparrow looked at Billy directly. 'What are you talking about?'

'You should leave Pa,' Billy said. 'You should leave Monument, Sparrow.'

'I'm surprised at you, Billy Cross,' Sparrow said. 'You've drunk too much.'

Billy now brought his (wide) hand up and covered Sparrow's, which lay undefended beside her bread plate.

'I would kill for you, Sparrow Love,' Billy whispered.

Breaking out from under Billy's hand, Sparrow saw Lyle's interest in their conversation from five places away, his weasel-like nose twitching above his Harry Amis moustache. Defiantly, Sparrow shook her head like a blood filly that senses a challenge.

'And where would you suggest I go?'

'Anywhere would be better.'

'I don't know "anywhere".'

'But you have thought about it.'

It came to Sparrow in a sudden wave of sadness that she had not had an intimate conversation, let alone a relationship, for eighteen years. No one to confide in, or to share pain or secrets with. No one to run to. Sometimes she spoke at length to Borneo, who gazed at her with his big, iridescent but empty eyes.

'I had this . . . extraordinary dream last night,'

'A dream?'

'It's still so clear.'

'Tell me about it.'

'It's very silly.'

'Nothing you could dream about would be silly,' said my mother's new son-in-law.

Sparrow described her dream, but in censored form, omitting the physical details and sparing Mag the fate dealt to her by Sparrow's unconscious.

'You dream is a message from God, Sparrow,' Billy said urgently.

'You think so?' my mother asked, although since waking she had formed the same conclusion.

'Your dream is telling you to leave Pa Shortcourse,' Billy said. 'It is telling you to fly away.'

'Ladies and gentlemen!'

Oscar Shortcourse was on his feet.

'Today I have been favoured by the exigencies of the situation . . .' began Oscar to cheers.

'I have often dreamt I could fly. When I was a small child I thought I could fly away with my father, just the two of us.'

'That is how I see you. A bird.'

'My lovely niece has found her husband in the outer reaches of what is still a great empire, an empire as great – greater – than the Holy Roman Empire, itself the mightiest empire . . .'

'Hear, hear,' murmured some of the older Monument fixtures.

'I have never forgotten that feeling,' said Sparrow.

'You mean you have not forgotten how to fly.' Billy smiled. 'You are, after all, a sparrow,' and this time when he put his hand over my mother's, she allowed it to stay there just long enough for her to feel its warmth.

'We have thrown away our riches at the very moment they were within our grasp! Empire. Gold. Silver. A way of life. I curse this Gaelic League, this Celtic twilight, so called. We are not fit to govern ourselves! I say we should fight for the Empire! I am an Empire man!'

'Hear bloody hear!'

'The world is so big. Even this wee country of ours. But the world in the mind of a man like Pa is so small. It's nothing. He is nothing and that makes my heart weep for you.'

'I think we have said enough now.'

'We pride ourselves on the fact that Ireland escaped the Reformation and the Industrial Revolution. But what are we left with? We have no business, no wealth. Are we also to be called cowards who will not fight by the people of civilised nations? We are hostage to our blindness!'

'Sit down, ye old fool, ye're drunk!' came a shout and Billy smiled brightly, turning to include Sparrow in his approval for the heckler.

'Cods' heads for the cat, Oscar!' cried a voice recalling Oscar's profession.

Billy's disdain for the Empire as espoused by Oscar was balm to my mother's view of anything to do with British soldiers in a way that Pa's drunken Republicanism could never be; each further time Billy laughed at Oscar's rambling rhetoric and the growing shouts it attracted from the guests, Sparrow felt a thrill at being able to associate herself publically with sentiments that further consigned the reputation of Harry Amis and his like to the dunghill of Irish history.

'If you ever need help,' Billy whispered above the noise, 'if ever he touches you, you know you have one friend. You see these eyes?'

Sparrow, despite herself, looked. She would recall later, in the years ahead, that she had seen warm embers of admiration.

'These eyes can see, even from a great distance,' Billy said. 'Remember that.'

'Even our chieftains are dead! We are left with only magistrates to lead us!'

'Thank God you're not one!'

'Give us six fresh mackerel, Oscar!'

'Will you remember?'

'Yes.'

'Say, "I will remember".'

Sparrow laughed. 'If it makes you happy, I will remember.'

'What we want in Ireland', Oscar shouted at the top of his voice, 'is a king!'

'Someone rip his head off!'

'And I will always remember you, Sparrow.'

'Oscar, you can be the king on Fridays!'

'Bad cess to all of you and your . . . mediocrity!' Oscar cried.

Father Whittle stood up amidst the consternation. 'In the name of the Father and of the Son . . .' he bellowed, closing the breakfast.

Sparrow glided back through the hall on Billy's arm. Pa was propped against the counter, singing obliviously. Mag joined Pa. Emboldened with drink, men brought women out to dance to the bars of an accordion. Music filled Sparrow's head – like the wheels of a train! She took the floor with Billy, and although it was years since she had danced, Sparrow allowed him to guide her haltingly through a reel. As the music quickened Billy became surer. Sparrow felt bolder sorties of his hands around certain contours of her body, manoeuvring her. The relief that had followed Sparrow's dream surged to fresh ground. Bodies spun in the mixture of smoke and sweet whiskey to the urgent beat of a badhran. Speed made one of Sparrow and Billy Cross. They held the floor. Sparrow threw her fox stole off to the ground. She was the dance. To the clap of hands. The suddenly deft young groom with the pretty but neglected wife. Old recklessness flowed like old wine. Sparrow and Billy danced with the unity of supple water currents, pulsing together and breaking whitely. They danced with a fever that was outside time. They danced together all evening under Pa's (seemingly) unfocused eyes.

Mag was passed out on a bench when, two hours later, Billy led Sparrow quietly out the hall of the hotel. Only Lyle saw them. Lyle followed.

Nine

Rain blew in great gusts out of the west and across the midland bogs, descending on Dublin like bands of demented spirits. St Fel's was packed, an island sanctuary in a howling sea. It was two weeks since I had met Lyle; somehow the urge to ring him had not been sustained and I had drifted along, unwilling to confront history in quite the way my brother had seemed to suggest.

The occasion in St Fel's was the visit of St Matthew's Singers from Belfast. As I stood robed in my stall I heard as if for the first time a voice of utter purity from the dense ranks of the arrayed regalia opposite. I tied the voice to a mouth. She was in her early thirties. Small, but you only noticed this because of the size of the choristers either side of her. Perfectly small, in fact. I suddenly realised there was a whole world of pleasurable diminutiveness from which for reasons unknown I had until that moment been excluded. I watched her mouth as she sang 'Jesu Joy of Man's Desireth', and without warning I felt a rush of excitement, which because of its rarity, fed voraciously upon itself and defied my efforts at containment. She looked across and saw me staring. Her smile was like the single beam of sunlight into the dark, prehistoric passage of my soul.

St Fel's became a cafeteria after singing had taken place. Disrobed, we sat in pews and on altar rails with our tea and biscuits.

'Small but perfect,' she said, looking at the ceiling of the nave, pausing with her tea in hand, and possibly speaking to herself if the outcome of her foray demanded it.

'Imitating the best in nature,' I observed, rising to the challenge. I wondered how a woman of her size could simultaneously appear to have such long legs.

'No doubt,' she said, showing me big, grey eyes, a feature that came as an unexpected bonus when she looked straight at you. A smile grew from the corners of her mouth.

171

'You have a difficult voice for a choir,' I said.

'You think so?'

'Restraining it is difficult, I could hear.'

'Restraint is difficult in certain circumstances,' she replied, 'and not always sensible.' Her lips for a moment went naughty, as if to tell me she was willing to flirt with danger if it came with the possibility of pleasure attached. 'The spirit will be free, I suppose. That's the main thing, don't you agree?'

I had always read about certain manifestations of infatuation and doubted them. I realised then, in St Fel's, that I had been wrong, and that the urge to drop everything, to abandon all assets and responsibilities and to fly without further thought to a faraway place with a person one has met only minutes before, not only happens but is advisable.

'Yes, I agree,' I said. 'I'm Theo Shortcourse.'

'I know.'

'How?'

'I asked.'

'Why? Did you ask, I mean.'

'Because I wondered who had been staring at me all evening.'

Everything about her was so tidy – in the way of Sparrow. My own relative size and height had never before seemed to me to be of any particular advantage, but now, somehow, confronted with this exquisitely miniature lady, I felt potent in the way of mountains.

'I'm sorry,' I said and pretended diffidence.

'I'm not,' she said and smiled again, making it a secret between us. 'My name is Elizabeth. Elizabeth Wedlake.'

All I could find out about my brother Lyle was that he had ten thousand pounds on deposit in a bank in Dublin, information I obtained irregularly. I was prepared to give Lyle the benefit of the doubt in most things and to put the suspicions he aroused in me down to an unfortunate aspect of his personality and nothing more; yet I would have been happier to meet someone he had done business with, or to ascertain if he had ever discharged a liability, before landing him as a partner on Bain. On the other hand, if Bain was so badly in need of funds it seemed churlish of me to act as the arbiter of someone who might so easily help him out.

172

My middle-aged life had suddenly blossomed the previous six weeks the way hyacinths suddenly do in midwinter. I had forgotten all about the mysteries of the past in the heady aftermath of my encounter with Elizabeth. I had never met anyone like her before, anyone whose zest for pleasure was so basically uncomplicated. As a younger man – as Juliet's young man – I would never have been able to handle Elizabeth Wedlake. Elizabeth! She kept peeping out behind the clouds of my mind and recharging the heart of my day whenever it succumbed to the frost of the past!

Yet I rang Lyle and arranged to meet him, telling him I had some information on Shortcourse Sausages. I was, of course, tantalised by Bain's story, which had told so much, yet had left so much to be told; and Lyle's promise of revealing matters that had remained hidden, his reference to the things that only he, Lyle, knew, seemed all the more interesting after what Bain had described. Lyle and I met in the upstairs lounge of a pub near Aungier Street where the barmen and Lyle seemed to have a familiar association. I told him I had met Bain.

'How is he?'

'You'll have to promise me that what I tell you will be confidential.'

'Consider me a tomb, old son.'

'He's strapped for cash,' I said. 'He wants an investor.'

Lyle shook his head.

'In debt, I suppose.'

'Yes.'

'He got that business debt-free,' Lyle said. 'No one would lend Pa sixpence.'

Lyle smoked cigarettes with the lighting end held inward between his thumb and first two fingers, like people do who spend their lives out of doors. This added to the shiftiness.

'What's in this for you, Theodore, old son?'

'I think I'm doing both of you a favour, that's all,' I replied.

Lyle looked at me warily.

'There are these grants nowadays,' he said. 'They *give* you money to buy machines.'

'The Industrial Development Authority,' I said.

Lyle gave a little, burping laugh. 'Imagine if thirty years ago

173

someone had told Pa they'd *give* him money to buy a machine! He'd have bloody choked himself.'

My brother went to the bar for another whiskey and a gin.

'I'll be honest, I have been thinking about it,' he said, settling back. 'All right, it should be my business but it isn't. It's Bain's. And that's the problem I have. I keep confusing Bain in my mind with Pa and anyone who would ever invest money with Pa would need his head examined.'

'I can't deny the similarities,' I said.

'What're your memories of our late, departed, shall we call him father?'

' "Shall we call him"?'

'Well, the bastard wasn't my father, as you well know.'

'Does that annoy you?'

'Quite the opposite.'

'Nor was he Bain's father.'

'*That's* a point in Bain's favour. A very good point indeed.'

'Was he actually my father?'

Lyle looked at me. 'Why do you ask that?'

'Pa once told me I wasn't his son. I tried to ask my mother, but it's an area I could never get her to discuss.'

'It is a very difficult area, Theo, very tangled, old son.'

'But one which you can unravel.'

'Yes, but only very slowly.'

'Why only very slowly?'

'Because, my old son, I think I like you, and I don't want to see you hurt.'

I liked him then too, and from that moment on. Beneath the sharp bookie there was gentleness and the wish to be kind. The warmth in the pub suddenly melted whatever armour he had years ago felt the need to put on and with the melting went all his shifty ways. He sat with his legs crossed and a little smile on his face as I got us fresh drinks.

'Do you know who the most mixed-up person in the world is, Theo?' he asked.

'Who?'

'Sparrow Love Shortcourse,' said my brother Lyle.

The story of Baby Love was always obscure. Sparrow was born

when Bernard was already seventeen, Hugo nine, and Baby Love, my mother's sister, fourteen years of age, which means that in 1939, the year of Mag's wedding, Baby was forty-eight. There was the framed snapshot of Baby that showed a beautiful young woman with loving eyes; there was the stock answer to any question about Baby: Baby went away. Baby in fact went away with a nephew of Nanny Morrissey's, a Frank Fox, four years Baby's senior. They went away to Atlantic City, New Jersey, where they lived happily, proprietors of a laundry business.

During her years in Balaklava, Sparrow managed to make contact with her older sister, and although she succeeded, the ensuing relationship was one-sided, Baby Fox being a reluctant correspondent. However, Sparrow's interest was stimulated. She undertook a further questioning of Nanny Morrissey about Baby, but Nanny's vague answers were unsatisfactory and left Sparrow more puzzled than before.

Baby and Frank Fox had had enough money when they arrived in Atlantic City to set up a laundry. But why had they gone in the first place? Baby, after all, was only fourteen. There was no child born to her at that time, no evidence that unwanted pregnancy had been the overriding motive, nor had a miscarriage or other tragedy been reported. And from where had the money come to set up a business? Frank Fox was the son of a poor farmer outside Monument, he had no education to speak of and could not possibly have accumulated wealth of that kind by the time he left for the New World, aged eighteen. The money had to have come from Sammy Tea. But why? Why did he pay his daughter of fourteen to run away with a semi-illiterate farm boy?

Sparrow accepted in the end that life invariably unfolds in the least expected directions. She gave up corresponding with Baby as a futile exercise and was therefore surprised when six months before Mag's wedding she received a letter from Baby informing her that, to much surprise, at forty-eight Baby was pregnant, and that a month after hearing this news Frank Fox had dropped dead on the Atlantic City boardwalk.

Lyle had drunk too much at the wedding. At eighteen drink sat heavily on his stomach and caused gagging. He had done so once on the Long Quay within sight of the Commercial Hotel, wherein the dancing was still in full swing. Moneysack, Palastine and Priests' Way all bore evidence of Lyle's homeward journey, yellow pools of gin with little red scabs of undigested pig's foot floating in them. Lyle, like everyone else who had seen Billy Cross and Sparrow dance, had been swept up by the excitement. Lyle had seen a new Sparrow; he had seen Billy Cross's eyes. But now Lyle's prurience ended on the cobblestones of Balaklava in involuntary retching.

Scarcely aware that Sparrow and Billy were in the kitchen of Prince Consort Terrace, it was all Lyle could do to climb the stairs and crawl on to Sparrow's cot. Sometime after collapsing, Lyle was awoken by the sound of soft voices. He heard Sparrow, then Billy. The night outside had turned to rain. Lyle heard Sparrow's and Billy's whispering laughs in the setting of peculiar stillness that persistent rain creates. He heard Sparrow say, 'Oh! Oh God, Billy! Oh!' Then he went back to sleep.

Lyle could not tell how long he had slept between his first awakening and the second, but abruptly reawoken he was by the crash of breaking glass. Through the rain's even beat, the sound of breaking grew. Of cups and plates. Chairs.

'No Pa!' Sparrow screamed.

'Sow!'

'Billy!' Sparrow cried. 'Billy! Quick!'

Pa was roaring.

'Bitch!'

There was the rapid clomp of Sparrow's heels on the stairs. She burst into Lyle's room and slamming the door, put her weight against it. Down on the cot, Lyle was hidden from Sparrow by the empty bed. He heard her pant. Then he heard Pa on the stairs, like thunder. The door flew inward and Sparrow was bowled back on to the covers.

'Filth!'

Pa was in and on Sparrow. He dragged her upwards by a hank of her hair and cuffed her solidly across the mouth. Lyle, terrified, remained invisible on the floor.

'Bitch.'

Pa hit Sparrow with a cold madness. Sparrow sucked in her breath. Pa hit her and she cried and spat out.

'Soiled goods! Good enough for anyone but not for me! That's what I got. I'll have them so, my soiled goods!'

Pa ripped Sparrow's skirt away from her body. Lyle could hear it rip. Pa caught Sparrow's blouse in both fists and in a single, expansive movement frittered it.

Sparrowed cried weakly, 'Billy . . .'

'*Billy?*' Pa jeered. 'Tryin' to find his trousers, the bold Billy is!' He slapped her face twice, forward and back. 'Sammy Tea's daughter is looking for Billy! I'll give you Billy, you filthy bitch! I'll give you Billy!'

With Sparrow's scalp in his fist Pa was breathlessly fumbling his buttons.

'It's in your blood, but I'm not good enough for you!' Pa shouted. 'Sammy Tea left his rod in every girl in Monument, but it drove him mad when he left it in one too many! Billy, is it?'

Springing up into Lyle's horrified vision was Pa's angry member, florid and slightly oozing semen.

'Do you know who she was, eh? Sammy Tea's doxy? Have you never been fuckin' told?' Pa roared. 'Look at the state I'm left in!'

Pa squeezed Sparrow's neck with such strength that only by opening her mouth to take him in could she find relief. A soft, wet noise brought abrupt silence, punctuated by Pa's groans.

'Oh Jesus . . .' Pa cried hoarsely.

Pa worked Sparrow's head like a glove for all of a minute, then, fist on her throat, he pushed her back and began to try and enter her. Without warning, as if wired, Pa careered backwards.

'Fuck you, Pa, but you're a bad mon!'

Billy Cross caught up Pa for all his weight and butted him in the face with his head. Pa was caught hard by the edge of the already ruptured door. He stood, hands flattened out, eyes round with astonishment.

'What the fuck . . . ?' he gasped.

'You're bad, Pa,' Billy said and this time kicked Pa up between his bare legs, a good, well-aimed kick.

Blood was everywhere. Spancelled by his trousers, Pa lunged at Billy. Billy butted Pa again, full in the face, and when Pa went down, Billy dragged him back up and repeated the treatment. Lyle had never before thought of a head as a weapon. Billy's head slammed repeatedly into the paste of Pa's face with the regularity of a rock-breaker. When Pa's weight at last defied his further

177

hoisting, Billy stood heavily on Pa's throat with the heel of his new boot until Pa's tongue crept out on the floor like a dying serpent.

'She's . . . my . . . wife . . .' Pa choked.

'More's the pity,' Billy said and kicked Pa in the head. 'You don't deserve one little bit of her. You're filth.'

'I . . . saw you downstairs . . .' Pa gasped.

'You saw nothing, Pa,' Billy said, 'but a lady who wanted minding,' and he carefully kicked the place where Pa's shirt was parted.

Lyle looked to Sparrow on the bed. She was lying where Pa had left her, mostly naked, staring wide-eyed at the ceiling of the little room.

Billy kicked Pa without urgency. A pause followed each time Billy's boot struck.

'Don't ever do that again, Pa.'

Pa joined together his two hands, prayer-like, and rose up slowly, bleeding and ridiculous, his ginger pubic hair streaked with Sparrow's blood and his own ejaculation.

'Please . . . you can have her . . .' he said from broken teeth.

Billy flew his two fists together like cymbals and caught Pa's ears. Pa went down on big, white knees.

It stopped when Pa could no longer speak, and even then Billy treated the supine figure to unending kicks to his midsection until, finally exhausted, Billy went downstairs.

Later, Lyle heard Pa dragging himself out to his own room.

Later still, Lyle heard an unsettling, animal-like noise in the corridor. Something out there, awake. It took Lyle some minutes to understand that Borneo had come in from where he slept outside and was lying across the narrow doorway.

The following morning at five to six Lyle cocked his head to light footsteps, but still groggy and not a little shocked by the events of the night before, he soon went back to sleep. Pa did not come downstairs that day. Mag, who with Billy had slept by the coal fire in the back room, attended Pa in his bedroom. Mag said Pa had no memory of the night before but she was shaken by his injuries. By nightfall Sparrow had been gone twelve hours. Bernard Love arrived to find Pa unavailable. In bed, weeping, sober, word came downstairs that Pa was unable to offer any reason for his wife's unannounced departure.

Pa was a sight that only Mag could appreciate. Never mind his nose, crooked and swollen, or his ribs, which would remain strapped for six months, or the many livid bruises and cuts on his face that betold the wreckage of his mouth and the fact that he would never again be able to eat meat unless minced, for Mag the most repulsive sight was that of her father's genitals. Pa roared for all of Balaklava as Mag tried to cold-sponge them. His sac was the size of a cabbage and the colour blue, all the little veins swollen to bursting, and his ragged penis reminded Mag of a turkey's throat.

A search party for Sparrow was formed. First house to house. Then out to Eillne. Lyle was questioned but he said nothing. They asked Borneo, who had returned to his hut, but Borneo sat in a corner and covered his face with his arms and groaned. At dawn the following morning, with mounting dread, they began to probe the mud-banks of the Lyle, big men in boots with staves, leaving their zig-zagging imprint for the incoming tide. Mag looked at Billy, but Billy was mute. It would not be the first time, said the Balaklava men, that a poor woman found her final release in the strong arms of the river. Of course, they were wrong.

So who was my father? Pa? Or Billy Cross? I look like neither Mag nor Lyle. Nor Bain. If I was the son of Billy Cross, whom Sparrow so admired, why was her attitude to me always so reserved, and that to Bain so indulgent? Could I be the son of Pa Shortcourse if his semen, although *intended* to be me, had ended up on the unfertile soil of his own scrotum? Or was there, I asked Lyle, another possibility that he was keeping to himself?

But Lyle would not be rushed by my questions. Lyle loved me like a brother, after all.

There was no nonsense about Elizabeth Wedlake. To meet her you would never think of a Senior Executive Officer in the Security Division of the Northern Ireland Office at Stormont. You would see a petite woman in her early thirties, with every hair of her auburn head in place and eyes that looked at you unforgettably and without blinking. She was not beautiful if beauty is measured only in the classical way, if a woman has to qualify against a check list of perfection. In that case, Elizabeth's teeth were not perfectly straight, her nose was a little too big and her mouth in a laugh showed off too much upper gum. She was too buxom for her light frame but her bottom acted in the way of ballast. These are, however, inanimate descriptions. Elizabeth could look at you sideways when she was both serious and trying to think what you were thinking, and that look conveyed such basic, womanly instinct that it thrilled me unfailingly time after time. Her buxomness also meant that she flowered, especially in my arms, and her legs, especially her thighs, bespoke such femininity that all I ever saw in Elizabeth was beauty unending.

The first night we spent together she told me matter-of-factly that she was married to Eric Wedlake, an officer with the RUC Special Branch. From the very outset we would seize the bonus aspects of our relationship; we would live on the foam where our two waves met. I do not know over the ages how much sin has taken place under the guise of choral singing, but I question if any of it was as pleasurable as that which I enjoyed with Elizabeth.

'I have this sense of space in Dublin that I don't in Belfast,' Elizabeth said.

It was two months after our first encounter. Elizabeth stood in my flat without shoes in that soft light of evening from the direction of Kish which is just a reflection.

'Belfast is compact, you know? A village. We go to the mainland once in a while to let off steam. Down here I get a feeling of more space but at the same time of being more limited. There's no mainland down here.'

Our separate cultures were analysed between us with a mixture of voyeuristic curiosity and genuine interest.

'When we say "mainland", it would be reasonable to assume that is because we are on an island,' Elizabeth continued. 'That is not actually the case. We in Ulster think ourselves an extension of Britain, not an island, even though we talk about "mainland". There's a difference, you'll agree. Like Wales and Scotland. If we were in London, for example, we would never say, "I'm back home to the island" or anything like that. But I like Belfast, bombs and all. I like the . . . warmth, you know?'

'Then you'll like chillis,' I said.

Elizabeth let me get on with it in the flat without feeling she

180

needed to weigh in in some way. We never discussed the regime in the Wedlake household, or her two tiny daughters, although I would in later years see photographs of them, blonde girls with nearly all the allure of their mother.

Elizabeth peered into my kitchen. 'Dublin Bay prawns,' she sniffed.

'God forbid. They come up on the train from a fisherman in Leire.'

'Followed by?'

'Vegetables. Glazed, sautéed and au gratin.'

'In season?'

'In Israel.'

She took my hand and we went and sat looking out to sea. John Coltrane was playing something from *Stardust*, his saxophone teasing out little fluid thrills.

'Oh to be music,' Elizabeth said.

'Saxophone is like being part of a stream. I never hear piano that way.'

'Choral music?'

'Sometimes. But there the marriage is music, voices, place.'

'I want to know all about you, Theo,' Elizabeth said, snuggling up, 'but I'm not in any hurry to find out.'

'Is that not a risk?'

'Hmmm.' She rubbed the back of my hand. 'Leave things as they were the first night, you mean?'

'Yes.'

'Anonymous.'

'That's too hard a word.'

'Will I think any less of you, you mean?' she asked. 'When you tell me about the wreckage of your past life, if such exists, or if I tell you about mine, will we see each other differently? Will the chemicals go flat?'

'I fear the future more than the past, I think,' I said.

'You mean, you fear repeating the past,' Elizabeth observed.

'Life is a constant repeating of the past,' I said.

'You see, I like the philosopher in you too,' she said.

'As well as what?'

She had slid her hand in between the buttons of my shirt.

'As well as the beast.'

181

'What about the prawns?'

'I want meat,' Elizabeth growled.

She did everything at the outset. With the precise little fingers of a seamstress she plucked my apron strings and shoelaces, and hurried down my shirt and trouser buttons, wordlessly, till I sat undressed and Elizabeth's only concession was still her shoes. Frowning in concentration she caught me, hard and gentle. In her groomed pertness, her professional exactness, bringing the pleasure on, letting it off, it was as if she were a pilot, coaxing forth the last ounce from a big plane. She worked me until every last possibility of power had surrendered its cover and nothing existed in my mind but the starkly opposite nature of our sexes.

She then quickly undressed and we made love on the carpet. We ate on the floor, too, in towelling robes, licking each other's fingers and dousing the chilli flames with iced beer. Later, from my bedroom, the winking lights of Howth and Dun Laoire on either side of the bay looked part of an elaborate system of transmitting information.

'Do you want to do this again?' I asked.

She nodded.

'Why?' I asked.

Elizabeth looked at me thoughtfully. 'Does there have to be a reason beyond pleasure?'

'No, but there usually is.'

Elizabeth laid her fingers across my lips. 'Do *you* want to do this again?'

'Yes.'

'Then let us just keep on doing it until we are either too old or get fed up with one another,' Elizabeth said. 'But let us not waste any time analysing what we both agree we want.'

She lay in my arms and I thought she was asleep.

'Tell me, who are the people in these photographs?' Elizabeth asked.

'That's Sparrow, my mother,' I said.

'She was very pretty,' Elizabeth said.

'Still is,' I said.

'And is that you?'

'Yes.'

'You look so suspicious.'

'I always look like that in photographs.'

'And who are the boys standing with you beside the river?'

'Pax Sheehy on the left,' I replied, 'and my nephew Bain on the right. He's our current Minister for Justice.'

'Hmmmm. What was he like as a child?' asked Elizabeth sleepily.

A business relationship, like an affair of the heart, cannot be ended with the same facility with which it began, and thus, four weeks after my meeting with my brother Lyle and my excursion with him into the devouring past, I again found us together, in a taxi, on our way to meet Bain.

'He must expand,' said Lyle, using his hands. 'He's being stolen blind, believe me, I can tell.'

'How?'

Lyle tapped the side of his nose like Frenchmen do in films. 'Been down there half a dozen times since we met, old son. Talked to people, you know what I mean? A whiskey here and there, a bottle of your fancy and they'll tell you the size of their old ladies' bloomers. It's my town, Theo.'

It was, too, in a way I could never claim.

'They're all at it. Bloody thieves, none worse than Batty, the manager. Half of Balaklava is eating gratis, believe me. And that's only the shop.'

'Only?'

'There are a dozen people in the factory on full wages doing the job of a twenty-thousand-pound machine'.

'People mean votes to Bain'.

'He doesn't *sack* them, I've got that covered. He gets grants for bigger and better equipment and he increases production, that's the answer. He'll be employing more people in twelve months, not fewer.'

Despite my wish to remain apart from any dealings between Lyle and Bain, there seemed to have evolved a duty for me to be present, at least for their first meeting, since I was the link that was bringing them together. I hated business.

'Have you decided to invest?' I enquired, wondering whether my taste for the past had led me into compromise.

'That will depend on a lot of things,' Lyle replied impenetrably.

183

Bain's flat was in Rathgar, in a compound whose architect was a devotee of the roof garden: young terraces of plants jutted out at every opportunity and in some cases had already begun their spill downward over new brick. I paid the taxi and we walked to a door where a man with the look of a guard on minister's duty let us in.

'You're to go up,' the man said, having spoken on a telephone.

Upstairs, the twin of the man below was waiting. I gave him my raincoat. The hall was turn-key new with pictures that had been hung by an interior designer.

'Very nice, thank you very much,' Lyle murmured, looking around and brushing down the shoulders of his jacket.

'Mr Shortcourse?'

A lady who introduced herself as the Minister's secretary brought us inward.

'The Minister is just finishing a meeting,' she explained. 'Can I get you gentleman a drink?'

I declined because I did not intend to stay, but Lyle went for gin. The large room was the child of a mind that saw perfection in magazines. Fabrics and pictures and carpets with the dreamy seamlessness of mail-order lithographs. Lyle put his briefcase on the table and we sat on a settee in colour and design like the segments of an orange. I could smell the legacy of Bain's salty flesh.

'Hello, Theo.'

He was standing at the back of the room. How long he had been there observing us, I didn't know. We stood up and he came forward and we shook hands with odd formality. He wore a new three-piece suit and his black shoes shone.

'This is Lyle,' I said.

'Ah, yes,' Bain said and nodded as he shook hands with Lyle.

You could feel the power in him, the arrogance, the sheer weight of the apparatus whose levers he now controlled. His smell, despite sweet oils, meant energy to me. The moustache, his trademark, was not as ginger as I remembered, but it covered more of his lip. He had grown very wide, a fact that emphasised his lack of height. He was losing hair on top too.

'I'll go now, Bain,' said a man's voice from the hall.

'Hold on, Jack!' Bain was suddenly grinning. 'Theo, I have a surprise for you.' He beckoned inwards. 'Jack, look who's here.'

184

'Ah, if it's not Theodore,' said Father O'Dea. 'How are you at all?'

'I'm fine, Father,' I replied.

'Theo, I must pull you up,' said Bain, wagging his finger. 'It's not Father O'Dea any more.'

'Ah now, Bain,' the priest laughed.

'It's Bishop O'Dea,' Bain said and inclined his head, 'or it will be soon, if my information is correct.'

I congratulated the priest, or bishop. 'What do I call you now?' I asked.

He touched my arm lightly. 'Jack,' he replied.

Lyle, who had been standing somewhat excluded from the flow of events, cleared his throat and stepped forward. He reached for the Bishop designate's hand and then, genuflecting, kissed it.

'Your Lordship,' he murmured.

'God bless you,' said Jack O'Dea, somewhat disconcerted.

'Well now,' said Bain and rubbed his hands for something to do.

'I'm actually on my way,' I told him.

'You're going, he's staying?' Bain said bluntly.

'I'm not familiar with any of the details,' I said, 'but Lyle tells me he's has done all his homework.'

'Is that right?' Bain asked Lyle suspiciously.

'Absolutely, Minister.'

'I'm Bain, right?' Bain told him. From the hairs on his wrist a gold wafer gleamed and he checked it. 'Very well. I haven't got very much time. It's a strange life nowadays, Theo, mine. Five men on the detail here, just to look after me. What do you think of that?'

I shrugged. What was I meant to think of it?

'Would you swap, Theo?' He reached up and put his hand on the nape of my neck. 'D'you know, Jack, this fellow and myself, we're like brothers.'

'Sure, I know,' Jack said.

'Whoever would have thought it in Eillne thirty years ago?' Bain asked, his thumb caressing the smooth cleft at the base of my skull. 'Two boys smoking fags and terrified of being caught. Now one of them is Minister for Justice and the other is . . . What exactly are you now, Theo?'

185

'Inspector,' I replied, trying to wriggle out from under his paw without appearing to offend.

'Theo is the boss man,' Bain said. 'Theo has more powers than you or I do, Jack.'

'And what about Pax Sheehy? Assistant Garda Commissioner,' Jack said and his words fell like coins into an empty bucket.

Bain walked the Bishop and me out to the hall.

'Theo,' Bain said quietly, drawing me to one side, 'is this joker for real?'

'He's keen,' I replied.

'Jesus, he gives me the creeps, always did.'

'He's OK.'

'The way he caught the Bishop's hand, I thought he was going to eat it.'

'He's not the worst, Bain.'

'Pa never trusted him.'

'Is that important?'

'Pa knew the fucker, Theo. Pa lived with him.'

'You've got to make up your own mind, Bain.'

Bain glanced back at Lyle, who had lit up and was smoking in the standard manner.

'Pa said Lyle couldn't lie straight in bed,' Bain said.

'Hear him out for himself,' I said, trying to get away from Pa as the bellwether of probity. 'He's got cash. Forget the way he goes on and what he looks like. Personally, beneath it all, I'd trust him.'

'You sure he's got the cash?'

'I think he has.'

'God knows where he got it.'

'What do you care?'

'I've got to care about everything nowadays,' Bain said. 'They're hanging out of the trees waiting for me to put a foot wrong.' He took a deep breath, then gave me a playful slap on the back. 'If I get the sack because of this fucker, you can bail me out, Theo.'

'No way,' I laughed and joined Jack O'Dea in the hall.

Outside I noticed the huddled figures at gable ends, the Special Branch cupping lights to cigarettes as they watched us, the hint of radio static you could get every now and then over the drone of Dublin.

'I put my foot into it about Pax, didn't I?' said Jack grimly.

I said, 'It's not your fault they don't like each other.'

'Can Pax not see that Bain has changed?' Jack asked. 'That Bain has thrown off all that old trucking with the North that he used to be at?'

'Pax believes that half Bain's heart will always be up there,' I said. 'That it's in his blood.'

'I'll pray for both of them,' Jack said delicately.

The rain had eased off. We walked along, glad of the air.

'Your mother is in fine fettle, Theodore,' Jack remarked. 'She complains she doesn't see enough of you.'

'She's still getting around all right?'

'Sparrow? Not a bother on her. She's in town three days a week about her business, and then calling into David Wise. David Wise is out in Eillne himself three days out of the other four. He never married, you know.'

'I often thought there might have been a move there after Pa died,' I said.

'Sparrow chooses her own time,' the priest said. 'You're a fascinating family. She talks all the time about Sammy Tea, you know. Sammy Tea this and that. She idolises that poor man, God rest his soul. I admire your mother for that, Theodore. I admire the respect she still holds, even at her age, for the dead. It's an inspiration. I often put it into my sermons, you know, our debt to the dead. For all their sins, we owe them everything, after all.'

'But they can owe us too, Jack,' I said.

'What on earth could they owe us?' the priest blinked.

'Explanations,' I replied.

The very infrequent nature of my association with Pax I allowed my mother to believe in was not entirely accurate. It must have been a measure of my fear, even as a grown man, of Sparrow's reprobation that made me portray Pax's and my connection as intermittent; Pax's old enmity with Bain meant that Pax could never be good in Sparrow's eyes, and for me to ally myself with such a person risked my own demeaning.

187

We got together at least once every couple of months to play jazz tapes, or for me to listen to little pieces that Pax had learned on his saxophone. We usually met in Pax's unpretentious house in Malahide. I don't think he had many friends and certainly no cronies. He was utterly upstanding, but always standing on his own, like a lighthouse. Even his family, I suspected, was secondary in Pax's fondness for his attachment to duty. He would always be the Pax on whose shoulders the great moral dilemmas rested and for whom music was the only skylight from a dark world.

'You hear the way he *coaxes* that horn?' Pax asked.

Pax's wife, whom I always suspected looked upon me as a diverter of her husband's affections, usually went out on our jazz nights. His two young sons were watching TV in the kitchen. The trumpet-coaxer was Woody Shaw on a track from *Moontrane*.

'He's as good as Dizzy,' Pax said. 'He can take you anywhere you are prepared to go.'

I came out to Malahide not just to hear the latest hard bop, although listening to jazz on my own at home always brought Pax and our childhood vividly to mind but for Pax's company. Jazz in the end meant more to Pax than it did to me, he was much more a part of it. For me there was always a dark side hovering on the edges of the music, a dangerous flavour that oozed from the notes and betold a sadness. I never said that to Pax because to do so, I felt, would be to intrude into a private place where he admitted no one.

'Will this music be played in a hundred years?' Pax asked.

'Probably not.'

'Why not?'

'It's not music that stands easily apart from its performers,' Pax said. 'Beethoven never stood up and performed like Miles Davis. They worked out of different mediums.'

'Jazz is a butterfly,' I said.

'Yes,' Pax agreed. 'But then, we're all butterflies. Jazz is the most human music.'

Like most Catholics in Ireland, Pax went to Mass every Sunday, but jazz was his principal religion. When he played his saxophone, although he was an amateur, he still managed to bring a spiritual dimension to it.

Pax's windows had Venetian blinds; the street-lights made everything in the room wear a striped, yellow uniform.

'What is it to be human?' Pax wondered aloud.

'To love?'

'To love,' he agreed. 'To feel.'

It was a week after I had met Bain and introduced him to Lyle. I had not heard the outcome of their meeting and did not want to; I certainly did not want to tell Pax, because however close he and I were, the instinctive duty I always felt to protect Bain from Pax remained perversely alert.

'What's the hardest part of your life, Theo?' Pax asked.

The question came from the same outlook on life that on the day of my wedding had wanted to discuss cremation. I refused to let myself be swallowed by Pax's metaphysical gloom.

'There isn't one.'

'Not at all?'

'No.'

'You're lucky. Of course, I'd forgotten you're in love.'

Pax knew about Elizabeth, in the most general sense. Where once he would have disapproved, I think that in this case when I told him he had been happy for me in a qualified, Pax-like way.

'It's good,' I said, knowing I sounded like someone who *wants* it, above all, to be good.

'Will she leave the man she's married to and come down and live with you?' Pax asked.

'No,' I replied. 'But maybe that's for the best. Maybe it wouldn't work if we could see all we want of each other.'

'Is that what she said?' Pax asked.

'No,' I said, but I caught more than friendly interest in the question. 'Why do you ask?'

'Just wondered.'

But Pax never just wondered, he was always riding shotgun for something that began with a capital letter, such as the National Interest or the Constitution.

'Come on,' I said, 'what is it?'

'What's what?'

'You have something to say on the subject of Elizabeth.'

'You're too touchy, Theo.'

I laughed. 'Look, I remember when Redden used to swing you by your locks. Say it.'

Pax sighed. 'I don't know the lady, Theo. I have nothing against her.'

'I accept your statutory disclaimer.'

'But she's part of a very grey world up there, all right?'

'All right.'

'*Very* grey. The Brits are unbelievable. They have this insatiable hunger for information.'

'I know all that, Pax.'

'Then you know that's she's a professional.'

'What the hell's that meant to mean?'

'That maybe she's paid to hunt around down here. To carry out decisions made in London. She's on the same team as the interrogators in Castlereagh and the listeners in GCHQ Cheltenham. Professionals always play to win.' The cd had run its course but Pax made no attempt to change it. 'She works for their intelligence, Theo,' Pax said.

'So what?'

'I'm serious.'

'So am I.'

'Doesn't that make you ask yourself certain questions, Theo?'

I didn't care. I wanted to tell him I didn't mind helping Elizabeth, or being used by her now and again, supplying her with little bits of local colour that would not come to her naturally, or helping her interpret the general mood in Dublin at certain times, mood being as important to politicians as gold fish is to cats.

'You work for a shady outfit yourself, Pax,' I remarked. 'Special Branch slither in and out of the North the whole time when it suits them. You use informers. Even I work for a shady outfit that spies on the citizenry as a whole. We all have jobs.'

'But you're an Irishman,' Pax said.

'A very minor one,' I said. 'I mean, I don't exactly hold the nation's future in my palm.'

'You have certain connections.'

'You mean Bain?'

Pax nodded.

'I know no more about Bain than she can read in the paper,' I said.

'That's not altogether true, Theo.'

I burst out laughing. 'You want to *protect* him, Pax?'

'It doesn't matter to me who's in power,' Pax said, a little too primly.

'You think Elizabeth's seeing me because . . . because she wants to *destabilise* us down here?' I asked in disbelief.

'Don't joke, Theo,' said Pax tightly.

'Don't joke? This is a joke!' I cried. 'It would be a very bad joke were it not so fucking bizarre. And the best part of it is that you're on Bain's side!'

'He's a good minister, actually,' Pax said.

'I'm amazed. This is Pax Sheehy talking about Bain Cross.'

'He's energetic, he fights for his department.'

'And the past is gone as far as you're concerned.'

'Don't you think so, Theo?'

'I did not think you could ever change your opinion like you have,' I said, resigned to his seriousness. 'Ever. But good luck to you.'

'Do you see him much?'

'Bain? Three or four times a year.'

'But you *understand* him. You understand him better than anyone alive, *that's* the point.'

'And that makes me valuable to some Whitehall puppet master?'

Pax nodded. 'It's possible.'

'I don't care, don't you see?' I said. 'I read the papers too. The people you work for turn a blind eye to the IRA when they cross the border. It's a lousy world. The CIA destabilised the entire South American continent. I don't care. I'm too old to change the world. I don't care, OK?'

'If you don't care, if you don't make a choice between right and wrong, then when the moment of decision arrives you will not be able to handle it,' Pax said calmly.

'Right and wrong,' I said, exasperated. 'So what am I going to tell Elizabeth? That Bain persecuted poor Uncle Hugo to the point where he nearly drove the poor man mad? That Bain used to lie a lot? That he once screwed my wife? I'm a forty-year-old bachelor with a ladyfriend who just happens to be –'

'Married to a top RUC man.'

'A Stormont employee,' I finished.

'You know what the Unionists think about Bain,' said Pax quietly.

191

'Yes.'

'They think he's a gunman,' Pax said anyway. 'The British Conservative Party is also the British Conservative and Unionist Party and if the Conservatives are to stay in power in Britain, they'll need the Ulster Unionists with them.'

'I told you, I read the papers,' I said.

'They say anything is possible in politics, Theo,' Pax said. 'If Bain is a marked man in Whitehall, then your ladyfriend, whom I'm sure is a very fine person in her private life, will follow her orders.'

'Elizabeth will not use me for some cheap political gain, Pax,' I said.

We sat quietly in the cramped front room that spoke so much of where Pax placed duty in relation to material ambition.

'I wish I had your faith in people, Theo,' he said eventually.

'Thanks,' I said. 'For nothing.'

'You said one thing this evening, though, that I can't let pass,' Pax said.

I looked at him.

Pax said quietly, 'I have changed my opinions on nothing, Theo. Nothing. Remember that.'

When I got home to Sandymount that night it was after twelve. A message showed on my machine. I half expected it to be Elizabeth, although she rarely left messages, but when I replayed it I heard Sparrow speaking in the formal voice she used for telecommunications.

'This is Sparrow Love Shortcourse. The message is: Theodore, your Uncle Hugo is dead. Repeat dead. End of message.'

192

Ten

Uncle Hugo's funeral was in reality no more than a tidying away that most people assumed had taken place years previously. The only ones who really cared that the stubborn old man had finally let go his grip on life were young nurses from the county home. They put on their best uniforms and cloaks and stood in two straight rows outside the cathedral and at either side of the grave, lending the occasion an oddly military air.

During my trip down from Dublin I thought about Uncle Hugo. His furtive pleasures, his hymns, his withered leg, the way he wore a hat, his horse and trap, his harmless parsimony. His life. If he had fallen dead in a heap ten years before, then we would all have run round in shock for at least a short time, our lives would have reverberated with short-term consternation; but instead he went out in the softest way possible, like a traveller with a lamp fading one step at a time into the night of a great heath. It was a measure of my new feeling for Elizabeth that she had been the first person I rang the morning after Sparrow's call.

'Just in case you were trying to call and didn't know where I was,' I said. 'I'll stay on in Eillne for the weekend.'

'You're sweet to let me know,' Elizabeth said. 'You must feel sad.'

'It's a happy release for Uncle Hugo,' I said.

'I'll be thinking of you down there,' Elizabeth said.

I came down to Eillne the night before the funeral and drove into Monument with Sparrow the next morning. All the descendants of Bernard Love turned out and some Samuel Love & Sons employees. There was a scattering of people from the town, like Mr Wise, and people with whom Uncle Hugo would have dealt for his whiskey, his flies and tackle, his books. His burial was attended by no friends because he had had none.

Bain arrived late to the cathedral and sat beside Mag. He was no longer just Bain Shortcourse from Balaklava whose elevation to the Cabinet had left men and women dumbfounded; he was the man you saw on the front of your daily paper, waving aside questions about the young Irishmen he had sent in handcuffs for trial in England. Bain's past was suddenly irrelevant to his public persona.

Out at the open grave the ends of other coffins peeped up at us: Uncle Bernard, Sammy Tea, my grandmother whose heart had been so inexplicably broken. Their coffins looked up like the faces of children hidden for years in a deep well.

'*May the angels lead thee into paradise.*'

I was picking out the plain-clothes men in Bain's entourage when I came to the woman.

'*Grant to Thy servant departed, O Lord, we beseech Thee . . .*'

Her grey hair was tied in a bun. Heavy-set, her lowered face stared at Uncle Hugo's coffin, perched between us on planks.

'*. . . by Thy mercy he may have fellowship . . .*'

But her bosom! It was the angle it stood at to her broad body rather than its fullness that I recognised. I could not believe it. As if to confound my disbelief, she looked straight across the grave at me. Her face was tear-streaked. Those same eyes had shed tears in the kitchen at Eillne! Those same breasts had known my humming ears between them!

I said, 'La.'

'*Through the bowels of the mercy of our God . . .*'

Standing ten yards distant, La could not hear me, and her eyes, if they saw me, did not register the fact, for she dipped her head once more in the direction of the black grave. La! I could never forget the fondness we had shared and it came to me with a jolt that the first time I had been able to claim La for my own had been on the day of another funeral – Pa's. Of course La had loved Uncle Hugo! Of course he had one friend to see him go down! But had she remained all these years in Monument – of course she had! – perhaps visiting Uncle Hugo so that Sparrow would not know, as all the while I had lain lonely in Dublin? La, whom I had so long sought! Her now grey-white hair, although obviously ahead of its time, nonetheless added an elusive, archetypal maternalism to La's established attraction.

194

'*Lord, who gave your servant Hugo the gift of life* . . .'

There was the bustle of activity that is involved in feeding a grave its coffin, the taking away of cross planks and the paying out of straps. Having no doubt that La would also remember the peculiar coincidence of events – the funeral tradition! – and rushing onward to the conclusion that the recalling of my first, fond performance was what was making her cry, I became aroused at the thought of history repeated. I could have sworn by her appearance that she had not married, a vain, yet compelling view: she had come into the Nanny Morrissey look of being bundled into what she wore, no doubt a family trait, but a not surprising one given my knowledge of La's generous thighs, her welcoming rump, and, of course, her breasts. I remembered how the various parts of her had spilled out like delicious gifts for my hands and thirsty lips. I yearned for La's warm love again!

'*May his soul and the souls of all the faithful departed rest in peace. Amen.*'

As the dispersal began – in this case people immediately began to talk animatedly to one another and to light cigarettes, Uncle Hugo, if they had ever remembered him, now definitely forgotten – La became hidden behind the ranks of the nurses. I could see Bain giving me the eye. I elbowed my way around the grave. La's rear was within touching distance if I forced my arm through, but then I decided that to reopen acquaintanceship by means of such a lunge risked misinterpretation. My cousin Johnnie stopped me and shook my hand. I could see the grey bun receding in the direction of the gate. I excused myself to Johnnie.

'Theo!' Bain had me by the arm. 'I need to talk to you.' He steered me around as Sparrow came towards us.

'I hope I haven't hanged myself,' Bain muttered to me obliquely.

I said, 'Bain, just give me –'

'Boys,' Sparrow smiled. 'The end of an era.'

'Poor old Hugo,' Bain said, but his mind was elsewhere.

I looked behind me, but there was no grey bun now.

'Theodore, aren't you going to invite Bain to Eillne?'

'I'll give you a lift,' Bain said.

'Just a moment,' I replied.

The grey bun was out on Military Parade, talking to two of the nurses. Her back was to me. I had begun to consider the practical problems that might flow from our reunion, and yet, if La now lived in Monument, the possibility that I could, given time, explain my behaviour of years before and reinstate myself in her affection made the prospect of coming down on weekends suddenly sweet. Sex, particularly the sex La and I had enjoyed, is not something that time can take away. You never forget it. Walking towards her rear, as I was, I could describe, if called upon, the texture of each buttock, and what they hid, just as I could portray in detail the constellation of her breasts and the rubbery-wet texture of her nipples.

One of the nurses saw me approaching and said something. They all turned.

'La –'

I stopped short and stared at her. A strange woman looked politely at me. Her enquiring face betrayed no sign of the tears I had seen back in the graveyard, and with the tears went the resemblance upon which my imagination had seized. And yet I could not swear it was not La. This woman's face had a shining hardness, so if she was La, all the change had taken place in the cheeks and mouth and around the eyes, from the neck up, whilst from that point down she was La beyond a doubt. I stopped, confused.

'Theo.'

Bain was speaking to me from the back of a black Mercedes. I could not bring myself to say her name again, and if she had recognised me, then not a hint of such recognition showed in her face, which meant that either she was not La, or else that bitterness had erased me from her memory with the thoroughness of an enema.

'Get in,' Bain called and I could see the nurses nudging each other, for it was Bain they had been staring at, not me.

I got in. If she were La, she was never going to say, and thus the only way I would ever know this woman's true identity would be to have access to her body, to run my hands over her rump and taste her breasts, to sleep with her, in other words, which even in my most liberal fantasy I had to admit was now unlikely. The ministerial Merc edged us off up Captain Dudley's Hill towards Balaklava.

'He's torn the arse out of the factory,' Bain said.

We had come along Prince Consort Terrace, our car leading, another behind filled with Special Branch. The incident outside the cathedral had left me drained. I remembered the narrow street we were turning into, I remembered walking up it with Bain and listening to his descriptions of what Pa had done to half the British Army, yet it was a street I might have been seeing for the first time.

'Who?' I said, not really concentrating on Bain.

'Who do you think?' Bain snarled. 'Your brother, Lyle.'

It was not the time to split hairs about the precise nature of my blood relationships.

'He's knocked out the back wall to get in his fucking machines,' Bain said as we drew up. 'There's been no pigs killed in here for three weeks because no one is going to work in the pissing rain.'

What is the past, exactly? I wondered. A woman whose body I knew like my own could confound me as to who she really was; a street I had walked a hundred times now denied that I had ever been on it before. All there was to connect the present with the past was something extremely tenuous called myself.

'He's got Balaklava's back up against me by accusing people of stealing meat,' Bain said darkly. 'Fuck him and fuck you, Theo. I could have done without this, let me tell you.'

'Maybe he's right,' I said. 'Maybe that is one reason the business is losing money.'

The shed or factory beside which we were now parked was in the advanced stages of demolition. A mound of rubble to one side was the resting place of the old gable wall, allowing sight of the bare interior with its ceiling hooks and rails and the wooden tables shaped in a sloping 'V' in whose grains and niches, I knew, was secreted the blood from uncountable lambs and pigs. But then I could see where a new concrete apron had been poured and foundation walls begun.

'Go out to Eillne,' Bain instructed his driver. 'The machines arrived sometime last week,' he told me.

We went over Buttermilk and through James's Place. I saw with surprise that where Wise's grocery had snugly resided since time began, a supermarket now stretched half the length of the block beneath huge letters bolted to the building and spelling WISEMART.

197

'They're meant to be the latest in German technology,' Bain went on. 'They can mix the meat and case the sausages in a thousand different sizes if you want them to.'

'Did he put in his own money?' I asked.

'Five grand and said he'd do the same again once the machines were up and running,' Bain said.

Each time I made the trip the houses stretched further along Captain Penny's Road.

'The machines arrived last week,' Bain repeated and shot out his cuffs. 'What does he want to do? He wants to send them to England for modifications. A hundred and twenty thousand quids' worth of machines. God knows what he has in mind. I don't trust the bastard now any more than I ever did. Pa was right.'

'Where did all the money come from?' I asked.

'The IDA,' Bain said and sighed deeply.

But the IDA's grants were only ever a proportion of the full costs, I knew.

'Did Lyle get you to use your political influence? For the grants?' I asked.

'No more than any voter would,' Bain said aggressively.

'So what did you do?'

'Oh Jesus, I don't know,' Bain said.

But Bain did know, I could see, and his knowledge was what was upsetting him.

'I rang the Minister,' Bain said. 'I told him the story. I mean, the employment projections if they were half right were fantastic. Twelve new people by the end of the year. Thirty to fifty in three years if we got the sales.'

'So you got the Minister to apply the lubrication,' I said.

'You make it sound obscene,' said Bain and looked at me. 'Yes, yes, yes. I signed the grant applications, I don't know what I signed. Here's the file. I want you to read it.'

I took a thin plastic folder from him and folded it into my inside pocket.

'But you got the government money,' I said.

'Yes, yes.'

'So what's the problem?'

Bain shook his head. He looked at his driver. He looked out at the houses and sudden little hills of countryside and at children

198

playing in front of the new national school for Eillne that had been built with the old school left intact behind it.

'He readied up the grant application,' Bain hissed. 'He got someone in Germany to say the machines cost a hundred and twenty grand; the IDA grant was sixty-six per cent, or so they thought. Eighty grand. The application went through so fast, the usual channels were avoided, but I swear to God I didn't know what he was at. Now I know the machines only cost eighty grand. He ripped the government off.'

We came up the hill with the acre of escallonia where in better days Bain and I had hid and made the cob carrying Uncle Hugo's trap bolt by springing out at her with masks of papier-mâché.

'What if he sends the machines to England and then flogs them?' Bain asked. 'They're brand-new. Paid for with government grants. He puts in five grand, he gets, say, forty grand for the machines. Jesus, I'll never see him again!'

'I don't think he'll do that, Bain.'

'Imagine the papers if they get hold of this. My name on readied-up grant applications for government money. I'm the Minister for fucking Justice, you know. Jesus Christ, I wish I'd never set eyes on the little bastard. *Fuck* him. Fuck you, Theo!'

'I think you're worrying about nothing,' I said, although the level of anxiety was somewhat contagious.

'Easy for you to say,' Bain snapped. 'If you've landed me with a con man, Theo, fuck you for all time!'

Bain's fear had nothing to do with principle, just with self-interest. He would have signed a thousand phoney grant applications if he thought no one would be the wiser.

Quite a few people had made the trip out to Eillne, up to twenty cars were parked on the gravel sweep, making the house seem smaller than usual. There was a little van with 'Wisemart' on the side and through the windows I could see waitresses going around with plates and teapots. Time was when the first thing I would have thought about was a swim. Down the front steps of Eillne with his usual smile came Lyle Shortcourse, dressed in a new suit and walking with a little spring in his step like the floor manager of a dodgy car salesroom.

'Look where I've put my future,' Bain muttered. 'Just look.'

'Let me talk to him,' I said.

'I'd have him arrested this minute if I thought there'd be no publicity,' Bain said, ignoring the fact that he was the one who had signed the applications.

Lyle waved to us.

'This is all your fault, Theo,' Bain said.

'Let me talk to Lyle,' I said.

That was the last day I ever saw my brother Lyle. I have more experience than most with con men and tricksters: theirs is a skill that hides slyly and allows their faces the probity of judges on the bench. Lyle Shortcourse was the opposite. He wore all the mannerisms of a swindler on his sleeve, but only there; at heart, I would swear, he was straight.

He and I walked together that afternoon along the swimming river's banks and he told me all the plans he had for the Shortcourse business. He was absorbed in what he was doing and saw his padding of the grant applications as nothing more than normal practice. The modifications to the machines on which he was insisting were essential and something to do with the way in which the sausages would be cased. He had moved to a flat in Monument, on Ladies' Walk, he told me. Despite everything that would be said later, I know Lyle had no designs in the way Bain feared, none at all. If he had, he would not still have been in Monument.

'Bain is nervous,' I said. 'You need to work on the trust between you.'

Lyle shook his head. 'No use. He's more Pa than I could have imagined. He *is* Pa, without the booze.'

'That should be an improvement.'

'At least if I pull a stroke I'll admit it,' Lyle said. 'Not Bain. He's the "I-seen-nothing" school. Pure Pa. I have this bad feeling, Theodore.'

Lyle's customary assurance had left him.

'What?'

'Of danger,' he said.

'You mean . . . ?'

'Everything about Bain,' Lyle said. 'He's trouble. I can't quite put my finger on it, but I know. I could get the same feeling as a bookie when someone was out to pull one over on me. Call it instinct, if you like.'

'I'm sorry –' I began.

'It's not your fault, Theodore,' Lyle said. 'It's hard to explain, that's all. I just have this feeling that getting involved with Bain Cross is the worst decision I've ever made.'

What he wanted to say was that from Bain he got a feeling of malevolence. And whilst poor Lyle, as it would turn out, was prophetically voicing his own imminent and never-to-be-explained fate, I could not tell him that I understood precisely how he felt, although in my case the feeling had always been attended by excitement.

It was September but the browning of the river fields and ways had only just begun. We sat together and I could see the light pink and frail heads of soapwort along the bank beneath me, and the blue heads of brooklime that is properly called *Beccabunga*.

'I've had these bad dreams, too,' Lyle said quietly. 'Dreams of death.' He put his hand up to stop me protesting. 'Maybe they mean nothing, who knows. But I've also had time on my hands down here at night. I've written it all down, what you want to know about yourself – or may not want to know, Theodore.'

Suddenly I would help this older man in any way I could. His wellbeing was something I felt accountable for and could not leave neglected.

'You see, I know you love Sparrow very much,' Lyle was saying. 'I don't want to ruin that.'

'Can I see what you've written?'

'It's a tough old world, you know,' Lyle said. 'People do the most unthinkable things for their own reasons. My own philosophy has always been never judge, because you never know what has led those people to do what they've done. Even the worst crime may be explicable in the light of something that happened before.'

'I won't blame you, if that's a worry,' I said. 'I trust you, Lyle. I told Bain that.'

Lyle sighed. 'I'll send it on to you,' he said, 'but don't push me, old son. I'll send it on to you in my own time.'

'You can always walk away from Bain,' I suggested. 'You have no long-term responsibility down here. He knows that.'

Lyle looked at me, but his nose was thrust up in the air like an old retriever. 'What's that smell?'

We hurried back along the swimming river's bank. The smell was of burning. Noise like a wind, except there was little wind, could be heard above the hill. Rounding a bluff, Eillne came into view, black smoke hosing out two of its windows.

'It's on bloody fire!' Lyle cried and we began to run.

There was shouting the closer we got. Cars were being started and driven out on to the road.

'Don't block the gate!' I heard Lyle call.

Thick smoke poured from the right-hand side of the one-storey house, from the part that was the kitchen, and drove me back in the direction of the terrace. Faces were comically black, making their owners difficult to recognise. The wind-like noise came from within, but was less now than the sound of cars revving and people callling for each other. Window glass broke in a series of tiny but sharp explosions.

'Somebody do something!' I heard Sparrow cry, although where she was I could not tell.

My eyes streamed. I stumbled further in the direction of the house through smoke and found Bain, Sparrow and half a dozen people standing opposite the hall door, looking anxiously in. Every few seconds another figure would come stooping out the door, coughing, and Bain would do a count. He turned as he saw me.

'Thank God!' he said. 'Where's that other fellow?'

'He's all right,' I said. 'What happened?' but Bain had turned back to the door, shouting instructions. I saw Mr Wise arranging a coat over Sparrow's shoulders. I asked, 'What happened?'

'We think it may have been the temporary staff in the kitchen,' Mr Wise said grimly. A girl in a smoke-blackened uniform was being comforted by another. 'She says the gas flame caught a tea towel,' said Mr Wise.

'Somebody *do* something!' my mother cried. 'Somebody get some water!'

Bain's driver came up to him. 'Monument says two fire-brigade units are on their way, Minister,' I heard him say.

'All out and accounted for here, at least,' Bain said.

There was a helplessness about our group, as if our bearings and best intentions had been lost in the smoke. The impression that a greater force had taken charge was hard to alter as a further series of explosions was heard, and then the wind, with a sense of predetermination, suddenly went around to the north-east and rose in strength, like a destructive agent arrived late to its business. Two men had found buckets and had filled them down in the river, but by the time they got back up they had spilled most of the water and seemed to lack a target for the little that was left.

'Someone *do* something!'

The smoke, although noxious and despite the freshening wind, appeared to lack the teeth for terminal destruction, but as I was taking comfort from this apparent fact the roof above the kitchen exploded. It went up like the tail-end of a rocket. Smoke suddenly gave way to searing heat and any notion that the smoke was ultimately harmless was replaced by the awful understanding that Eillne was doomed. With dismay tempered only by awe, we retreated further. The fire had a grip on the house to the right of the hall door, but all the windows to the left, the rooms where we ate and sat and read, although yet untouched, showed the wild reflection of the flames that would soon consume them and gave the impression that they too were already ablaze.

'Listen!' cried Mr Wise.

We turned as one to the river valley. From the heart of the river, as it were, came the sound of sirens, and we all cheered. I looked back to the house and saw, like a hallucination, Sparrow entering by the hall door.

'Sparrow!'

I went after her but ran into a wall of heat.

'Theo, for Christ's sake!' cried Bain as I stumbled back.

'Sparrow!' I shouted.

Bain whirled around and scanned the gaping faces.

'What?'

'She's gone back in!' I cried. 'She's mad!'

Bain looked in alarm at the crowd as if I might have been mistaken.

'Look!'

People were pointing. The unmistakable figure of my mother, in black, could be discerned moving about the drawing room, the reflected flames licking around her, like the depiction of a fallen angel in hell.

'Jesus Christ!' Bain gasped.

203

Ripping off his jacket he plunged it into one of the idle water buckets. Then, sticking his head into the jacket, he ran for the house, and I, without really knowing why, followed.

Heat was everything. Heat wrapped my lungs. It made my eyes stand out. I felt my liver roast and leap. Touching my hair, I scalded. Along the hall I screamed out but my voice grilled before it could be born. The terrible roaring. The sense of dying needlessly. Bain had kept going and had disappeared. The knowledge that I had been in this situation before, on the day I was married, when Sparrow had stolen the limelight by putting her own life at risk, seemed elemental. Now poor Uncle Hugo could not even be buried without giving rise to fresh antics from my mother. My breath had been replaced by a searing wound within my chest. This time Sparrow was lost to me. But Bain? I lacked, without warning, the resources to save even myself. I cursed Sparrow.

Two firemen, sudden apparitions in helmets, dragged me back out through the door and on to the terrace where they wrapped me in a blanket. Then, almost biblically, as everyone dumbly watched, Bain appeared with Sparrow in the hall door of Eillne and the firemen with their blankets rushed forward once again.

'They're all right,' I heard a firemen say.

Bain had lost his eyebrows and most of his moustache.

'A snapshot,' he gasped. 'She went back to get a snapshot.'

My mother's hair was singed to half its normal length. Surrounded by everyone, she sat happily in the way of a little girl, something clutched to her chest.

'Give her some air, please!' the fireman said.

'Theodore,' she smiled.

She was holding the old silver-framed photograph of Sammy Tea.

Eleven

I liked Dublin best in autumn and winter when the pubs in the Liberties seemed warm and intimate; in summer I found them cold and best avoided. I left the Castle Yard at ten to five on a Friday in mid October and walked uphill to Christ Church, then down past the tenements. Elizabeth knew our snug, which held just the both of us, in Cranleys, out whose ancient window is a wobbly view of Dean Swift's cathedral. I got a whiskey and a pint and we sat in silence on the leather-topped bench, Elizabeth and I. She dabbed her finger on the creamy head of my pint, then landed the blob on her tongue.

'Hmmmmmm.'

She was most beautiful when she was in some degree serious; seriousness revealed a girl that was otherwise hidden, a serious waif.

'When do you leave?' she enquired.

I was off to Salonika, as Thessaloniki is called, to mingle for three days with my European peers and discuss the finer points of revenue enforcement. Greece was about to become a member of the European Economic Community and our jamboree had been organised as a sideshow to a conference of Western finance ministers.

'Monday,' I replied. 'Back on Friday morning. Tell me what to expect.'

'Feta cheese,' Elizabeth replied. 'The smell of Asia. Blue and white taxis. The view across the gulf to Mount Olympus. Churches that were changed into mosques by the Turks and changed back again.' She made languid tentacles in the air. 'Octopus.'

'I wish you could come with me.'

'You'll be working, Theo,' she said softly and kissed me. 'Are Customs and Excise well, or does one ask after each separately?'

'I think we'll soon be a department of Brussels,' I replied. 'My next boss may be a Dutchman.'

'Who knows who our bosses really are.'

'Exactly,' I said, amused. I could sit for hours and just watch her face. 'Pity you can't stay down.'

'Next month, I promise,' she said. 'How is your mother? Has she recovered from her fire?'

'She has, but the house is finished,' I said. 'She's moved in to stay with Mr Wise in Monument until a new house has been built.'

'Is she sad?'

'I don't think she paused for a moment. The symbolism of the whole event seemed quite lost on her – the house burning, Uncle Hugo dying. She's too concerned about herself.'

'You liked your uncle, didn't you?'

'I used to, certainly. He'd been an invalid for fifteen years.'

'But you have your memories, you love what you remember.'

'Exactly. Poor Uncle Hugo. He had boyfriends.'

'Quite daring.'

'Bain used to torture him, lay traps for him. Uncle Hugo was defenceless?'

'Did he attend the funeral?'

'Bain? Oh yes.'

'How is he settling into the job?' Elizabeth asked.

In the emerging shorthand of our relationship, Elizabeth had begun to make regular little tidying-up sweeps of knowledge about Bain whenever she and I met. She reminded me of a fastidious gardener who at every visit compulsively goes around deadheading the results of your incompetence.

'I recently met no less than a bishop who believes Bain will be the best minister that Justice ever had,' I remarked.

'It's possible,' Elizabeth agreed. 'He's taken tough decisions already. He's a new man.'

'You don't really believe that.'

'Yes, I do in fact. Theo.'

'You don't trust him. You believe he's still a wild man,' I said recalling Pax. 'The Unionist view.'

'*What* view?'

'The Unionist. They're paranoid about Bain being a minister. Whitehall listens to what the Unionists have to say.'

'It may well do, but I can't see the relevance to what I think.'

'What do you think?'

'About Bain Cross? I think he's made the change from young firebrand to government minister very well.'

'You don't believe he's a liability to North–South relations?'

'Of course I don't, Theo. What's got into you?'

Pax's observations suddenly seemed crude and parochial; Elizabeth lived on a higher level than the one Pax was obsessed with.

'I'm being mischievous,' I said. 'Bain's got business problems. It's a shame that he should be deflected from doing a good job in Justice because of a miserable little business in Monument.'

'What about your long-lost brother, what's-his-name?' Elizabeth said.

'Lyle.'

'Didn't you say Lyle might be able to help Bain out?'

'I put them together. Lyle's moved in and he's tearing the factory asunder.'

'That's *good*, Theo.'

'He's upped the stakes, he's doubling the size of the business, too fast for Bain's liking.'

'That doesn't have to be bad news, Theo,' Elizabeth said. 'You can't worry for everyone.'

'Bain has had to sign a raft of grant applications as chairman and principal shareholder,' I said. 'Lyle's used Bain's political weight and got the Industrial Development Authority to buy over a hundred thousand pounds' worth of German machinery for Shortcourse Sausages. Bain's worried sick.'

'So what's wrong with that?' Elizabeth asked. 'Think of frankfurters. It seems to me that Bain badly needs someone like Lyle.'

'Maybe,' I allowed. 'It's all happening too fast for Bain. If anything goes wrong he could be badly hurt, politically.'

'You make it sound dramatic.'

'He gave me the file to read,' I said.

'But everything's above board.'

'Of course.'

'Sure?'

207

'Of course,' I repeated. 'Of course.'

It was unworthy to consider for any more than the merest second that this warm, attractive woman who meant so much to me could, in the way that Pax had suggested, have motives beyond those to do with our mutual emotions; and yet, perhaps because of old hurts, in times and with people Elizabeth would never know, I stopped short of telling her the full extent of Bain's possible compromise at the hands of Lyle.

'Lyle has given me new insights into the past,' I said.

'The past is a monster,' Elizabeth said.

'With many heads in our case,' I said. 'So many mysteries, so much avoided. Do you know, I'm not sure any more who my father was?'

'Your mother sounds like she was quite a gal,' Elizabeth said.

'You two should meet.'

'Probably not the best idea, Theo,' Elizabeth murmured and took out a cigarette.

The way she initiated things thrilled me: sex, conversations, cigarettes.

'I wish we could be together more,' I said.

Elizabeth made a little wince. 'So do I.' She looked at her watch and then at me. There was a quality of sorrow to her that disturbed me.

'What's wrong?' I asked.

'Nothing. I don't like goodbyes.'

'Ring me,' I said.

'It can be difficult.'

'I understand.'

She gathered her handbag. I pushed up beside her under the closed hatch of the snug and kissed her. We stood up and she kissed me again, this time her way, the softest, tasty graze of her yielding lips.

'Good night, whoever you are,' she whispered and went out of the pub before me.

Salonika is a chessboard, a port city that for two thousand years has been ravaged by siege, fire and earthquake, and you fly direct from London. The faces one sees at these gatherings. The canvassers and lobbyists, the kingmakers and back-room men, the

208

wheeler-dealers, the brokers for obscure but organised pressure groups. Our hotel on the Avenue Egnatias, 'Hotel Egnatias', was shiny as a Rubik cube. Early Tuesday I strolled along Salonika's waterfront, the air pinging with cosmopolitan zest. The city was already crowded with commuters and Elizabeth's blue and white taxis; I watched early light warm a basilica of glistening, mosque-like dome and realised how much I wanted her.

You never see much of the real face of your host's city on these trips. You follow their master plan. On that Tuesday morning was held the first session of a conference of customs chiefs to endorse a common strategy for the new age. We had luncheon on a yacht in the Bay of Salonika but had to cut it short because of bad weather. That afternoon was spent endorsing a master plan of our own procedures for five more years. Evelyne-Mary fed me position papers in flawless succession. Tuesday night twenty people sat down at a popular quayside restaurant where I ate octopus.

By Wednesday's small hours I knew I had trouble. If I had eaten the octopus alive it could not have caused my stomach to writhe and leap more. I spent six hours mostly on my knees, themselves bled of their ability to support my shivering torso for more than a few minutes at a time. Crawling like a wounded starfish to the telephone I rang Evelyne-Mary and within another two hours, sustained by brandy, I flew out.

Dublin was wet and grey in its early afternoon but the sight of it was happiness itself. I took a taxi to Sandymount, feeling the beginnings of a rally taking place. I would call Evelyne-Mary, who was standing in for me on the final day, then I would put on my pair of galoshes and tramp the frill of the tide for twenty minutes by way of convalescence.

I paid the taxi off. What was the song about it being so much nicer to come home? A van was parked along the kerb beside a striped tent set up on the footpath. Yes, it's so much nicer, yes, it's so much nicer . . .

My flat was in a purpose-built block of six, two each on three levels, mine being the left-hand of the middle pair you walked up the steps to. Humming, I unloaded my post. My latchkey would not turn. Putting down my grip and the post, I reapplied the key to the lock and added my shoulder. The door went in all of a sudden. Standing in my hall looking at me was a man in a hood with, in his hands, what was left of my hi-fi system.

I went for him, bluntly. Despite years of reading in newspapers what not to do in such situations, I took the intruder with me back on to a stand of bookshelves that promptly sundered and covered us with their contents like rubble. He was a cat. Every part of him rippled with dangerous muscle. I went for his hood and he bit me on the hand. We rolled across the floor in the classical manner. It was my mistaken impression that we were causing the mayhem that I fleetingly perceived all about us. The advantage I had gained by my spontaneous attack was being eroded by my opponent's experience. He caught my nostrils between clamp-like fingers and began to tear my nose away. I shook him off. He made to throttle me, reducing my resistance with a succession of well-practised knees to my groin. I, in turn, hammered my knees into his arse, provoking him to grunt. The greatest pain for me was being caused by the corner of the ruptured coffee table, which was pointing up into the small of my back. I lunged sideways with all my strength, bringing the man on top of me into a less effective position and allowing me to smash what would later prove to be an ashtray into his face.

Physical combat of this kind, I can attest, takes place without words: words for my adversary would have betrayed his voice and for me would have demanded resources I lacked. A satisfactory dribble of blood appeared from the mouth-hole of his hood. Wondering if I had perhaps gone too far, speculating on the sudden emergence of a resource I had previously not recognised in myself, I sat back for a breather. Thumps of protest sounded from my neighbour downstairs. I slapped the tiled floor feebly, an effort at communication, but my arms and legs suddenly began to go the way they did after a very hot bath, or when I ate octopus.

He came at me without a sound, this time catching my hair in one hand and bringing his knee up into my down-swung face. My mouth went sticky. I hit him on the chest, but I could tell he had gone into top gear and that I had not misjudged, over forty years, my own inability in such encounters. Lashing out with my foot, I then got to my feet and began throwing whatever objects came to hand. They bounced from him, ominously. I caught up a biscuit box and flung it; the lid came off and the contents, old photographs, hung prettily and all too briefly in the air between us.

I made for the hall, but he yanked me backwards and snapped his elbow into my face like a sprung hinge. I lost all vision. I hoped he would use his knee again, which, although solid, was less sharp than his elbow. Refusing to accommodate even such a joyless wish, he belted me one between the eyes with his fist and floored me.

Even were I not carrying the remains of Greek poison in my gut, I doubt if I could have done much better. I had only fear left as an incentive to fight. I crawled once more for the hall, flinging a standard lamp between us and using the tiny diversion it created to get up. He was bleeding freely from his mouth, spitting as he came at me, and hissing. My hand felt the shape of a bottle. Using it as a club, I lunged and caught him on the shoulder. The bottle (of malt whisky) flew away and hit the far wall where it disintegrated odorously. My opponent swung his fist. I ducked and, hearing the whistle of air above me, was beginning a moment of self-congratulation when he chopped his forearm into my throat so hard that as I crumpled I thought I would never draw breath again.

I had no way to convey my acceptance of his superiority, or to apologise, or to flag the fact that he had won and I would now be happy to call it a day. Indeed, my main concern was the amount of blood coming from my own mouth, spraying outward from it any time I was unwise enough to let it open, and the feeling that something other than my tongue was flapping around in there.

My torturer dragged me up by the collar and staggered me into the ruin of my kitchen. I choked. He beat me with his fists. I searched desperately for the sharp implement that might later be called 'Exhibit A' in my trial for manslaughter, and actually wondered humorously at my own ability to be optimistic in the face of such obviously hopeless odds. A wooden spoon was all that came to hand. I jabbed it – spoon end, of course – into his eye, but in response he powered down his head into my face, as if my nose had been too long overlooked.

His rhythm was no longer urgent, just slow and deliberate. I put up my hands but he picked his blows as he pleased. The pain was nothing extraordinary, but the fear was. My blood was on his fists. I had now slid to the ground and knew what was coming next.

211

Steel-capped boots; I actually noticed them. Then I saw two pairs of boots. I prayed it wouldn't hurt.

St Vincent's Hospital overlooks a golf course. Beyond the golf course are the Dublin mountains. The golfers seemed to grow out of the mist at the base of the mountains, pulling their little carts. Against the landscape their clothes jarred when they were meant to gaily amuse. Who were they? How could so many people in midweek afford to play golf in a country crippled with debt? Perhaps, like me, they were temporarily laid off, but for different reasons.

My life is peppered with only partial recall of vital events. The day I stole Charlie Blood's flag; the day I learned my wife was adulterous. Thus I could tell Pax nothing about my assailant that might have assisted in a capture and arrest. I remember calling Pax in Harcourt Terrace, doggedly dialling out his private number and watching the telephone turn a jolly red beneath my mouth. But nothing else. I did not even realise there had been two men until Pax told me.

'One in a van outside,' Pax said.

'Ddtthh clipe clen . . . ?'

'Don't try to talk. Yes.' Pax nodded. 'The striped tent.'

My ribs and assorted bruises pained madly, but, they said, that was a good sign, it meant healing had begun. I believed them. I would have believed anything that would get me through those days. I had tried to spit out my tongue, which had been 90 per cent severed by my own teeth. They had expertly sewn it back in place, then lashed my gums together with loops of wire that were then clamped.

Any leads on the burglars? I wrote on a pad.

Pax was sitting by the end of the bed, noting, with the professional interest that had become a part of him, a four-ball in progress below.

'They were pros,' Pax replied.

Who? I wrote and tapped the pad impatiently.

'Who is the question,' Pax continued. 'Rip-off merchants would have been in and out of your flat with every item of value in their van within six or seven minutes. These people were looking for something. They either found it and were breaking the

212

place up to make it look like a burglary, or they were breaking the place up in order to try and find what they were looking for.'

Pax looked at me searchingly and I replied with the body language of innocence.

'You must tell me who they were,' Pax said.

I had no enemies that I could think of, just as I had few friends. There was, of course, a Budget in the making, and anyone who could learn where the pennies would go on could make a killing of sorts. I wrote this down.

Pax shook his head. 'This wasn't to find out whether a penny or tuppence goes on the pint, Theo,' he said.

Ever so gently he brought me around to Elizabeth. Looking out at a golfer addressing his shot, I remembered Bain's file. The grant applications for inflated amounts signed for his own business by our Minister for Justice. It was too hurtful to consider that this information might be of interest to Elizabeth, and even if it was, that she would go to such lengths to get it.

'She knew your plans,' Pax said.

I nodded.

'She understood you would be in Greece until last Friday. That your flat would be empty.'

I shook my head. I wrote, *Others knew too.*

Pax looked at me with a mixture of fondness and exasperation, the way he might look at a child who refuses to learn. It frustrated him, I knew, that the main element of an otherwise perfect friendship, total trust, would always be lacking between us.

'Is there anything you can think of, Theo, that you have in your flat and that this lady might want?' asked Pax. 'Anything at all?'

It was as if Pax was challenging my right to love someone. There was more. To divulge to Pax the contents of that file would be to put Bain at risk from the one person who would never be truly converted to Bain's new respectability. I was trapped again, and not for the last time, between love for Pax and an obscure responsibility to Bain.

I shook my head.

'It's just, if there is anything, I could check your flat to see if it was taken,' Pax gently pressed.

I sighed, a whistling sound.

'She's a pro, Theo,' Pax said. 'It would not be personal, just

213

business. It does not diminish either of you. It probably went beyond her control.'

'Hm-hn.'

'She's using you, Theo,' Pax said grimly. 'She's using you like others have in the past.'

I wrote, *Fuck off*.

Generators or engines made the building throb like a ship. I may have slept.

'I'll come in next week,' Pax said and got up. 'Be grateful for the rest. Is there anything you want? Anyone you want me to tell?'

'Hm-hn.'

'By the way, a car knocked you down,' Pax said quietly. 'Hit-and-run. You were lucky.'

I wondered whether the subterfuge was for my own protection or part of some greater strategy.

My flat? I scribbled.

'Forensic should be finished with it by now,' Pax said. 'I'll see they make an inventory and a list of everything broken so that you can claim your insurance. Then we'll put the place back together best we can for your return.'

I stuck my thumb in the air and gave him a metallic smile. Did Pax ever get fed up putting things back together for me, I wondered? I felt sinking guilt that I could never commit myself to him the way he deserved and that my loyalty was never something he would be able to take for granted. Pax stood looking down at me, his big knuckles standing out where he held the bed end.

'Maybe they were burglars,' he said. 'But if you think there's anything you've overlooked, anything you want to tell me, then tell them to get me. I'll be right over. It's what friends are for.'

'Hnn,' I said.

I wished I did not suspect Pax's friendship for me as springing, at least somewhat, from a misplaced sense of duty. And yet, as those next days in St Vincent's went by, much as I longed to see Elizabeth and tell her – or have her told – about what had befallen me, I hesitated each time I went to do so. Even though she might be trying to ring me at home, so long as she never rang the hospital it meant that she had no knowledge of my predicament, thus making Pax's inferences groundless. Each further silent day was proof of Elizabeth's innocence and balm to my soul.

214

I lost a stone in six days. My food came in glasses and bowls and was sucked through a straw stuck between a hole sculptured in the palisade of my mouth. On the Wednesday following the attack, some bandages came off so that only a few inches of sticking plaster remained on my head. The golfers came and went. I began to stroll corridors in my dressing-gown and get the strength back in my legs. I would be discharged soon, the doctor promised. I gave a nurse a tenner and wrote her to buy me some whiskey. Bain's face appeared on my silent television, and pictures of Monument; I didn't even bother to turn up the sound.

Later that evening the nurse put her head around the door. I presumed the whiskey had arrived.

'You've a visitor,' she whispered and I heard noises different to the usual ones out in the corridor.

I thought it might be Pax, but in walked Bain. He turned to a plain-clothes type at the door. 'No one,' he said grimly, 'and that means *no one*, is to come into this room.'

Bain was ashen. He had not shaved properly. Some of the bulk had gone out of his face.

'It's taken me twenty-four hours to find you, you cunt,' he whispered.

I pointed at my mouth; I held up my pad. Why was I so terrified? I wondered. I was in a hospital, after all.

'Have you seen the news?' he asked.

I shook my head.

'He's gone,' Bain said grimly. 'The machines are gone, like I said they would be. Vanished. He's a crook, your famous brother. Some dividend for a couple of month's work. Theo, you've got to help me!'

I wrote, *What? What?*, underlining it forcibly.

'The British Sundays have the whole story,' said Bain in short breaths. 'They've got copies of the grant applications signed by me. They've got the real invoices which show how the price was inflated. They're even suggesting that I'm in on the stealing of the machines. You've got to help me! You got me into this!'

How?

'Can't you fucking talk?' he shouted.

I shook my head.

'That's all I need, a fucking dummy,' he cried. 'How? How the

215

fuck do I know how? I thought you might know how.' He went suddenly dangerous. 'I gave you the file. Where is it?'

'Hm ay at.'

'*Where is the fucking file, Theo?*' Bain screamed into my face.

In my flat, I scrawled.

'You're sure? I mean, how do you know it hasn't been taken whilst you've been in here?' Bain asked. 'What happened to you anyway?' and he pressed the pad into my chest.

Car.

'I'm fucked,' Bain said and suddenly sat down. He looked at me with tears in his eyes. 'I'm fucked and I've done nothing. The system took a chance on Bain Cross and lost, that's what'll go down in the history books. He abused his position. When all I was trying to do was to keep a few jobs going in Balaklava. Jesus Christ, Theo, the shame. The whole country is cheering. I'm ruined.'

You're innocent.

'That's what's so unfair,' he wept.

I tried to exclude everything from my mind and to get him to seize on his practical options, if any existed.

Fraud Squad?

'They've sent the details over to London, what more can they do?' Bain replied. 'Do you think Scotland Yard are going to drop everything to find a couple of sausage machines? Jesus, I'm ruined. I'll have to resign or I'll be hounded out of Dublin. Oh God, what would poor Pa say if he was alive?'

Don't resign!!!!!

Bain wiped his eyes with his hand and looked at my vehement note curiously. 'Why not?' he asked.

I clenched my two fists in an attempt to signify holding on grimly, and made animal-at-bay sounds.

'What can I do not to resign?' repeated Bain.

I did not believe that Lyle had absconded; something more sinister overhung these events, and that, along with the genuine innocence of Bain's position, seemed to me to warrant tenacity.

Set up? I wrote and gave him the pad.

'Set up?'

'Hm.'

'What could give you that idea, Theo?' asked Bain narrowly.

I shrugged as if to say, it seems obvious.

Enemies.

'But who, Theo?' Bain asked. 'Who do you think might want to set me up? Which enemies? I think you know more than I do. Do you, Theo?'

I shook my head.

'I mean, I know you could not be involved yourself, Theo,' Bain went on, a little too calmly, 'but maybe you know more about Lyle Shortcourse than I do. Or about other people altogether who might want to set me up?'

'Hm-hn.'

'There's something,' Bain pressed. 'There must be something or you wouldn't have suggested this. I was set up, right? By who? Who?'

I spread my hands emptily.

'I don't believe you, Theo,' Bain said and stood up. He came to the side of the bed. 'I'm dying, politically, Theo,' he said with great intensity. 'This is crucial information to me. Life and death. I must have it. Who set me up?'

'A clo clo.'

'Who, Theo? Yes? Who?'

'A clo *clo!*'

'Here, write it down, Theo!' Bain said and thrust me the pad and pencil.

I don't know.

Bain sprang on to the bed. He caught the lapels of my dressing gown in his hands and dragged me upright.

'*Who set me up, Theo?*' he screamed. '*Who fucking destroyed me?*'

I put my hands on his face to push him off, but he was crazy.

'I'm going to kill you, Theo!' he screamed.

A pair of arms appeared as from nowhere. Bain was dragged back, his eyes locked on mine.

'You cunt . . .'

'Minister!'

'I'm going to kill him. He's destroyed me.'

'Minister, get a grip on yourself,' said Pax Sheehy.

It must have been further proof to Bain of his fate that it was Pax who had intervened. Bain sat, trembling and white-faced, panting

217

like a man who's run a mile, tie and collar over to one side. Pax stood between Bain and me, his back to the door.

'Are you OK?' he asked me.

I nodded. I wrote, *Nurse. Whiskey* and pointed to the door.

Neither Bain nor I broke the silence as Pax went out. Bain's eyes were red and their surrounds were red and swollen; he glared at me with red hate. Pax came back in and put the whiskey beside the bed and I poured out three half-tumbers.

'What's going on?' asked Pax quietly.

'I have a business problem,' Bain said.

Pax's face said he knew; the whole world knew.

'His brother Lyle swindled me,' Bain went on. 'He also swindled the IDA, but it's my signature on all the forms. How, I want to know, did the papers get hold of it? Who gave it to them? I gave Theo a file with the whole thing in it, invoices, my signature, the lot. I want to know, does he know anything about what happened? The fucker can't even speak.'

File in my flat OK, I wrote on the pad for Pax.

Pax's eyes as he watched me did the most extraordinary thing. They smiled.

'I checked Theo's flat at his request, Minister,' said Pax, turning to Bain. 'No one's been near it. Everything is secure. The leak must have come from another source.'

Bain was slumped. He was dead and we all knew it.

'What happened to Theo, Pax?' he asked quietly. Dead, but still dangerous. 'Why is Theo in here? Pax? Remember your position, mind!'

'As I understand it, Minister, Theo got hit by a car,' Pax replied.

Bain should have resigned, but didn't. If my advice in any way toughened his resolve to stay in office, then it was advice he would have been better off without.

Lyle was never found. Never. Neither were the machines. Pax told me later he doubted if the UK police had ever so much as lifted a finger in the inquiry. Bain clung on in the hope of brazening it out. First he denied everything; then he made a full admission, but said he had been set up. The press, which one suspected had long lain in wait for this day, slaughtered him. There was initial support from the Cabinet and from the

218

Taoiseach, but when it became clear that Bain had lied early on in the affair, that he had pretended he knew nothing about grants or about Lyle, he was abandoned. He lost not only ministerial office but the Party Whip. There was a clip of him on the six o'clock news, leaving his office on the Green. He looked an old, beaten man. If you had been asked then, you would have said Bain Cross was finished.

Bain believed I knew more about the Lyle business than I let on and until the day, almost twenty years later, that we buried his mother, my sister Mag, we never spoke. We never met. The occasion just never arose. I lived out my career in Dublin. Bain moved back to his power base in Monument where he founded a new political party, Daonlathas Láir, which means Democracy of the Centre, and which began in the dying years of the eighties to contest by-elections in those constituencies where history matters more than jobs.

What I remember most from the time of Bain's fall from grace are not the doubts and suspicions it all raised about myself and the people close to me, such as Elizabeth and Pax; my most vivid memory is of what occurred the day I was discharged from hospital.

I was kept in a week longer than I expected. I did not really object. The thought of going back to the empty flat, to the memory of what had happened there and to the realisation that I would have to confront the truth about the wretched file, all combined to make life in hospital more attractive. I eventually left on the Thursday of the week following Bain's visit. The Irish media had a fixation with Sausagegate, making Bain appear as a figure somewhere between scandal and outright farce. I took a taxi the short journey to Sandymount and felt uplifted by the sight of the sea.

My mind refused to grapple with the problem that would arise if the file was missing and the possibility that Elizabeth had engineered Bain's disgrace therefore became more likely. I knew on the one hand that the file was gone; I also knew, or wanted to know, that Elizabeth loved me for myself and not because of the strategic opportunities I might provide her with.

I scarcely noticed the neatness I came back to. A number of messages lay waiting on the machine. I went straight to the desk in my bedroom, pulled back the lid, found a little key in a box and opened the bottom right-hand drawer, the one nearest the floor. I was ready for the shock. I wasn't ready for the file to be there. I fumbled it out and spread it open. There were all the forms and sheets, copied and intact as I remembered them.

I groaned in relief. Relief for Elizabeth. For Bain. I went and poured a whiskey and, sucking it through a straw, replayed my messages. Elizabeth four times.

I groaned again, this time in dismay at myself, for all my self-inflicted doubts and misery.

I sat down and went through my post. The first envelope I opened was thick to the feel and addressed in a sloping, uncomfortable hand. It had been posted two weeks before from Monument. My brother, Lyle, was delivering his promise.

Sparrow was not dead, she had just flown. With the travel documents arranged nearly two decades beforehand for evacuating with Harry Amis and never used, Sparrow at last left Monument. She went aboard a steamer and the sun rising over the River Lyle was her last sight before she slept. Six weeks later, in deep snow, the train between New York and Atlantic City, New Jersey, broke down and froze over. Sparrow looked out at men singing as they sawed logs to build a fire by the trackside. Everyone disembarked and formed a circle. The fire, when it got going, seemed big enough to Sparrow to unfreeze the world.

The photograph taken of my mother at Mag's wedding is all that remains of the Sparrow from that time. The flirting look across the eyes. The ripeness. The mixture of disdain and apprehension.

If Baby Fox was glad to see her younger sister, she kept it to herself. She scarcely spoke to Sparrow, who was given a job in the laundry with its own living quarters. Baby in middle age was a big, powerful woman with an ample bosom but a hard face that become even harder when Baby set eyes on Sparrow. It was as if in Sparrow Baby was being forced to confront memories she had long resolved to forget.

For the first weeks the most Sparrow saw of Baby was up in a glass-fronted office above the laundry floor, surveying the work in progress beneath. Sparrow learned that following the death of

Baby's husband, her sister had become wildly neurotic about the care of her infant son, Dan. Sparrow, when she stole a glance up at the office, could see a black nursemaid tending a pram.

Atlantic City throbbed with New Deal change. On cornfields rose libraries and schools, hospitals and athletics pitches. Old, crooked streets disappeared, new ones took their place. Hotels went up for people who came to prosper from the air.

In the week leading up to Christmas, when the steam irons were flat out and money was being made, Baby came home from a visit to her downtown bank and found Dan and his nursemaid missing. The pandemonium was phenomenal. Baby ran in fury up and down the floor, berating women for not keeping the whereabouts of her son uppermost in their minds, and then rebuking them for remaining at their posts when every corner of the laundry premises and of her residence had not been searched. Everyone was culpable. Outside it was five below and dark. She went crazy, Baby. She shouted that a nigger girl had kidnapped her child. The laundry delivery men were dispatched on their bicycles and in their vans into the night. Baby's anger turned to fear and she began to cry, accepting comfort from her women, beating the walls with her hands, and once or twice running out into the freezing night and screaming Dan's name.

The police arrived and began a systematic questioning of all employees as Baby reeled about her office, alternating between hysterical rage and helpless despair. She called the mayor of Atlantic City. She raged over the ineffective police and called up Pinkertons. She called the governor and said she wanted the coast-guard called out. At seven thirty Dan was found safe and well, up an alley beside the railroad track where he had been left by his nursemaid before she jumped a freight train and headed home for Christmas in New Orleans.

It took Baby all of Christmas to get over the shock. She could not let Dan out of her sight. But after Christmas business resumed and Baby realised that she could not run the laundry and look after Dan. The very thought of another stranger looking after her infant made Baby feel faint. Then she remembered Sparrow.

Sparrow's life was transformed. She was given a bedroom beside Baby in the centrally heated house (although the laundry, it has to be said, was never cold). Baby's whole attitude changed.

221

She watched Sparrow bathe Dan and watched Dan smile at Sparrow. A bonding had taken place, straight off. The sisters began to go for walks together. They listened to *Amos 'n' Andy* each evening. Sparrow told Baby about Pa Shortcourse and what he had done, and Baby held Sparrow as they cried together. Baby gave Sparrow an old cony coat; Baby had a whole wardrobe full of redolent furs.

Sparrow's letters of that time to her bother Hugo give a picture of a happy domestic situation whilst Hugo's speak of the progress of the war, of the fall of the Low Countries and of rationing and hardship.

'Ireland will fight no war,' Baby said. 'They just fight each other, the Irish.'

They sat in the front room of Baby's wooden house, two Irish sisters in New Jersey.

Baby said, 'A penny for your thoughts.'

Sparrow frowned. 'I was shopping at the grocery yesterday. The owner reminds me of young Mr Wise.'

'Their store doubles as a synagogue, d'y'ever hear the like,' Baby laughed, one eye twinkling.

'God is what you make Him.'

'That's a mouthful for an Irish girl,' Baby said. 'It's kinda blasphemy, I'm thinking.'

'The Jews are fleeing everywhere,' Sparrow said.

'These people are survivors.'

'They're coming here by the boatload.'

'I used to hear it said that when Old Mr Wise arrived in Monument, he was some other name than Wise,' Baby said.

'He looks foreign,' Sparrow said, remembering.

'That's Irish!' Baby laughed. 'Here everyone looks foreign.'

Sparrow bathed Dan twice a day. She sponged water gently over his blond curls, her hand supporting his neck, and watched the water run down his pink body.

'Do you remember Monument, Baby?' asked Sparrow.

Baby bit her lip. 'Monument. Eillne. I learned to swim in the river at Eillne, you know. Sammy Tea told us he would build us a house there. Jesus. Me and Frank Fox, we stood on the back of the boat going down that River Lyle from Monument. We were laughing and crying because we knew we were never coming back. Can you believe that was thirty-five years ago?'

222

'I often think of Monument in those days, days you must remember so much better than me,' Sparrow said. 'It was always sunny. You smelt Mazawattee everywhere. No one hurried, dogs slept in sunshine – it all seems so safe now, looking back.'

'Safe?' Baby asked sharply.

'You know.'

'Sure I know,' said Baby dryly.

'Why did you leave?' asked Sparrow.

'Oh, I don't know.'

'You were only fourteen,' Sparrow said. 'Why did you leave Monument? Papa gave you money, didn't he? Why?'

'You do funny things when you're in love,' Baby said.

'D'you remember Papa, Baby?'

'Oh yeah, sure.'

'I mean, when he was well?'

'Sure.'

'I envy you that.'

Baby's mouth took on a tight smile.

'I used to climb the wall of the mental home to see him,' Sparrow said. 'I used to try and compare him with his snapshots.'

'Yeah? What was he like?'

Sparrow paused. 'Sad, I suppose. Like all the other men.'

'Describe him.'

'Oh, you don't want to hear, Baby. You want to remember him as he really was.'

'No, I want to hear what he was like in the mental home. Go ahead, Sparrow.'

Sparrow took a deep breath. 'They were all shaved to their scalp for lice,' she said. 'Even his moustaches.'

'They shaved his moustaches?' Baby said. 'What was he like without them?'

'Not like Papa,' Sparrow said. 'It was as if he had a white patch over his mouth. They all wore the same clothes as well, tweed trousers and jacket. There were no pockets in the clothes, so he'd be always plucking at them as if his fingers thought there were pockets they couldn't find. He had no idea who I was. He looked tortured, Baby. That's how I remember Papa. Tortured.'

'Tortured, eh?'

'What really happened?' Sparrow whispered. 'Who was the girl?'

'How would I know?' Baby shrugged. 'I went away.'

That evening Baby gave Sparrow a coat down to the ankles made from the pelts of chinchillas.

There follows one of the many impenetrable interludes that pickle our family history. Months fly by, unchronicled. It is suddenly September. France has fallen; the Battle of Britain has the world on the edge of its seat.

'D'you ever think of going home?' asked Baby mildly, checking her newspaper as she did each morning to see how Wall Street had closed.

'Home?'

'You have a husband, a family,' Baby said. 'It's been nearly a year.'

'I can't go back, do you not understand?'

'I understand that we can't always have everything we want in life, Sparrow.'

It was still warm enough for iced tea. Dan began to cry and Sparrow picked him up.

'The nest is cold in Monument, Sparrow,' Baby said with a click-click-click of the tongue and folded her paper. 'There's a good business. Even I remember the sausages. People have to eat, war or no war.'

'I'll never go back,' Sparrow repeated, frowning.

'Even so.' The business side of Baby sat on the stoop, her glass propped up by her elbow on a rocking chair. 'Think of your own position, Sparrow. Your position here.'

'What do you mean?'

'What arrangements last for ever? I ask myself.' Baby shrugged. 'A sister does what she has to in a crisis, but every home can only have one mistress and every woman wants to be the mistress of her home. It's only natural. It's what a man wants to find, that's if he looks, of course, you understand.'

Sparrow could not believe what she was hearing. She *loved* Baby and Dan. She had assumed that with Baby and Dan she had a home for life.

Nonetheless Sparrow said, 'Yes, Baby.'

Baby said, 'You should get yeself a man, Sparrow.'

'I'm already married.'

'So who knows? Plenty of single men in America and none of them don't care nothing about the past.'

'I couldn't.'

'Suit yeself,' Baby said.

Sparrow began to pick up the old hardness from Baby again, a tendency to be easily irritated with her younger sister, or pointed questions concerning Dan that suggested Baby had some misgivings about Sparrow's stewardship.

'You never leave Dan, or anythin', do you?' Baby asked. 'Even for a minute?'

'How do you mean?'

'I read in the paper about kids bein' snatched from their strollers in Chicago.'

'Of course I never leave him,' Sparrow said. 'How could you have such a thought?'

'Sometimes I have these bad dreams,' Baby said. 'I wake up like I was in a fever. I have to go in and check on Dan, I have to see his face, you know? It's as if my dreams are tryin' to tell me a secret or something.'

'About what, Baby?'

'About you, Sparrow.'

Winter came suddenly to New Jersey, flurries of early snow swept up from northern wastelands and scattered down the Fall Line. Sparrow learnt there was a laundry for sale in Camden County and that Baby had been back and forth over four weeks, although Sparrow had been told nothing. In the last days of October Baby went off again and this time was away from home for nearly a week. Two days after her return she was followed by a man her junior, a Philadelphia launderer. The talk was all money and merger. He had an oily way with him and treated Sparrow like a hired girl.

'Sparrow?'

'Yes?'

'We need to talk a moment.'

The launderer had been gone a week, and Sparrow had begun to perceive in Baby a restlessness and a reluctance to meet Sparrow's eyes.

'Sit down, Sparrow.'

Sparrow sat on the rim of a chair and noticed fresh aspects of

Baby, such as Baby's fine bosom, her bright blue eyes, and her jewellery, which Sparrow had never seen worn before.

'I gotta think of the future, Sparrow.'

Ledgers and other portentous books were piled on the floor behind Baby's desk.

'A woman doesn't stay young for ever. I'm not kiddin' anyone that I'm any chicken, so if a man looks my way more than once, then I'm going to sit up and take notice, and who's there to say I'm wrong?'

Sparrow gasped. 'You're getting married?'

'A boy needs a father,' Baby said. 'I'm nobody's fool, believe me. We're forming a joint-stock company to run the new business. I'll have shares in my name. I told you before, this country's full of single men.'

Sparrow felt giddy. 'I'm very happy for you, Baby.'

'I've had an offer for this place which I think you'd agree I'd be foolish to turn down. Thirty thousand. With that sort of cash think of what we can do in a city like Phily.'

'Of course.'

'It's kinda tough on you, I know, but life is tough, who am I tellin'?'

'Who has bought this place?' asked Sparrow hoarsely.

'People come down from Trenton for their health,' Baby said. 'Don't worry. I've put in a word for you, Sparrow. You'll be looked after here, that's my guess. But if not, you can always go home. Why not? A year is a long time. Who knows what's changed there?'

Sparrow turned her face away. 'Let me think about it, Baby,' she said.

'I'll miss you, Sparrow,' Baby said.

It began to snow in earnest. Snow covered everything it fell on, people said it would never thaw. Baby would move before Christmas to let the new owners in. Baby went in November to be outfitted in Philadelphia for her wedding, leaving Dan to Sparrow's care.

Sparrow never waited for Baby to come home. It was wartime, the future was uncertain and Atlantic travel had become a perilous undertaking. Sparrow decided she should go with all her good memories of Atlantic City intact. She did not want to wait around for Baby and Dan to move to Phily and then find herself at the mercy of new owners.

There used to be a photograph from that time, I could have told Lyle. It was taken on the deck of a ship beside a lifeboat by an amateur, it would seem, for the camera is too far from its subjects for their features to be distinct. However, Sparrow always said I'm in the long infant dress and a bonnet, and it's Sparrow who is peering at the distant camera from the high collar of one of Baby's red sable coats. The name of the ship, however, can be seen clearly on the side of a lifeboat. It is, *Theodore Roosevelt*.

Records are something we take for granted nowadays, but in the days before the war they were often of the most arbitrary kind. During the best part of twenty years, following my reading of poor Lyle's last testament, I spent many fruitless days, lonely days if the truth be told, in Atlantic City, that town of garish casinos and hotels crammed with conventioneers and hookers, trying to find anyone – *anyone* – who worked at the outbreak of the war for Baby Fox and who remembered her pretty sister Sparrow. How we are condemned to seek comfort from the past! A building of thirty floors faced in mirrors stands on the spot where Fox's Laundry once operated. Americans are never still; they disperse with the regularity of the seasons. Not one voice remained to talk of that (to me) precious time. Despite placing prominent notices in the local papers and offering what I would regard as substantial cash inducements, I came up with nothing.

The hospital records in Atlantic City are all mute as to my birth. Sparrow always told me that I was a war baby, a Yank, born in the July of that year and able to kick my heels at its Indian summer. Sparrow might, like thousands of other women at the time, have given birth to me at home, that is, in Baby's laundry, but the official register of births in Atlantic City on the coming into the world of a son for a Sparrow Shortcourse (or Love) is silent. Given Baby's autocracy and business bent, it is possible she insisted my mother remove elsewhere, to Philadelphia for example, to have me, in the process absolving Baby from any suggestion of responsibility. But if so, *where did it happen?*

Then there are the letters of the time between Sparrow and Uncle Hugo. Even the most frigid communication – which this was

227

not – would surely allude, if only by way of postscript, to the successful birth of a child, even an unwelcome child, to one of the correspondents?

The most damning indictment of all is the disappearance of Dan Fox. Sparrow did indeed speak on this incident, but she always put Dan's mislaying by his black nursemaid as occurring in December of 1939, thus establishing the occurrence beyond doubt, but perhaps preparing the ground for future archivists such as myself to believe that the official date of the event came somehow to be misrecorded. She was never stupid, Sparrow.

The records of the Atlantic City Police Department that I have examined show that on 13 *November* 1940, Mrs Fox of Fox's Laundry reported her infant son missing. A telephone communication from the office of the mayor is logged. There was considerable activity. On 27 November, two weeks after reporting Dan gone, Baby Fox took a train to New York and a boat to England. She arrived in Southampton at midnight on 28 December and, after a long wait, took a train to London. Baby was exhausted. She booked into a hotel in Charing Cross. She did not know that 29 December would bring the climax of the Luftwaffe's bombing fury. Baby went to sleep. She must not have heard the sirens.

In Atlantic City a businessman from Philadelphia was able to show that he was the owner of Fox's Laundry, which he promptly sold, vanishing with the cash from the easiest windfall ever likely to come his way.

In the end I gave up torturing myself, gave up trying to find a Dan Fox in the orphanage records of Pennsylvania, and being haunted by the fact that I am him. Sparrow never altered her version of the Dan story and refused point-blank to discuss Lyle's journal. I settled down to deal with the more pressing problems of my life. You are what you are, after all. I am what I am, even if my mother is someone long dead, a poor, frantic woman driven across an ocean in my pursuit. My memories from that time are all phantoms. Deep green swells. Mist and fog. Even today, whenever I hear the fog-horn of a ship, I feel the past stirring like giant within me.

PART III

Twelve

When I jumped from the toll bridge and hit the water, my sense of freedom came not only from being immersed in what for me has always been the most benevolent medium, but also, I now know, from the prospect of death. I felt the deep churn of water from the sailing boat's wake and wondered whether it would drag me irrevocably under. It actually tried but I was not bothered. Had not the swimming river taught me all the tricks of negotiation I needed in such circumstances? When to fight and when not? Carefully husbanding precious thimbles of air, I bowled along the bottom, my compass intact. I could tell the incoming Liffey was funnelling me and all its other flotsam towards its south bank. I surfaced only when a dark cliff appeared and I felt comforting hanks of sea moss in my hands.

I broke the surface and was oddly reminded by my view of the (distant) bridge of my wedding day, surfacing in the swimming river beside Pax and seeing the rapidly contracting knot of anxious guests on the bank. A good three hundred yards down-river of me I could discern my escorting party still stranded on the north side of the bridge, which for some reason remained open. A chain hung hidden in the moss. I climbed it and crawled on to an empty quay. No purpose now remains in concealing the clarity of my intent. I set out for Bain's flat in Rathgar.

That journey was my first taste of freedom in over a year. I felt no fear. I helped myself to a jacket from a selection outside one shop and to a jaunty cap from another. My squelching soon stopped. The sun came out. Forethought made me calm, not anxious. I wondered if things would really have turned out any differently had I not made Bain's reacquaintance at Mag's funeral.

It had been a funny old twenty years, near enough, since I had last met Bain, although not everyone would agree.

Oscar Shortcourse had died on Long Quay, whose length he had walked every day of his adult life at least half a dozen times. Supervising the unloading of fish boxes for his shop from a trawler and losing his footing in the process, Oscar slipped between the heaving boat and the quay and bobbed out of reach but in sight for at least a minute. Shouting to the people on the quay, calling them by name, he clawed alternately at the trawler's teak and the granite quay until a wave married the two and finished him. Oscar could not swim. A bachelor when he died, his business went under the hammer. The proceeds went to an obscure foundation in Belfast whose aim was to bring the Irish Republic back into the Commonwealth.

David Wise died in Israel. He died unexpectedly and on his own in the bedroom of a kibbutz outside Jerusalem. An unfinished letter to Sparrow was found by his side. Sparrow had his body brought home for burial in Monument, despite strenuous representations from Wizemanns in Israel who wanted their cousin interred on the Mount of Olives. But Sparrow's wish prevailed. She had by that time become Mrs David Wise.

Johnnie Love's death took place in bizarre circumstances. One December, wildfowling in the river delta after torrential rain, Johnnie shot a goose. According to Johnnie's sole companion, the great bird appeared to fly on after the shot, but then suddenly dropped like a meteor straight between the two men into the flimsy punt. The damage seemed minimal at first. Johnnie's companion shook Johnnie's hand excitedly for such a shot; Johnnie held up the heavy goose, in awe at his own achievement.

Without warning, the punt began to sink. Johnnie's companion screamed in fright and, throwing his gun away, launched himself for an island of weeds. But Johnnie seemed paralysed. He sat in the punt, his gun in one hand, the goose in the other, until the gunwale of the boat disappeared and was (in the speedy way these thing unfold) swept away by the hastening river, until only the barrels of his gun were visible. He was fifty-one. He couldn't swim either.

Johnnie's widow entered a convent – which perhaps she should have done originally instead of marrying Johnnie and putting up with his philandering – and the business went to their youngest son, Samuel, who was sixteen and still at school. Samuel went on to become a Columban Father, working in India. The business of Samuel Love & Sons was run by professional managers until it was absorbed into the growing empire of Teddy Batty.

The Shortcourse meat business was the seed that gave Teddy Batty his start. He literally got it for nothing from the receiver after Bain's downfall; miraculously, the shed and shop immediately began to make money in a way that had eluded them all the years Teddy Batty had been merely the manager.

The old premises in Balaklava was sold. Shortcourses – the name was retained, albeit as 'A Member of Batty plc' – operated from a twenty-five-thousand-square-foot boning and chilling plant (one of several strewn around Ireland; Teddy visited them regularly in his own helicopter) on the road to Deilt. Teddy Batty took over Samuel Love & Sons, as mentioned, and thus cash succeeded in making a permanent unit where matrimony had tried but failed. Teddy also purchased the Love residence and farm when the widow retired. He was not as lucky in his personal life. His marriage was a childless one. His wife choked to death when her string of pearls became entwined in the gates of an old-fashioned lift in Moscow during a business visit to that city with her husband.

It was always widely believed that Teddy Batty had bankrolled Daonlathas Láir, Bain's new political party, and by the ease with which Batty plc got every grant and subsidy going, particularly after Bain came to power, and from the funds of cash that Daonlathas Láir had at its disposal for election advertising and other forms of self-promotion, it is likely this was the case. Bain would not have been offended by such an arrangement. Bain would have seen it simply as his dividend from Pa's business by another route.

And Bain himself? Does anyone now remember the political tumult of the days after that election and before the Government was formed that brought Bain Cross to power?

It was six months before Mags died. The Government in office concluded a series of gross misjudgements by going to the country. The numbers returned did not work and Ireland foundered for eight weeks without a Government because none of the parties involved could agree upon a Taoiseach. Then, with our currency being hunted across the foreign exchanges of the world like a

233

snipe, events imposed a compromise. Daonlathas Láir, Bain's breakaway party of twelve whom no Government had wanted, suddenly became the party no Government could be formed without.

The price was Bain as Taoiseach.

The unthinkable became reality.

'He told you *what* about his son's horse?' asked Elizabeth.

'Someone mutilated it, killed it,' I replied. 'With carpet cutters.'

'That's horrific!'

The fate of the mare that had belonged to Brendan, Bain and Aggie's afterthought son, had galvanised Elizabeth. 'He sounded rattled,' I conceded.

'I don't blame him. Who did it?'

'He said he didn't know.'

'He didn't *know*?'

'He said perhaps the guards knew but couldn't prove it.'

'He's the Taoiseach of Ireland, Theo,' Elizabeth scoffed. 'Of course he knows.'

We had become a single act over the years, Elizabeth and I. Her pretty daughters were grown and gone to lives of their own. Elizabeth's marriage was a thing whose coldness I knew like an unwelcome part of myself, something I yearned to be rid of, whose severing was long awaited. All that remained for her in Belfast was a job.

'He's got the whole State working for him,' Elizabeth said.

'Perhaps.'

'His Minister for Justice, Miss Twinkle, is said to know what goes on in every corner of the land, yet she's only had the job six months,' Elizabeth went on. 'Don't try and tell me she hasn't been told about this incident.'

'You really follow these people, don't you?' I said.

Elizabeth shrugged. 'It's hardly a secret that it was drinks all round in Miss Twinkle's father's pub the day Airey Neave was killed.'

I would retire, but not quite yet. I had gone the distance that the old Surveyor in Monument had predicted and was enjoying my power at the summit of affairs in Dublin Castle almost as much as I enjoyed Elizabeth. Of course after almost twenty years I knew what she did, just as she knew my routine, but the nature of Elizabeth's job, the almost weary acceptance nowadays that there are two sides to every story and that governments as well as terrorists bomb and kill, these specifications of Elizabeth's career did not lend themselves to common chat in the way of your ordinary day at the office.

'Do you think the Provos are getting to Bain at last?' I asked, handing her a whiskey.

'That's what I hoped you'd tell me,' Elizabeth said.

'If they are, then he didn't give me that impression,' I said. 'He's put all that old business long behind him.'

A spring evening, people were out and about. The tide was full and had made a great, deep bay out of Sandymount for those who knew no better.

'I'd like you to meet Sparrow,' I said, moving off Bain. 'It's been on my mind.'

'She terrifies me,' Elizabeth said.

'I've built her up too much for you.'

'She's like some kind of icon that I've heard so much about. Like the Queen, or the Pope.'

'She's just another old woman,' I said. 'She'll soon be dead. Cheers.'

'Cheers,' Elizabeth said. 'I remember the story you told me years ago about her performance when the old house burned down. The photograph of her father that she went back in to get. That's not just another old woman.'

'That happened. She venerates Sammy Tea's memory.'

'It's where Bain gets his resilience from.'

'Don't change the subject.'

'I'm serious. He's the Lazarus of Irish politics.'

'Will you come down to Eillne?'

'I'll think about it very seriously.'

'We can stay the night.'

'Will Sparrow approve?'

'She won't mind,' I said. 'Although she's an old woman, she's become quite the liberal. She's a television addict as well.'

'I envy you such a mother.'

'She's a wonder. She's all the time attending to improvements about her new bungalow in Eillne. She can't read the papers any more, but she has them read to her, especially the business page and every word that's written about Bain – and dare whoever's reading leave out a word! She's razor-sharp.'

'She sounds amazing.'

'She said last month when I was down, in no uncertain terms, "That Teddy Batty is a thief. Stole Bain's business," she said. "The Battys were nothing, now Teddy Batty has bought Bernard Love's old house and farm. He *has* to be a thief, Theodore," she said.'

'You're so *sweet* when you do imitations,' Elizabeth said and kissed me.

My old tongue wound had never completely healed; I had been left with – in addition to the need for glasses and a slight limp – a furry collar of flesh that made me fluff the ends of my words sometimes and which Elizabeth found amusing. However, we laughed together at my mimicry. I knew this end of the day in my Elizabeth so well. Having served her masters for more than ten hours by concentrating on the pinheads of what was, or was not, said, she was left tight as a fist until gradually the whiskey unclenched her and her eyes began to go dangerously dreamy.

'Do you like Sparrow, Theo?'

'What a question.'

'I'm sorry.'

'I don't know, is the answer,' I said to my own surprise. 'I don't know if she's the light or the dark. I'll only know when she's dead.'

Elizabeth stayed in Sandymount that night. She liked to draw the gauze curtains at my bedroom window, to pull my bed over to it and to undress me as I stood there with just a flimsy veil between us and the world. She liked me to stay standing. She liked to remain fully clothed, which meant keeping on not just whatever suit she'd been wearing that day, but also all items of adornment such as rings, bangles, wristlets, chunky gold bracelets with tinkling charms, and heavy, pendulous necklaces and chains. It was to her, I think, as though, in the middle of whatever intergovernmental conference she had been attending that day, she had knelt at the feet, as she now knelt at mine, of whatever male had taken her fancy, and, in full view of everyone, had taken him like a hot kebab. She licked and nibbled, every now and then raising her arm to shake her jewellery out of her way, working her probing way deeper and deeper whilst families strolled up and down and cars passed us by the hundred.

I wanted her for ever. I did not want to share her, however nominally, with some man I had never met. She would come to me in the end, I knew, yet I did not dare to hope, as I once had, that sole possession would bring with it greater happiness.

I undressed Elizabeth. Her clothes were expensive, inter-governmental conference clothes that packaged her figure as trim and petite, hiding the full wonders of her breasts and thighs for the unwrapper. Her gold and platinum required closer quarters for their catches and hidden clasps. She liked to offer no assistance. She liked to feel the swinging rub of my penis against her pubic hair as I bent to her neck. She liked to catch hold of the curtain rail and appear to swing there, a figure of bondage, whilst I picked my way around her ornaments like a satyr picking the fruit from a magic bush.

I did not dare to visualise a day when we would get married, such was my memory of the previous occasion. I entertained only flashes of fantasy. It would be a registry office with, again, Pax as my witness. He had mellowed over the years. It would do him good as Assistant Commissioner to attend the wedding of a woman who he had once, long ago, told me worked for a hostile government's intelligence network.

We now stood in a pile of our own clothes and Elizabeth's baubles.

She stood up on the bed so that our heads were level. Taking off my glasses, I used the benefit of this adjustment between us to accomplish at length what might otherwise have been limited in time due to the strain of her weight.

'My God,' she panted, 'my God, my God.'

She gave me self-esteem over the years, Elizabeth. She patiently gave me back my pride and the mastery of my loins. She restored what had once, in the only-guessed-at past, been cruelly removed from me and took as her reward, and mine, long, sweetly shuddering climaxes, my hands on her backside, her arms around my neck, her legs around my waist, her head thrown back with its mouth wide open, her breasts flowered and receptive, our joined bodies moving like a single muscle. Her sinking back and down on the bed, never breaking, had me off with a single flip of her hips.

237

Two weeks had elapsed since I had last seen Elizabeth. One morning my assistant, Evelyne-Mary, informed me of a request that I attend, that afternoon, a meeting at the office of the Minister for Justice.

'The Minister's private secretary apologises for the short notice,' Evelyne-Mary said.

'You'd better come too,' I said.

We had a light lunch in a pub off Grafton Street. Evelyne-Mary carried that inner bloom of maiden ladies. She was pretty, in a slightly porcelain way, and spent her free time popping around dolmens and stone forts and other physical testimonies of our hunter-gatherer past. Where work was concerned, Evelyne-Mary was a pro, an irreplaceable source of legislative minutiae. Over the years we had met many ministers together, Evelyne-Mary and I. Some had been farm boys to whom their ministry began and ended with a chauffeur-driven saloon car; others, like Miss Twinkle, came to the job with a reputation for endless ambition.

'What do you think she wants?' I asked as we entered the Green.

'My guess would be just a general briefing,' Evelyne-Mary said. 'She's still settling in. The present Taoiseach, when he had Justice, made the same request, if you remember.'

Tulips quivered upright in their short-lived splendour.

'Look at the areas where we overlap,' Evelyne-Mary continued. 'Enforcement. She'll have been briefed separately about drugs. There's been a bit in the press recently about illegal gaming operations. Maybe that's on her mind. Or arms.'

'Yes,' I said as I saw the distant windows of Newman House. 'Or arms.'

There was a traditional neurosis on the subject in Ireland, not without reason: a generation before, when the North had burst alight, great political reputations had gone down with an attempt to import arms for our beleaguered kin in Ulster. As a mere unattached officer I had seen mighty men humbled, whilst Bain, just a minnow then, had survived. In the aftermath of it all you couldn't get a catapult into Ireland without the say-so of the Department of Justice, but nowadays, although its permit was still needed, pragmatism had relegated its role to that of a rubber stamp for decisions taken by my section.

'What sort of an old trout is Miss Twinkle?' I asked.

Evelyne-Mary shot me a token scowl in defence of womankind.

'Very capable,' she replied. 'Some people thought she could be Taoiseach last time round, but her rivals started a whispering campaign. She's beside the border up there in Sligo. She rubbed shoulders in her day with a lot of the current incumbents of Long Kesh.'

'Comes from a wild Republican family,' I observed.

'At least in name.'

'And is poised to take the top job here if Bain so much as stumbles – or so I heard on television.'

'Who did you hear saying that?' asked Evelyne-Mary.

'What's-her-name, the columnist. Big,' I said, using my hands. 'Her articles have a bitter taste to them.'

'Hah,' said Evelyne-Mary. 'Joyce Ogar.'

'Why "hah"?'

'She's . . . she and Miss Twinkle . . . they say Miss Twinkle and Joyce Ogar are friends.'

'I see.'

'Not that I believe such rumours, of course. Nor if I did would it be up to me to disapprove.'

'Of course not.'

Evelyne-Mary gathered her thoughts. 'Anyway, Miss Twinkle's father was a TD who advocated armed insurrection in Ulster – after he'd had his share of drink, of course.'

'Of course.'

'Miss Twinkle won all before her on the dance floor and when her father died she won the seat easily. She's fifty-one now, never married.'

'So who's right, apart from Joyce Ogar?' I asked.

'I'm sure as a longtime member of Fianna Fáil Miss Twinkle has a soft spot for the aspirations contained in the Irish Constitution, but I doubt now that she's Minister for Justice that you'd find timing switches in her corsets, Theo,' said Evelyne-Mary.

I looked down. My longtime assistant's cheeks each glowed with a little, round spot, her jaw was set and her eyes were fixed on the Department of Justice.

It was a building of the sixties, which is to say it had not altogether stood the test of time. Outside it dripped of grey

239

concrete cladding and inside, everywhere you looked were aluminium right angles and grubby walls. We were taken to the uppermost floor and here, against the odds, taste had joined battle with the surrounding limitations and some nice paintings had been seconded from public galleries. In an office with a view over the Iveagh Gardens, we had scarcely had a chance to admire them before the door reopened and a big, untidy man came in.

'Superintendent,' he said, giving me my functional title, and we shook hands.

'Secretary. You know Evelyne-Mary O'Grady.'

'*Conas tá tú?*' he said in Irish.

Evelyne-Mary replied, '*Go maith, go raibh maith agat,*' in regulation.

We sat. John Codd had lived for many years in Justice in the shadow of a famous predecessor and was now, as Departmental Secretary, reaping the rewards of his patience. Once a guard, his link to the force was seen as an advantage. Today he had had onions for lunch.

'Sorry for the rush, Superintendent,' he said, somewhat warily, his way with everyone, as I remembered. 'It's all go with this Minister.'

'We're at your disposal, Secretary,' I said.

'She's seeing a, ah, a friend of yours at the moment,' Codd said. 'Assistant Commissioner Sheehy.'

'I see.'

The Justice Secretary had the narrowed eyes and swept-back bush of hair of a man whose livelihood depended on his ability to count his sheep from a windy hillside.

'The Minister is acquainting herself with every aspect of the Department,' Codd explained. 'She already has a tremendous grasp of the job. She's going to be very much a Minister for us in here, Superintendent.'

'I'm glad,' I said.

'The Minister wants you to outline to her the procedures for the importation of arms and explosives, Superintendent,' Codd said.

'I'll be happy to oblige, Secretary,' I replied and mentally gave Evelyne-Mary ten out of ten. 'She could, of course, have obtained at least as good a briefing on the subject from yourself.'

'Nevertheless, that was her request.' Codd stood up and he

could have been someone about to ask airline travellers to empty their pockets before boarding, or, at any rate, someone whose job it is to unsettle. 'If you'll follow me in now, please.'

The Codds of Ireland's civil service were people from humble villages who brought these whole villages with them to Dublin, intact in their heads. It meant that the country's affairs at the highest level were run by those for whom the dictates of a Roman Catholic bishop took precedence over all other laws and conventions, who saw the Irish language, although moribund in fact, as deserving the same deference as a spoken tongue, and who painted the courage that went with the intellectual espousal of worthy but perhaps risky causes as ungodly liberalism, thus ensuring that the country in their care would in every way remain an island.

Down the corridor, Codd's stride had a shape to it from his days on the beat. In the Minister's outer office a male secretary made a call, and moments later inner doors opened and a woman whose name I can't remember but who was Miss Twinkle's personal private secretary smiled and shook our hands and led us in through what was, I'm sure, her own considerable office and then through yet more doors to the lair of Ireland's Justice Minister.

They say impressions gained in the first few seconds are the lasting ones. Miss Twinkle sailed around her desk and out to meet us. Although her skin had the colour and texture of lint, although she was incontestably a middle-aged lady with foaming white hair, Miss Twinkle's movements came from an intrinsic athleticism that refused to let old glories be forgotten. She came directly for me with both hands held out like a bird about to perch. Her bright blue eyes danced with excitement and her bottom lip curved out and up in a smile that anticipated generously the prosperity of our relationship.

'Superintendent Shortcourse,' she said in a deep, most non-*danseuse* voice, and caught me two-handed.

'Minister.'

She rounded off perfunctorily with Evelyne-Mary, then glided at the head of affairs to armchairs near the window where Pax had been standing. The Minister's calf-length dress matched her eyes, and was made of material that shimmered and emphasised her grace of movement.

241

'Pax.'

'Theo.'

Pax was dressed in full uniform.

'Gents, ladies,' Miss Twinkle purred, settling down like a leaf.

Codd was put at his Minister's right side, the lady secretary at the other. Evelyne-Mary and I sat opposite, whilst Pax occupied a no-man's-land. The man from the outer office reappeared with a tea tray, which he set down. Miss Twinkle's secretary poured and Codd handed out, although I noticed Miss Twinkle herself took nothing stronger than a glass of water.

'Years ago a tourist came into Daddy's public house in Sligo, Superintendent,' the Minister resounded, 'and asked him for a glass of water.'

She had picked up my glance.

'Daddy didn't, shall we say, approve of water,' Miss Twinkle twinkled, and Codd put back his head and opened his mouth in silent mirth. ' "Excuse me," the tourist said when the glass was put up on the counter, "but is this water clean?" "Indeed it is, sir," Daddy said, "I washed it myself." '

Codd laughed as if to some invisible colleague over his right shoulder whilst the rest of us joined in the general spirit of breaking the ice. Elizabeth, I remembered, had spoken of the same Sligo public house in different terms.

'Congratulations on your appointment, Minister,' I said.

'Ohh.' Miss Twinkle brushed aside such considerations with airborne fingers. 'I would much rather be in Sligo, Superintendent. Mountains. The smell of turf fires. Springtime in the West of Ireland.'

Codd nodded quickly as if to say we were all victims of circumstances that saw us separated from our natural habitats.

'The Assistant Commissioner and you are both from Monument,' the Minister thrummed. 'Childhood friends.'

'Yes, indeed.'

'And, of course, the Taoiseach himself,' she said.

'It's a very small world when all is said and done,' I said, 'but as children we never realised it.'

Miss Twinkle crossed her legs to show me a firm, unstockinged ankle. 'Tír na n'Óg,' she smiled. 'Do we ever leave that land of our youth, I wonder? Happy the little children, Superintendent. I grew up on a strand, myself and my younger brother. We chased oystercatchers. We swam. Daddy was away, up here, in Cabinet like me now. My mother was always working, working. My brother and I never knew sadness. We played on the strand all day and in the evenings when we came home we turned on the wireless in the kitchen and we danced. We danced.' Miss Twinkle's upper body seemed for a moment to be detached and her arms thrust through the air like the pliant necks of swans.

I looked over at Pax. He had not, in truth, changed much from the Pax of Tír na n'Óg. I could see the Pax Sheehy who wanted first to believe the good in everyone, his endearing trait, which some might mistakenly take for weakness. And yet, although he was the trimmer of the two of us, although his hair and eyebrows were inky and his step the more vigorous, nowadays a weight seemed to sit perpetually on Pax like a morose black cloud on the peak of a mountain, so that for all his outward success in the battle against age, inwardly he was the older. Pax sat, a worn leather briefcase beside his gloves and cap on the adjacent chair, his face attentively composed for his Minister.

Miss Twinkle recrossed her legs: the left ankle for small talk, the right for business.

'Superintendent, you are the man to whom the army and the gardaí now look when they wish weapons to enter the State,' Miss Twinkle throbbed. 'You are therefore the man to educate the Minister for Justice on the safeguards and procedures that currently prevail.'

She sat back, her smile expectant and unwavering, as her personal secretary quietly brought a notepad up ready.

'Your own Department, Minister,' I began, expansively I hoped, 'is of course the ultimate authority in such matters, which is entirely appropriate and universally acknowledged as such.'

Codd's body language – he had gone into a foetus-resembling curl – bespoke siege. Pax listened politely, and Evelyne-Mary concentrated on a detail in the carpet. I wondered as I briefed her, as Miss Twinkle nodded me on, how much alienated in this new job she felt from her grass roots, or if, like a dancer, movement would be everything, the only constant.

I concluded, 'Therefore, where official arms importation is involved, Minister, the concern is to limit knowledge of such importation to those people who need to know about it, and only to those.'

243

'Which presumably limits advance documentation,' Miss Twinkle said.

'Indeed,' I replied. 'Our senior official at the point of entry, our customs Surveyor, is voice-briefed by the gardaí or army as to the imminent arrival of a shipment of arms in his jurisdiction.'

Miss Twinkle nodded and gave Codd a quick glance that may or may not have been a rebuke. I looked Evelyne-Mary's way to unleash her, and she said: 'There are three signatures authorised between us and the army, and they change on an arranged monthly basis. Our Surveyor has copies of such signatures and knows the details of their monthly rotation.'

The Minister looked amused.

'Our Surveyor then independently voice-confirms the signature,' explained Evelyne-Mary. 'A confirming panel of three further names exists, separate to the signatories. The panel is also rotating. Our Surveyor must have it confirmed to him by the correct name on the panel that the signature has been properly applied to the order.'

'The same procedure applies to arms for the gardaí,' I said, and Pax nodded.

'And the Department of Justice?' asked Miss Twinkle.

'The Department's procedures are something of a mirror of what has just been described,' I said.

'Yet their input is in arrears,' said Miss Twinkle. 'After the event. A rubber stamp, in reality. What if there's fog?'

A little silence took hold, the way it had in class years ago when Mr Redden decided to wrong-foot everyone.

'Minister?'

'Fog,' Miss Twinkle boomed. 'The plane's diverted because of fog, from Dublin, say, where your Surveyor has been making his clever telephone calls, verifying and cross-checking his rotating panels, squinting at signatures, and the plane thunders overhead in thick fog and puts down in Bally-go-God-knows-where with a ton of hand grenades. What then? Where's the documentation?'

Codd was nodding furiously as if some basic and neglected truth had been wilfully overlooked.

'There's no documentation in that case,' I said, allowing the Minister's eyes and mine to flirt briefly. 'Air-traffic control in Dublin alerts the AFISO in Bally-go-God-knows-where. AFISO stands for Aerodrome Flight Information Services Officer. The AFISO will only allow the plane to land and unload if someone from customs is present. Therefore, in the example you give, Minister, the grenades remain the sole responsibility of our Surveyor in Bally-go-God-knows-where.'

'Which means no problem exists,' said Miss Twinkle and looked brightly at the other faces around her.

Whether she saw no problem in the round, or if the procedure in fog was her major preoccupation, now put to rest, or whether she had had other, unspoken concerns entirely, in regions sinister or benign, which we had managed to allay, I cannot say, for the Minister for Justice made a graceful half-pirouette in Pax's direction, and paused, her long, upper body leaning forward, her fingers unfurled, the choreography for changing the subject.

'Assistant Commissioner Sheehy and I have been in discussion,' she said.

'Yes.' Pax took his cue and sat forward with his most intensely worried frown. 'The Brits are concerned.'

'Think of how much more concerned they might be were it not for your altogether remarkable achievements, Assistant Commissioner,' purred Miss Twinkle.

'What do you hear?' I asked Pax.

Pax said: 'That surface-to-air missiles could soon be used against troops in Ulster.'

All the faces turned to me, the way people, in a sudden gust of wind, look instinctively to their roofs.

'From our point of view,' I said to Pax, to the Minister, 'our procedures have succeeded in stopping this kind of thing before and I'm confident they'll succeed again.'

Pax nodded, as if to say that's exactly what I've said. Miss Twinkle floated to her feet.

'I love meetings that free people from the need for further meetings,' she hummed and took my hand. 'I also love information that's cool and clear, like mountain air.' Miss Twinkle shut both eyes for half a second and, using me as a lever, increased her height an inch or so, all the better to fill her lungs. 'Whatever kinship we feel to those poor wretches up there – and we *do* feel it – we must let them know that down here we are *civ*ilised people. Lovely to meet you, Superintendent.'

Codd brought Evelyne-Mary, Pax and me to the lift. Its doors first shrank and then erased the Departmental Secretary. We swept down through the air to the warm clatter and bustle of normal life in the street.

'It's quite unusual for a Minister to be that interested in procedures,' I remarked.

'She's different all right,' Pax allowed.

'But why all the detail?' I asked. 'Why 'What about fog?' and all the rest? Is she holding a brief for someone whose need for arms outweighs Miss Twinkle's view of her own responsibilities?'

Pax shot me a look and then dropped a glance in the direction of Evelyne-Mary.

'I thought she was going to kiss you, Theo,' he said with diverting cheerfulness as we walked along the Green.

'You were always the dancer, Pax,' I responded. 'I note she had you in alone first.'

'Ah, she knows you're unattached, Theo,' Pax said, keeping it up. 'I'm no good to her, married with three children. You'll be back in there now on a regular basis, mark my words. Did you see the size of her office? A little gramophone in the corner, I bet. Pull back the chairs. "We danced." '

Evelyne-Mary was enjoying herself hugely at my expense. We went by the ornate door of University Church.

'Listened to any jazz lately?' I asked.

'No, but I heard a good Stan Getz story,' Pax said.

His need to be cheerful had fed upon itself, so that the black cloud had momentarily lifted from the mountain and it was suddenly Pax of the swimming river, Eillne's Pax, standing there in fancy-dress uniform on sunny St Stephen's Green, the world going by in its confusion.

He said: 'One cold winter's night, Hod O'Brien was playing piano at Gregory's in New York. Joe Puma on guitar. Ronnie Markowitz on bass. Only other people in the place are some Japanese tourists. A big limo pulls up outside and Stan Getz emerges with a lady. They come in and have a drink, and after listening for a bit, Stan gets out his horn and sits in. While he's playing, the door opens and this guy with a few too many drinks comes and stands swaying by the door for a minute, listening to the saxophonist. The doorman asks him to leave and as the drunk is going out he looks back over his shoulder and says, "Well, he ain't no Stan Getz".'

Pax shook Evelyne-Mary's hand and made his way up Harcourt Street as we pressed on for the Castle.

' "He ain't no Stan Getz",' I chuckled.

'Who is Stan Getz?' asked Evelyne-Mary.

'Someone who played the saxophone,' I smiled. 'Someone Pax and I grew up with, if you like.'

'From Monument?' my assistant politely asked.

I didn't laugh but I made a mental note to store it away for the next time Pax and I had a swim together.

'No,' I replied. 'By the way, full marks back there, on every score.'

'Thank you,' Evelyne-Mary said and reddened happily.

I put on Stan Getz that evening. 'Early Autumn' cascaded over me, making the muscles in my neck and shoulders yield to it the way they do to water. I thought of Miss Twinkle and, in an odd way, sitting there on my own I found the spinster Minister had her attractions, whatever her preferences might be. She was someone born with a political philosophy intact, fashioned by the choice of her forbears in a civil war and handed down the way red hair is handed down in families, or an ability at games. She had strong ankles. I recalled her remarks about kinship and wondered, when it came to it, how she would define civilisation. Perhaps it was her power that appealed to me, the way she had seized me like an eagle and used me to bring herself up to my eye-level. Perhaps it was the concept of being used.

I wondered about Pax's sharp look in my direction. I would ring him in a few days and we would get together. I went to sleep and had a dream.

I was in a familiar house. I knew its location in the town, the wooden porch outside its front door, and its narrow stairs. The house was not just familiar in that I recognised it from memory; it was familiar from a hundred other similar dreams, like a film set that is dragged out again and again.

247

I climbed the stairs. In a bedroom, in a red-velvet setting, lay a young woman seductively attired.

'What's that smell?' I asked her, sniffing.

'Starch,' she said. 'For the love of heavens, ride me.'

I obliged the young woman, but during our intercourse she changed into an older woman with white hair and quite extraordinarily enormous breasts. They wept milk. I sucked them. The woman wrapped me conscientiously in a skin-kissing, slinky fur wrap and then lay warmly beside me, clutching me to her.

So far this was all standard stuff. The bed began to roll, the woman began to shrink. I began to panic.

In my dream that night I was suddenly standing alone in the carriage of a hurtling train. It was night-time, or at least dark. I was still naked except for my fur. Then I came upon a box in the carriage and upon opening it, found inside a shoulder-mounted, surface-to-air missile, the type you sometimes see on the television news being shown off by guerrilla groups. I looked outside for a target, but it was dark. Hefting the missile from its box anyway, I discovered it was a plastic toy.

Miss Twinkle said, 'For the love of heavens, ride me.'

I was not surprised that Miss Twinkle was on my train, she had been there all along, sitting on the seat in the lotus position. I admired her litheness at her age. I admired her ankles. Accepting her invitation, we lay together and made love about the vibrant regularity of the tracks.

'This is a great breakthrough, Theodore,' Miss Twinkle said.

Thirteen

Sparrow was not so much the person I had always known grown
very old, as a completely different person who might well have
always been the way extreme age now left her. Life for Sparrow
had been in one sense not a gradual progression but a series of
reincarnations, as her final persona as Mrs David Wise attested.

Her skin had become translucent. The shape of her face told of
the skull beneath. It was impossible to think of her as a warm
vessel within which children had hatched. A remorseless shrinking
was afoot as if, like a voyager trapped in frost, she was receding
ever more into her centre until all that would remain penulti-
mately would be the frail pilot light of her eyes.

Sparrow was a wealthy woman. She owned all of CityWise, a
considerable complex of malls and shops and an underground car
park on the site of the old ice rink. Even without David Wise's
inheritance, Sparrow's careful handling of her own and then Uncle
Hugo's legacy from Sammy Tea would have ensured her comfort.
Three nurses attended her round the clock, giving her a daily bath
and feeding her calf's-foot jelly brought out specially every day from
Monument. Sparrow had not left Eillne for over a year. A few
people, such as Bishop O'Dea, made a point of coming to see her.
Mostly she slept, but at invervals, like an old radio receiver, she
would crackle into life and a period of transmission would follow, its
clarity surging through the ether of her mind.

'Sparrow, this is Elizabeth.'

My mother smiled benignly, although the cold scales on her
eyes must have denied her nearly everything but light.

'I'm so pleased to meet you, Mrs Wise,' Elizabeth said. 'I've
heard so much about you.'

'From Theodore.'

'From Theodore, of course. He's very proud of you, let me tell
you.'

'Theodore is impressionable,' said my mother and we all laughed, Sparrow included, although I doubted if the remark had been humorously intended.

'I see you have acquired a tape recorder, Sparrow,' I said, picking up a plastic sleeve from beside her chair. The machine worked by batteries and was small enough to sit in her hand. There was also a packet of tiny cassettes.

'I can't bring myself to use it,' my mother said. 'It's the Bishop's idea. He said I should tell my memories into it – he even showed me how.'

'You should, Sparrow,' I said.

Sparrow looked in Elizabeth's direction. 'I took it to please the Bishop,' she said.

We sat in a semicircle at the double-glazed bay window overlooking the swimming river and its bluebells. The views were indeed as good as those I remembered from the house whose roofless shell still stood within fifty yards.

'You have a wonderful view,' Elizabeth said as through the connecting doors came a woman with a tea tray.

'My father built this house out here when my brother Hugo picked up a disease in Monument,' Sparrow said. 'What is the cake?'

'Carrot cake, ma'am,' said the woman.

'Carrot cake,' said Sparrow to Elizabeth. 'Would you pour, please . . . what is your name?'

'Elizabeth.'

'Elizabeth. He's dead now, Hugo. Sammy Tea is too, of course.' Elizabeth poured fragrantly.

'Sammy Tea died when I was a young girl,' Sparrow said. 'Just dropped dead.' She lifted and dropped her hand with its vivid blue veins. 'He was a lovely man, but he didn't want to live after my mother died.'

'Poor man,' murmured Elizabeth.

'It was he who called me Sparrow,' said Sparrow and trailed off, her milky eyes seeing something for themselves out the window.

It was too late to probe Sparrow about the one question that had always refused an answer, or about any question. Too much time had covered the tracks of unhappiness. Anyway, Sparrow probably did not know the mystery of the headstone; in the end she had been left with Sammy Tea's memory in her clasp, a personal memento.

'This is wonderful tea,' Elizabeth nodded.

'Mazawattee,' I said.

'Rats,' Sparrow said. 'Rats gave Hugo his disease. But he could swim. Bernard taught him.'

'Uncle Bernard was a good swimmer,' I ventured.

Sparrow's mouth went sour for a moment. 'Bernard thought he was good at everything,' she said. 'He was vain.'

'Theo always talks about the swimming river, Mrs Wise,' Elizabeth said. 'I've heard so much about it I'm dying some day to find out how it's different to any other river in the world.'

'Are you a good swimmer?'

'Not as good as Theo is.'

'Theodore is quite a good swimmer, but you must know the swimming river,' Sparrow warned. 'You can't demand of it, you must accept it, and hope it will befriend you. It will if you take the time to learn. It's far too cold to swim today, Theodore. I don't advise it.'

'I agree,' I said, and wondered how many summers had gone by since I had joined the currents.

'Are you married to Theodore?' asked Sparrow. 'What is your name?'

'Elizabeth. I . . .'

'We hope to get married soon, Sparrow,' I said and looked in Elizabeth's direction.

Elizabeth reached for my hand. I was suddenly thrilled because I remembered the last time and with whom a similar show of affection had been made in front of Sparrow.

'But you *are* married, Theodore,' Sparrow said in confusion. 'To . . . to whom?'

'I was married, Sparrow, many years ago, to Juliet,' I said. 'We are no longer married.'

'Juliet,' my mother affirmed. 'A girl came here the other day. Juliet's daughter, a doctor.'

I looked at Elizabeth and shrugged that I had no idea.

'Dr Denny,' said the nurse from the back of the room. 'An English lady who was a locum for young Dr Armstrong last week. She says her mother came from around here.'

'Did she mention her mother?' I asked the nurse.

'No, she never mentioned her,' the nurse replied.

'Juliet's silly brother drowned down there the day Theodore married,' Sparrow told Elizabeth.

'Elizabeth knows,' I said.

'Donald Blood. Always drunk. They're all dead and gone, Reggie Blood included. Imagine, not a Blood in Monument,' Sparrow said.

'Reggie's brother still lives over at Cruachan,' I said.

'He is mad,' Sparrow explained to Elizabeth.

'A hermit,' I said. 'What about the sister, the one in Monument?'

'Reggie always believed she had married beneath her. Who's living in Drossa now, Theodore?' Sparrow asked.

'A German, I believe,' I replied. 'An industrialist.'

'A German industrialist,' Sparrow said to Elizabeth. 'We had such parties in Drossa.'

'You must have wonderful memories, Mrs Wise.'

'I think I had a very happy childhood,' my mother said. 'First in Monument, then out here in Eillne.'

'Which was the happiest of the two?' asked Elizabeth.

Trouble entered my mother's face like a worm. 'Monument, I think,' she replied. 'We were more a family in Monument. My father.'

The nurse with a rather bored look about her came over and sat down. She tried to spoon something into Sparrow's mouth but was dismissed.

'Billy is coming out this evening to see me.'

Elizabeth and I exchanged looks.

'He's the Taoiseach you know,' Sparrow said to Elizabeth.

'Bain, Sparrow,' I said. 'Billy was his father.'

'I know his name, Theodore,' my mother said. She smiled to Elizabeth. 'I never turn on the television at night but I hear Bain. He was in the White House last week, in America. He comes out to Eillne and tells me all his problems.'

'What are his problems?' asked Elizabeth like someone who never took time off.

'Oh, he thinks I don't understand,' Sparrow replied, 'that I'm too old to know what's going on. But I understand everything.

This name and that name. Enemies and friends. Bain tells me them all. Men want to tell their problems to a woman. It's how a woman holds on to a man, remember that.'

Elizabeth smiled. 'I will.'

'That and a proper kitchen,' Sparrow said. She looked around her. 'These girls nowadays can't cook. Nanny Morrissey's apple tarts were as big as cartwheels.'

I said, 'You must eat more, Sparrow.'

'I shall eat when I'm hungry, Theodore,' my mother said.

'Theodore is going to show me all the walks along the river tomorrow,' Elizabeth said.

'Theodore, you must help Bain if you can,' my mother suddenly said.

We sat, a little, silent island.

'Help him in what way, Sparrow?'

I saw in my mother a curious anxiousness.

'In whatever way you can,' Sparrow said. 'In whatever way Bain asks you, Theodore, do you understand?'

'I understand, Sparrow.'

'Now take Juliet for a walk, Theodore,' my mother said.

She closed her eyes and was instantly asleep.

Bain came at six. First a squad car and two guards on bikes, then two long limousines swept in. Bain's arrival was a surprise, even though my mother had said he was coming. She seemed to have developed her own rules as to time present and past, which tempted one to discount her forecasts. I saw Bain from the bay window, pausing for a moment and looking down on the swimming river. He turned and saw me. He waved.

'Your big day,' I said to Elizabeth.

Bain entered the room like an impresario walking on to a stage. The nurse became immediately unbored. The woman from the kitchen put her excited face around the connecting door, then ran back, calling, to the kitchen. Bain knew them all by name. Sparrow sat animated. The crackle of radio static seemed to electrify the air. Suddenly there were men on the gravel and men in the hall. It was as if someone had switched a slow-motion picture to its proper speed.

'Theo, Theo.'

'Good to see you, Bain. This is Elizabeth.'

'Well, you always had taste, Theo.'

'Taoiseach,' Elizabeth said.

Bain was most unsubtle where an attractive woman was involved. He looked Elizabeth up and down appreciatively, the wind from his nostrils making little momentary ridges in the hairs of his moustache.

'I'll have a cup of tea,' he said to no one in particular and we all sat down. 'Isn't herself looking well?' he asked me and nodded in Sparrow's direction.

'As well as ever,' I agreed.

A little pause ensued in which Sparrow could be admired. She was staring at Bain, or, rather, gaping at him with eyes that lacked the hardness of focus. Her mouth was slack. I had seen her look at the television in this way, and I suddenly realised that for Sparrow Bain on the box or in the flesh was the same. She saw not the boy she had once known, but, like the whole country, the image he had created. I inspected him for myself. He had grown extremely broad and only the attentions of a good tailor prevented width making him grotesque. Seemingly unfit, he wheezed a lot. He had taken up smoking again, although this could not dilute the ever salty marinade of his flesh.

'Are you down for a few days?' I enquired of the Taoiseach.

'Not at all,' Bain replied. 'I had to open the new wing of the barracks in Monument today. Grand job, totally refurbished. Cost five million.'

'Good turnout?' I asked.

'The usual. I'll tell you a good one,' he said, more to Elizabeth than to me. 'You've heard of General Hegarty?'

'UN High Command?'

'Correct,' Bain said and gave her a rewarding smile. 'He's old now, but forty years ago, he told me, he was sent out secretly to advise Haile Selassie. Ethiopia. "My problem, General," the Emperor says, "is that these blighters of mine won't stand and fight. They run every time a shot is fired." "I'll tell you what you'll do, Emperor," Hegarty says. "Every time a man runs, you catch him and put him in a tar barrel out in front of the lines where all his comrades can see him. Have no doubt about it, put them in tar barrels and that'll end your desertion, Emperor." '

254

Bain laughed, anticipating the punch.

' "And so, did it work, General?" I asked him. "Not at all," the General said. "The blighters ran out of the tar barrels." '

I could see Elizabeth's eyes shining in a way I thought I owned the rights to.

Bain repeated, ' "The blighters ran out of tar barrels," ' draining the last drop. 'Isn't it grand here?' he said. 'Warm and cosy. The draughts in the old house would have skinned you on a day like this. Bloody old tomb. I hated the place.'

I looked Sparrow's way to see if she might be in anyway troubled by Bain's remarks, and to protect her in the event that she was, but Sparrow just smiled like a little girl whose happiness is beyond the danger of words.

'Has Theo brought you for a swim yet?'

'Not yet, Taoiseach.'

'Oh, you have a treat in store. God bless you,' said the Taoiseach, and took a cup and plate from the kitchen woman. 'You look down there now and you see an old river twisting off down to the delta beyond. A few trout in it, maybe, you think. Not worth putting a boat on – where would you go? Coots and ducks in the reeds, a heron or two, so it has a bit of wildlife as well, you might say.' Bain swallowed cake and gulped tea, then put the cup down and lit a cigarette. 'But Theo knows that river better than anyone. He's like a pagan with it. I'm only joking, but that's what comes to mind. That river and you speak the same language, Theo. No one else knows it.'

'Sparrow knows it,' I said.

'Nah,' Bain said as if my mother wasn't there. 'Not the way you do. *Thought* she knew it.' He rubbed his hands together. 'Is this your first time to Eillne?'

'Unfortunately, yes, Taoiseach.'

'Elizabeth's from Belfast,' I said.

'I know.' Bain laughed, pleased with himself. 'I picked it up from her first word. "Taoiseach". My father was from Belfast,' Bain said to Elizabeth. 'I know the people there. I'm half Ulsterman. Where do you live?'

'In Holywood,' Elizabeth said.

'County Down,' Bain said. 'What do you make of things up there at the moment, Elizabeth?'

255

'They're . . . uneasy,' Elizabeth replied.

'That's for sure,' Bain said. 'But what's going to happen?'

'To what?' Elizabeth asked.

Bain shrugged impatiently. 'To the situation up there,' he said, waving his cigarette around. 'You're living there. What's going to happen?'

'I would hesitate to say,' Elizabeth replied, and blushed as I imagined she might if caught on the wrong foot during official business. 'Particularly to your good self, sir.'

Bain handed his cup into midair and the woman from the kitchen was there with the teapot. He frowned.

'Have we met before?' he asked.

'Once in Dublin and once in London, Taoiseach,' Elizabeth said. 'Anglo-Irish conferences. I work for the Northern Ireland Office.'

'Hah-hah,' Bain said and appraised Elizabeth anew. 'And Theo is showing you the real Ireland, eh?'

I said, 'Elizabeth and I have known each other for years.'

Bain made a face. 'I'll tell you what's going to happen up there, Elizabeth, no offence to you, I hope, but I'll tell you which way the situation will go. As long as the Unionists hold the balance of power in Britain, the Union is secure.' Bain made a flattening chop with his hand. 'No question of it. But as soon as that political situation changes, then Ulster becomes redundant. Seven billion quid a year redundant. And the Unionists know that. You may disagree with me.'

Excess energy flowed from Bain in his movements, the way he spoke and gulped his tea and sucked at his diminishing cigarette.

'I have no opinion, really,' Elizabeth said. 'I do what I'm told.'

'A Unionist has two plans,' Bain hammered on. 'A and B. A is to stay and fight, but if he loses the fight, then plan B comes in, and that's to evacuate. You have to ask yourself, what plans have the people on the Falls? They have no plan B, let me tell you. Their life is plan A: this is our place, it always was, we stay. That's the difference, and it's the crucial one.'

'I saw you on television.'

Sparrow, whose blind gaze had remained fixed on Bain since he came in, was nodding.

'In the White House, in America,' she said.

256

'With the President,' Bain said and smiled as if given inner reassurance. 'I presented him with a bowl of shamrock.'

'Shamrock,' Sparrow said. 'Why ever shamrock?'

'It's the bowl really, not the shamrock,' Bain said. 'They . . . What's the word, Theo? They do something to each other. Explain to her, she doesn't understand.'

'They complement each other,' I said. 'She's not deaf, you know.'

'That's it, they complement each other,' Bain said to Sparrow.

'I hope you were well received,' Sparrow said.

Bain winked at me lewdly. 'I was,' he said, 'and I'll tell you something else. I knew you were watching me. I said to myself, I bet my granny's watching me this minute.'

'On television,' Sparrow said.

'On television,' Bain said. He looked at his watch. 'Fancy a walk, Theo?'

Two men followed at twenty yards as we left by the front door.

'Classy lady you have there, Theo,' Bain said. 'Will you marry her?'

'If she'll marry me,' I replied.

'Do,' Bain said firmly. He stopped at the head of the first flight of terrace steps. 'Can I ask you something personal, Theo?'

'Ask me what you like.'

'The old thing with Juliet. Do you hold it against me?'

I could see the toughness in his eyes as they saw me for what I was worth to him and nothing more, and yet I felt his vulnerability too, as if I had some ability that he lacked and envied.

'I won't ever forget it,' I replied. 'But I don't hold it against you, no. It was a long time ago.'

'If I never told you I was sorry,' said Bain, 'then I want you to know I was and still am. There was nothing much in it, if that's any consolation.'

'It was thirty years ago,' I said. 'I'd hate to be married to Juliet. She was crazy. Maybe you did me a favour. With La as well.'

'With who?'

'With La.'

'Who's La?' asked Bain.

'La Fox,' I said. 'Sparrow wouldn't have her for me, remember? You agreed with Sparrow.'

Bain shook his head in genuine puzzlement. 'I don't remember any La,' he said.

For Bain to disremember a person of such importance caused my perception of the past to be cast in momentary doubt.

I said, 'Anyway, Juliet would never have worked out.'

'Do you mean that?' asked Bain.

'Her daughter is a doctor and came out to see Sparrow last week,' I said in an attempt to get off the subject. 'The nurse told us just before you came.'

'Her daughter,' said Bain reflectively and as we went down the steps I could see calculations sweeping across his face like clouds running before wind.

Sammy Tea's old house presented itself all the more the lower we went. It had about it an air of suffering, like something wounded that begs for its end. Weeds sprouted everywhere, at every level. All the eyes that had watched us down in the swimming river, the windows, were gone, but the door and the white front step remained as if they were unaware of other events and were awaiting a resumption of old ways.

'I think she should have it knocked down,' I said.

'Sparrow? She doesn't even know it's there,' Bain said.

'Sparrow knows exactly what's there, Bain,' I replied. 'She remembers everything.'

Bain looked at me with sudden interest, the way he did when he suddenly saw an advantage he had previously overlooked. Then we wound on downwards. I wondered what he wanted – there was always something, after all. I wondered if the now ancient business with Lyle was still rankling him; I thought about it rarely, but when I did it sometimes clutched my heart most uncomfortably.

Most of the terrace gardens had been left to grass over and many of them already needed cutting. Hedges had grown thin from being too tall. Once there had been stones to mark the sides of paths and each stone had been whitewashed twice a year, but now the paths themselves had gone winters without scuffling and the stones were almost indistinguishable from the earth around them.

'Remember Dalton,' Bain said and shook his head. 'It seems only yesterday Dalton was telling us Germans were coming up the river.'

We reached the bank and stood for a moment, watching the face

258

of the water moving in its own patterns and in a dozen different places, like a great, black beast whose intelligence you dared not doubt. We went upriver. I wore a topcoat, but although Bain's jacket flapped open, leaving only his shirt against the wind, he did not seem to care.

'How did I sound back up in the house?'

I looked at him. 'You sounded fine.'

'Not like a man who thinks he's losing his mind?'

'Of course not.'

'Just goes to show.'

'Are you?'

'Mag's death probably took more out of me than I realise. Her dying was actually a relief. She lived with us up in Brambling the last two years, you know. One morning I got up at six o'clock and found her in the kitchen with a bottle of gin. She was kneeling at a plastic basin, crying. She'd slop gin into a glass, put it on her head, shudder like she was having convulsions, then vomit into the basin.'

Bain stopped and looked over the racing water.

'I took the bottle off her. You wouldn't credit the names she called me. They made her up for her coffin. She looked like a whore.'

Bain glanced over his shoulder; the two men behind us had their hands in the pockets of raincoats. One wore a hat.

'But it's not Mag,' Bain said. 'It's me. Ever since the thing with the mare.'

'You told me.'

'Don't tell anyone this.'

I shook my head.

'I'm always first up in the morning when I'm home on weekends,' Bain said. 'I love the view up the Lyle, up to the mountains. That's why I built the house up there, you know.'

'I know.'

'She was an old pet, almost white. She was brought in every night and let out into the paddock every morning. 'The first thing I saw was the door of the stable open, but the paddock was empty. There are a few stables in a row with a concrete path outside them. I could see something dark in the grooves of the cement. It was blood, Theo.'

From reeds beside us a heron erupted. Bain jumped.

'God,' he wheezed. 'See how quickly that happened? No warning.' He looked back grimly to his two protectors. 'A lot of good they would have been if it had been someone with a gun just there. Bain lit up a shaky cigarette. 'I'm going mad, Theo.'

'You need a rest.'

'I know, I know.' We resumed, almost reluctantly on Bain's part, our progress along the river. 'Anyway, the mare was still alive, that's what made it so bad,' Bain said, tugging on the cigarette. 'I mean, Jesus, think of all the pigs I've stuck over the years. I'm used to blood and carcasses and squealing. This was different. She was still alive. You couldn't tell she'd been almost white, the job they'd done. They'd cut the length of her in little strips, including her head. It was like she was wrapped in a red net. All I could see was this one eye looking at me. She could still see me, Theo.'

'It's an obscenity,' I said.

'It was a message, Theo.' Bain shivered. He threw away the cigarette and put his hands in his pockets, burrowing his head lower as he walked. 'Do you know the grey world, Theo?'

'No.'

'There's the black-and-white world that most people like you live in,' Bain said, 'and there's the grey world. The grey world is whist drives and hops. Poker classics run by priests. Traditional Irish music evenings. "The Men Behind the Wire." Always a rousing bar before the collection. No coins now, lads, remember your comrades. The grey world is commemorations like Deilt, or stone crosses at the side of lonely country roads. It's people bussed down from Derry and South Armagh and from the Falls. It's day trips south of the border, it's standing to attention in remote graveyards with the same faces down the years. Shoulder to shoulder. At Gaelic games and *feis-ceoils*. It's marching to prevent the extradition of young men to England, and marching behind their coffins when they starve themselves to death. The grey world extends into money and business. It's cash funnelled from the United States into bank accounts in Monaghan and Dundalk. It's the faces you see in the Bronx or Boston at the same whist drives and hops and poker classics run by priests and traditional Irish music evenings. Your blood becomes grey blood, Theo.'

260

We had stopped again and Bain was looking at me intently, as if he was wondering whether any process existed whereby our identities could be exchanged.

'You see this river?' he asked. 'Do you remember how hopeless, how completely fucking helpless I was in there?'

He nodded bitterly. We had reached the boundary of Eillne where the river curled back out of sight behind a hill and the path ended. I remembered that near where we stood, during a faraway summer, Bain had once lain in reeds and looked at me with the same quality of pleading in his eyes.

'Do you know how people kill in Ireland?' he asked quietly.

'What do you mean?' I asked.

'I remember the reports from the time I was Minister for Justice,' Bain said. 'Reports dealing with assassination. Entry and exit wounds. Millimetres. The time of death. Quantities and types of explosives. Urea mixed with icing sugar. It was that simple. Do you know how men and women do it? How they can kill in cold blood?'

I shook my head.

'They come from outside the target's area,' Bain replied. 'They travel. They come down from Cookstown to do jobs in Craigavon. People in Fermanagh are murdered by people from Coleraine. Strangers to each other. A man in Omagh means nothing to a man from Ballymena. They kill on Sundays. Look at the statistics. They travel on Sundays so they won't be missed from work.'

He rubbed his hands diligently, the busy butcher.

'Ask yourself, Theo, how far did the blade travel that carved up the grey mare? I can't sleep any more. I wake up in sweats. Pa used to talk about men losing their nerve, losing control of their water. Now I know what he meant. I sometimes feel like getting drunk, but I hate drink.'

Part of me felt sorry for him, but another part was asking, why me? Why have I been chosen to hear all this? It was a question I preferred not to answer. Bain's lips were quivering.

'I take a pill to make me sleep,' he whispered, 'but I'm afraid of going to sleep, because I know what's going to happen, Theo. I'm going to have a nightmare and it's always the same. I'm stuck to the ground with blood and the grey mare's eye is staring at me as if I'd just murdered one of my own children.'

261

*

That was the first weekend in April. Bain went straight off to Dublin when our walk was finished and Elizabeth and I spent the night in Eillne. The next day I brought Elizabeth down to the river. It was still too cold for us to swim, although I had often swum in April, but nevertheless I explained as best I could how the river worked, pointing out the crucial currents – mere sighs in the overall narrative, yet clues to the fiercest twists – and the world that existed beyond the bend, the vast world of the river delta. Because they had yet to bloom, the flowers along the river could only be described, but I tried, using love as my pollen, to bring them as alive in scent and colour for Elizabeth as if we had been there on a day in summer. Bog orchids with their tiny green bulbils. Lady's- tresses that once I had believed had come from the hair of a drowned lady. Redcurrant and bedstraw; woodruff, mallow and devil's bit.

That morning Sparrow sat in her wheelchair overlooking the swimming river, scrawling a letter in the morning sun to Jack O'Dea, the Bishop of Monument. She wanted a side window put into the cathedral for David Wise.

'There's a wing of a hospital in Tel Aviv called the Wise Wing,' she said. 'I'll never see it, of course. But I think there should also be something here in Monument.'

Sparrow wore a pink blouse beneath a white woollen cardigan. She must only have been able to see the outline of the writing pad and wrote each word with great deliberation. I kissed her goodbye. She was cold.

'Look after Theodore, dear,' she said to Elizabeth.

Elizabeth was enchanted with Sparrow. She talked about no one else all the way to Dublin.

On the first of May for many years Pax and I had entered the sea together at the Forty-foot. It had been a ritual governed by the date and nothing more: we had swum on May Days on which there had been sleet and equally on days when afterwards we could dry off on the baking rocks. We had, however, missed two years. Once Pax was in the United States, and the year before I had been in the old Soviet Union, tutoring emerging governments on how to

262

impoverish their people. But that last April of my freedom, with two days to go before the month changed, Pax rang me to revive our May Day expedition.

We swam for half an hour in sharp temperatures that were forgiven by hot sun. The sea was viscous compared with the swimming river. It was also impersonal because of its expanse; there were no private corners or hidden currents to contend with, just a limitless green swell. We swam back in together and rode on the upward surge, gaining the rocks before the drag could suck us back.

We were both nearing sixty. We were both tall, well-made men with all our hair, but Pax had never allowed his body an inch of middle age; he had kept it relentlessly fit and his regime could be seen in the tone of the long muscles in his legs and the stark width of his shoulders that gave him the gaunt look of a Roman cross.

'So, what *do* you think of our Minister for Justice?' I asked as we sat on towels.

We picked up conversations like that, as only old friends can.

'She's a lady who will have her way,' said Pax, his fatal disposition intact.

'Which is?'

'Tell me your impression,' Pax said.

I trusted no one more than I trusted Pax, which means I trusted no one completely. In my genesis as Theodore Shortcourse were the seeds that made complete trust impossible.

'I wonder what was really on her mind last month,' I replied. 'All this attention to detail about arms importation. What's her real interest?'

'She's the Minister,' Pax said. 'She has a right to know, apart from a duty.'

'She's died-in-the-wool republican,' I said.

'That's permissible,' said Pax.

'Her constituency is the border,' I said. 'Let's be honest, the present situation in the North is hurting her people. They badly need arms – her people. So, she has to know all about procedures in case they ask her.'

Pax sighed. He was boy and man at the same time, a seedling that had crept up into a big, leafy tree.

'Do you want to know something?' he asked. He prodded his

263

chest, the head of his stomach, just below the pediment of his ribcage. 'There's a little, hard ball that's right there nowadays and it won't go away. I should have retired last year. I should be taking my grandchildren on hikes through the Deilt Mountains. But what am I at instead? Sitting in an office surrounded by files. Master files and subfiles. Files of press cuttings and photographs. Of sound tapes and video tapes. Of the records of interviews. Of the transcripts of court hearings. Of confidential reports. Of faxes and internal memoranda. Of legal opinions. Of the opinions of chief superintendents.'

Poor Pax, I thought. The keeper of last principle for us all.

'People have given me credit for all the arms finds,' Pax went on. 'I have even been described as a hero. Do you want to know how I really feel? Tired. Reduced. I feel a terrible inevitability hanging over my life like a day that refuses to lift. I can see everything utterly clearly, but, like a fly on a window, I can't change or even become a part of what I see. You see, I know too much, Theo. That's cruel, to know too much.'

I had often envied Pax his wife and children and now grand-children. His neat house and sense of order. The way he saw everything clearly defined and read his compass without confusion.

'Why don't you retire?' I asked.

'That's what . . . would be liked,' Pax replied, so that I knew he wanted to say but couldn't: 'That's what Bain would like.'

'Are you under pressure?'

He nodded.

'To retire?'

'The whole time.'

'But you won't retire as long as Bain has his hands on the levers of power,' I said, understanding. 'You don't trust what will happen.'

'No comment,' said Pax defiantly.

'And Miss Twinkle is your only ally, she's the only person standing between you and Bain's camp, which wants you gone,' I concluded.

'No comment,' said Pax again.

I laughed. 'And there was me thinking Miss Twinkle was on the other side. I thought she was trying to find a way to get guns in for some of her constituents.'

Pax shook his head and arranged the towel over his shoulders. I could feel the granite between my toes and smell the salt smell of the bay.

'You beat me to it,' he said.

'I did?'

'I was going to ask you when you are going to retire.'

'I have a few years left to make up my mind.'

'But you're in the zone. You could go now if you wanted.'

'Yes, if I wanted.'

'I envy you, Theo. If I were you I'd retire tomorrow. I'd go back down to Eillne and work on the gardens. Maybe restore the old house. Money is no problem to you. Your mother is still in good health. Not many people get the opportunity to look after a parent like that.'

'I'd moult,' I said.

'Buy a horse and trap,' Pax said. 'Get away from all this pollution. You have a set-up down there that people would pay millions for. All the shops you want in Monument and the best library outside Dublin. I'd be there like a shot.'

'I'd feel I was hanging on, just for the sake of it,' I said. 'I have no family. I'd be the last link in a chain started more than a hundred years ago. I don't like that feeling.'

'You're crazy.'

'Maybe. But I've stated my case in Eillne. The swimming river and I know everything about each other there is to know. We have said to each other everything there is to say. Now it's time to move on. There's a new century coming soon. The swimming river needs a new partner to teach and learn from. That's how life goes.'

'That doesn't mean you can't retire.'

'Of course not. I'm looking forward to it in a few years,' I said. 'Not on my own, either, let me say.'

That was Pax's cue to come out bubbling for my happiness, but instead it was if he had planned a set piece that had not worked as he had intended. The price for Pax's integrity had always been the transparency of his purpose. Now, as he dressed, his mood plunged, either because I had not agreed to retire immediately and go and live in Eillne as suggested, or perhaps because he knew

I had just referred to Elizabeth, his sudden taciturnity was a signal of his long-standing reserve concerning that relationship.

'Have you time for a drink?' I asked. 'You'll have to pass my flat to get home.'

'Thanks, Theo,' Pax said and shook his head. He filled his big chest with sea air and let it out aggressively. 'When did we last swim here?' he asked.

'Two years ago?'

'Two years ago.' Pax nodded like an old man whose world is reduced to the confines of his immediate surroundings. 'If two years ago someone had told us that in two years' time Bain Cross would be Taoiseach, what would you have said?'

'That it couldn't happen,' I said, glad that at least in an oblique way we had reached the ground that for the past hour we had been avoiding.

'But it has,' Pax said.

'Is that why I should retire, Pax?'

'Just be careful, Theo.'

He dropped me off on my road along the sea. Pax believed positively in nothing any more. He had drained the last drop from the concepts that had kept him going for all these years and now, dry and treacherous as columns of sand, they were a-crumble. To continue he needed a spiritual apparatus, and that he lacked.

I waved him off. It was Pax who should retire, I thought, not me. Pax was the one who really wanted to go back to Eillne.

I had no intention of retiring. You might think that as sixty loomed, like an old apple gently going off with age, I was ready for the shelf. Nothing could have been less true. I had never enjoyed life as much or as fully. I was the intellectual master of my brief and widely respected as such. I could outwalk and outswim men half my age and the physical intimacy I enjoyed with Elizabeth – the mutual satisfaction it engendered – showed my past stumblings for what they were and gave the present a meaning that made each day's dawn an event designed for my personal relish.

A week after my ocean dip Bain rang me at work. It was a call I might, but for other reasons, have forgotten.

'I want to apologise,' he said.

'For what?'

266

'For whining when we met in Eillne. I was depressed.'

'We all get like that, there's nothing to be sorry about.'

'I was talking rot. Pure rubbish. Maybe, unconsciously, it was Mag's death.'

'I'm sure it was.'

'I'm getting on well. There's no pressure, and if there is, I can handle it.'

'Good, Bain.'

'All that business about dreams, I'd prefer it if you forgot all that, Theo.'

'I already have. Forgotten.'

'You didn't tell anybody? I mean, you didn't let anybody know the state I'd let myself get into?'

'No. It was between the two of us.'

'Good, good, that's good, Theo. You don't mind me calling you like this?'

'I'm glad you're over it.'

'So am I, let me tell you. We must get together again. When I'm free I'll call you.'

I actually then considered myself the luckier of the three boys who had smoked Woodbines in Leire: luckier than Pax because I had been spared the burden of his moral crusade, luckier than Bain because I had not inherited the burden of history. My feelings were a measure of the extent of my happiness, but they also dazzled me and left me otherwise blind.

Jack O'Dea, Bishop of Monument, lived a life in the style of his countless predecessors, which is to say, his only remaining goals lay in spheres metaphysical since those temporal had long been taken for granted. Thus, as well as a palace, so-called, in Monument, Jack enjoyed a penthouse flat in Ballsbridge and an apartment in Rome. It was at the Ballsbridge location that on the last weekend in May Elizabeth and I were invited to dine.

My association with Elizabeth was well known to Jack and it suited the liberal and, to an extent, the Christian streak in him not to impose his views concerning the essentially adulterous state of affairs in which I was firmly embroiled. Politically, of course, it would have been out of the question for Jack to have entertained us in Monument, where his image of traditional shepherd with

267

adoring flock had made his reign an episcopal success, and where men did not go out with women who were otherwise married. In Dublin, however, Jack was much more the cosmopolitan.

The Bishop's flat was perched in a new development built for princes of industry as well as of churches. I spoke into an intercom and we entered a hollowed-out building with a glass lift shaft. The world yearned for atriums. Elizabeth and I soared four floors like astronauts. Jack, who eschewed rings and crosses and favoured grey suits, awaited outside his door.

'Theo, I'm so pleased. And you must be Elizabeth,' he said.

Jack had succumbed to the clerical fault of caressing with his left hand what his right had already rendered defenceless.

'Your lordship,' Elizabeth said.

'To Theo's friends I'm Jack O'Dea,' said the Bishop, patting. He added, 'Another "d" and I'm dead.'

The demands of office had not blunted Jack's boyish edge. He led us with little, springy steps in to a very large sitting room with Dublin lying at its feet. He pivoted so that his back was to the window.

'Theo and Elizabeth, this is Joyce Ogar,' he beamed.

A large woman with the face of a doll was staring up at us. In a tent-like patchwork dress and plaid shawl, with dramatic eye-shadow and hair flattened to her skull by a scarf before it spewed out in a torrent on her shoulders, she resembled a fairground fortune-teller, but twenty years before she could have been a Romany princess.

'Pleaure,' she said.

Jack fussed over drinks and olives and sat in an upright, throne-like chair to one side of Joyce.

'Anything you say tonight, Theo, may be taken down and published in evidence against you,' said Jack cheerfully. 'To Theo and Elizabeth, their first visit here. Health and happiness. Hmmmm.'

As Jack quizzed Elizabeth about herself and about Belfast, and as Elizabeth acquainted Jack with her views on current affairs, which meant the North, I watched Joyce Ogar, the lady journalist. I liked her bigness. Although gone to fat, it was obvious she had taken pleasure in doing so, and when you realised that you also understood that pleasure for her would be a dam-bursting affair.

Voluptuous is not a word that sits easily on a woman in the presence of a bishop, but it was nonetheless the one that came to mind.

'All we can do is pray,' Jack said, presumably about the North of Ireland. Looking beyond us to where a girl in her twenties had appeared in an apron, he said, 'Ah, I think the young lady is ready for us.'

We began with smoked salmon, the real, sea creature, tweezered of every tiny bone.

'Has anyone heard about this new play at the Gate?' Jack asked. 'A new lad, name of Walton or Wallace, silly of me not to remember. Waller perhaps. Extraordinary. About Muslims, God bless them, in Dublin. In Dublin.'

'I haven't been to a play in years,' Elizabeth said.

'I don't see what's extraordinary about it,' Joyce said. 'I don't see why God shouldn't bless the Muslims any more than he blesses us.'

Although this was the woman of whom dark things had been said in heterosexually intact Ireland, especially about her relationship with Miss Twinkle, the chemicals I discerned across the table were all of the basic man–woman variety. That Joyce might take her pleasures where they arose and without regard to convention added spice to her undoubted attraction. She looked up and rewarded my instincts with a smile.

'Their poor women,' Jack winced, still on Muslims. He held aloft for visual inspection the proffered wine; he sniffed, sipped, allowed a millisecond for an informed decision, nodded. 'A religion that so mistreats its women . . .'

'Like your own Church did in the past, Jack,' Joyce suggested.

I had to confront the fact that as much as Elizabeth's diminutiveness had made me a slave to her perfection, the pull I felt in the presence of well-endowed women was something that would always reside in the marrow of my bones.

Jack smiled. 'We can't live in the past.'

'Islam isn't the dark place that, forgive me, your Church has led us to believe, Jack,' said Joyce. 'The play, by the way, is by Jonathan Waldegreve.'

'Ah, an Englishman,' said Jack, as if that explained it.

'No,' said Joyce. 'He's as native as bog oak. Before this he spent five years translating Proust into Irish.'

269

To have Joyce sit on me – which was the sudden, shameful image I was indulging – to sweat on me, in fact, would, I knew, be a festival of the senses sharpened by the weighty if remote existence of danger.

'*Swann in Love*,' I said. 'What's the Irish for swan, Jack?'

'*Eala*,' Jack beamed. 'But it wouldn't be the same thing . . .'

'I love "*Eala*",' said Elizabeth.

The quarter-hours were marked from the sideboard by a reproduction carriage clock. Soup came.

'Are you a Proust fan?' I asked Joyce.

'I have the video,' Joyce said and looked at me with mild interest.

'Ahhh,' said Jack, dabbing his mouth. He looked for the young lady. 'That soup's the grandest. Cauliflower, is it?'

'Fennel, Your Lordship.'

'Fennel.' Jack smiled and nodded at all of us as if to say, how the world had changed.

The image of Joyce's breasts, which must needs overhang my fantasy position like soft, weeping vats, coaxed my foot across to rest insouciantly against her (unretracted) ankle. After our toil I would arrange animal pelts on the rounded bluffs of her naked shoulders. I saw Elizabeth looking at me.

'Are you political?' Joyce asked and made me feel the press of the soft bone in her ankle.

'I have never voted in my life,' I replied with a cavalier smile.

'You're Bain Cross's cousin.'

'His uncle, technically.'

Joyce worked her foot bone in little, roundy motions. This seemed to say that every square inch of her territory, like an oil-rich desert, would yield handsome dividends.

'Even better,' said Joyce for some reason.

'Are you talking about Bain?' asked Elizabeth.

I nodded. Joyce had loosened a scarf at her throat, revealing entire bays of flesh.

'I met Bain when Theo brought me down to Eillne a few weeks ago,' said Elizabeth brightly, saying 'Bain' as if she had knocked around with him for years.

'Oh?' said Jack. 'For the first time?'

'Socially, yes.'

270

Joyce had brought her right foot into play, and had slipped her shoe from it. Her bunching toes pinched the hair on my calf whilst above table her face maintained a look of intent enquiry.

'What were your *pre*conceptions of Bain?' asked Jack of Elizabeth, and gave me a little, knowing wink.

'Not tremendously impressed,' Elizabeth said.

'But . . . then?'

'Bain has very strong views,' Elizabeth replied carefully. She made a little show of making her mind up, then she looked at me with a touch of defiance. 'Quite attractive, I should think, if you're into raw power. Also an element of hesitation. Perhaps because he didn't know me. That hesitation, strangely, is attractive too.'

'Interesting,' Jack said.

'You didn't tell me that at the time,' I remarked to Elizabeth as Joyce reached the back of my knee.

'Darling, a woman doesn't blurt out her feelings on the spot,' Elizabeth replied.

'What about all the years you people looked on him as a gun-runner?' enquired Joyce sweetly of Elizabeth, gouging.

'I find that makes him somehow more rather than less attractive,' Elizabeth replied.

'An interesting slant on policy,' Joyce observed to me.

'My goodness me,' Jack said and laughed. ' "God has chosen the foolish things of the world to confound the wise." Corinthians. Ah, fish.'

'Monkfish, Your Lordship.'

'You see, Theo? I didn't forget your fish,' said Jack.

Garlic rose tantalisingly in little wafts. Elizabeth's interest in Bain had always arisen in the unspoken context of her profession. Women *wanted* such a man, I realised; they wanted the weight of power on them, brutish and uncompromising. As the sudden chill of Bain's shadow crossed my relationship with Elizabeth, my arousal for Joyce shrank, which, of course, was what Elizabeth had intended.

'There is a rumour that the subversives have been active recently in arms-purchasing in the old Eastern bloc,' Joyce said to me as I took my limbs back out of range.

Stripped of desire, her face now appeared cute where before it had seemed lascivious.

271

'Really?'

'That's my information.'

'Another exclusive, Joyce?' asked Jack with the air of someone who likes to be in on things in advance.

'Hopefully,' Joyce replied. She gave me a curious look. 'It depends on how exclusive my information is.'

'I bet Theo here knows more than all of us put together,' said Jack, not helpfully.

'I'm sure he does,' Joyce said. 'My information is that this current effort has the support of certain elements in the Government.'

'I can assure you, even if that were true, I'd be the last to know,' I chortled.

'We mustn't embarrass Theo,' said Jack.

'Any names in these rumours?' asked Elizabeth mildly of Joyce.

'They're exclusive, dear, remember?' Joyce said.

'Now, Joyce,' said Jack cheerfully and wagged his finger. 'It's well known who you'd like to see in office in Merrion Street.'

Joyce looked at me and rolled her eyes. A telephone rang. The young woman approached Jack's shoulder and whispered.

'Excuse me,' Jack said, getting up. 'I won't be a minute.'

I was drawn to the view of the city from Jack's picture window. The vastness of light that represented so many people, and so much power, made me suddenly envious of Bain in a way I had never felt before. More than a century had passed since Sammy Tea had come up the Lyle and now his descendant ruled the whole country. The ladies, I became aware, were staring. I followed their eyes. Jack was standing in the middle of the room. He seemed perplexed.

'We must watch the nine o'clock news,' he whispered, speaking as if angels were falling from the sky behind him.

An image grew from the television screen. Bain's face. It was as if he had been there the whole time, listening.

The newsreader said: 'An Taoiseach Bain Cross is tonight fighting for his life following a car accident in Brussels.'

Fourteen

Sparrow rang me after each news bulletin. Although I knew no more than she did, she assumed otherwise. I dissuaded her from travelling to Dublin for a Mass in the Pro-Cathedral presided over by Bishop O'Dea. Joyce Ogar must have rung my office half a dozen times; Evelyne-Mary was told to report me unavailable. Although I did not personally attend Jack's Mass, twenty thousand others did, filling the streets for half a mile and following the prayers relayed outside on loudspeakers.

After a week in Brussels on the lip of life, Bain began to rally. The nature of the injuries to his head, the photograph of his car whose tyre had blown out going through an underpass, and the pictures of Aggie, Bain's wife, and his sons had consistently been on the front page of every day's newspapers and the first item on television bulletins. A poll by a national newspaper reported that should a general election now be held, Bain's party would win a seat wherever it fielded a candidate. Following the poll, Miss Twinkle, widely perceived as Bain's main rival, went on television and said that contrary to malicious rumours she would serve Bain Cross as long as he honoured her to do so. Bain was a true hero for Ireland, Miss Twinkle said to camera, fighting back a tear as bravely as any man. Perhaps, someone said, these developments had been whispered to the Taoiseach and the news had pulled him back from the brink. I had no doubt about it. Sparrow rang me to say that Aggie had come home from Brussels to Dublin. I took a taxi to Rathgar.

I had not been to the flat in nearly twenty years, not since, ominously, the time with Lyle. There was a young guard on duty. He spoke on the intercom, then punched a code into a keypad on the door, the soft tip of his gloved finger giving way as it carefully depressed four successive digits.

I knew Aggie Cross only from occasions such as funerals, and her three sons, the youngest of whom was with her when I arrived, I knew not at all. Aggie was squarely and strappingly built, an uncomplicated-looking woman except for her eyes, which were the colour of limes. An air of acceptance sat about her.

'Brendan, get your Uncle Theodore a cup of tea,' Aggie said to her lad of sixteen, unaccountably tall and thin as a clothesline.

'How is Bain?' I asked.

'He's all right now, thanks be to God, Theodore,' she said with the familiarity of crisis.

'He was lucky.'

'The Blessed Virgin and no one else saved him,' Aggie told me.

'The country is behind him as never before,' I said.

'I wouldn't like to depend on that for long,' said Aggie with commendable wisdom.

My tea arrived, some of it in the saucer. Brendan had a foxy look about him. He had extremely long hands, like those of a basketball player.

'What exactly happened?' I asked Aggie.

'The tyre of his car blew out, Theodore.'

'The government car.'

'The government car,' said Aggie grimly. 'From the Irish Embassy in Brussels. The driver is dead. The poor ambassador will be in a wheelchair the rest of his life, God help him.'

'They hit the wall of an underpass.'

'They scraped along it for a hundred yards,' Aggie said.

'Four people in the car.'

Aggie looked at me. 'As far as I know, Theodore.'

She was the type of woman whose innocence about the darker side of life was her greatest asset.

'Bain mentioned that awful business you had with the horse,' I ventured.

'Oh!' said Aggie and covered her face.

'Who did it?'

'Punks, Theodore,' Aggie said firmly, recovering herself. 'Bain said it was punks.'

'Mammy, I'm going to get a video,' said Brendan. 'How do I get back in?'

Aggie told him the numbers and he loped off like a wolf in search of food.

274

'I don't know how people live in these places,' Aggie said.

I sat with her for half an hour. We talked about Monument, where she was happy, and about Sparrow, whom she admired, and about the family she had joined when she married Bain. I liked Aggie. She was far better than someone like Bain deserved and would spend her life being unappreciated. At six o'clock after the Angelus on television came the news. Aggie blessed herself and turned the volume up and we sat watching as Joyce Ogar's intense face filled the screen.

'What I am saying in tomorrow's article is that there are a lot of things the public is not being told,' Joyce said to camera. 'What I am saying is, this was no accident. There has been a massive cover-up by everyone concerned. Why? What really happened in Brussels that morning? If the Taoiseach has enemies, then these are also enemies of the State and we as citizens of the State have a right to know who our enemies are.'

'Are you saying this was an attempt to assassinate the Taoiseach by persons unknown?'

'I am saying, we have a right to know what's going on.'

'That was journalist Joyce Ogar talking earlier to . . .'

Aggie turned, her hand to her mouth. Her eyes were so green, you wondered if they had somehow been contrived.

'Is everything going to be all right with Bain, Theodore?' she asked me.

The buzzer sounded from downstairs.

'Is it, Theodore?'

'What are the numbers, Mammy?'

Aggie spoke the code for the door into the telephone, but she kept watching for my answer.

'I'm sure it is, Aggie,' I said. 'Yes, I'm sure.'

Elizabeth did not usually stay down in midweek for more than an overnight.

'I have the urge to be wifely,' she said, kicking off her shoes. 'Give me your sewing, Theo.'

Sometimes our love was a mad, irresponsible sea; sometimes, like that night, it would be a deep but barely stirring pool.

I asked, 'Did you see Joyce Ogar on TV?'

'No. But I read her article.'

275

'And?'

In a kimono I had given her for Christmas, with glasses on her nose, Elizabeth began sewing a button onto the jacket of a suit.

'She's right. The tyre didn't blow out,' Elizabeth said, eyes on her sewing.

'It didn't?'

'It wasn't an accident, Theo.'

'So what happened?'

'The tyres were shot out as his car went into the underpass.'

'By whom?'

'By a man on the back of a high-speed motor bike.'

'How do you know?' I asked. 'What do you and Joyce Ogar know that the world doesn't?'

Elizabeth made brisk jabs with the needle and sharply tightened the thread. Then she looked up at me, letting loose the full-grained texture of her irises.

'It was a totally professional operation. The underpass was not on the approved route between the Irish Embassy and the European Commission. There are two regular drivers attached to your embassy in Brussels. Both called in sick the morning of the accident. The substitute driver was a Turk with a history of drug abuse. He was paid a thousand pounds to drive that morning.'

I had the sudden feeling that I was the only one not in on this business.

'Both the regular drivers revealed to the Irish Special Branch that they and their families were intimidated the night before,' Elizabeth continued. 'By men with Belfast accents. In both cases, the first names of the drivers' wives and children were known to these men. The implications were obvious: we know everything about you, including the way to hurt you most. Classic IRA.'

'The IRA always claim responsibility for such acts,' I said.

'I know, Theo,' Elizabeth said calmly. 'But it was still the IRA.'

'The Irish Government has said nothing,' I said.

Elizabeth shrugged.

As if being irritated might keep reality at bay, I said, 'I don't believe this. It's too . . . predictable.'

Elizabeth finished her job. She put down the jacket and wrapped the needle and thread in a little pouch. The luminous rounds of her knees begged for my attention.

'Would you carry me to bed, Theo?' she asked quietly.

'I mean, why does there always have to be a deeper truth than truth itself?' I asked her, now in my arms. 'Why can't Hitler be allowed to have shot himself in the temple, or Kennedy have been shot by a man acting alone? All this other stuff is just an industry.'

Light in a single spear fell across the bed. From way out at sea the last tremor from a ship's foghorn made it to the window.

'What's going to happen?' I asked quietly.

'I don't know,' Elizabeth replied.

'Will they try again?'

'It depends on him.'

'In what way?'

'It depends on whether Bain now decides to help them or not, now that he's been warned,' Elizabeth said. 'How deeply has he been shaken? Who knows.'

'He's suddenly much more popular,' I said. 'There's been a closing of ranks.'

'That may help the paramilitaries.'

'In what way?'

'Now *their* man is completely in the driving seat, or so they may think.'

'Their man?'

Elizabeth nodded.

'How might that affect matters?' I asked.

'Take people like Pax Sheehy,' Eilzabeth said. 'He's hated by the republicans, understandably, since he's had his foot on their throat for twenty years. In some ways, people like Pax stand between you lot and anarchy. But Bain and his like *hate* Pax. He's too strong. They want him out and have done everything they can to achieve their aim.'

'But Miss Twinkle's a zealot when it comes to the law and arms,' I said with understanding. 'She was on Pax's side.'

'Exactly. Was,' Elizabeth agreed. 'But Miss Twinkle is a politician and it's always a mistake to think that politicians do anything for other than political reasons. She's now come behind Bain a hundred per cent. Pax is finished. And those like him.'

I knew Pax knew this too. Pax would go into retirement and feel a sense of failure until the day he died.

'Why are you telling me all this?' I asked.

277

'Because anyone close to Bain is at risk,' Elizabeth said. 'Because you are and always have been close to Bain. Because I love you too much not to tell you.'

'I owe Bain nothing,' I said. 'He has no hold on me.'

'I know that, Theo.'

'I don't think you do,' I said. 'I think you believe the opposite.' I sat and caught both our hands. She was blinking. 'You and I have always managed on our own up to this. Elizabeth! Tell me none of this matters to us. Tell me!'

'It doesn't matter to us, Theo,' Elizabeth sniffed.

'Say, "Bain can't make you do anything you don't want to do." '

'Bain can't make you do anything you don't want to do,' Elizabeth said. 'Now, make love to me, Theo. Please.'

Across the hill leading to the inpatients' block of the Blackrock Clinic had been thrown up aluminium crash barriers. An outside broadcast unit stamped their feet in litter mulch, awaiting to update the nation.

'Theo Shortcourse to see the Taoiseach,' I said.

The young guard retreated a pace and spoke into a hand-held device. That morning the call had come to my office. I almost rang Elizabeth in Sandymount to tell her. Almost. But then the old feeling whereby Bain caused my judgement in everything to be suspended reasserted itself as easily as if he had just called me from one of the terraces in Eillne or from behind a rock in Leire.

My name was hurled in static from the guard's walkie-talkie. The barrier was pulled back.

In a stand of bare trees, perhaps believing himself to be inconspicuous, I saw a Special Branch man, and on the roof of the building I was approaching, outlined bleakly against the sky, one of his colleagues. The lobby housed a water garden. At a makeshift desk my name was written into a three-and-one system and a sticky-backed name tag issued. Twenty men on the ground, minimum, I estimated. I was assigned a big, youngish-faced lad and we boarded a lift designed for stretchers.

'I'd say it's cold outside,' my escort politely said.

'You're better in here than on the roof,' I remarked.

His small eyes suggested he might smile, but he looked away instead. The lift doors opened on a man exhaling smoke and facing

278

the lift with a Uzi in the ready position. Nervous. Done in browns, the corridor smelt correctly of hospitals. Ten yards on, two more Special Branch men stood silently aside as out a door walked the Bishop of Monument.

'Theo.'

'How is he, Jack?'

Jack blew out his cheeks. 'He came close, Theo.'

'Too close,' I said.

'Death is like a dark continent, you see,' Jack said. 'Bain has sailed the waters off its shore.'

'But he's all right now.'

' "Death hath no more dominion over him", Romans. But listen to him, Theo. Hear him out,' Jack said and looked at his watch. 'Goodness, is that the time? Hear him out, Theo. He needs you now,' he said and hurried off at a trot.

Two young nurses were hauling Bain from the pit of a bed. At my appearance he started.

'. . . Theo. God . . .'

White, beret-like bandages together with vivid eye bruises gave him a beaten boxer's look. Tubes from an upturned pouch and from a machine with dials led to his arm and chest.

'There you are, Taoiseach. OK?' asked a nurse.

'Give me . . . some of . . .'

Bain swallowed jerkily, then faded back, a nurse dabbing at orange dribble. His mouth was that perfect triangle, small and inverted beneath his – I almost said moustache, but his moustache was gone.

'Theo . . .' Bain was gasping and held up an arm for me to squeeze. 'Let me get my breath back.'

Smoothing and settling, the nurses pecked. On a trolley scrambled eggs and toast lay untouched. I suddenly realised his front teeth were gone too, making him look like an enormous infant.

'. . . no visitors,' Bain whispered as a nurse arranged the call bell over his shoulder. 'Do you know who just telephoned? Sparrow. God, she's some woman, Theo. Wanted to be driven up to Dublin there and then.'

'What did you say?'

'I told her I wasn't that bad,' Bain said. 'To stay put. She's too old to make that journey. Sit down, Theo.'

279

'I got your message this morning,' I said. 'I had assumed you'd have callers enough.'

'I just want my family,' Bain heaved. 'If they let the Dáil sit out there in the corridor, it would. Everyone wants me.'

'The country wants you,' I said. 'It needs you.'

'I know that, Theo,' Bain said.

Despite his circumstances, despite the fact that he could speak in no more than a whisper, he provoked in me that quiver of exhilaration I still valued more than I would ever admit.

'We were going from the embassy to the Commission, half three in the afternoon. Myself and Sharkey,' said Bain.

Tom Sharkey, the Irish permanent representative in Brussels.

'A big Merc, thank God. We're flying along through a tunnel. The next thing we're out of control, all I can see is a wall coming for me.' He blinked. 'It was a sign from God, Theo.'

'A sign?'

'I had an extraordinary experience. I just told Jack. They rushed me to an operating theatre. I could see myself down there, from a great height. My scalp was shaved pink and marked in blue the way you mark bacon. You know what I mean, Theo. You know.'

It pained him to breathe. Bandages for his broken ribs augmented his girth.

'The surgeon took out a little silver drill and went in through my head, same as you'd drill a hole in the wall. I saw everything. I knew if they didn't drain the fluid off my brain I was gone. Two inches from the first hole he drilled a second. I suddenly felt this happiness, Theo. It was as if I was at the gates and the man upstairs said, "This fellow can't come in yet, there are people down there who *need* this fellow." '

Bain struggled up on his elbow and checked towards the door. Out the window, across my line of vision, walked a man over a flat rooftop, a tinted sun perched behind him.

'I thought, Jesus, how many people get it put to them like that? I said to myself, I'm being sent back to do something for our people.'

A nurse appeared in the doorway. Checking. A smile for Taoiseach Cross. Bain sank back.

'Then you know who I thought of, Theo? You. I swear to God.

You and my own father, Billy, who I never knew, and poor Mag, God be merciful to Mag. And Pa.' He gave a laugh. 'Pa. If Pa could only see me now, what would he say, Theo? You and me, we don't have blood, we have the history of Ireland in our veins.'

It was difficult, because of the missing teeth, the suddenly overlarge upper lip, the bruises and the bandages, to make accurate comparisons with, for example, the Bain I had last met in Eillne. But even if his appearance had dramatically changed, there was still the briny smell to confirm this was the person I had known since time had begun, that and his readiness to flatter when he wanted something.

'There'll be no settlement in Ulster,' Bain said suddenly. 'The Loyalists talked our people into a cease-fire, codded them into giving up their guns, then what happened? The same Loyalists held the British Government to ransom in return for their votes and shut the door on negotiations with the Ulster Nationalists. Cunts.'

I knew then that Elizabeth was right. I knew it from the way my belly died.

'I have to help them, Theo. It's why I was spared. But what can I do? I can trust no one. Everyone is watching me. The Brits. Dáil committees. The media, fuck them. My own Cabinet. Jesus. My own Cabinet.'

I wanted to get out of that place. I did not want the conversation, if that is what it was, to go on, but as if my thoughts had appeared in text across my face, Bain caught my wrist in a grip whose strength belied his recent sail along the shore of death.

'I want you to give me a help-out, Theo,' he said. He looked at the ceiling and began to pant. 'All I want you to do is to be present somewhere. To just appear.'

'Bain . . .'

'Hear me out, Theo, at least have the guts to hear me out.'

He was wringing wet. I remembered Pa's grip on my arm like that forty years before.

'There's a plane coming in from Eastern Europe in four days' time,' Bain whispered. 'You don't need to know what's on it, Theo. It'll be meant to come to Dublin, but then it will change its destination. It's going to land in Deilt.'

A head appeared beside the bed like a seal breaking water; a

281

tiny woman bore away the untouched tray. Bain drank a deep breath.

'Bain, don't tell me any more. I'll forget what you've already told me –'

'Deilt, Theo! The crowd in Dublin Airport will ring your customs man in Monument. One phone call from you, Theo, his boss, will do it. Just tell him you know all about it, you're on the case. You know what's going on. One call from you, Theo, and he'll forget about the plane.'

'Bain –'

'You have the power to help your countrymen, Theo! I can't even do that and I'm Taoiseach. If you're in Deilt the plane can land and unload. Theo!'

I broke his grip and got to my feet.

'Look, I know you've had a terrible experience,' I said, trying to bring sanity between us. 'I'm going to put this down to your condition, Bain. I'm sorry if you don't like that, but you'll thank me later, I assure you. This discussion never took place.'

Bain pulled himself up into a sit. 'Oh by Jesus it did!' he cried. 'What kind of a man are you to stand there and look at me and what I've been through, and then deny me the first real thing I ever asked you? One favour?'

'You're making a huge mistake,' I said. 'You've got to stand up to them now, after what you've been through, not give in.'

'So you know the truth about Brussels.'

'It's all going to come out, Bain. But everyone is on your side.'

'What do you know?'

'That it wasn't God who sent you the sign in Brussels, it was the Army Council of the IRA.'

'Who are all that's left between their own people and a holocaust,' Bain said.

'That's a political opinion,' I said grimly.

'Isn't that convenient,' Bain sneered. 'You're in the lifeboat. Your own flesh and blood stretches up a hand to you out of the water and you make a political decision.'

'Bain, I'm not going to help you break the law of this country,' I said.

I watched him sink down into pillows. His red gums had taken away the edges from his words.

282

'That plane will be met in Deilt by people who are desperate, Theo,' he said softly. 'The consignment will not even be unpacked on Irish soil.'

'Why not say "the weapons"? Or even, "the missiles"?'

'All right, the missiles,' Bain said. 'They'll go north and be over the border in two and a half hours. A whole race of people depends on them. All you have to do is pick up the phone, make one call and give me a few hours of your life.'

I could have said I had already given him a lot more than he now asked for.

'It's simply not possible.'

'Or instruct someone else to make the call.'

'Even less possible,' I said. 'Bain, you can't do this. You're not thinking right.'

'One consignment is all they need from me,' he said. 'One little bit of recognition that we owe them the means to defend themselves.'

'Not that it matters,' I said, 'but it would never stop at one.'

'I will do this once and once only,' Bain said with vigour. 'There is no doubt about that in my mind.'

'Look,' I said, 'all right, now that I know what's going on, let me give you the best advice anyone ever has. Call it off, Bain. It won't work. The missiles may appear to help the republicans in the short term, but in the long term they won't. There are too many people watching attempts like this. There are too many procedures in place.'

'And you', the Taoiseach said, 'are probably the only person in Ireland who can get round them.'

I had been standing at the end of the bed for the latter part of this dialogue, keeping, if the truth be told, one eye on the door. I could hear toing and froing out in the corridor and every so often, through a tiny gap, could see a white uniform snap past. If only they knew out there what was being said within feet of them.

'You mention laws,' Bain said, pulling himself up again. 'There are laws and there are political contrivances. The only real law is the one that you make with your God. That's my law, Theo.'

'Then we see things differently,' I said.

'Decent humanity alone would allow you to help them,' Bain said and his voice caught. 'Human decency.'

'I can't do what you ask,' I said. 'I am sorry for your predicament. I have to go now.'

'Don't do it for me as Taoiseach, Theo, or for me as someone who has nearly given his life for *your* principles. But will you not do it for all the good years we had together? And Jesus, we go back like no other two men I know. Will you not, Theo?' He had begun to weep. 'Do you *hate* me that much, Theo? Do you want me to kneel down and *beg* you, is that it, Theo? All right, I don't mind, I don't mind.'

He threw back the bedclothes and struggled his legs towards the side of the bed, dragging along tubes and pipes as he did so. I went over to him. The russet body hair of his chest and belly leapt at me shockingly.

'For Christ's sake, Bain,' I muttered and pressed him back.

He looked up at me, open-mouthed.

'Will you help me, Theo?'

'No,' I said firmly. 'I won't, I can't.'

Bain sighed. 'I must tell you something, Theo,' he said.

I had forgotten how it felt to be afraid of Bain. I had always looked forward to his coming to Eillne, but part of that feeling had had to do with fear.

'We all see responsibility in different ways,' he said, but there was now venom in his voice for my punishment. 'You see it as upholding a law, I see it as helping a race of people whose very identity is threatened. Very well. Very well.'

He tapped the telephone beside him, in the process turning it into a threatening weapon.

'I've also carried a heavy responsibility around on my shoulders for forty years, Theo. It's called the truth. And do you know what? I'm fucking sick of the weight of it.'

'What are you talking about?'

'I'm talking about what Pa told me one night,' Bain said. 'Not when he was drunk, because no matter how drunk he was he never talked about this. Fair play to Pa. No sir, this was a piece of information that was sealed inside his head the way a yoke is sealed inside an egg. But one night we were talking. He had no drink taken. Do you know who we were talking about, Theo?'

'Me, I suppose.'

'No, Theo,' said Bain precisely. 'Sparrow.'

That kicked me somewhere soft, and it must have showed.

'You don't like that, do you, Theo?' Bain asked knowingly. 'You hate anything that might upset Sparrow, don't you?'

This was the Bain I knew.

'Go on,' I said quietly.

'Now how did Pa view this information?' Bain mused. 'You see, Pa, behind it all, admired Sparrow in a funny way. He would go so far, brutally far, but never the full way. She was his *wife*, after all. He might be rough with her, but there was a limit to how much he would *hurt* her.' Bain tapped his head. 'He didn't want to destroy her, not his wife.'

'Because of how that might reflect on him,' I said dryly.

'Perhaps. But still, that's how Pa was,' Bain said. 'Also, maybe Pa then, like me now, was fed up with carrying this information on his own back. Maybe he wanted to share the burden. Who knows?'

Bain had forgotten the circumstances from which the necessity to so torture me had arisen and was enjoying himself. He took a drink.

'What really happened all those years ago to Sammy Tea?' asked Bain rhetorically. 'There was a man with the world at his feet. One day he's walking the Long Quay, the dandy of Monument, the next, hey presto! he's in the nuthouse. What happened?' Bain looked at me slyly. '1905, Theo. That's the year you have to look at. 1905.'

'Sparrow was born in 1905.'

'Exactly. But when?'

'February.'

'February 1905. Well done, Theo,' said Bain. 'Go down to the Town Hall in Monument and look up the births. You'll find Martha Love there, born February 1905. Father's name, Samuel Love. Mother's name, Mary Love. Mother's former name? For some reason, not given.'

'Is this your big secret?' I asked.

Bain was smiling, his finger held up. 'Give me a minute, Theo, please, give me a minute. Now, you're in the Town Hall. You've looked for Sparrow's birth registration. While you're there, I'll tell you what you'll do – look up the deaths.'

He fell on the word 'deaths' like a dog who has been playful suddenly falls with intent upon a bone.

'Go back three months,' Bain whispered. 'Into 1904. Don't look for Love, but for Sweeten. Mary Sweeten she was entered as, Sammy Tea saw to that. Died 26 November 1904. Three months before her daughter was born, Theo!'

Of course. I smiled, I think. Of course.

'And if that amuses you, Theo, then you'll die laughing at what comes next,' said Bain tightly. 'Where is Baby Love, Sammy Tea's lovely daughter, during all of this? I'll tell you where. She's up in a cottage six miles from Monument with Nanny Morrissey's in-laws, the Foxes, with a belly on her out to here. And what does Sammy Tea do? As soon as she has her child – within a few days – he gives young Frank Fox five hundred pounds, a fortune, to take her to America. But Baby was a pet name only. What was Baby's real name?' Bain was nodding. 'Mary was her name. Called after her poor mother. Sparrow was Baby's daughter, as well as her sister, Theo. Sammy Tea put his own daughter up the pole.'

I could not hate Bain because I could not hate the truth.

'Why did they register Sparrow's birth?' was all I could think of asking. 'They could have left it and in twenty years no one would have remembered.'

'Nanny Morrissey did it,' Bain chuckled. 'Without telling Sammy Tea. Nanny Morrissey went off on her own and registered the birth and the mother's name. Once registered, nothing could then be done. When Sammy Tea realised what had happened, he lost his reason.'

It was a funny place and time to learn the answer to an old mystery, perhaps the final mystery. I was not my mother's son, but her brother by another man. Then I suddenly remembered the context in which Bain's story had just been told.

'Sparrow must never know this, of course,' I said, somewhat unwisely. 'She's too old.'

'She's too old not to know,' Bain said bitterly. 'Why should we have to carry around this knowledge? Isn't she entitled to know that she's a freak? That her father, whom she still adores in memory, was nothing better than an incestuous old bastard? Eh? I think so, Theo. I have no doubt, in fact.' He lay back. 'It's been on my mind for a long time. I'll send a car to Eillne for her. She wants to see me here, after all. That's exactly what I'll do.' He grinned fleshily. 'I'd actually like to see the old bird, you know.'

There was no point in discussing the quid pro quo. I knew, and Bain knew I knew. I needed time to think. I stood up and wondered for a moment if there was a machine to which Bain was hooked up whose switch I could throw and give him what he deserved. If this had all happened a week before he would have been weak enough to let me smother him.

'I need some time,' I said.

'You can have twenty-four hours, no more,' Bain said.

'I won't tell you now what I think of you,' I said from the end of the bed. 'It would be pointless, anyway.'

'And don't try to negotiate with me, Theo,' said Bain. 'There's no time for fucking around. This time tomorrow you either tell me you'll do it, or she comes up and hears the story for herself.'

My limpet was still waiting in the corridor. He clung right out to the barriers, through the ring of steel. I walked a hundred yards or so for the sea. I needed some stiff sea air in my system. If I thought that praying would have made Bain die, then how I would have prayed! Looking back at the clinic in the distance, I could see a bronze sculpture on its roof. Two snakes, mouths open, intertwined. Bain and Pa, I thought as I hurried away, trying to shake off the panic I felt tearing at me. Pa and Bain.

Fifteen

Elizabeth said, 'You've been walking in the rain.'

I went into the bedroom and changed from my wet clothes.

'Have you seen the evening papers?'

'No.'

'Rumours of a big shake-up in the guards. They say your friend Pax is for it.'

Maybe we could go back to Eillne together, Pax and I, just the two of us. We could play jazz.

'Is there anything the matter?' Elizabeth asked from the door.

'No.'

'Where were you, darling?'

'Seeing Bain.'

'In hospital?'

'Yes.'

'How is he?'

'He looks terrible. His head is bandaged. He's lost all his front teeth, his face is bruised and his moustache is gone. But he's over the worst.'

'Why not just put on something, you know, minimal,' Elizabeth murmured. 'I want you to cook for me.'

'I'm not hungry, unfortunately.'

'I bought some scallops,' Elizabeth said. 'I have this yearning that won't go away.'

'I don't want to cook this evening.'

'I'll cook them.'

'I want to eat out.'

'In that case I'd better get ready,' Elizabeth said.

I did not want to be alone in the flat with Elizabeth and burn up all my energy fending off the questions that would inevitably arise now she knew I had seen Bain. I sprang from one solution to another. I considered, for example, if not for long, removing

Sparrow and with her Bain's threat. Yes, killing my mother, or whatever she was. She was old. My hand over her mouth and nose. She would die in a minute, with less resistance than a farmyard hen, and no pain. She was ninety-three.

I put on a checked shirt and looked at myself in the dressing-table mirror. I did not look, I thought, like a man actively deliberating murder. I looked calm, if slightly haggard. I wondered if I was going mad.

'Walk, I drive or taxi?' asked Elizabeth in her coat, with her bag, again at the bedroom door.

I did not want to risk walking again. Minutes ago, walking from the Blackrock Clinic I had suddenly become convinced that hairy warts had sprouted all over my tongue. It was as if at the moment I wanted to tell the world my problem my imperfect tongue had become perversely afflicted. The feeling was loathsome. I had rushed over to where cars were stopped at traffic lights and tried to examine the reflection of my offending member in a driver's window; the woman at the wheel had – in retrospect, understandably – broken the lights and screeched off at speed.

Elizabeth drove us out to Dalkey, a journey that entailed passing the Blackrock Clinic. In there was a monster whose shadow had ruined my whole life. And yet, even at that point, with the guillotine of the past honed and ready above my head, I found it difficult to blame Bain. I found myself inventing excuses for him, not just to do with his own self-preservation in the face of assassins, but more lofty justifications involving patriotism and decisions based on ancestry and blood. After everything that had been done to me, I did not even have the capacity to sustain hate.

We would normally, on such a night, Elizabeth and I, drool over the preliminaries, eking out pleasurable forethought from the descriptions of the food.

'You order for me,' I said and went to the gents.

Again, a mirror. I searched my face for a reason – any would have done – that would explain my feeling of responsibility for Sparrow's happiness. Why should I care? Did not Sammy Tea deserve to be ultimately exposed for what he was, a beast, and be stripped from the comfortable position he had occupied for ninety-three years in my mother's memory – if mother to me she

289

was? *I am insane*, I said to my face. *If you say that, then you are not insane*, my face said back.

I actively wondered if this was the middle of a (very bad) dream, something that would dissolve with the sunrise of my mind. Or perhaps I had died and was a phantom, my real self deep in the earth of Monument, hatching out grubs.

My bowel was swollen and reassuringly demanding. Corpses cannot shit. I bolted the door of the cubicle. What was needed was a great leap, a bold and liberating bound of imagination, but one that did not involve murdering either my mother or the Taoiseach of Ireland. That was sufficiently amusing to make me laugh out loud for ten seconds or thereabouts. My laughter resounded in the cramped toilet. The only thing, in truth, that linked me to reality was the waste product of my body, which, again shameful but true, nosed into the bowl on which I sat in a huge, unbroken coil, as long and as vigorous as a mature python, or so I imagined.

I wanted proof of my being. Biting my unsteady tongue till it bled I tried, athwart that porcelain bowl, to break out of the loop in which my whole life had been spent. It should have been such an easy decision: to call Bain's bluff; to inform Pax, although Pax was no longer the force he had been; to drive to Eillne and tell Sparrow myself what I had heard from Bain. But the moment I tried to visualise that eventuality, I immediately knew it was doomed. I stood up and looked down curiously into the toilet for evidence of the robust movement I had given birth to. All that was there beneath the water were three little nuggets of shit, less than a rabbit would produce during its morning stroll.

I found myself crying. Was that the most that I, Theodore Shortcourse, could call upon in my hour of direst need? Was that all I amounted to, despite my notions? How could I tell the woman waiting outside, ordering pan-fried brill or nut cake for me, the extent to which my life had been abruptly reduced? How could I tell anyone? Why had the preservation of so much happiness been left in my totally incapable hands? Why was a race of people, not to mention an old woman, now deemed to depend on the choice of a man so frail as Theodore Shortcourse? Killing myself, of course, was the option I had been avoiding. Could death be any worse than what I now was having to endure?

I expected Elizabeth to have ordered and be halfway through a bottle of wine by the time I returned, but instead she had her glasses on her nose and was still studying the menu. I realised I had been away not for half an hour but for only five minutes.

'They have fresh John Dory,' Elizabeth said. 'Or monkfish.'

'Jack O'Dea!' I cried.

'Darling?' Elizabeth smiled quizzically.

'I'm sorry,' I said. 'I have to go and see Jack O'Dea.'

Elizabeth, perhaps from a lifetime of crisis management in the political arena, was exactly the type of woman needed in the circumstances.

'I'll drive you,' she said.

'You stay here and eat.'

'No, I'll drive you. Then I'll go home and cook the scallops,' she said practically.

Jack was a priest, I reasoned. Jack, who would carry the sins of others to his grave, would not blanch in the face of my dilemma and might even have advice to offer.

We drove back into Dublin in uncharacteristic silence, rolling in along the foreshore like a marriage that has lost the joy of words. Elizabeth was not angry with me, just biding her time. I began to watch the cars either side and behind for signs of unusual interest, as if the flowering of my guilt were already a foregone conclusion. It was all, for me, uncannily like the past: the guilt, the inevitability, and – yes! – the excitement. Not so much the thrill of the looming crime itself as the degrading and mysterious attraction of being the equivalent of a whore. But that was only one part of it, of course, and highly inappropriate at that. Waves of dismay about betrayal of my duty washed over me and not even the warm, uterine lap of memory could tide me away from the sorrow of my position.

Dún Laoghaire was oddly empty. I could, of course, unleash Pax, who had been a lifetime awaiting this opportunity. This might *save* Pax! The neatness of justice! A raggle-taggle band of subversives arrested. Their missiles seized. But how could any-thing be proved against Bain? My part in the betrayal would be obvious. Bain could pluck the pride from Sparrow with all the leisure of plucking wings from a fly. Not Pax, then. But had I not made that very choice decades and decades ago?

As we arrived outside his Ballsbridge address, Jack O'Dea was

291

leaving. He was standing with the key in the door of his car, a blackthorn stick wedged under his elbow. He invited us in but when it was explained to him that Elizabeth was not staying he proposed that I join him in a nocturnal burst of exercise.

'A most attractive lady that,' Jack said, driving me once again in the direction of the sea. 'Did you ever get a dispensation from that old business, Theo?'

'You mean my marriage to Juliet?'

'Yes.'

'I never bothered.'

'Is she still alive?' Jack enquired.

'I don't know.'

'If she was dead you'd be elected,' Jack remarked.

To contemplate Juliet, lovely Juliet, dead, and to seize advantage from the fact, added a new level of disillusionment to the evening. Jack parked and we set out along the Bull Wall that thrusts into Dublin Bay like a barnacle-encrusted digit.

'So, what's on your mind?' asked Jack. He walked on my right side, swinging his stick with a regimental flourish. 'Not that there has to be anything on it, of course. I'm always delighted to see an old friend from Monument.'

'I've got a real problem, Jack.'

Jack made a little pastoral gurgle of sympathy and touched my arm.

'I was told Bain wanted to see me today,' I said. 'You met me in the hospital. He's lost the run of himself, Jack. He's gone over the edge.'

'Over the edge,' Jack said.

My narrative, I felt, merited a break in our stride, even a pause, but Jack kept up his pace as if exercise and my revelations about the Taoiseach's intent to subvert justice were in synchronicity. Ahead, the night sea, illuminated by the sky and by Dublin at our backs, seemed far higher than the wall on which we walked. The further down the wall we went, the stronger was the feeling of being lost at sea. I told Jack everything except Bain's delivery of the final instalment of my mother's family history. I left Jack in no doubt that Bain was in hospital because the IRA had put him there and that his sudden conversion to saviour of the republican cause was founded not on conviction but on terror.

292

'And what do you want from me, Theo?' asked Jack when eventually we could go no further. 'How can I come between you and the pain of your conscience?'

Jack, to whom, over the years, the murderers of children must have whispered their unspeakable sin, looked at me implacably. He had learned the body language of forgiveness which the very good use in the presence of the very bad and which at moments such as that on the sea wall comes across as withering kindness. He touched his chest with the gathered tips of the fingers of both hands.

'What to you want me to say, Theo? What do you want me to do?'

'I suppose I see you as an old friend,' I said haltingly, feeling very compromised, and adding, 'and also as a priest,' to emphasise the confidential nature of the discussion. 'I suppose I need someone to talk to. Damn it, this has enormous consequences for everyone, Jack.'

'Granted, granted,' said Jack and we turned for home, faces now to amber Dublin and into a hitherto unnoticeable breeze.

'Did Bain tell you his dilemma?' I asked, then shouted, 'In the hospital?'

Jack had his head down. He appeared to be picking his footsteps in a way that had been unnecessary on the outward leg, and thus needed, I imagined, more time to formulate a reply. But we had gone fully twenty yards before Jack broke the silence.

'You know how I became a bishop, Theo?' he bellowed. 'I'll tell you how. I always took the middle division. There's good and evil, but there's also grades of both, and if that's the case, then by definition there's a state equally made up of both. I'm a limbo man, Theo. When you're sitting at home at dusk with the light on, you look outside and you think, goodness, it's dark as pitch out there. But it never is. When you go out you find you can see quite easily, and the room you've left appears bright as a star. But it isn't, you know, it's just the one light you left on when you were in there.'

Jack shouted into the wind, as if into a gigantic scrambler that allowed a mere instant for the broadcasting of each of his words before sucking them irretrievably away.

'A man may try to be good,' Jack bawled on, 'but he may be

diverted by a number of opposing attractions. He may be vain, not in itself very evil, but incompatible with being very good. He may wish to be important and run into the same problem. In the East they judge jealousy a greater evil than almost anything, yet here we covet as an unspoken way of life.'

Dressed in a zip-up jacket as opposed to my madly flapping mac, Jack was the more aerodynamic of us.

'That's how I became a bishop, Theo. I never preached absolutes, not even in the matter of the word of God, which is as absolute, you might say, as they come. I was never tagged as a liberal or a conservative, even when it came to the most satanic evil. I was and am a priest, a shepherd, an anointer of the dying, a confirmer of the young, a confessor, an alms giver, a healer of souls and a comforter of those stricken with grief. But I am also a lobbyist, a flatterer, a committee man, a financial brain, a judge of markets, a man become wealthy in his own right and with his own ambition. In other words, I am a politician, Theo, as are in one way or another all successful men. And that means not seeing life in terms of moral absolutes, but in finding the middle way.'

We had regained the car.

Jack said, 'That's why the Catholic Church is the supreme institution she is, Theo. Supremely political. She can be on the side of the left on one continent and the champion of the right on another. Having invented and then perfected advertising five centuries before anyone else, she then moved into politics. She made politics a civilised profession when America was still a swamp and the ruling families of England were engaged in internecine warfare. She did not achieve that with daily torment on matters of moral philosophy. She always looked to her assets and then made political decisions.'

We drove in by the warehouses and depots where oil is stored.

'Look to your assets, Theo, and then pick the middle way,' said my friend the Bishop of Monument. 'Forget absolutes. I recall that even where your own organisation is concerned, you have, over the years, offered frequent tax amnesties to evaders. In other words, you have suspended the rule of law, presumably for the sake of expediency.'

Jack laid his hand gently on my arm.

'That's a grand lady, that Elizabeth. You're lucky to have her, Theo, at a time like this.'

I asked Jack to drop me a mile short of my flat. My disappointment at his refusal to make my decision for me was somewhat tempered by the studied nature of his advice. Darkness, if it could still be so described, had settled on the bay. The distant, opposing lights of Howth and Dún Laoghaire created in me the wholly unrealistic expectation that my predicament could be solved by moving to a faraway place. I wondered, cruelly, what middle way Jack took in matters of the flesh. Titillated by perceptions of my own good chance in that area, the slow burn of desire for Elizabeth began in me. I wondered, genuinely, how a man in my position could have time to entertain his own arousal when every moment should be employed in solving the crisis about to engulf him. And then I understood what Jack meant.

I ran home. It was a short distance from the place my revelation occurred to my flat, but run I did. I ran up the steps. I ran into the building. As if I were a chess grand master, all the many moves that would make my strategy victorious were laid out in stark but sublime clarity.

'Your friend Pax Sheehy was looking for you,' Elizabeth said, slightly alarmed at the sight of me, over her cup of coffee.

That already cluttered evening is notable in several further respects. Firstly, there was the frenzied quality of our love-making. It had to it a definite, if mutual, element of wishful pain. Unusually, if not uniquely, I played the dominant role. Our longstanding subtleties were swept aside in the full-blooded expression of my needs. If I was a different man, then Elizabeth was another woman, a harlot whose nails scored the length of my back as I tore down her tights and presented her with my considerable engorgement. Elizabeth walloped her right knee into my chest and rolled me on my back. The bed grumbled under the crash.

'Bastard!' Elizabeth hissed. 'Shit!'

Flattening my legs, Elizabeth sat on me so abruptly that I thought I would break. She manoeuvred first one heel, then the other, so they sat on my shoulders. Then, moaning, she began to seesaw back and forth like someone rowing a boat. When she leant fully back the pressure on my erection was unbearable, relieved at the last moment by her relaxing the position.

'Jesus!' I gasped.

'Bastard!' Elizabeth said from clenched teeth.

Back she went again. And forth. Like all aspects of this encounter, her orgasm was abrupt and accompanied by violent shuddering. I caught her on a forward stroke, my hands cradling her head into my chest – which she bit hard, but I wanted it – and knelt and then stood on the bed with this groaning lady clamped to my midsection, her head between her legs, her heels on my shoulders. I came suddenly. My entire body skin gulped like an iguana's throat. Floridly I roared.

We lay on the bed antipodally, gasping and, in my case, slightly ashamed. Sharp, protesting knocks sounded on the floor from the long-suffering inhabitant beneath.

'Elizabeth?'

She did not reply. On her back, she had her eyes on the window and appeared to be thinking.

'Elizabeth?'

She looked up at me strangely.

'Will you marry me?' I asked.

She did not answer at once. Nor did she dissolve the way women are alleged to at such moments when lifetime commitments are unveiled; instead she continued to look at me rather in the way she might first consider someone who stopped her in the street and asked her if she could change a pound.

'I might,' she said eventually.

'I need to know, Elizabeth.'

'I said, I might.'

'It's not ruled out?'

'Of course not,' she said with a hint of old huskiness, and rubbed my hand with her knuckles. 'Why the sudden rush?'

'I need . . . I need to be sure of my position,' I said, rocking back on my heels. 'Sure of my ground.'

'In what way, Theo?'

'I need to *involve* you in something,' I said. 'Something awfully important.'

'I see.'

'And I suppose what I'm saying is, that although we love each

296

other, we are not married to each other, and legally marriage contains certain mutual safeguards, which is what I'm after, to be honest.'

Elizabeth became thoughtful. She slipped down from the bed and put on her knickers and a little vest thing that gave expression to her breasts, and then a light robe that she belted and knotted firmly before she returned to sit cross-legged on the duvet.

'You should tell me what's going on, Theo,' she said calmly. 'I will agree to marry you, but not at the end of an evening in which your behaviour has left me worried silly.'

Her eyes were two enormous pools of sanity that suddenly offered me, as I had imagined they would, immeasurable relief. Jack had been right.

She said softly, 'You can tell me as a wife, Theo, if that will make you feel better. After all, it will hardly be the first secret between us.'

Put like that, in context, my shoulders shed the weight they had been carrying since I had met Bain. I told Elizabeth. Everything. I told her about Bain and the missiles and the plane. I did not spare her the fact that my grandfather had been a monster who had violated his own daughter when she was no more than barely pubescent. All the forgotten days in Atlantic City I recalled for Elizabeth anew. I was not Sparrow's son, but her brother, stolen by her from her sister whose daughter she also was. The caravan of my life and that of Bain's had met at a great crossroads.

'But there is a middle way,' I said smugly.

'I'm glad, Theo,' said Elizabeth quietly. 'What is it?'

'I'm going to let the plane land and the missiles be taken north,' I said. 'But as they cross the border, you're going to have them intercepted.'

'I see.'

'Everybody fulfils their obligations,' I said happily. 'Bain has done what the IRA are demanding of him. I've helped Bain. The terrorists are deprived of their missiles, but they won't know how it happened. And their money is lost, making it difficult for them to try again in the near future.'

'And Sparrow is spared the truth,' Elizabeth said.

'Yes, Sparrow is spared.'

I expected some token resistance to my solution and was

297

prepared with an array of rebutting arguments, but instead Elizabeth nodded slowly.

'It can be done,' she said.

'Naturally I now see Bain for what he really is.'

'Naturally.'

'And whatever his long-term plans are, he won't be able to involve me in this fashion again.'

'Really? Why not?'

'Because I'm going take my retirement at the end of this year and use my new-found time to spoil my wife,' I said.

Sixteen

Time is the only real mystery to me. All the others, even those to do with the random nature of God's mercy, I can satisfy one way or another by philosophy or by great leaps of faith. Time is the open-ended conundrum. I can imagine anything except the absence of time; and since the corollary is to say that time is inherent in everything I can imagine, it frustrates me beyond words to realise that something upon which I am so dependent remains so incomprehensible.

Thus it now seems that the events of the days that followed occurred not in a distant part of my life, but in a distant century and not one necessarily in the past. The relevance of events to the man I was and am seems tenuous in the extreme. And yet, as if I am a student who has devoted his time to the study of that peculiar person, me, I can recall all the minutes of those days, bled of emotion and set in the permafrost of memory.

Elizabeth went home the following morning. We did not discuss the night before, each preferring to consider the meaning of our unusual encounter when the other was absent. It had at worst brought out a wantonness in both of us that we might have otherwise preferred to deem absent; at best it showed us to be up there with the best when it came to acrobatic sex.

There was nothing excessively conspiratorial about the arrangement we reached regarding the missiles shipment. The day, the time. The place. I asked Elizabeth that no one be killed and Elizabeth, within the limits of what could reasonably be expected in such circumstances, undertook to emphasise, albeit anonymously, my request. My almost omnipotent intervention on behalf of the wretches whose strategy I had ensured was doomed added to my sense of elation. Yes, I was elated. A small intervention, a telephone call, and I could thereafter call the future mine. No little feat in the conditions. 'THEODORE

TRIUMPHS', or headlines to that effect in the weary Grub Street of my soul.

I did not want to see Bain again, so I telephoned him at the clinic. Suitably curt in manner, I told him, it is done, the message can be delivered, or words of intrigue to that effect. Bain wanted to linger on the phone, to become sentimental, or to get me to pretend for his own peace of mind that it was me helping him voluntarily and not him fucking me ragged that had achieved his illicit goal. I terminated the call. My momentum would carry me only so far when it came to Bain. If he started to cajole and wheedle, for all I knew my voice might betray a spiteful satisfaction that came from knowing the enterprise would never succeed, or I might break down entirely and confess my duplicity. I never knew myself with Bain.

'You won't regret this, Theo,' were his last words. 'You're doing the right thing.'

In order to land at Deilt and take off again, the plane would need daylight. Saturday had been chosen. I assumed this was for strategic reasons: security forces more stretched, customs offices on tick-over for the weekend. If I was the customs man present, then the only other figure of authority who would attend the landing would be the AFISO, a gentleman from Monument whose corruption obviously no one had been able to mastermind.

'You're in Brussels twice next week,' Evelyne-Mary told me on Friday morning. 'I assume you'll stay over.'

'I assume,' I said and off she went to make the necessary arrangements.

There was comfort in so planning ahead. This was Friday; on Monday night I would be in the Grand Place sipping a tankard of beer and considering the chocolates I would buy for Elizabeth. Yet I was circumspect in leaving the office that evening. What did I expect? Pax, to be honest. He had tried once more to speak to me, probably on no more pressing a subject than a swim in Sandycove together, but I had told Evelyne-Mary to say I would call him after the weekend. At five o'clock, I stood in the portal shadows of my office, scrutinising the cars and activity in the forecourt and the shadows of the other portals, which might easily, to the uninquisitive eye, be harbouring someone as lurking as myself. Then I walked all the way home to Sandymount and, if the truth be

300

known, cooked myself prawns and ate them to the accompaniment of a bottle of good chablis that I had intended keeping until these happenings were over but am now very glad I did not.

I rose at seven the next morning. I made sure I had all the telephone numbers. Unlocking the basement garage, I took out my car and with, it must be said, mounting apprehension, set south for Monument.

I can drive. I owned a car. During one of the transport strikes in the early eighties I purchased a showroom-new Volkswagen, a bright orange Beetle that I kept like a neglected horse under the apartment and brought out only twice a year, each time back to the garage to be serviced. Sixteen years later my car still had the plastic on its seats and smelt like a pair of new brogues. The point had been reached, I was informed on the last occasion, where my Volkswagen was now worth more than it had originally cost me, although that singularity was about to be eroded.

In all these years I had never driven myself to Monument. A creature of habit, I saw no reason not to be transported by train and bus. I set out at eight on the Saturday morning. Weather? Sublime June. The Deilt Mountains would be at their best and most welcoming for an airborne arsenal. I left the great midland plain and purred southwards with all the concern of a travelling salesman out on his rounds. I could not overcome a certain flippancy in my attitude, as if the nearer to my assignment the more unlikely it all seemed. Or, on the other hand, perhaps it was the first sight of the aforesaid mountains, in whose bedrock were conceived the springs that went on to become the river delta and whose grandeur buoyed my heart, that made the forthcoming afternoon seem petty by comparison.

Monument bustled. I could see scaffolding down one side of the cathedral and strapped to it the tarpaulin – green in this case – used when an old building is being power-washed of ancient grime. I parked under CityWise and walked the short distance to the Commercial Hotel. Buildings on both sides had been acquired by the hotel in recent years. Carpet of deep pile and a teak-fronted reception graced the expansive lobby. I dialled the home of the Area Surveyor. I told him he would be getting a call around midday from the area AFISO. It would concern a flight from Europe heading for Deilt. He should call me when he heard from the AFISO, I said.

'You're handling the case yourself, Superintendent?' the Surveyor asked.

'Yes, I am.'

'Do you require me to assist you in any way?'

'I'll fill you in the next time I see you,' I said with the verbal counterpart of a wink.

'No problem, Superintendent,' the Surveyor said. 'I'll ring you immediately the AFISO calls. And thanks very much for filling me in.'

I put down the telephone and turned around. Standing in mid-lobby and staring at me like a yak was the journalist Joyce Ogar.

'What's going on?' she said.

'I'm sorry?'

'There's something going on,' she said, standing her ground.

'What do you mean?' I asked and looked at my watch.

'Movement,' Joyce Ogar said thoughtfully. 'Certain key players missing up North. The same people reported in this area in the last few days. Suddenly my usual contacts in Branch and the like are unavailable. Now you.'

'I'm down to see my mother,' I said making light of it. 'She's ninety-three.'

'Look, I was having coffee when I saw you come in here,' she said. 'Would you like to join me?'

My attraction for Joyce, first born in Jack O'Dea's, was now absurdly strengthened by the fact that we were both (probably) alone down here in Monument and that Elizabeth was absent. There was something warmly dissolute about the woman. I considered the possibility of asking her to wait a few hours, then rejoining her in Monument when the day's business had been taken care of. Then I thought of the Surveyor, about to call me.

'I don't have the time,' I said. 'My mother lives in Eillne.'

'I don't believe you, Theo,' Joyce said. 'Something's up.'

'I'm sorry,' I said. 'Nice meeting you again.'

I hurried out of the hotel with Joyce following me. I cursed her. Hurrying up Bagnall's Lane and across Mead Street, I cut in through the lanes behind MacCartie Square, stepping over the foul-smelling and prostrate body of an old man at the corner of Ladies' Walk. He lay on one side, his begging hand open and

302

outstretched, his long, white hair hanging across his face. Our eyes met. His lips moved.

'Fawdoluvagaw,' he whispered.

It would have suited my mercurial sense of guilt to have discharged alms, but I was being pursued and lacked the time to do so. What had it meant, fawdoluvagaw? I rounded two corners and made a dash for CityWise. My old leg injury began to nag. Entering a paper shop on the main mall I hid behind a magazine stand, creeping down the titles like a stork. Sure enough, into the far end of the mall, looking like a restless tepee, came Joyce. I crouched. Joyce trundled past. I slipped back out and down the steps into the car park. The hotel was now out of the question. I jumped into my car and scurried for Eillne, turning my lie to Joyce into a prophecy.

Where time had been on my side, now it was suddenly against me. I needed a telephone. I could not stay in Monument and risk having Joyce follow me out to Deilt. I imagined her returning to the Commercial Hotel, swallowing coffee, listening to my name being paged when the Surveyor called and intercepting the precious information. I considered going to the Surveyor's house and waiting there until the AFISO rang him, but that would mean my having to deflect inevitable questions about the mission on which I was engaged.

I passed the ever-encroaching houses along Captain Penny's Road. The holy well. New bungalows in fields that rose into little hills. Passing the national school I paused to wonder how tiny the old schoolhouse looked beside the magnificent new construction, taking my eyes from the road for a moment too long and almost ending matters in a head-on encounter with Sheehy's shrieking, klaxon-blaring bus. My watch gave the time at twelve o five. It had been Mr Redden, I realised, occupying the pavement by Ladies' Walk. He had begged for years in Monument, and I had often dropped to him, which now made me feel better, but in those days his hair had not been white. But 'Fawdoluvagaw'? I breasted a little rise and saw the river. For the love of God.

One small car was parked outside the hall door. There was still time, of course, to change my mind as to my intentions. It struck me that Joyce Ogar may well have been an omen. Here was my opportunity to reveal to Sparrow that her mother had been other

303

than whom she had for a lifetime assumed, her sister in fact. In a great, sweeping explanation, I would level the landscape of ninety-three years' misapprehension. I turned the Volkswagen into the gate and got out. The river winked up in the sunlight. Villainy had no place on such a day. The hall door of Eillne was open.

'Mr . . . Shortcourse,' said a young nurse, surprised.

I was looking at my watch with obsessive regularity.

'Mrs Wise is sleeping,' said the nurse.

'I must use the telephone,' I said, going to it.

'I'll tell the cook you're here for lunch,' the nurse said. 'Your mother was trying to ring you this morning.'

That stopped me too. Why would she do such a thing on such a crucial day? Did she *know* something? From the moment of Joyce Ogar's appearance, the day had proceeded like a slow but progressive derailment of my earlier elation. Even the appearance of my old schoolteacher, whom I had long assumed dead, seemed pregnant with fateful if complicated symbol.

'I must make this call,' I said and did so.

The Surveyor's number was engaged. Was *this*, then, how providence would deal out the hand? An unstoppable chain of events that would be initiated when the Surveyor failed to find me, his duty – a concept I did not wish to dwell on – being to attend a lone plane now landing, thanks to me, in mysterious circumstances in the middle of nowhere? I dialled again. Hard bars of unavailability.

'She'll be out in ten minutes.'

I whirled. 'Who?'

'Mrs Wise,' the nurse frowned.

In my confusion, I had thought she meant Joyce, and in the resulting atom of time allocated to this misreading, during which Joyce had been delivered to Eillne, I actually entertained the beginnings of a speculation as to how Joyce might react to a straightforward proposal.

'Would you like a cup of tea?' asked the nurse.

'No thank you,' I snapped. I wanted to be left alone in the hall where my anxiety could flower in comfort. 'Yes, yes, I will,' I amended, guessing correctly that tea might remove the girl and allow me to swing the numbers again on the old telephone.

'Won't be a moment,' the nurse said pertly and pecked her way in the direction of the kitchen.

The number rang once.

'Hello?'

'It's Theo Shortcourse.'

'Superintendent,' said the Surveyor. 'Are you in the hotel?'

'Yes. No, no! I had to see someone. Were you trying to ring me?'

'Twice,' the Surveyor said. 'The hotel insisted you weren't there. Never mind. The AFISO's been on and is already on his way to Deilt. The flight left LATCC at eleven fifty. ETA Deilt one o five. It's now twelve sixteen. Where exactly are you?'

LATCC was London Area and Terminal Control Centre; ETA, estimated time of arrival. Acronyms seemed to underline the soullessness of the situation.

'I'm near the landing site,' I said with a satisfactory tone of conspiracy. 'I can't say too much.'

'Take it as read,' the Surveyor chirped. 'Aircraft's a Quiet Trader, four turbo fan engines, ready-made for STOL situations, two POBs. Are you sure you don't want any assistance up there?'

'No,' I said and looked at my watch, 'and listen. Forget any of these conversations between us or between you and the AFISO ever took place.'

'No problem, Superintendent,' said the Surveyor.

'I think she's waking now,' said the young nurse, cup and saucer in hand. 'I've told her you're here.'

'That was unnecessary.'

'Superintendent?'

'I'll ring you next week,' I said and put down the phone. My watch said twelve eighteen.

'Theodore?'

Sparrow's voice came from the bedroom, but all I could think of was a plane lumbering through the sky to its bog rendezvous and, because customs were still on their way, a hapless AFISO refusing to clear it and being shot dead in the process.

'I'll be back,' I said, running out the hall door of Sparrow's new house. 'I'll be back this evening for a swim, tell her.'

I can't blame Joyce Ogar for everything, I can't blame her for the fact that I did not stop to take the time even to look in at Sparrow, an opportunity forsaken that would later come back to taunt me. However, at sometime in the last hour and a half, like a

305

plane – a plane! – crossing an invisible border miles below, I had crossed the line from facilitator to conspirator, as Bain no doubt knew I would.

I lost no time between Eillne and Monument. Chivalrous would be overstating my mood, but I was feeling quietly satisfied that I had spared Sparrow the brutal truth. As I left Monument in what was suddenly a very hot afternoon for June, a cargo ship was rounding the bend of the river. With the appearance of the ship, the bustle of cars and people on Long Quay, the solid voice of my Volkswagen's engine, and the unexpected weather, I had a sense of decency triumphing over baseness and not an inkling that I might be grievously mistaken. The hedgerows had filled with green in the sudden countryside, the side of Monument that for reasons topographical and because of the lack of river views had not been built on by property developers. I passed Batty plc and wondered what Elizabeth would do; how she would trace the cargo; whether the border would be a bottleneck of cars and infantry. Who bestrode the occasion? I asked myself. Who presided at the summit of affairs, tweaking the strings that made planes land, engines start, men drive from one end of the country to the other and soldiers check their rifle magazines? Bain, but not just Bain, because in the end he was just someone's tool. Some so-called chief of staff, but not just him, because he without doubt was also a tool – of the hard men, of people in the Falls and South Armagh, of the ballot box . . . I was the tweaker supreme, I realised with awe. This day had dawned and would set because of yours truly.

I felt the foothills of the mountains beneath my humming wheels. The Volkswagen, my steed, devoured the twisting, climbing road with a hunger that testified to its years of captivity. It was ages since I had been up here. My watch said twelve forty-five. I began to check the sky, as well as my watch, happy that the car had innate German perspicacity when it came to navigation. I checked the empty road. My watch. The sky. The terrain climbed, turned. I opened my window to listen for airborne engines. I looked up. Suddenly my windscreen was filled by a white horse.

I cannot have been going too fast. We slid rather than crashed off the tarmacadam, all rather gracefully and without discomfort, into a gateway located on the downhill side of the road. The white horse, a huge beast, was attached to a cart and was cast by my impact into the relative hospitality of a deep ditch. Two men, farmers, I thought, had for some reason climbed on to the roof of my car and were hanging upside down, peering in at me and shouting. I wondered if I was being attacked.

'Are you *all right*?'

'Yes,' I replied, 'yes, thank you,' and then realised that we'd gone belly up.

My forehead had taken the rear-view mirror with it and was bleeding, although no pain was involved. The back window was gone.

'Give me your hand.'

They pulled me out and away from my so recently pristine machine, which lay, wheels still spinning madly, like a small, fat dog with a broken back. One of the farmers had a squint. He sat me down and handed me my glasses, one eye of which bore an overlay like spider's web. The other farmer attended the horse. He unbuckled straps and ropes and following a great thrashing and pitching, the animal lunged from its recess in a spasm of energy and stood out beside the car, trembling hugely and heaving for its frothy breath.

'No one hurt, the main thing,' the squinty farmer said.

He was cute-eyed, despite his squint, suggesting an inborn dislike of authority and the complications that the formal treatment of this incident might entail. The world through my spectacles was somewhat crisscrossed.

'You were going a right lick,' the other farmer said. 'Do you know these roads at all?'

I dabbed red blots from my forehead. A pair of asses had appeared in the field and were looking with interest at the scene over the gate.

'Are you from these parts?' asked the squinty farmer curiously.

'No, no. Well, yes. I live . . . I'm not from here, really, not any more,' I replied.

'Haven't I seen you up this way once before?' asked the squinty farmer. 'Couple of year back?'

They may have thought that in my disorientation I was searching the sky for an answer, but I knew better. I reached to my wallet and extracted two twenty-pound notes.

'Do you think this car will start?' I asked.

'She's upside down, mister,' the squinty farmer said.

'Can we right her?'

They looked at the Volkswagen dubiously.

'We'll tip her down into the gate,' I said, standing up.

'We'll never swing her,' the farmer said.

It was twelve fifty-five. I took out another two score.

'Hitch up the horse to her,' I said.

The gate was opened and the asses shooed off, although they continued to linger on the edge of affairs for nuisance value. The withers of the horse were fitted with a waistcoat-like apparatus in leather, full of buckles and straps. Ropes were run from the central pillar of the car, the one between the two windows on the passenger side, as the animal was stood in the field at a secure distance.

'Now lads!' the squinty farmer cried.

The rope went quiveringly taut. With that tiny shuddering that marks the birth of momentum and so many other things, the Volkswagen twitched. Then off down the hill in a magnificent marriage of science and nature went the white horse, and over once and then twice crashed my maiden car, settling doggedly if filthily on her wheels with an expression that I can only think of as uncompromising.

I leapt in. One o'clock had passed. The engine started at the first touch in a great roar of justification for a choice made sixteen years previously. The two men put their shoulders to the once nubile rear section and I shot up from the gate to the road to the cheers of the enriched farmers and perhaps even of their horse.

I kept my foot to the floor. Breasting the hill, I careered downward and passed a wood of beech trees either side of the road, their trunks the colour and consistency of granite. A continual rasping from near the road suggested a fender abrading a wheel, but time did not exist to amend such faults. It was ten-past one and for all I knew the innocent AFISO was plugged and dead and the missiles already unloaded and on their way.

I left the cover of the trees and immediately the surrounding countryside and perspective changed. Instead of fields with boundaries and trees it was limitlessness: a bog that spanned the entire potential of the eye, and hazy, purple mountains that took the place of the sky ahead like brooding gods.

I took the left fork of the road. To have gone straight on would have brought me down into Deilt village where an American manufacturer of computers had set up a sprawling facility whose stacks oozed smoke columns up into the clear afternoon. The road ahead of me was straight and empty as the sky. Turf, cut and stacked in black, porous mounds, stood in lines marking the confines of people's plots. I thought I could see vehicles parked along one side of the road, half a mile distant, but knew I must be mistaken. No one else could possibly be in Deilt this day; Deilt had been chosen because of its remoteness.

I slowed and checked the sky for an aircraft, but as far as the distant horizon was uninterrupted blue. Looking ahead, I now thought I could see a tree by the roadside, but as I approached it became a man. In fact it became a guard in uniform. I stopped short. He seemed to be on duty in some way. Then I saw the buses upon whose livery sunlight had recently glinted for me, half a dozen buses at least, pulled in along the left-hand side of the road to the Deilt Ambush car park and a hundred yards short of it. I halted. This was all, I knew, a dreadful, dreadful mistake.

'*Baaaaaaaaaarrrp!*'

Yet another bus towered behind me. Its driver spread his hands rhetorically for my benefit. Forced to proceed to where the guard held the road, his eyes taking in my overall get-up with considerable misgiving, I rolled down the window.

'Out for a spin?' he suggested warily.

Buses loomed to my left, faces within them peering down at me. Other people were spreading rugs up on the bog, a few yards off the road. There were women and children. Picnic boxes were being opened. It was a lovely day for a picnic.

'Customs,' I said, sounding ridiculous.

The guard began a little inspection of my recently immaculate car, from which steam was now rising as impressively as sweat. I could see the large and now clearly empty car park over to my right.

'Are you the owner of this vehicle?' the guard enquired.

It was then I saw the young man in dark glasses, pullover and jeans, a telephone clipped to his belt and an authority-bolstering black shoulder bag with the aerial of a mobile radio protruding from it, standing near the entrance to the car park.

'Are you the AFISO?' I called.

'Mr Shortcourse?'

He came over and we shook hands.

'It's all right, guard,' the AFISO explained. 'He's expected.'

As the guard stepped somewhat reluctantly aside, I drove down on to the tarmac and got out.

'I thought it was going to be a disaster,' the AFISO said, rejoining me in a cloud of radio static. 'These buses need to park. But she's nearly here. Only a few minutes more now.'

'What are they all doing here?' I asked in dismay.

'It's the anniversary of some battle,' the AFISO told me wearily. 'Is this flight to commemorate it or something?'

I wasn't aware until that moment that Bain might have a sense of humour. Buses kept arriving. I could see cars and vans as well as buses, camper vans included. In festive mood – a credit to them considering the way they were being inconvenienced – tiers of spectators lined the bog above the perversely empty car park. Occasionally, brave sorties in the direction of the car park were made by small children, but their parents reined them back up the hill. Perhaps two hundred people were now ready to witness an event that was intended to take place in the most deadly secrecy. In the last century military engagements had been viewed in this way.

The AFISO began to talk into his radio, walking to the middle of the car park and peering into the sky. Wishful thinking aside, I began to give weight to the overall events of the past weeks and from them tried to make sense of the scene I was now part of. With a sudden rush of happiness, what had actually happened was blindingly revealed! In his post brain-surgical trauma, Bain had scrambled a perfectly legitimate commemorative flight into a Pa-like conspiracy to bring in missiles and I had been foolish enough to believe him. I laughed! I looked up at the faces of children and I waved! Some of them waved back. I felt the sun on my face. Even my Volkswagen, its journey completed, seemed to smile ruefully. I was about to stroll to the plinth whereon my uncles' names and this very date seventy-six years ago were engraved, I was just about to take a wander round and try to imagine what it must have been like for poor old Pa, as Bain called him, all those years before, when the plane suddenly appeared.

The engines, four of them, were slung two each under overhead wings, giving the machine as it readied up the appearance of a portly seagull. She seemed to be gliding, because over the sound of yet another arriving bus there was no noise to speak of. She just crept in from the hills, did a single circuit of the intended landing place at a hundred feet, went out ahead of us in a little climb and then came back in, equally quietly, and settled on the tarmac with no more fuss than a kite.

Back up beyond, on the high road, I heard engines start. The AFISO looked at me and then walked to the halted plane. A pilot emerged and stretched his arms, then another did the same, staring at all the activity.

Past me a Hiace van was driven slowly by a man with a beard and wearing a knitted tea cosy. A twin van followed. They pulled up one behind the other as, responding to a switch activated in the cockpit, a rear cargo door opened like the mouth of a fish.

I was twenty-five yards away. The AFISO was looking at me enquiringly. I could not believe what was happening. I could not accept that anyone in their right minds would smuggle a consignment of deadly weapons into the middle of a picnic. The AFISO was still looking at me; I nodded OK. I did not believe the plane was carrying what I had been told, but the evidence was suggesting otherwise. Four men, two from each van, began to carry wooden crates from the plane. A fifth man, the one with the beard, stood to one side of the first van's open door, watching me suspiciously.

Just as I was beginning to accept that what I had first imagined as a disaster of judgement was, in fact, a brilliant coup – everything was so *normal*! – a number of things happened simultaneously, as if to demonstrate that in my case the birth of any assumption heralded, as in the way of certain species of insects, its immediate death. Joyce Ogar got out of a car and came bustling down towards the car park. I swore. Pax – *Pax?* – ran from behind a bus to block her progress. Pax was holding a sub-machine-gun. The tea-cosied man standing beside the van lunged for something on the van's seat. There was, even to my untutored ears, the unmistakable crack of a rifle and the tea cosy slumped inward. Dropping their crate, the remaining four men assumed a

311

variety of tactics from hands in the air to sprinting for the bog, whilst the AFISO flung himself on the tarmac beside one of the two pilots, leaving the other, perhaps slower of reaction, in the process of lighting a cigarette.

I sat in the Volkswagen. The next half a minute, now copiously documented elsewhere, is perfectly clear in my memory. There were people running everywhere and at least three guards in uniform, rather like the end of a football match where the pitch is invaded by spectators. I edged for the road. Pax alone stood in front of me. No detail of those seconds is too insignificant to evade memory: Pax's windcheater (black with a jagged, purple stripe), his deep, brown eyes, his steelgrey hair, the white earphone with its thick loop of grey cable leading into his collar, his gun, which remained pointing down his leg. I passed the engraved names on the Deilt memorial at gathering speed. Pax, standing directly in the way of my exit, did nothing dramatic, made no point-duty signals, just the barest flutter with the fingers of one hand, as if he had a message to relay. But I wasn't going to speak to Pax. In fact, it seemed crucial, with an eye to posterity, that in view of what was happening there be no contact whatsoever between us, and so I pretended not to heed Pax at all and pushed the pedal of my car to the floor. Pax leapt aside. As if the top card of a deck had been peeled away and the queen revealed, so appeared Joyce Ogar. I may have grazed her is my recall. *May* have. I could not have gone over her or anything; there was no impact and Joyce was a very big woman. She just rolled to the side, out of my way, and I pointed for Monument.

For a few miles it went well. I considered myself the blunt instrument that had somehow been used to foil a major crime, and it was thus consistent that I should be allowed to slip away, my duty accomplished. How else could Pax have known? Loose ends remained, assuredly, but would no doubt be tidied up: for example, Bain's part in the whole fiasco. I would not then have been surprised to learn that far from capitulating to fear, he had set the whole thing up and formed an historic alliance with Pax in the process. Pax's barely moving fingers to bid me stop back in the car park had had about them a quality of almost Renaissance-like intrigue; his had certainly not been the attitude of a man who harboured any malevolent intentions in my direction.

I left the bog, went through the great stand of beech, up the hill and past the gateway, scene of my earlier contretemps. My car had aged that morning with the suddenness of an old person robbed of long-standing routine, and proceeded with whatever is the mechanical equivalent of a limp. Clearly Pax had known all along about the attempted importation. I laughed at my own naïvety. This was an everyday incident to men like Pax. Wondering if Elizabeth would think I had for some reason intentionally misled her, my ears popping, I squealed down the successively declining mountain foothills. Monument was now a necessity rather than an option: Citywise was sure to have a man who would know how to sort out whatever was impeding my car's litheness and ensure I got to Eillne. I saw the town in the distance and the car in my wing mirror at the same moment.

Pax came up close and flashed his headlights. He was pointing to the side of the road, telling me to pull over. Disinclined to comply with his instructions for the same reasons I had not stopped back in Deilt, I continued. Pax bore up the grass margin on my inside and if he had mounted the ditch instead of pulling up as he did when we came to the corner, it would have been his own fault. I gained a hundred yards. Through my broken rear window I could hear Pax come noisily for me at a collected run, but I kept to the crown of the road and endured his blaring and flashing all the way into Monument.

We came down the Small Quay together, Pax on my rear mudguards, at times inadvisably close. Just beyond Samuel Love's premises an accident appeared to have taken place. Lights flashed on Garda cars. A man in a flak jacket aimed a gun at me. I veered right into Ship Street. Pax clung, hand on his horn. When he actually ground his car into my rear-engine quarters – steel gratingly mounting steel as if in some grotesque mating – I suppose I knew finally what no amount of hypothesis could dispel. Swinging left, I came to the railings of the cathedral, then tried to go left again, back in the direction of the river, at the same time that Pax, unfortunately, was trying to come up on my left-hand side. I lost control. We met the railings together and took them down with us for twenty yards in a graceful ripple of cast iron.

First out, I stumbled for the scaffolding-clad church.

'*Don't shoot!*' Pax screamed.

I was wondering why he was saying that when I saw a man at the far side of the cathedral gates slowly lower his gun.

'Back off!' Pax commanded. 'Theo,' he called. 'It's no use, Theo. It's over. I'm taking you in.'

I had my back to the end of the cathedral, to the great window that Sparrow had commissioned for my wedding day. Inside that window, in the sacristy of the church, was a book with Pax's and my signatures, side by side. Different people. Pax was walking slowly for me. I raised my hand to catch a bar of the scaffolding and swung up to the first level.

'Theo, the best favour you'll ever do yourself will be to come in with me now,' Pax said.

'I'm going to Eillne,' I said, knowing how crazy that sounded, yet feeling that to assert some purpose was essential. I scrambled up even higher, level now with the centre of the window, whose careful lead work I could touch.

'I swear you won't be hurt,' Pax called up.

'I've done nothing,' I said down to him.

'Theo, you've badly injured a woman,' Pax said. 'And you've conspired to import arms. I know it wasn't your fault, but make it easy on yourself. If it wasn't for me you'd be dead by now.'

'Stay where you are!' I called to Pax, picking up a concrete block.

Pax had climbed up to the section beneath me.

'Don't try and tell me this whole business was not set up from the start,' I said. 'Ask Bain your questions, Pax, not me.'

'Theo,' Pax said up to me, eagerly, 'I swear to you, give me the rope and I'll hang him myself. Yes, if you say so, yes, he did set you up. I believe you completely. Yes! But you'll have to go through the mill first after what you've done today.'

There persisted in my mind the conviction that Pax was mistaken.

'But', I said, 'was it not Bain who told you about the plane?'

Pax shook his head grimly. That was the worst part, looking into his eyes. Long years might not have passed. We might both have been back in my digs on Baggot Street, with Pax the one lumbered with shattering my world.

'Pax?'

'Theo,' he said gently. 'I'm so sorry.'

'Who told you, Pax?' I cried. '*Who told you?*'

'We got a call this morning from British Intelligence,' Pax spoke softly.

'I don't believe you.'

'She's always been working for them, Theo. I've always known that.'

'No.'

'It's true, Theo.'

'*No!*'

I was operating now by rote only. My outward appearance was that of any middle-aged man confronted halfway up the side of a cathedral, but inside I had started to die.

'We love each other,' I said. My poor pride.

'She wants Bain, Theo,' said Pax. 'They do. They want Bain's head. Do you remember that old business with your brother Lyle?'

'Lyle?'

'British Intelligence set it all up, Theo. They took the machines, they removed Lyle. No one but Elizabeth Wedlake could have had that information. She copied the report with all the shit on Bain, then fed it to the media. I've always known that too.'

'Elizabeth had my brother killed?'

Pax nodded. 'They wanted to ruin Bain at the time, and they thought they had succeeded.'

'We're getting married,' I said, wet-faced.

'Theo, she's happily married already.'

'No. She's leaving him. She's going to marry me.'

'They left Belfast this morning for London,' Pax said quietly. 'They're now on their way to South Africa.' He said, 'Sorry, Theo. Sorry.'

The concrete block in my hands had a gritty realism that I otherwise lacked. As I lifted it I could feel its density. Its ability. In truth the block had more potential than I did in that whereas I had failed utterly in everything, it at least could be used to build. Or kill.

'Don't! Theo!'

To kill Pax would only grieve me further in the scarce few seconds I intended to survive him; it would also delight Bain. To

315

kill myself would be to allow Bain to escape from the net in which he had caught me but which I might yet use to snare him; it would also sadden Sparrow. What I needed to kill was the past. I needed to extinguish everything that had led to my existence. Everything that stood in the landscape of my history needed to be destroyed and then the ground ploughed and purged of memory.

'Theo –'

'No, Pax.'

'Theo, don't give up now. Trust me. I have known you all my life. You know you can trust me,' Pax said.

'You don't know me, Pax,' I said down to him and I never felt sadder. 'How could you, when I don't even know myself?'

'Is that important, even if it were true?' Pax asked. 'Who a man may be is not important. It is what he is that really matters.'

I raised the block over my head and went on crying long and loud. I didn't care who heard me. Pain drove me, and the need to hurt. I would never have an easier target than Pax's face. Nor would I ever love a man more.

Turning, I launched the block at the window. It went through dully enough, leaving a hole the size of a head, but landed inside with a loud explosion. Then, piece by piece, the window began to disintegrate, great globs of lead and glass falling in larger and larger sections, the eyes and halos of Christ and his Apostles cascading on to the altar and into the churchyard and presenting the interior of the cathedral to my eyes.

PART IV

Seventeen

The cell keys turned in Dundrum at seven each evening, and for thirteen hours, until slop-out the next day, that was it. You could shout and scream all you liked, and some did. The old men who died before dawn were cold as planks by the time they were found. Staff cutbacks, we were told.

'Tuesday.'

The voice came from the cell next door. Constantly. I never knew why he kept repeating the weekday whose name he had come to share; Tuesday up to then had always seemed to me the most neglected day of the week.

I found the meat-and-starch diet hard. I missed not just the eating of fish but also its preparation and cooking. I liked the knife work that came with filleting, the way you had to lift monkfish by its eyes and then the contrast between its devil's head and its seductively muscular body as you uncoupled the two. Because I had not eaten meat in forty years, not since my days in Pa's abattoir, my choice in Dundrum was confined. I lost weight. I could feel the bones in my shoulders and shanks and after meals I could hear my bowels resounding like the old lead pipes in Eillne.

'Tuesday. Tuesday.'

He had killed his father and mother when they were very old with a county-council shovel in some forgotten part of the Glenties. He beat them lifeless, then buried them in shallow graves and went about the milking. That was before the war. Tuesday had been thirty then. He had never had a letter or a visit. What had happened to the farmhouse? I often wondered. The land? What residue of stalwart Donegal juices would become extinct with this anxious old man, always frowning, stuck for an answer? Or a reason.

'Tuesday.'

I went to sleep most nights with the Walkman Pax sent me, blotting Tuesday out with Bird Parker.

319

In the beginning Sparrow wrote once a week. The letters did not come to me personally, of course, but in the way these things are deemed most suitable, were read to me, or parts of them were, by a third party, usually Dr Croke. It was as if Sparrow knew everything but was restrained by good manners from saying just how much. The window, she reassured me, would be replaced: she was studying plans and the cost. She thought the inscription might be of a more general nature than before. As the months went by her letters became vaguer. They spoke of the injustices of overcharging and the wages of her nursing platoon.

Then, quite suddenly, she wanted to visit me. Her tone was urgent in the way of a woman anxious about time. She said she blamed herself for my position. There was much I needed to know, Sparrow said, crucial things, and she wanted to come and inform me of them before it was too late.

I demurred. The time for her telling, if it had ever existed, was long past. Not that I blamed her, far from it, but the knot of our lives – of all our many sad and happy lives – now defied untying and the dead cried to be left alone. Perhaps, of course, she had something else entirely in mind; knowing Sparrow, she probably did. And although to love someone truly is to love them in the round, I could not bear the almost indecent sight of an old woman's confession. So I let it be known that I could not imagine why a woman of her age would want to take such a journey and said I was sure she had never stopped to consider all the people she would put out with her vagary. I did not refuse to see her outright but played her along, saying something else had unfortunately arisen, hoping that time, like the swimming river in Eillne, would wash over her crazy old notions and that she would wake up a few days afterwards, her proposed escapade quite forgotten.

It seemed to work. The letters stopped. The suggestion that Sparrow visit was never relayed to me again.

Dundrum had none of the roughness and abuse that had attended my first days in Mountjoy; indeed, the prisoners from Mountjoy who came to Dundrum for observation but were later returned judged sane, did so howling like dogs.

'The prisoner exhibits symptoms of borderline personality

320

disorder. Specifically, short-term depression, occasional identity disturbance manifested by reference to himself in the context of imaginary persons, fears of abandonment, and intermittent impulsiveness as manifested by swimming in the hospital pool to a point where it must be considered to be self- damaging.'

The judge looked across to me with, I like to think, surprise in his eyes. We had met socially in the past. He was embarrassed by our relative positions, I think.

'What is the Minister's recommendation?' he asked quietly of the doctor for the Department.

'That the prisoner continue to be assessed in Dundrum, Your Lordship.'

In the third month of my first year a new patient came in at supper and sat beside me. Small and wiry with a flourishing moustache and inquisitive eyes, Doc reminded me extraordinarily of my dead brother, Lyle.

' "Did you know what you were doing?" the judge asked me,' recounted Doc. ' "My lord, it was a moment of the most total lucidity," I told him. "I have never enjoyed a moment of greater sanity in my life." '

I swam every day. In four strokes, if I wanted, I could devour a length of the little pool. Doc took to joining me. Togged out, he would sit on the side with his legs in the water, but would never venture further.

' " My lord," I said, "the whole world knows what is going on. Let us be frank. I am an accountant by profession. I have lived all my life in other people's financial procedures." '

Doc smoked at the pool, although it was prohibited. He smoked like poor Lyle, cupping the hot ash into his hand.

' "People dip into me like into libraries and I have always maintained the reciprocal prerogative. I admit I become estranged from the rudimentary. But," I said, "this is a very strange world where no one can point the finger. We live in a moral vacuum where the oddest things occur. Vinegar, for example, was used during the Crucifixion." '

Doc stood at the handrail of the pool, his hands resting on it like they must have on the dock.

' "I am just a midget. There is a controlling cadre without any fibre of the moral kind. They are in contact with one another. Their voices flash around the world ordering the transfer of money through satellites. Pick up the paper any day. The same people again and again. The same ultimate companies. Truly atomic in their construction. Molecular." '

Doc began to tremble.

'And then I said, "The truth is, my lord, I killed her for love." '

He once ran a charity for the relief of famine in Africa, Doc, but spent the money on a prostitute instead. When they found out and she shopped him for embezzlement, Doc killed her with the wheel brace of his car.

They shaved us for lice in a job lot one evening, then hosed us all down. Tuesday went to the infirmary after that and never returned. Influenza. There's a lot of it around, Dr Croke said. It became oddly quiet in my cell without the familiar chant through the wall. You become used to things. Like the ticking of a clock. Like the falling in early winter of dead leaves, each one a soul you have known. Like a woman's breath beside you. Regimenting the long hours.

I received only Sparrow's letters in the vicarious fashion I have already described. I wrote one letter only, to the sister in England of Joyce Ogar, regretting the needlessness of Joyce's death. No reply was reported.

I grieved quickly and efficiently for Elizabeth. When I overcame the shock of comprehending her position, I came to realise that the moment of Pax's revelation had been the worst moment of all. I remember saying to myself on the cathedral scaffolding, nothing will be worse than this, nothing more can hurt me now. I would have bared my chest to bullets without fear, having endured such duplicity. And yet, there was a part of me that could not blame her completely, some visceral department that was still ready, even though the situation would never arise, to put out little flags of appeasement and to show almost with eagerness that I had got no less than I deserved. For her part, I believed that my only real competitor for Elizabeth's affection had been her loyalty to duty. Duty alone had subordinated her attachment to me. She had not faked for twenty years. At worst she had used me, and if

322

that were true, then I had used her as well. I had realised my manhood through her. Such brutal standards of honesty persuaded me to accept the realities of life and to mourn Elizabeth for no longer than she would me.

But after those first months, when I came to accept that Elizabeth was gone in the fatalistic way that a man twenty years my senior might accept his lifelong partner's predeceasing him, I sensed that a part of me had gone with her. I could vividly remember desire's slow growth in me hours before my tumescence was ever suggested. I could remember the very jungle feeling in my skin and in my hair as the need for a woman distilled in me drop by drop. I had lost it. It had gone without further notice, like an ability in athletics or in letters.

When my only contact with the outside world was pretty April, my tenacious counsel, I worried a lot for Pax. Deilt had made Pax unassailable. An opinion poll revealed Pax Sheehy to be the most recognised – and admired – guard in Ireland. Anyone who sacked him risked political injury and he thus survived like a rose in the midst of briars. April's reports of Pax's physical appearance at remand hearings increased my concern. And although evidently he had frequently requested access to me but had been denied on the grounds of my adjudged unpredictability, from chatting to April now and then, and from the enlightenment that comes from sure instinct, I knew exactly what Pax was going through, and he I, as surely as if our places had been exchanged.

His marriage, never brilliant, was further losing its gloss under the weight of his obsession to bring Bain to justice. Pax's children were grown and gone. He knew exactly Bain's part in the Deilt arms affair, but without me to testify, he had nothing. Finding himself excluded from the crucial reviews of his peers, and isolated by Miss Twinkle, his own Minister, anyone else would have taken early retirement, and if I had not been alive and well in Dundrum, perhaps Pax would have done just that. But he clung on. He watched Bain prepare for another general election. Pax watched Bain grow and Pax grew old.

We were like three branches from the same bough, but only one of us, it seemed, could flourish, and then only at the expense of the other two. Bain had made Pa's myth a reality. He had taken the gases of history and like a medieval alchemist had made matter of them. To many people he *was* Ireland.

Bain won the next election with an increased majority that gave his coalition a mandate into the new millennium. He gave Miss Twinkle powers that no Minister for Justice had ever had, and with zeal unmatched since her ballroom days, she crushed the subversives one by one, as only a woman could. Bain soared in the polls. During the campaign, April told me, whenever the opposition dared to raise the spectre of the fiasco at Deilt they were jeered by the audience or by the crowd. Jeered. When I heard that, I felt they were jeering me.

In the end, Bain had destroyed Pax; he had destroyed me. It was not so much my spirit he had robbed, as everything I had ever held dear. He had taken my innocence. When I had wanted no one but Sparrow, Bain had stood between me and her affection. By his attitude, he had robbed me of La. By his lust he had robbed me of Juliet. Ultimately he had robbed me of Elizabeth. And yet, when on the news his face came up, smiling, his mouth like the spout of a teapot hatching out the words that now came so naturally, something stopped me from surrendering to the impulse to stand up and scream.

A weight on my shoulders stopped me from standing up.

A hard ball in my throat blocked my scream.

In May of this year, in the last year of this millennium which has now reached its final autumn, a week after the second anniversary of my confinement I was summoned to the office of Dr Croke. Behind his bonhomie, his cheery smile, his attempt to always make it seem that we were in fact two chums making the best of a bad draw together, there sat on Dr Croke the cold alertness of a man dealing with a caged beast. He knew too much about me and I too little about him for our relationship ever to be otherwise.

'Sit down, please, Mr Shortcourse,' he murmured solicitously, strolling around his desk.

I picked up the signals instantly. On the desk there was a bowl of fruit that Dr Croke was in the habit of offering from but which in this instance remained ignored. I had spent my lifetime out-guessing criminals and two years incarcerated in their midst; my antennae worked. I scented the medical director's fear.

'Are you well today, Mr Shortcourse?'

I nodded and looked around for clues. It was not much of an office, really, not for a man at the head of such an institution. I saw from a kettle in the corner that he even had to make his own tea.

'I want you to prepare yourself for some bad news,' said Dr Croke.

I closed my eyes. Dr Croke had promised his best efforts to bring my case for a proper trial before the Review Board. I had known that he would not, even if he really tried, be able to prevail against the weight of political pressure, but I had still hoped he might.

'Your mother is dead, Mr Shortcourse,' said Dr Croke quietly.

I looked at Dr Croke for a trick.

'She died in her sleep five days ago,' he continued bleakly, 'at home in Eillne. She was buried the day before yesterday with her husband in Monument.'

'Which one?'

Dr Croke blinked, then checked a sheet of paper on his desk. 'Wise?' he said.

'David Wise.'

Dr Croke nodded and joined his hands.

'I understand what you must be feeling, Mr Shortcourse,' he said with concern. 'I am very sorry for you. I regret your position, in here, in these circumstances, but . . .'

I noticed details about Dr Croke that had hitherto eluded me: the slight misalignment of his eyes; the cat hairs along the line of his collar.

'What . . . happened?'

'The end was, I understand, extremely peaceful. She, ah . . .' Again he looked down to the piece of paper as if to a script. 'She simply closed her eyes and died.'

'Thank you.'

'There was a very good turnout.'

'The Taoiseach?'

'And most of the Cabinet,' said Dr Croke, pleased with the news.

I said nothing; there was nothing to say.

'The Bishop of Monument remembered you in his prayers,' Dr Croke continued. 'You don't have to say anything at all. The

325

chaplain will be only too pleased to arrange any form of religious service you may wish – if that is your wish. Bereavement counselling facilities are available and I strongly recommend them. I am very sorry. If it is any consolation, I want you to know that I am pushing the Board very hard on your behalf. But I am very sorry.'

I walked out of the little office block, leaving Dr Croke looking after me. Rain from the Dublin Mountains rolled across Dundrum, driven by strong gusts. I went down by the new cell buildings and out to the all-weather football pitch that was like a wasteland of lava and ash and where, in the midst of a hundred sudden pools, rain beat into my face and blurred my bespectacled eyes. They could at least have brought me down and let me stand in my rightful place. Bain could have fixed that. They did not have to wait until she was two days buried to tell me.

But then something strange happened out in that desolate, rainswept place. I suddenly felt free. To be accurate, I first felt light, not light-*headed*, just weightless. As if air had entered hidden pockets of my body and made it curiously unheavy, I made a hop. I laughed because it was such a silly thing to do, out there in the sodden field on my own, hopping in a way that might make them rush out and drag me in for volts in the head. But I hopped anyway. I laughed, airily. It was a happy laugh. It brought on another hop. I laughed again. There was no weight to keep me down. Nureyev-like, I soared, landing a bit too awkwardly and going down in the mud. The fun! I roared! Getting up I sprang around the wide, wet pitch, my arms out in takeoff position. It had never happened before.

I gambolled in the rain like a happy fool. I rolled and shouted and did somersaults of delight. As if time had granted me an extraordinary amnesty from my huge, accumulated debts of sin and unhappiness, I roared with pleasure. Suddenly and un-expectedly all the dark sadnesses of my life had been taken away. No shame or guilt lurked to spoil the day. There would be no . . . consequences! I danced until at last the screws who had been sent to keep an eye on me beckoned me in for a hot shower and tea. I looked in the stainless-steel mirror of the shower room and despite its uncertain undulations could recognise a happy man when I saw one. I would eat the meals of two men that evening and sleep with the untroubled mind of a child. Behaviourally, of course, it would do my case no good. They wanted a sniveller to practise their techniques on. They wanted to slobber along with me, the bereaved son, and then go home and write up their notes.

Snivel? Slobber? Bereaved? I laughed. I didn't care.

I didn't care!

The sense of emancipation after Sparrow's death was like the resolution of an old, dogging injury. It was as if I had had to wait until her death to consider my own priorities, and then, when her death occurred, saw my horizons opening in a manner hitherto unthinkable. I was free in a way that walls could never limit. The feeling was a heady one. My only (inconsequential) regret was that I had waited nearly sixty years to reach this point.

Elation did not stop me from being sorry for Sparrow herself, nor from admiring her. Her birth was the result of a sin, and thus, like a little tree that has been planted in a warped brace, her whole life was distorted by this fact. I did not dwell on what she had done to me or the people whose lives she had destroyed in the process. Sin is endemic. Some are luckier with it than others. Sparrow had lived and died and with her death came to me not only the sense of freedom I have described but also, in terms of great clarity, the duty I now owed myself, and Pax, and, in a peculiar way, my family history.

Whereas before, if I had been a model patient I had also been morose, now I could not even be indicted on grounds of low spirits. At the same time, ever mindful of the emotional sterility by which standards as to reason are set, I curbed the new, inherent joy that drove me and concentrated instead on matching my outward blandness to that of my masters. I modelled myself especially on Dr Croke. His economy of expression whatever the situation became my set. I acquired a simultaneous if somewhat suspect generosity of interest in the misfortunes of others and began to look on my fellow inmates with a degree of clinical concern. I took Doc for swimming lessons. Although taller than Dr Croke, I began to walk like him, not in a mime or caricature, but just following the body language of his gait, the easy, strolling, ringmasterish way he had about the place which bespoke more than anything the gulf that separates the possession of power from impotence.

327

June began with a heatwave. I felt strong. Dr Croke and I now always met eyes in our daily encounters: a little nod, a smile, colleagues doing their best in a turkey farm full of the criminally insane. I began to study the television news rather than gape at it in the way of my peers. In July Bain began forcing the Dáil to sit late in order to hammer through some bill or other, I learned. They would sit into the summer recess as well, the Taoiseach threatened. Bain would cancel summer itself in order to get his way.

Two days later came the moment on which all my optimism was founded. My summons to the office – 'Mr Shortcourse'; 'Dr Croke' – the change in his slightly divergent eyes from the wariness of old to a, dare I say, new respect. I chose a mandarin following Dr Croke's invitation to do so and he, in an inversion of our usual roles, accepted my invitation to do the same. Our peeled shells of orange skin lay together at the base of Dr Croke's wastepaper basket; Dr Croke and I sank our teeth in unison on the fruit.

'You are being seen in Beaumont tomorrow,' Dr Croke said.

I inclined my head in cautious gratitude.

Dr Croke sighed. 'Look, I shouldn't be saying this, I know, but, well, yours is not like a case I've ever come across before. In lodge, all right?'

I allowed my hand a gentle flowering in the way I had seen Dr Croke do when showing provisional consent.

'There's big pressure in your case,' the Doctor said and made a ledge over his head with one hand. '*Big* pressure. From up here. I'm only a small boy when it comes to big decisions, I think you understand that, Mr Shortcourse.'

'Of course,' I diplomatically murmured.

'It's not *my* decision,' Dr Croke said. He winced. 'It's a political decision, as I'm sure you know, and they're the worst kind. All I can do and have done is push for a review. I've pushed hard and Beaumont tomorrow is the result.'

'Thank you.'

'Look, I'll be perfectly honest, it's not *only* me pushing,' Dr Croke confessed. 'Assistant Commissioner Sheehy has been on this case from the start.'

'Pax,' I smiled.

'That's right,' said Dr Croke. 'But try to remember that tomorrow is only a first step. I don't want you to get your hopes too high. All I can say is, before today's decision a review of your case was not even a possibility. Today's decision puts it into the range of the possible, but only into the range.'

'Any tips for Beaumont?' I asked.

'Just be yourself, Mr Shortcourse,' Dr Croke advised and gave me his most rugged smile.

'You've done everything you can,' I said and meant it.

Dr Croke seemed grateful. 'This may sound disgraceful,' he said, 'but I'll be genuinely sorry to see you go, Mr Shortcourse.'

He meant, of course, *if* I was released, but his anticipation of regret seemed nonetheless auspicious. It was, I imagine, as near as he would ever get to telling a patient that he liked him.

Dr Croke's was the last face in Dundrum I saw the next day. He came down to where we were all getting into the Honda Accord, the two screws from my block either side of me and the main-block screw with the car keys in his hand.

'Aren't you going to cuff him?' the driver asked.

My screws turned to Dr Croke.

'That won't be necessary,' said Dr Croke with a knowing little smile.

As we waited for the first, electronic gate to slide across, I turned around in the back seat and looked behind. Dr Croke was still standing there, still smiling. He saw my face and raised his hand to elbow height in a tactful wave. It was as if he not only knew what was going to happen, but that he also approved.

The visit to Beaumont Hospital that strengthened my sense of purpose, my despair at the cursory hearing afforded my most vital revelations, our little party's providential stop on the way home at the bridge that had been opened for the sailing ship, and my liberating leap, have all been mentioned elsewhere on these tapes. So, too, has my climb up the slimy quay wall two hundred yards distant, and my hauling out amphibian-like on the sunny quayside.

Dublin was having a cheerful day. I made my way happily in my purloined disguise through the noise level as I traversed the city.

329

For two years noise had lost its immediacy for me, like a pencil loses its point; now I revelled in the sharpness of brakes squeaking, in the sweet tingling of cyclists' bells, in the soughing of the heart of the city I had rejoined. I drank in the beery smell from the open doors of pubs. On College Green high-octane gasoline mingled coyly with dung from the horses of the tourist jarveys as silver water made an arch from the mouth of a fountain. Seagulls swooped overhead scavenging for offal. From the high bracket of a lamppost someone, perhaps students, had hung a human effigy by the neck and stuck on it the name 'Bain', but it hung gaily nevertheless, the day defying opportunities for being sinister, even to sham cadavers.

Crossing the Green along its northern perimeter, taking the crossing for Harcourt Street, I could see the distant Department of Justice with two guards pacing lazily outside. Was there an alert inside there yet? I wondered. Would the Dundrum screws initially try for damage limitation and go for the gamble that I had drowned? Or would a red-faced Dr Croke instinctively reject that notion and go public? Pax would know I would not so drown. But would Pax know anything of society's latest problem – yet? Pax came even more vividly to mind as I detoured around the side of Harcourt Square, wherein my old friend's office and those of his several hundred colleagues were located. A car with sirens erupted suddenly within the precincts of the red-bricked building and screamed for town past me, the detective in the passenger seat leaning forward with some urgency as if tying up his laces or topping up the Uzi that lay beneath his seat.

The canal looked deceptively uncontaminated; like cool, black ink it lay beneath its bridge. The flat land of Rathmines, or at least its repointed brickwork, gleamed. Once I had dreamed of La and I living in such a place, needing only our body heat and the odd loaf of bread. It was hard to recall that dream now. Like an old book whose details I could not remember, all that remained was the fact that it had given me pleasure at the time.

Leafy Rathgar. The subtlety of greater opulence than Rathmines, long, winding residential roads and culs-de-sac with the rainforest-theme developments wherein lived people such as Bain.

'Bain.'

I spoke his name softly to myself as I followed the gentle curve of a granite wall. Scots pine could be seen against the sky if I looked up, and now, to my right, laurels grown into a hedge. Someone nearby was cutting grass with an old, hand-push cylinder mower, rattling it back and forth with consoling regularity.

A single guard stood on duty, stripped down to his blue shirt, hands on hips, chatting up a girl on a bicycle. I observed them from behind the trunk of a tree. The girl wore a dress of muslin. The guard was tethered by duty to an ugly sentry box just inside the gates of Bain's apartment complex. The girl, a pretty child with notions of womanhood, would allow their banter to reach a certain point before pedalling off, her dress breaking deliciously over her knees. Then the guard would step out into the road, his back to where I stood, and call after her, reeling her back to him so that their ritual could recommence. I slipped in without a sound when next he turned his back; I slipped in like a salmon slips through a weir.

Other blocks of flats had been added in the two years plus since I had come to visit Bain's wife, Aggie, in this place. The rampant vegetation that burst and then fell from the upstairs terraces of Bain's building gave it the appearance of a gigantic dessert cart with organic problems on the upper decks. No one attended the door. I pressed four numbers on the keypad. Not any four numbers, but the ones I had seen pressed and heard called out by Aggie the last time I was there. Detail. I took the lift to the fourth floor. It struck me that Bain could have moved. Higher in this building. Or to a newer one. But somehow the smooth tracks of history on which I heard myself hum did not admit such last-minute difficulties. Another keypad outside Bain's door. Press four. A deep and satisfying click. He hadn't moved, no. I could smell him straight off, as soon as the door swung open.

'Bain.'

It was a modest flat, as I had observed at other times. Not a home it was just a suite for the Taoiseach to rest between divisions. At the same time someone had tried to make a home of it, but had not succeeded, because the pastels on the walls and the bowls of fresh fruit and curio items placed with designer careless-ness on polished reproduction chests and tables were alien to the

331

taste of the man they stood to serve. The kitchen was new and unused with an eye-level oven and a porcelain hob of the kind popular in the seventies but which everyone else had now thrown out. Yet Bain's tangy smell made the place uniquely Bain. I went into his bedroom.

The windows were surprisingly small but nonetheless were covered by nylon curtains, creating a perpetual twilight. Like a phantom, I moved around touching things. Over Bain's bed hung a heavy crucifix. Built-in wardrobes, stained black, were fully stocked. The picture of Sparrow on the dressing table amused me. It was the same one I had in my flat, the one taken at Billy Cross's wedding that showed her foxy, flirting eyes. How had Bain got it? She had been a most attractive woman in that almost sideways, seductive way you saw in the photograph. You could see from the way her chin sat in her fox stole that she was a sensuous person, that she would like to be stroked. After all, I just might have been conceived the night that photograph had been taken – mightn't I?

Following the events of the previous two hours, my general attire was unsatisfactory. My feet and underclothes were still wet and I stank unconscionably of the Liffey. Water of volcanic temperatures gushed from the bath tap and when I added crystals from a plastic jar the aroma rose triumphantly to greet my tentative shanks.

I was hungry. Washed and shampooed, I went to the kitchen and made myself sandwiches from fresh rolls. A little rack of wine yielded a dusty Burgundy. To fit the mood, I thought, and uncorked it with a chuckle, then crumbed my way back into the bedroom to select from wardrobe and drawers a suitable trousseau. The top drawer yielded a wallet with leaves of ready cash, the bottom drawer socks. Parking my glass, I rummaged fastidiously. My fingers furled around a hard, wedge-like shape. Everything, eventually, occurs with synchronicity; I took out the cloth. I unwrapped the gun.

It was a sombre-looking gun. It had a long barrel and snout and dull chambers. The oil and the weight defined it as a killing thing without a doubt. It fitted the man, of course. That's what Bain would have done after Brussels, coming back alone at night from the Dáil. Pa had slept with a knife under his pillow, hadn't he? The one he used to cut the tripes from Brits? Oh, yes. *The hero of Deilt!* I put it down on the bed. I assumed it was loaded.

Nothing fitted me, of course. I was head and shoulders above Bain and he was twice my span, so that when I got past the primary area of underwear and socks, the best of what followed were baggy, shin-high trousers, an expensive and probably never worn pullover, and a pair of equally neglected deck shoes that were ridiculous when you understood their owner's aversion to water. I looked around for tapes or records, but gave up when it became obvious – as it should always have been – that there were none. I switched on the television but all that came up was a race meeting somewhere. Nothing about my escape, not that I expected much. Nothing even about Bain. But he would come back here. He was still in Dublin, still holding the promise of summer trapped like a bird in his big fist.

Two hours must have passed. From where I lay on Bain's bed with Sparrow looking at me, I heard the outriders' sirens. They grew towards me like a chant from an unfamiliar church. I was in time to see power arrive below in full harness: two motor-cycle guards at the vanguard of two black limousines that, according to the press, had been specially fortified in Detroit, and a couple of Garda squad cars. Radio static gave the late afternoon an urgent quality it had not previously seemed to need. The crown of a hairless head presented itself to me from the back of one limousine and I realised that Bain was now completely bald.

I sat in the bedroom's only chair to wait. It had gone beyond the personal, it had gone into the very structures of dignity that man depends on, and realising this made me profoundly calm.

'Just put it on the chair.'

Bain's voice was suddenly in the flat. I could smell him, too, in a redoubled, fresh way as if his presence could never be done justice to posthumously.

'Can I get you anything, Taoiseach?'

A man's voice. His driver or bodyguard. I had feared Bain might have brought home some of his acolytes and continued to work or dictate, or perhaps, driven on adrenaline, he might have used his time here for a tryst.

'No, I'm all right. I want three hours, then I'll go back in for the vote.'

333

'Very well, Taoiseach.'

The door to the flat opened and closed. I heard Bain moving about the big room.

'Hello? It's me. Look, I'm in Rathgar, I'm exhausted. I want three hours' kip, all right? Any problems?'

I could hear him kick one shoe off.

'When? Jesus. Is this confirmed? Jesus Christ. Have they found him?'

Thump. The other shoe.

'Jesus Christ. But he's drowned. He's drowned, yeah? You're sure? Poor bastard. Anything else?'

I had been right to assume the extent of the authorities' wishful thinking about me.

'They can wait,' he said. 'Just keep everyone off me until I get back in.'

The telephone went down.

'Jesus Christ,' I heard Bain say.

He opened the door to the bedroom, dropping the jacket of his suit and loosening his tie as he made for the bathroom. I heard him urinate, a thing of long instalments. The toilet was flushed. Then the shower erupted with a throaty roar. Bain came back into the bedroom fully naked except for the gold watch he was removing from his wrist. Despite ginger body hair his appearance was that of a white frog. Whilst catching and drawing out the flesh of his scrotum as he might elastic, with an accompanying grunt of satisfaction, Bain saw me. He jumped, also frog-like. The fright he got made him croak. He had his watch in his hand and held it out to me like he might trinkets to a savage.

'Stay there, Bain.'

'Theo, thank God! I heard you were drowned!'

'No, I'm a good swimmer, remember.'

'Ah, of course, of course,' Bain said, steadying. 'Is it all right if I make a quick phone call? There's something I –' Then he saw his gun on the bed beside me. 'Jesus, Theo . . .'

'Bain, I want to tell you something.'

'Go ahead, Theo. I'm in no hurry,' he said, but his nerve had gone and his eyes kept flicking to the gun in almost stage alarm.

'You're a cunt, Bain,' I said as evenly as I could. 'And a bad one at that. Maybe it's not your fault, maybe it's the way you grew up, or Pa's fault, or Mag's, or some other reason, but whatever it is, you're the worst there can ever be.'

'And you're perfect?' He trembled, every inch of him. The rumbling shower noise stole his words, it made his voice frail.

'I'm so flawed it's a wonder I can walk and talk,' I replied. 'I'm a ragbag of imperfections. I'm defective to the point that I've been removed from society, remember? The Minister for Health has recommended that I be detained indefinitely in Dundrum Central Mental Hospital, in case you were wondering where I've been.'

'Listen,' Bain said, eyes three times on the gun in as many seconds, 'that's been on my mind, I swear to you.'

'You're bad for so many reasons that you are probably not aware of even a fraction of them,' I said. 'You've taken everything I ever loved in life, including my pride and my freedom. I'm sorry for your wife and children. I'm sorry in a funny way for all the people I understand have voted for you. If it's any consolation, you'll probably go down in history as a great Taoiseach.'

Bain saw me pick up the gun.

'Theo . . .' he gasped. 'Jesus, oh Jesus, what are you going to do, Theo? It's not my fault!'

'Say what you must,' I said, even though I did not care what it would amount to. I took no pleasure from his fear, I just wanted to end everything. To do my duty.

'OK, Theo, I was wrong,' Bain stammered, 'it was my fault about the missiles, OK. But what could I do? I was dead otherwise! I was easy prey in hospital, you saw me yourself, you didn't need me to explain what had to be done. We're part of the one family. I'd have done it for you, Theo, you know I would.'

'That all happened two years ago.'

'I was letting time go by, Theo, I was waiting until the whole Deilt thing was forgotten. Until after the election. Then, with winning the election and one thing and another, the time just didn't seem to be there. But next month, Christmas at the latest. Yes!' He was crying with sincerity. 'Oh, Jesus, I was looking forward to the surprise on your face the day I came – *personally*, Theo! – into that shithole. Oh, God, how I felt for you! I was going to pick the time and come in one day and say, "Theo, it's all right, old friend, get in here beside me now and we'll go off together to Eillne." May God be my judge and strike me down if I'm telling

335

one word of a lie, Theo. That was the greatest ambition I had left, in all the flying around the world and the meetings and all the rest – they were nothing, *nothing*, Theo! – to the happiness I was going to have the day I came and took you home.'

'Could you not have done it the day you buried Sparrow?' I enquired.

'I *wanted* to, Theo,' Bain said, hands spread. He clasped them back to his white but hairy belly. 'They wouldn't allow me, or at least, I hadn't the time to put the wheels in motion. I said to myself, be cool about this. Plan it out so it will work for Theo. Theo, put down the gun. Please put down the gun.'

'Bain, do you want to pray or anything?' I asked.

'Ah Jesus,' he blathered, 'ah Jesus please, Theo, please no, no. What do you want? Do you want Sparrow's funeral to be done again? No problem, Theo, I can do it. We'll dig her up and do it properly this time with you there. That's what we'll do! Why didn't I think of that! Stupid. Of course that's what we'll do. Let me set that up this minute now on the phone, Theo.'

I raised the gun and he froze.

'Theo! No! Just listen to me. I can give you anything you want. Any immunity. Any posting. Anything. I know! Do you want to be an ambassador? An ambassador? It's a fantastic life. One of these tropical countries. A big house. Theo, don't, for the love of God, I beg you. Tax-free money. I was wrong, but it wasn't my fault, it wasn't, God knows.'

It was so disappointing to listen to him and at the same time so entirely predictable. I pointed the gun and pulled the trigger. There was no sound that I heard, but the effect on Basin was that of a bullet. His knees met the floor with a sharp crack.

'Aggghhhhhh!' he screamed.

I pointed the gun again.

Bain shrieked, 'Theo! Listen to me, I beg you! Think of Sparrow, Theo. Think of her looking down on this now. I was with her before she died, Theo. For the three days she took to die, I never left her. Do you not want to know what she was like? I'll tell you, I'll tell you now, Theo. She was like that picture there on the dressing table again. Beautiful. Young. Like you and I must have remembered her. She told me things she'd never told anyone. No one. About you, Theo. Things you don't know. Important things that only I know. If you kill me you'll never hear about yourself or who you really are or where you come from. Put down the gun now, Theo, this has gone far enough. Theo! Do you understand what I'm saying? She told me *who you are, Theo*!'

Bain paused and I swear a little victorious smile began to build around his mouth.

'This is very important, Theo,' Bain said softly.

I thought the next chamber was empty too because when I pulled the trigger, although the weapon tugged, I heard little more than a click, but then Bain fell sideways, and before I could decide whether in fact he had simply fainted, I saw the deep red tongue of blood from the base of his throat where I'd shot him.

Stepping over his body, in his shoes, I turned the shower off. There was a strong smell of cordite in the air. He was quite unlike anyone I knew, lying there, and certainly not like the leader of a country. Funny, his salty smell was gone too. It was good that Sparrow and Mag and even Pa, not that I would especially worry on his account, had predeceased Bain. Before I let myself out I turned Sparrow's gaze away from the corpse on the floor.

The landing was empty of protectors. Everything waited outside for the next twitch of the Taoiseach's humour. It was all rather strange being the first witness to history, a vacuum. I circumnavigated the cars and outriders with cigarettes and bored detectives. I walked out the gates and no one gave me a second glance; they were watching for people coming in, not going out. Lovely summer evening for a swim. Not a hint of political or other crisis in the air, which just shows how deceptive appearances are. I set my face for Eillne.

The river delta is a vast, floating and shifting place. Years ago when Donald Blood went into it, they gave up searching after ten days and even then they knew they had not covered a small fraction of what lay waiting.

I went to Eillne first. I would have liked to have gone down by train to Monument and out in the usual way by Sheehy's bus, but I knew I could not afford such luxuries. From someone's front garden in Templeogue I took a motor bicycle, a big, shiny 350 cc Japanese machine with leather seats, and paid a little further along the way for a fill of petrol with the money I had found at Bain's. I felt bad about that, strangely. It seemed an abuse of my position to have taken money in that way.

No impediments arose to my journey. It was more than thirty years since I had felt the wind in my face on Pax's big bike. No way could they have stopped me anyway, even if they had tried: in customs we feared a speed bike above all else when it came to taking in a suspect. I approached Monument cautiously. But you can tell from the expressions on people's faces in a sunny afternoon street whether there has been a recent shock to the national psyche and my observations told me that none such had yet occurred. Guardian of the nation's most scandalous secret, I passed the grotto on Captain's Penny's Road, then gave her full throttle.

It was still only five o'clock, making it difficult to comprehend that the day was still far from over and yet had already been filled with so much. The bike ate up the miles. The little fields running into hills, the school, they flew by. I saw a car parked at the foot of the hill that was the back of Eillne as you came from Monument, and eased the revs. Four more cars were parked along the side and up the hill where shrubbery tumbled outward. Parking, I walked the last hundred yards, drinking in the gummy smell of the escallonia. A sign said 'Auction' beneath the name of a Monument auctioneer.

More cars, perhaps six or eight, were parked inside the gates. A couple with an infant in arms walked along the gravel towards me, the sound of their feet on the pebbles saying as persuasively as always that time has no real meaning. They smiled pleasantly. There were other people strolling in front of Sammy Tea's house, which had had a rough fence put up around it and signs saying *Danger!* I joined them. Some walls still stood. They might have been there a thousand years, not less than a hundred. Beneath the spaces where once had been windows stood small, dirty cones of melted glass. The kitchen was gone entirely, but the little yard behind could now be seen, with the lean-to sheds where coal and sticks had been housed, and the steps leading up to the garden and the paddock. You could see Nanny Morrissey puffing down with a basket of greens if you tried hard enough. You could see Theo Shortcourse, too, if you tried, him with the new job in Monument, following La with her coal bucket at winter's dusk, his hand lunging like open jaws for the luscious pleasures of her rump.

Sparrow's (no longer) new bungalow was now the centre of the gardens and lawns, leaving the old ruin in the rear, rather like Uncle Hugo stubbornly refusing to die. Inside the door I was handed a brochure. The auction was in five days' time, it said. I had joined the tail end of the midweek viewing.

The house meant nothing to me. It had been David Wise's house, which he had not lived long enough to enjoy. Apart from one good room that overlooked the swimming river, the house had been built with only two people in mind and thus the dozen or more to which I now added my one made what space there was inadequate. It was Sparrow's bedroom I wanted to see. She had gone from this place to the cathedral cemetery three months ago, but I hoped that she might have left behind some clue to her presence as a consolation prize.

The bedroom, too, looked out on the swimming river, but through a small window that cramped the perspective. I stepped back to allow out a small man with a hat before I could enter. He thanked me. There was no evidence that this was *her* bedroom, no smell of Sparrow, which I had somehow expected, remembering how Nanny Morrissey had once clung on in the fabrics of La's bedroom, her pungent old essence refusing to evaporate with her spirit. I listened: no whisper, just the chat of people in the other rooms, out for the day in the guise of buyers of property. Wardrobes took up one wall: they were empty. Sparrow had lain on that double bed more than two years before and called for me – a last call, if only I had known then – but I had decided to rush out to Deilt. The bed, firm and flat, looked as if no one had ever slept in it. On the wall side of the bed was a narrow oak locker I vaguely remembered from Eillne. It was easiest to lie on the far side of the bed to reach the locker's door. The auctioneer's man came in as I was so doing: he went out again, rolling his eyes. I pulled the catch and the door popped. I could see nothing. I don't know what exactly I hoped to find, but I went in with my hand anyway and on the bottom, at the back, felt the contours of a little, forgotten box.

'Oh dear! Goodness me!'

The little man with the hat had come to stand in the doorway. He had a radio the size of a pack of cards pressed to his ear.

'Goodness me!' he said again. He spoke in an English accent. 'Your Prime Minister's dead, I'm afraid.'

I was able to sit on the side of the bed and put the box on the floor between my feet to inspect it. People were chattering out in the corridor and saying 'Shush!' The plastic sleeve containing the recorder and packets of tapes I had once seen by Sparrow's side lay in the box. Transferring the package into my pockets, or Bain's pockets, I left the room for the sudden buzz outside, the drifting in of new people to the source of information, the man in the hat, who was still listening to his radio. I thought Sparrow's voice might be on those tapes. I never thought of the use to which I would put them.

'Some country,' said the auctioneer's man to me as if he suddenly knew me. 'I never voted for him, mind, but God, I don't know what things are coming to.'

The man in the hat was standing outside the front door, hands in his pockets, looking down the river as I emerged.

'Lovely place,' he said.

'It is,' I replied.

The news about Bain had, for a moment, brought everyone closer together.

'We're on holiday in the area,' the man said, explaining the presence of a woman hovering on the other side of the terrace. 'We just drove out, didn't know there was a sale on or anything.'

'Like myself,' I said.

'You know the area?'

'Yes.'

'My grandfather used to talk about Monument when I was a child,' the man said. 'He'd been in the army here. Seems he had a girlfriend, the old scoundrel, even though he was married at home. He used to tell me about a place downriver of the town where they used to swim together, below a big house. My wife and I wonder if this is it.'

I wanted to ask his name; I yearned to. But then I felt that my intrusion into history had been sufficient for one day.

The little man said, 'I've always had a picture of this place in my mind.'

'And does what you see here fit the picture?' I asked.

The man wrinkled up his nose. 'Not really, to be honest. But what does, you know?' He put his hand out. 'Nice meeting you.' He laughed awkwardly. 'Sorry about, you know, your problems,' he said and held up the radio.

The terraces still held the day's heat as I made my way down through them to the swimming river. It was not difficult to imagine that Bain might have gone on ahead and be lying in wait in some defile, or that when he sprang out and dragged me down with him on a bank, that Sparrow's disapproving voice would carry down from the house, summoning us to eat with her and Uncle Hugo. Turning and looking back up at the old house, now in shadow, only a small leap of imagination was necessary to restore everything to the way it had once been. But I put my back to it. I went to the river.

Pax would know the next steps exactly. Where the bog oak lay semi-submerged, like brooding crocodiles; how I would select one to fit and, stripped down, lie gently on it and paddle with the hurrying flow, crossing the edge of the delta proper at some point in the hour that followed. I did so with the tape recorder in its plastic package tied around my neck. I followed the red sun until it vanished that evening beneath the water I was skimming over. Dragging my boat behind me on to weeds, I slept the most untroubled sleep I remember, and when the sun had swung under my lapping bed and reappeared the next morning behind Monument, I resumed my swift course for the centre, the sun steadfast overhead, giving me my compass and gently licking my bare skin towards the colour it would soon become.

The weeks that have gone by here have never held a false promise. My head hair and my beard are long and white, but my skin is brown. My skin is taut and brown and shines where it lies on my muscle and bone. I need no glasses to talk into these little tapes. I rest on my back and feel the strength of the sun on my eyes.

I have always known how it will end: how Pax alone has held the line against the pack baying for my blood; how Pax alone will decide when to end it. He is the only person I feel I have let down, but then I realise how unavoidable that has always been. Torn between his love for me and his duty, I am saddened by the certainty of his approaching loneliness, but I am powerless to alter it in the same way I am powerless from now on to alter history.

I wonder about history. It seems to forever dissolve under my touch, to the point where I feel I might be better off without it. But what do you have if not history? A blank? Blanks won't do, as Sparrow might have said. We must have something, and history, for all its imperfections, is what we are left with in the end.

The river is now the only thing that matters, but this is something I have always known. From Sammy Tea back to the untold generations of Bloods and forward to the dead children of children who are not yet born, the river connects us all. I am not sure what that means, other than no one who swims in this river, even those afraid of water, is ever truly alone. That is more than can be said for those who stay forever on land, where aloneness has a grip from the very lowly right up to the powerful and exalted. As long as this river was here in Eillne, I was never alone.

It is the late afternoon now of the eighth week. I have heard Pax coming for two days. At least, I have seen in the sky the little explosions of bird activity that Pax is causing as he makes his way towards me and I can hear the slowly nearing screech of alarmed coots and the wing beats of herons and swans as he comes to them and disturbs them. Where did he rest these last nights? He must have set out at least five days ago to get in this far. On the same floating islands as I did, I know. In the old days on a trip like this we'd never have to talk or ask each other questions, it just happened.

The water is warm and running with deceptive vigour. It rained in the mountains last week. I could hear it, fifty miles away, and in the days that followed I could see it, in the busy water and in the habits of the birds, particularly those with chicks, anticipating the slightly rising level and making their arrangements to suit, like shopkeepers coming out to the footpath and with anxious glances towards the sky bringing in their wares.

I have made a loop of the plastic sleeve and tied it around my neck so that I can speak to my tapes even when I am in the water. I find that particularly relaxing: drifting on my back, sun on my face, the words that make up so many years – and lives – making their way on to my drowsily revolving spools.

I am sitting at the far side of a clearing on an island of weeds. When Pax comes through there will be only thirty yards between us. I'm sure he's got some way of getting home, some flares to attract one of the choppers that were around a few weeks ago, or even a radio. Pax will be back in Dublin tonight, sitting in his room with the streetlights making horizontal patterns through his Venetian blinds, and Glenn Miller for company. Straight out of the vegetation I'm looking at some three coots, dashing across the water on their laughable legs.

'Pax! I'm over here!'

I haven't seen a human face for the best part of two months, other than my own each time I stoop to drink. Pax comes through the reeds quite quickly in the end. Apart from shorts, he is wearing nothing. His white body glistens like steel. He stops and rises from where he has lain, straddling his piece of oak.

'Are you all right, Theo?'

'I'm very well, Pax. Really.'

'That's good,' Pax says.

We're looking at each other over this stretch of water. We *want* to just look at each other. Words are unnecessary to us. By just sitting we can see all the years between us, hear all the music, recite the words that were spoken, or shouted, and laugh or cry at all the jokes and miseries that all now seem such tiny details of one long, but very normal, day. It's this understanding that makes my fear of where I am going so very insignificant. I'm much more worried for Pax. He is not going anywhere. Pax is staying behind.

'Theo?'

'Yes?'

'Do you want to swim?' Pax asks.

'Yes,' I say. 'I do.'

'I'll keep my oak,' Pax says grimly. 'OK? I won't come any closer.'

'That's OK.'

I slip into the current. It's moving even faster than I thought; down where your legs trail it's hurrying along like an underground train. I can see Pax off to one side, but as a corner comes up and the river narrows and suddenly begins to rush, I lose Pax, who is less part of the flow than I am as he has to manoeuvre his bog oak and I have left mine behind.

'I can't go any further with you, Theo!' Pax yells.

It's really got me now. It's got me double-handed. It tugs my

343

head under and when I come back up it skids a wave into my face and makes me swallow water.

'Theo!' calls Pax from way back. He's calling something.

I've reached another bend and I can see froth on the water as if I've been living for two months beside a dangerous neighbourhood I never knew existed. Pax calls out yet again but now I can't hear him all that well because I'm being pulled under now more than I'm being allowed to stay on top. I have to spit. Islands are whizzing by, and I suppose if I really wanted to I could probably haul up on one of them. But my arms are not doing much any more. They're trying to guide air into my mouth. It's OK, really. I've been here before.

I suddenly know what Pax is shouting.

'Swim, Theo!' he is calling from a great distance. 'Swim!'

I am swimming. Yes. I swim.